VAULT

PUBLISHER **DAMIAN A. WASSEL**
EDITOR IN CHIEF **ADRIAN F. WASSEL**
ART DIRECTOR **NATHAN C. GOODEN**
EVP BRANDING/DESIGN **TIM DANIEL**
VP OF MARKETING **KIM McLEAN**
DIRECTOR OF PR & RETAILER RELATIONS **DAVID DISSANAYAKE**
OPERATIONS MANAGER **IAN BALDESSARI**
PRINCIPAL **DAMIAN A. WASSEL, SR.**

WRITTEN BY

MICHAEL MORECI

ILLUSTRATED BY

HAYDEN SHERMAN

COLORED BY

JASON WORDIE

LETTERED BY

JIM CAMPBELL

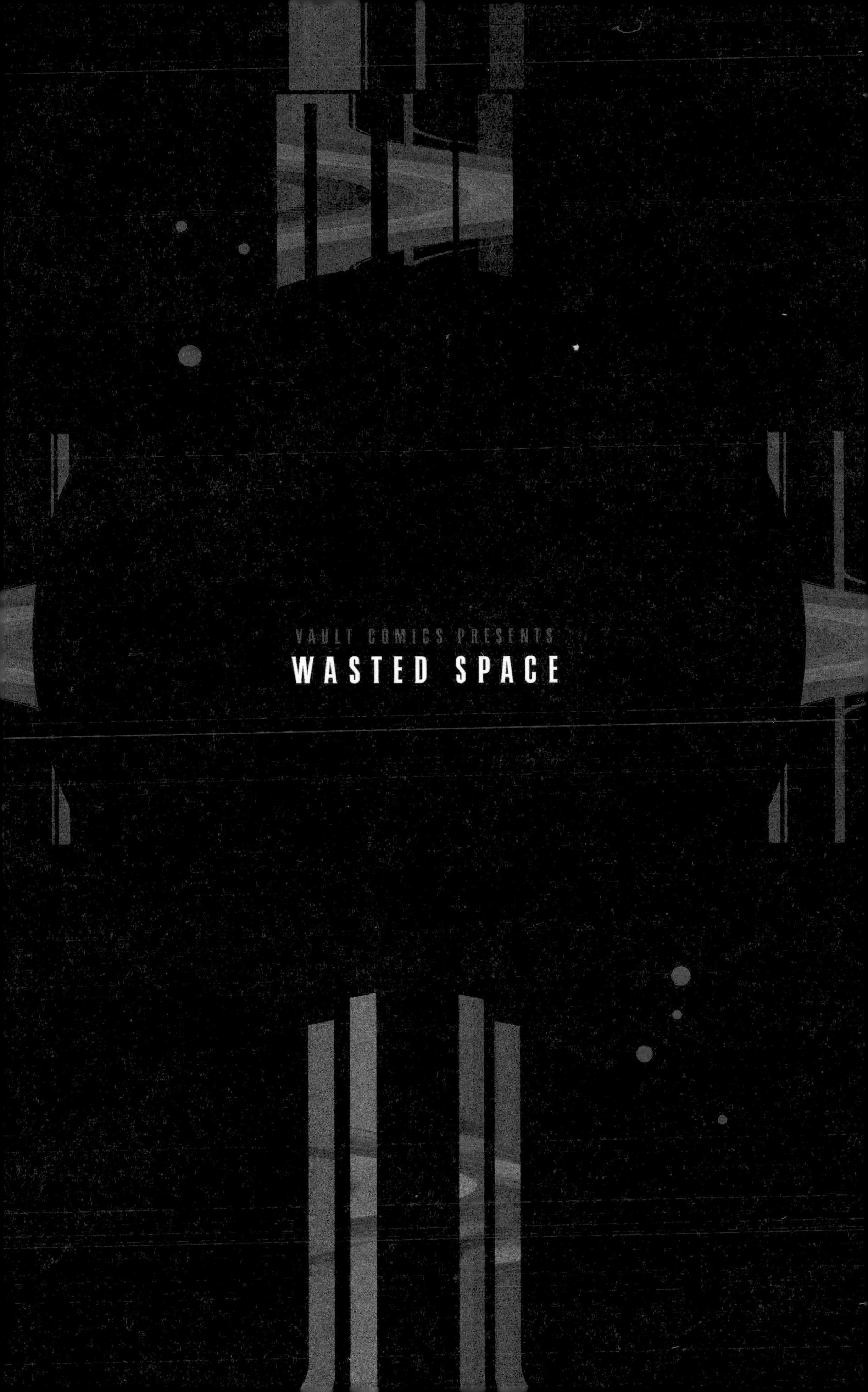

VAULT COMICS PRESENTS

WASTED SPACE

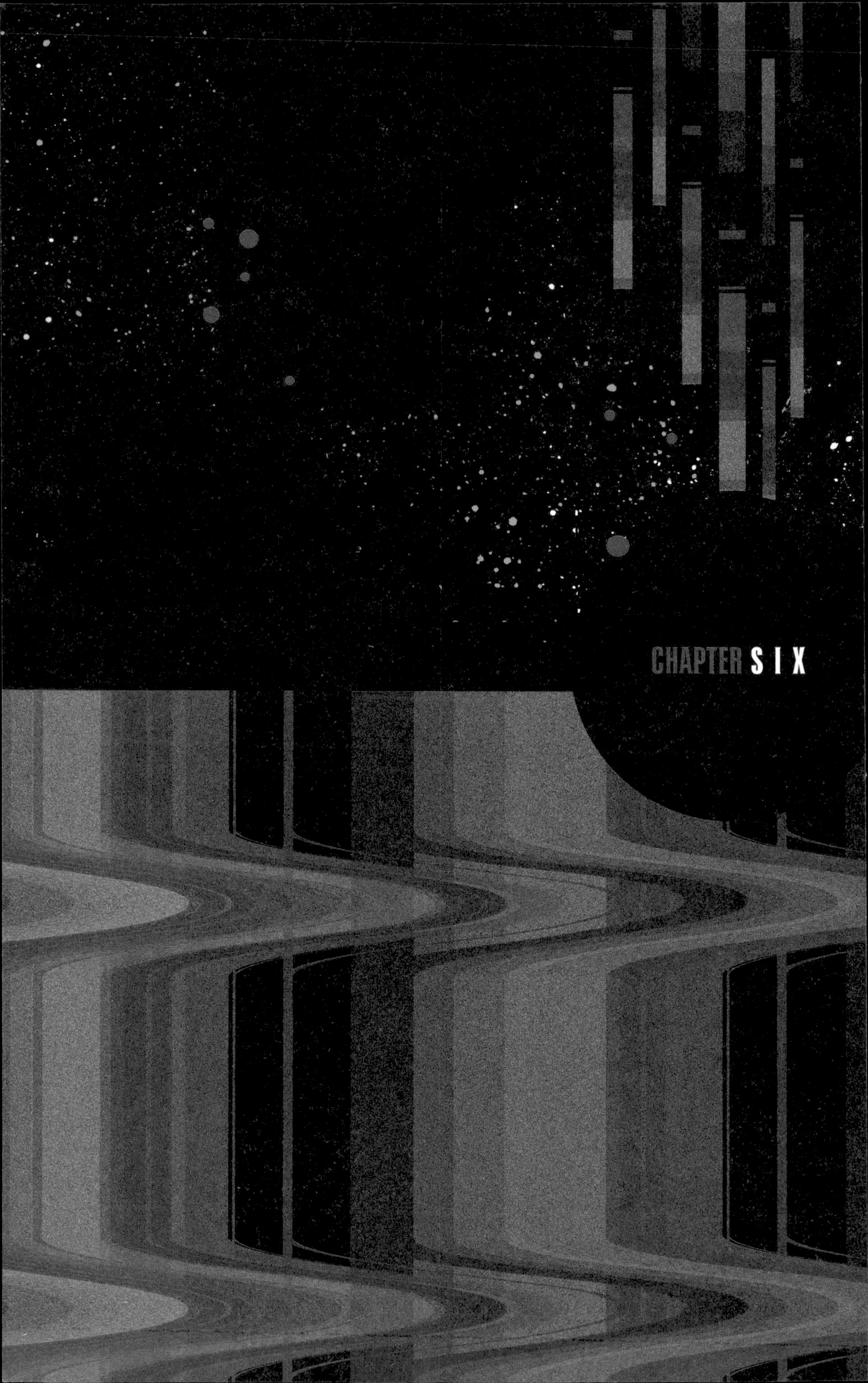

CHAPTER SIX

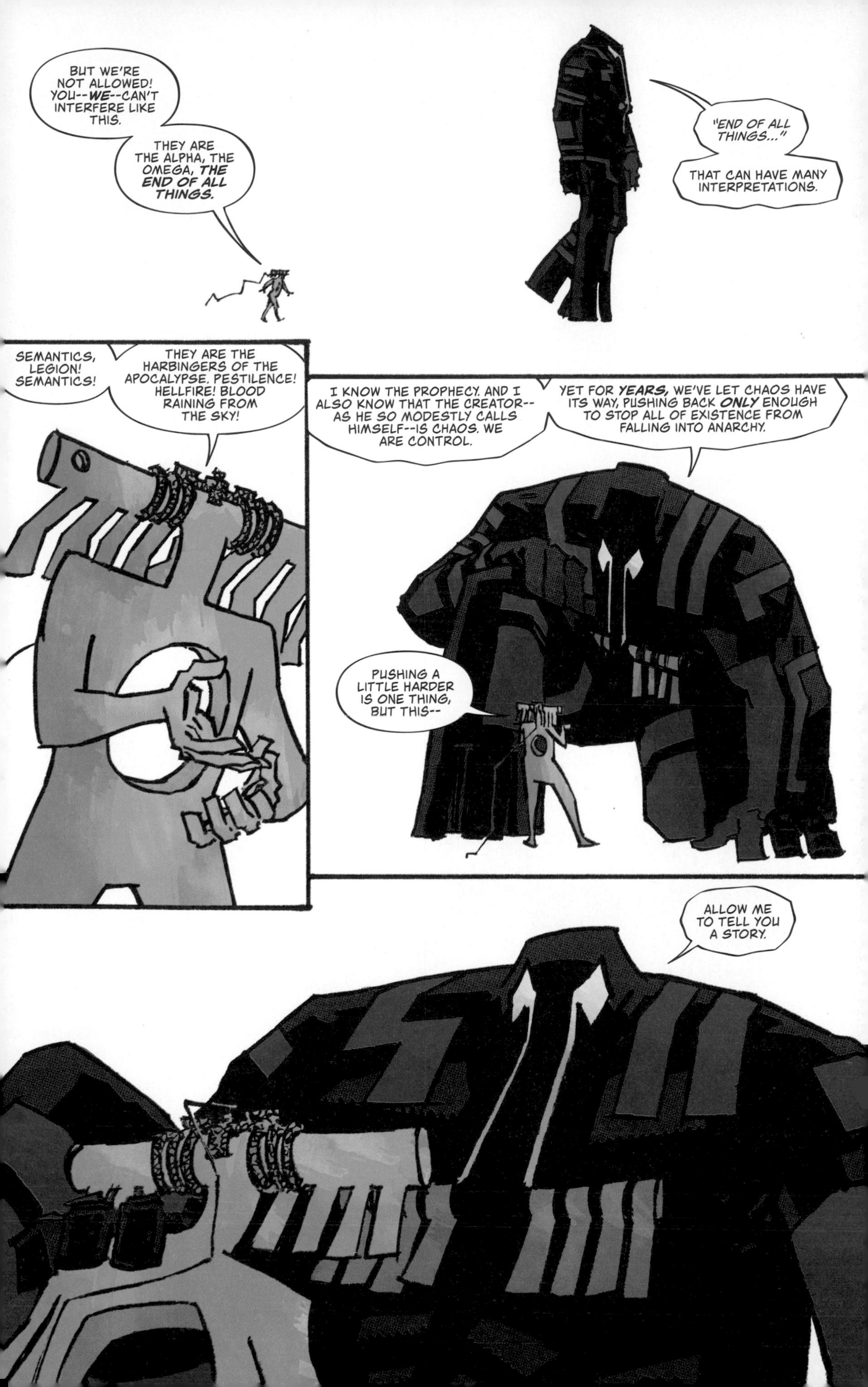
BUT WE'RE NOT ALLOWED! YOU--WE--CAN'T INTERFERE LIKE THIS.
THEY ARE THE ALPHA, THE OMEGA, THE END OF ALL THINGS.
"END OF ALL THINGS..."
THAT CAN HAVE MANY INTERPRETATIONS.
SEMANTICS, LEGION! SEMANTICS!
THEY ARE THE HARBINGERS OF THE APOCALYPSE. PESTILENCE! HELLFIRE! BLOOD RAINING FROM THE SKY!
I KNOW THE PROPHECY. AND I ALSO KNOW THAT THE CREATOR-- AS HE SO MODESTLY CALLS HIMSELF--IS CHAOS. WE ARE CONTROL.
YET FOR YEARS, WE'VE LET CHAOS HAVE ITS WAY, PUSHING BACK ONLY ENOUGH TO STOP ALL OF EXISTENCE FROM FALLING INTO ANARCHY.
PUSHING A LITTLE HARDER IS ONE THING, BUT THIS--
ALLOW ME TO TELL YOU A STORY.

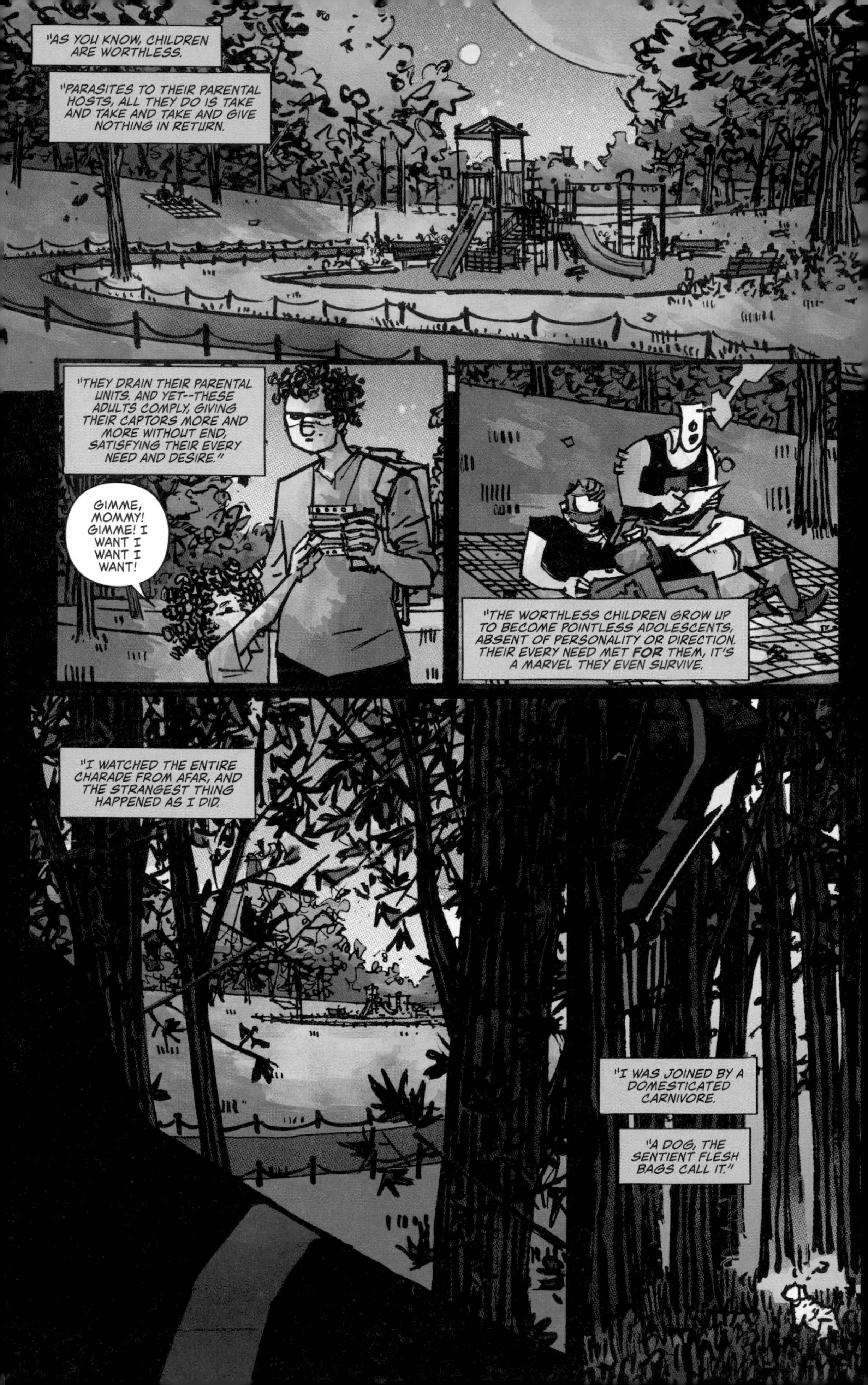
"AS YOU KNOW, CHILDREN ARE WORTHLESS.
"PARASITES TO THEIR PARENTAL HOSTS, ALL THEY DO IS TAKE AND TAKE AND TAKE AND GIVE NOTHING IN RETURN.
"THEY DRAIN THEIR PARENTAL UNITS. AND YET--THESE ADULTS COMPLY, GIVING THEIR CAPTORS MORE AND MORE WITHOUT END, SATISFYING THEIR EVERY NEED AND DESIRE."
GIMME, MOMMY! GIMME! I WANT I WANT I WANT!
"THE WORTHLESS CHILDREN GROW UP TO BECOME POINTLESS ADOLESCENTS, ABSENT OF PERSONALITY OR DIRECTION. THEIR EVERY NEED MET FOR THEM, IT'S A MARVEL THEY EVEN SURVIVE.
"I WATCHED THE ENTIRE CHARADE FROM AFAR, AND THE STRANGEST THING HAPPENED AS I DID.
"I WAS JOINED BY A DOMESTICATED CARNIVORE.
"A DOG, THE SENTIENT FLESH BAGS CALL IT."

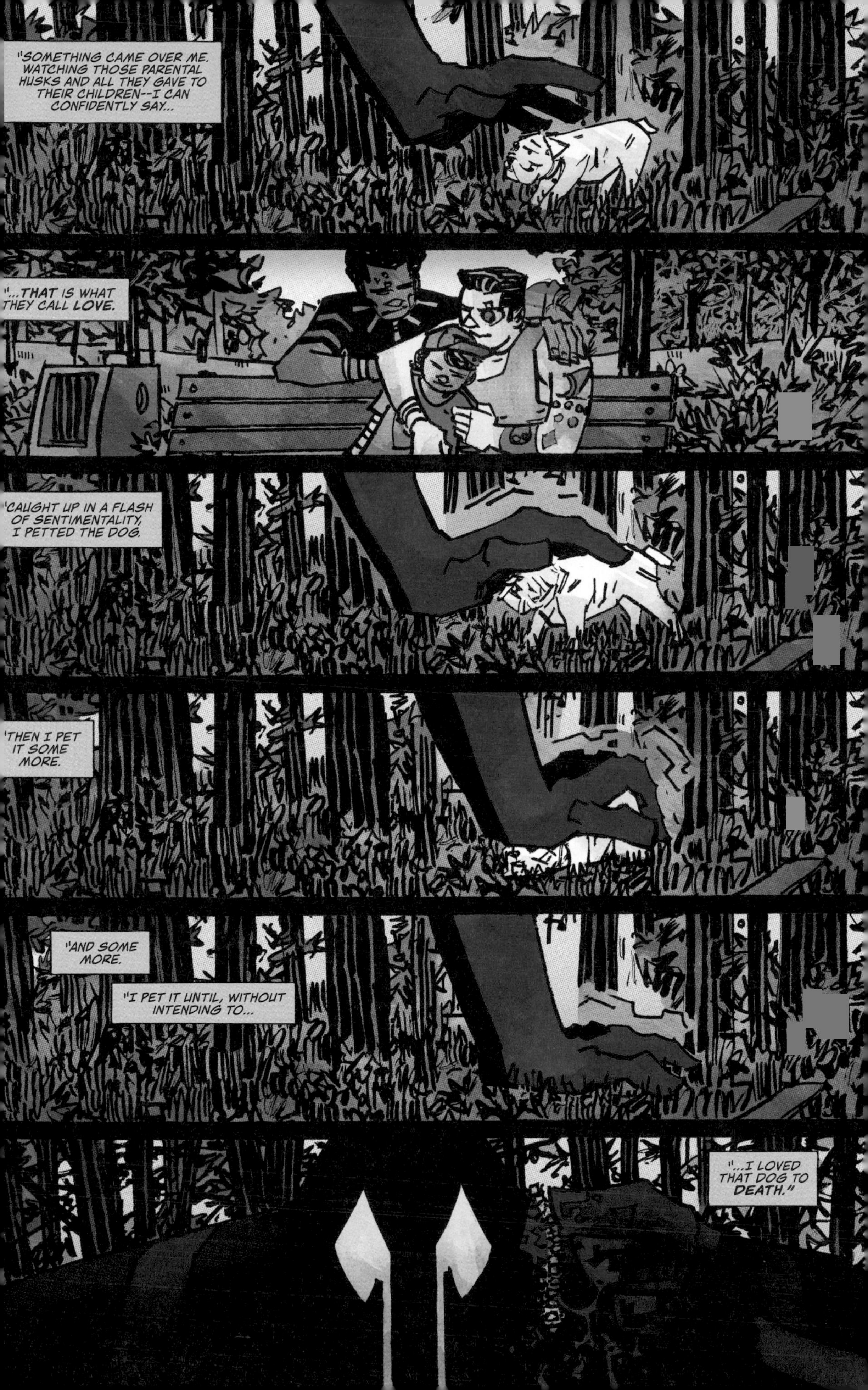
"SOMETHING CAME OVER ME. WATCHING THOSE PARENTAL HUSKS AND ALL THEY GAVE TO THEIR CHILDREN--I CAN CONFIDENTLY SAY...
"...THAT IS WHAT THEY CALL LOVE.
"CAUGHT UP IN A FLASH OF SENTIMENTALITY, I PETTED THE DOG.
"THEN I PET IT SOME MORE.
"AND SOME MORE.
"I PET IT UNTIL, WITHOUT INTENDING TO...
"...I LOVED THAT DOG TO DEATH."

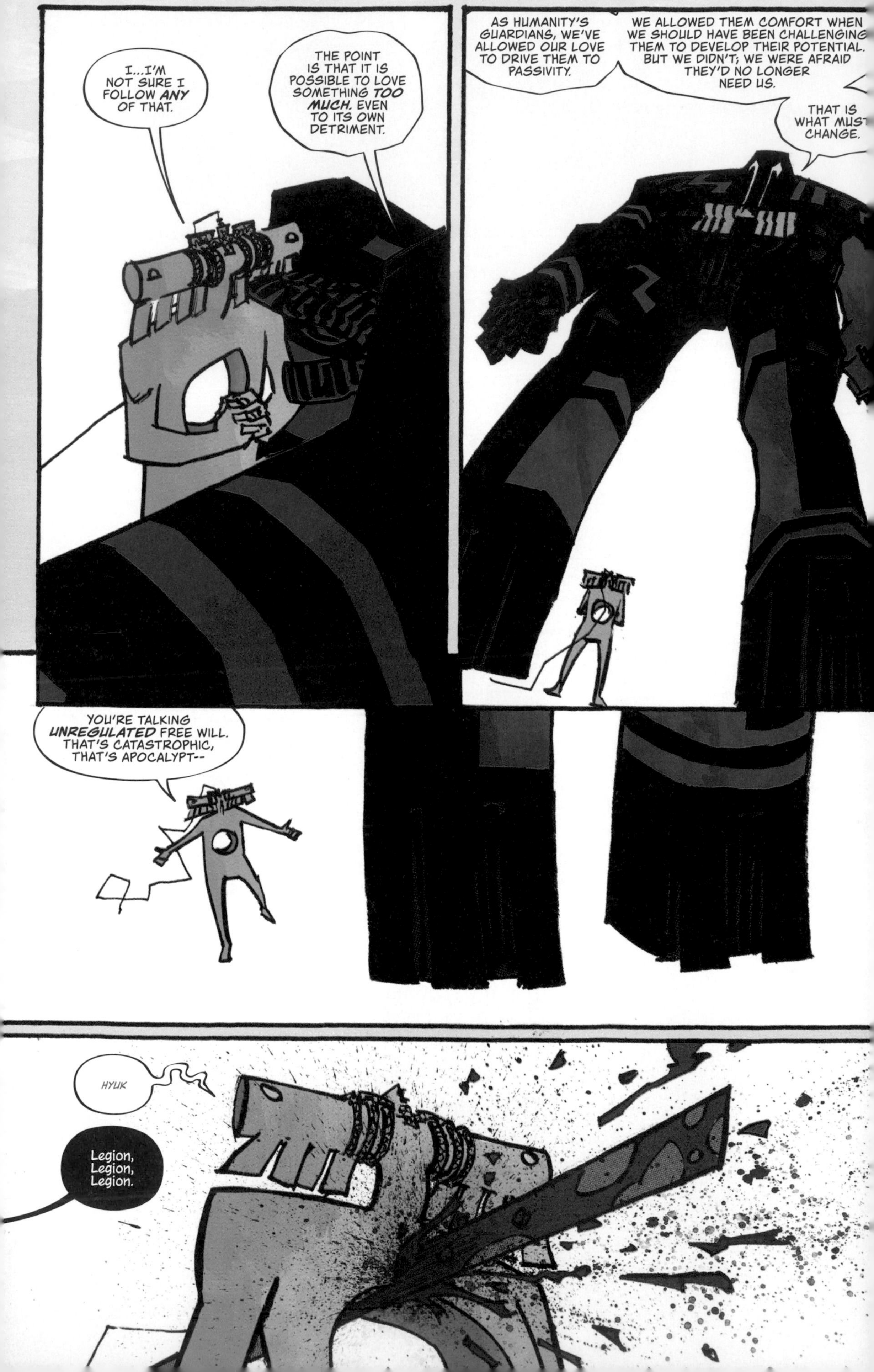
I...I'M NOT SURE I FOLLOW ANY OF THAT.
THE POINT IS THAT IT IS POSSIBLE TO LOVE SOMETHING TOO MUCH. EVEN TO ITS OWN DETRIMENT.
AS HUMANITY'S GUARDIANS, WE'VE ALLOWED OUR LOVE TO DRIVE THEM TO PASSIVITY.
WE ALLOWED THEM COMFORT WHEN WE SHOULD HAVE BEEN CHALLENGING THEM TO DEVELOP THEIR POTENTIAL. BUT WE DIDN'T; WE WERE AFRAID THEY'D NO LONGER NEED US.
THAT IS WHAT MUST CHANGE.
YOU'RE TALKING UNREGULATED FREE WILL. THAT'S CATASTROPHIC, THAT'S APOCALYPT--
HYUK
Legion, Legion, Legion.

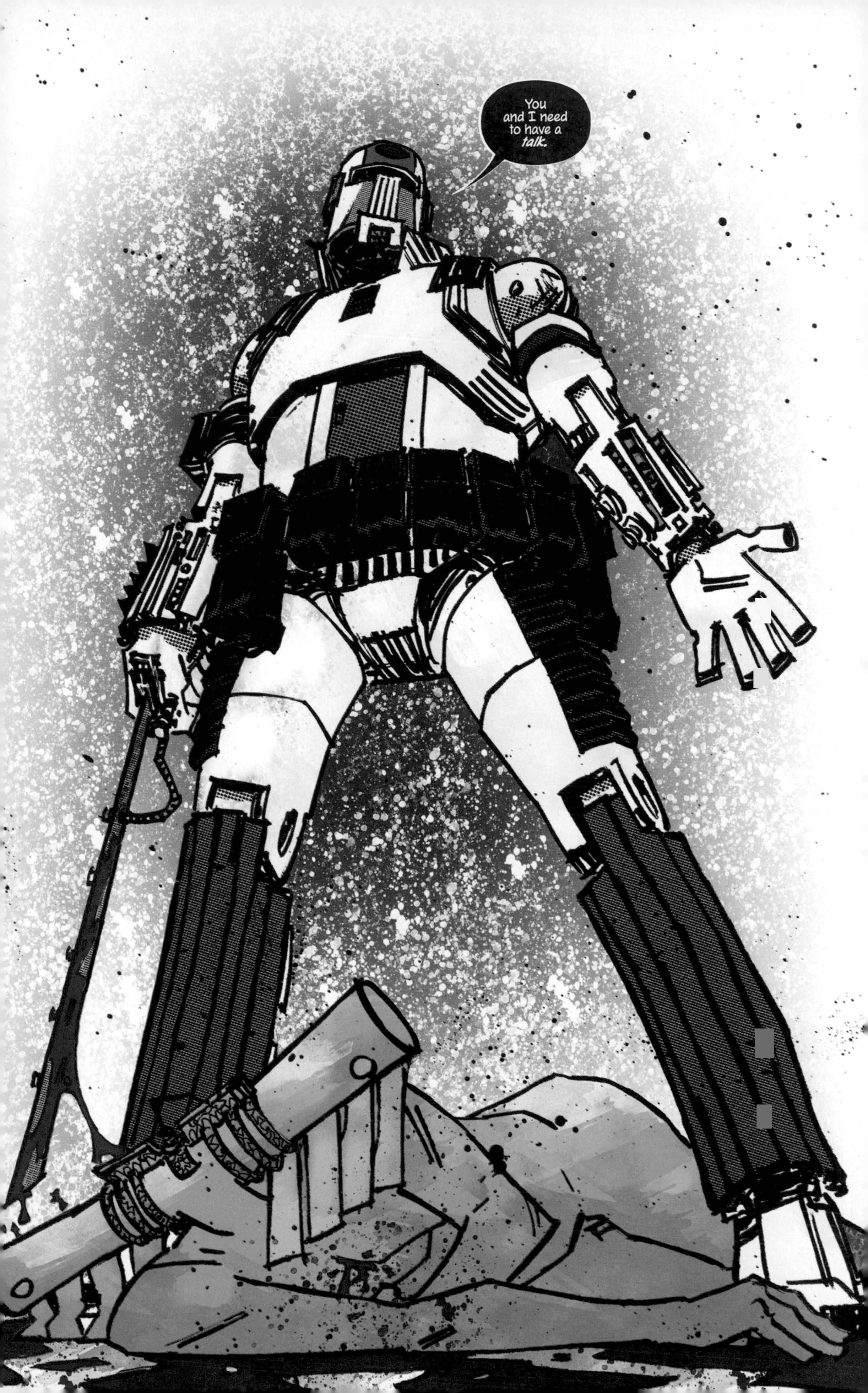
You and I need to have a *talk.*

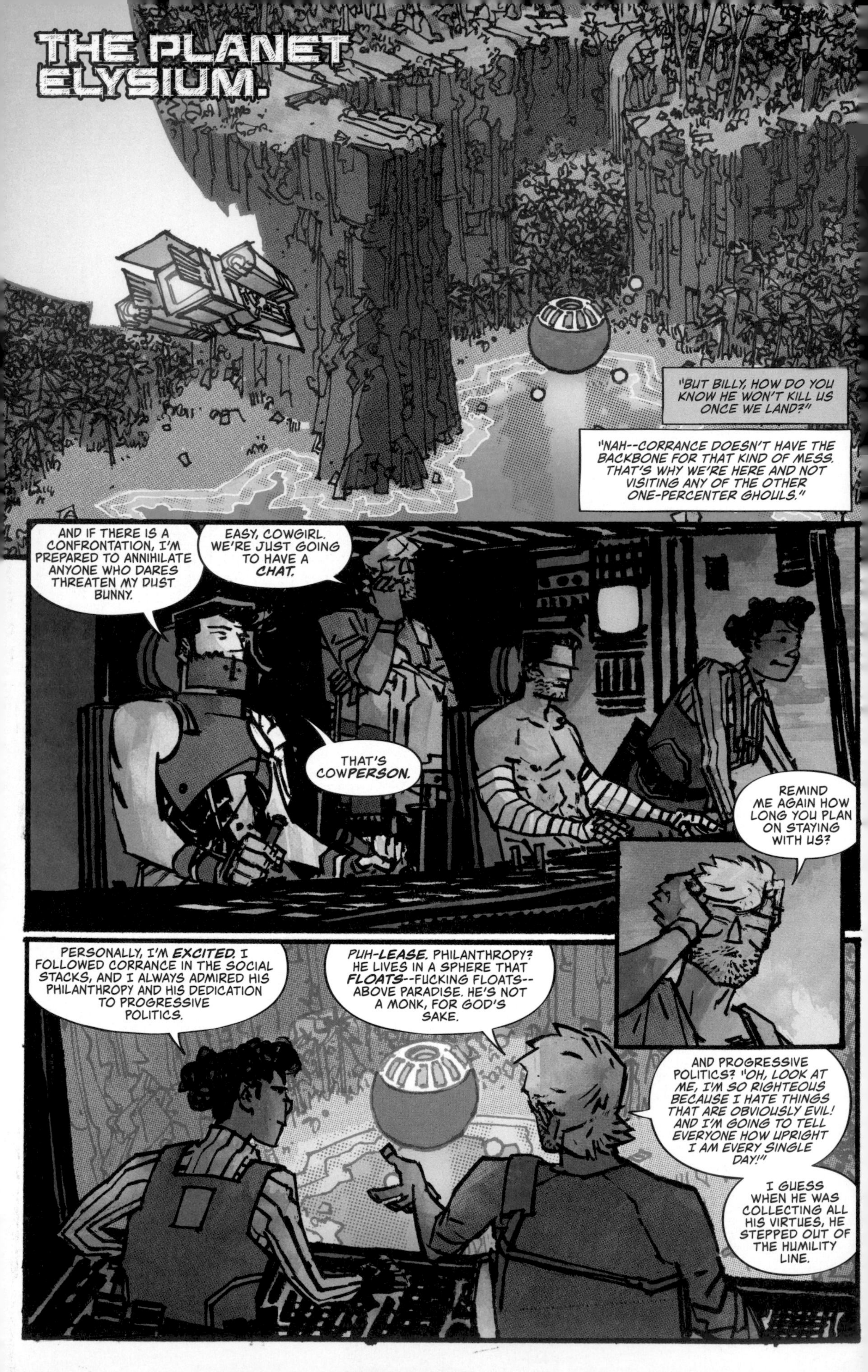
THE PLANET ELYSIUM.
"BUT BILLY, HOW DO YOU KNOW HE WON'T KILL US ONCE WE LAND?"
"NAH--CORRANCE DOESN'T HAVE THE BACKBONE FOR THAT KIND OF MESS. THAT'S WHY WE'RE HERE AND NOT VISITING ANY OF THE OTHER ONE-PERCENTER GHOULS."
AND IF THERE IS A CONFRONTATION, I'M PREPARED TO ANNIHILATE ANYONE WHO DARES THREATEN MY DUST BUNNY.
EASY, COWGIRL. WE'RE JUST GOING TO HAVE A CHAT.
THAT'S COWPERSON.
REMIND ME AGAIN HOW LONG YOU PLAN ON STAYING WITH US?
PERSONALLY, I'M EXCITED. I FOLLOWED CORRANCE IN THE SOCIAL STACKS, AND I ALWAYS ADMIRED HIS PHILANTHROPY AND HIS DEDICATION TO PROGRESSIVE POLITICS.
PUH-LEASE. PHILANTHROPY? HE LIVES IN A SPHERE THAT FLOATS--FUCKING FLOATS--ABOVE PARADISE. HE'S NOT A MONK, FOR GOD'S SAKE.
AND PROGRESSIVE POLITICS? "OH, LOOK AT ME, I'M SO RIGHTEOUS BECAUSE I HATE THINGS THAT ARE OBVIOUSLY EVIL! AND I'M GOING TO TELL EVERYONE HOW UPRIGHT I AM EVERY SINGLE DAY!"
I GUESS WHEN HE WAS COLLECTING ALL HIS VIRTUES, HE STEPPED OUT OF THE HUMILITY LINE.

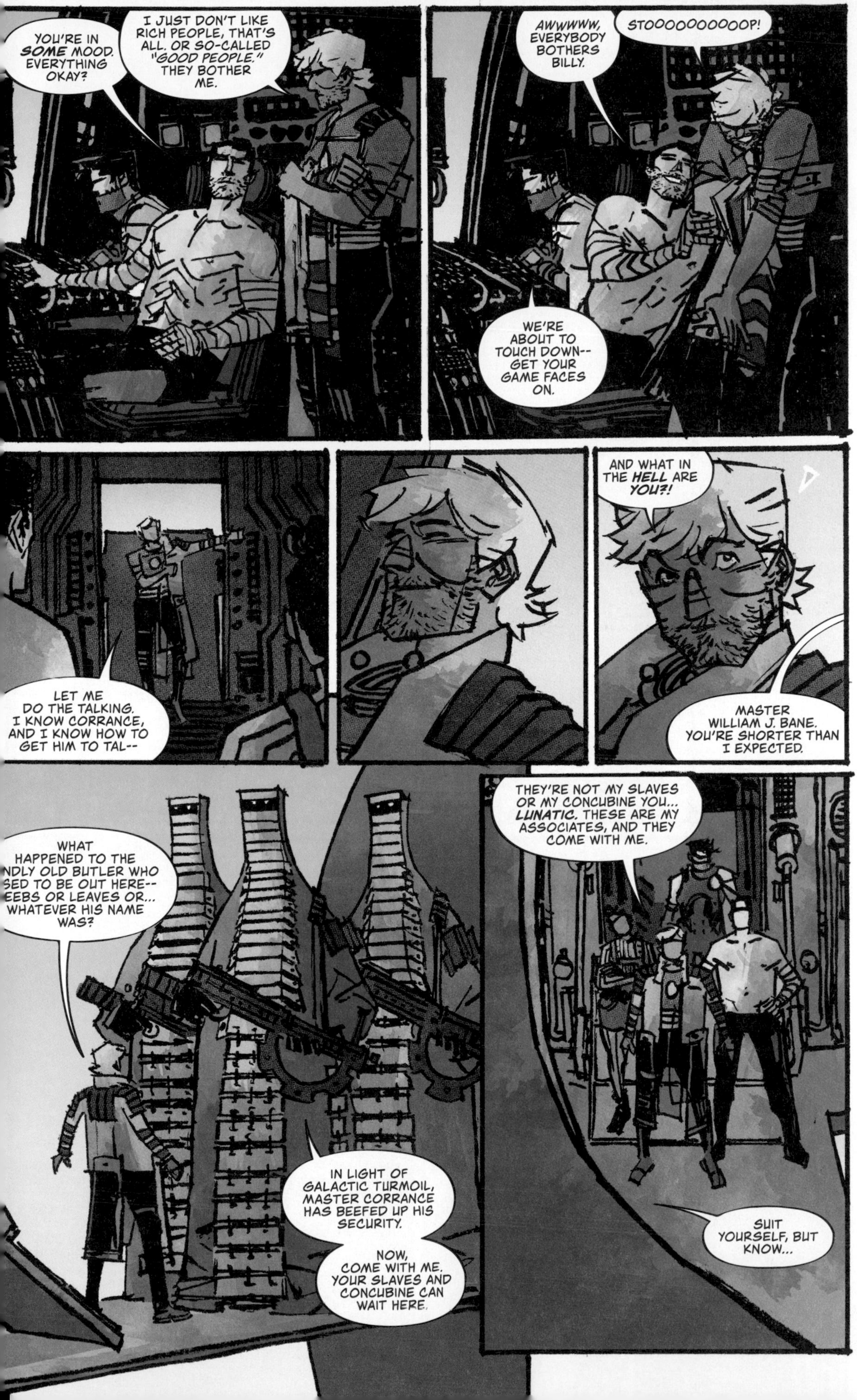
YOU'RE IN SOME MOOD. EVERYTHING OKAY?
I JUST DON'T LIKE RICH PEOPLE, THAT'S ALL. OR SO-CALLED "GOOD PEOPLE." THEY BOTHER ME.
AWWWWW, EVERYBODY BOTHERS BILLY.
STOOOOOOOOOOP!
WE'RE ABOUT TO TOUCH DOWN-- GET YOUR GAME FACES ON.
LET ME DO THE TALKING. I KNOW CORRANCE, AND I KNOW HOW TO GET HIM TO TAL--
AND WHAT IN THE HELL ARE YOU?!
MASTER WILLIAM J. BANE. YOU'RE SHORTER THAN I EXPECTED.
WHAT HAPPENED TO THE NDLY OLD BUTLER WHO SED TO BE OUT HERE-- EEBS OR LEAVES OR... WHATEVER HIS NAME WAS?
IN LIGHT OF GALACTIC TURMOIL, MASTER CORRANCE HAS BEEFED UP HIS SECURITY.
NOW, COME WITH ME. YOUR SLAVES AND CONCUBINE CAN WAIT HERE.
THEY'RE NOT MY SLAVES OR MY CONCUBINE YOU... LUNATIC. THESE ARE MY ASSOCIATES, AND THEY COME WITH ME.
SUIT YOURSELF, BUT KNOW...

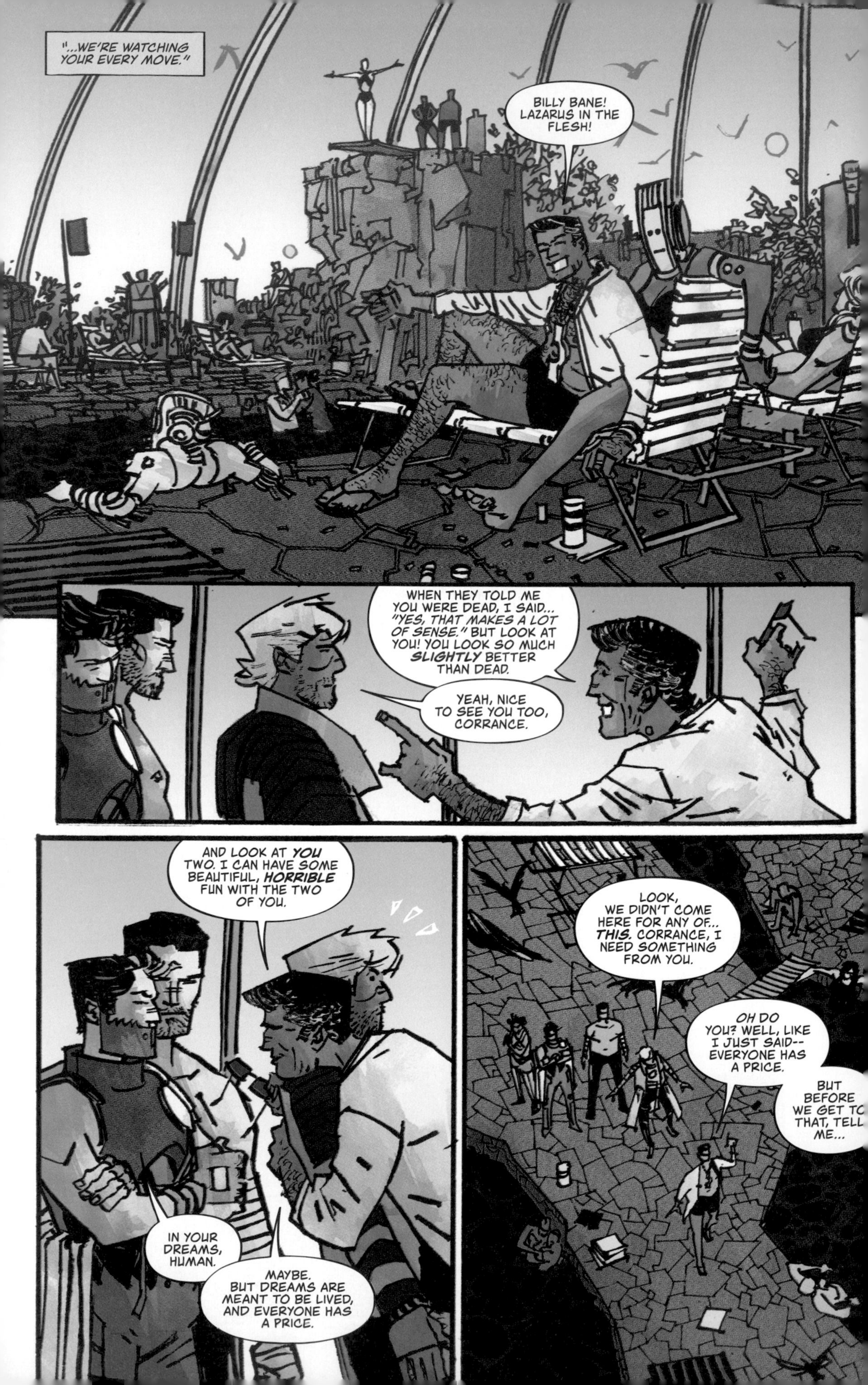
"...WE'RE WATCHING YOUR EVERY MOVE."
BILLY BANE! LAZARUS IN THE FLESH!
WHEN THEY TOLD ME YOU WERE DEAD, I SAID... "YES, THAT MAKES A LOT OF SENSE." BUT LOOK AT YOU! YOU LOOK SO MUCH SLIGHTLY BETTER THAN DEAD.
YEAH, NICE TO SEE YOU TOO, CORRANCE.
AND LOOK AT YOU TWO. I CAN HAVE SOME BEAUTIFUL, HORRIBLE FUN WITH THE TWO OF YOU.
IN YOUR DREAMS, HUMAN.
MAYBE. BUT DREAMS ARE MEANT TO BE LIVED, AND EVERYONE HAS A PRICE.
LOOK, WE DIDN'T COME HERE FOR ANY OF... THIS. CORRANCE, I NEED SOMETHING FROM YOU.
OH DO YOU? WELL, LIKE I JUST SAID-- EVERYONE HAS A PRICE.
BUT BEFORE WE GET TO THAT, TELL ME...

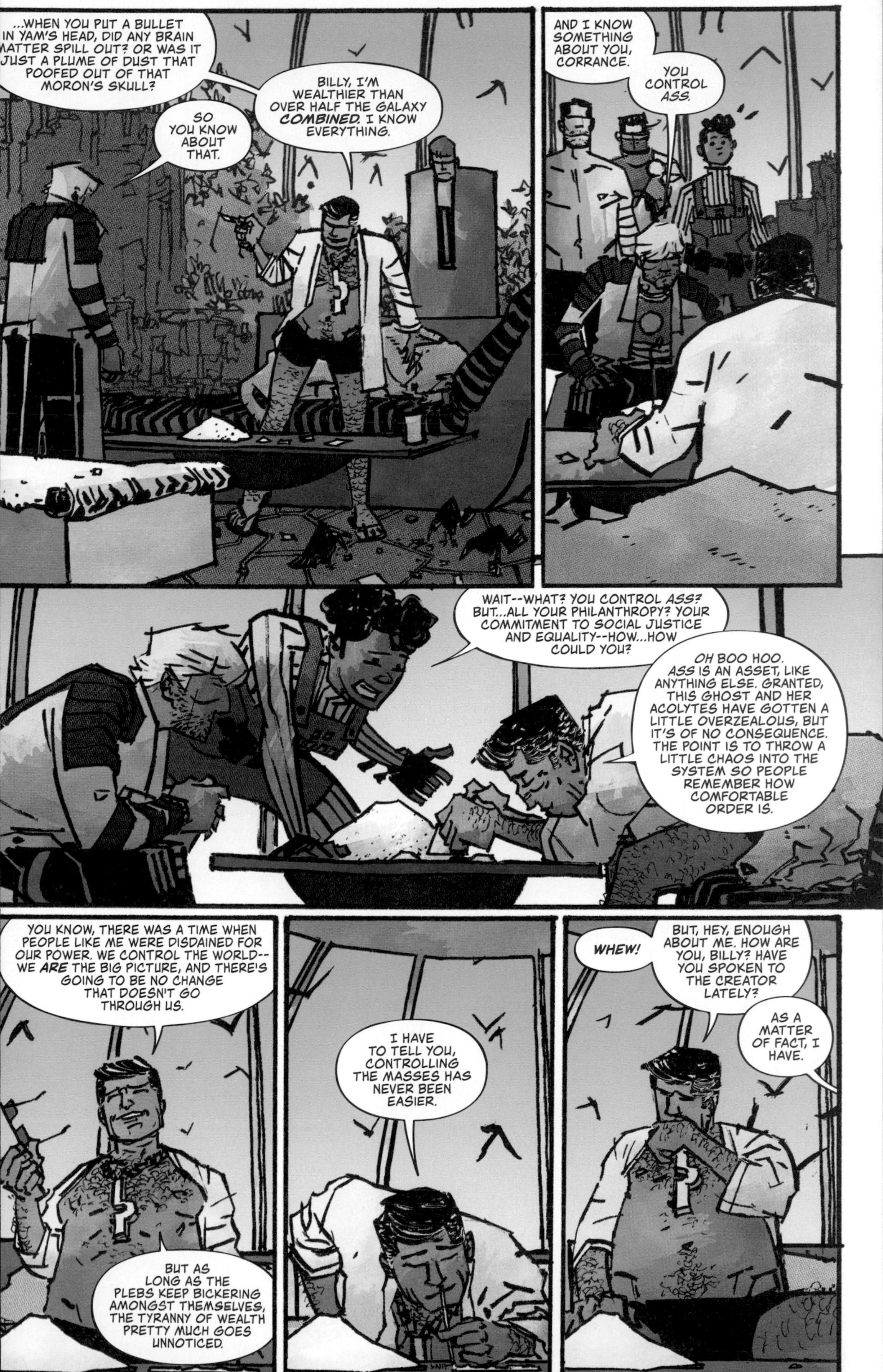
...WHEN YOU PUT A BULLET IN YAM'S HEAD, DID ANY BRAIN MATTER SPILL OUT? OR WAS IT JUST A PLUME OF DUST THAT POOFED OUT OF THAT MORON'S SKULL?
SO YOU KNOW ABOUT THAT.
BILLY, I'M WEALTHIER THAN OVER HALF THE GALAXY COMBINED. I KNOW EVERYTHING.
AND I KNOW SOMETHING ABOUT YOU, CORRANCE.
YOU CONTROL ASS.
WAIT--WHAT? YOU CONTROL ASS? BUT...ALL YOUR PHILANTHROPY? YOUR COMMITMENT TO SOCIAL JUSTICE AND EQUALITY--HOW...HOW COULD YOU?
OH BOO HOO. ASS IS AN ASSET, LIKE ANYTHING ELSE. GRANTED, THIS GHOST AND HER ACOLYTES HAVE GOTTEN A LITTLE OVERZEALOUS, BUT IT'S OF NO CONSEQUENCE. THE POINT IS TO THROW A LITTLE CHAOS INTO THE SYSTEM SO PEOPLE REMEMBER HOW COMFORTABLE ORDER IS.
YOU KNOW, THERE WAS A TIME WHEN PEOPLE LIKE ME WERE DISDAINED FOR OUR POWER. WE CONTROL THE WORLD--WE ARE THE BIG PICTURE, AND THERE'S GOING TO BE NO CHANGE THAT DOESN'T GO THROUGH US.
BUT AS LONG AS THE PLEBS KEEP BICKERING AMONGST THEMSELVES, THE TYRANNY OF WEALTH PRETTY MUCH GOES UNNOTICED.
I HAVE TO TELL YOU, CONTROLLING THE MASSES HAS NEVER BEEN EASIER.
WHEW!
BUT, HEY, ENOUGH ABOUT ME. HOW ARE YOU, BILLY? HAVE YOU SPOKEN TO THE CREATOR LATELY?
AS A MATTER OF FACT, I HAVE.

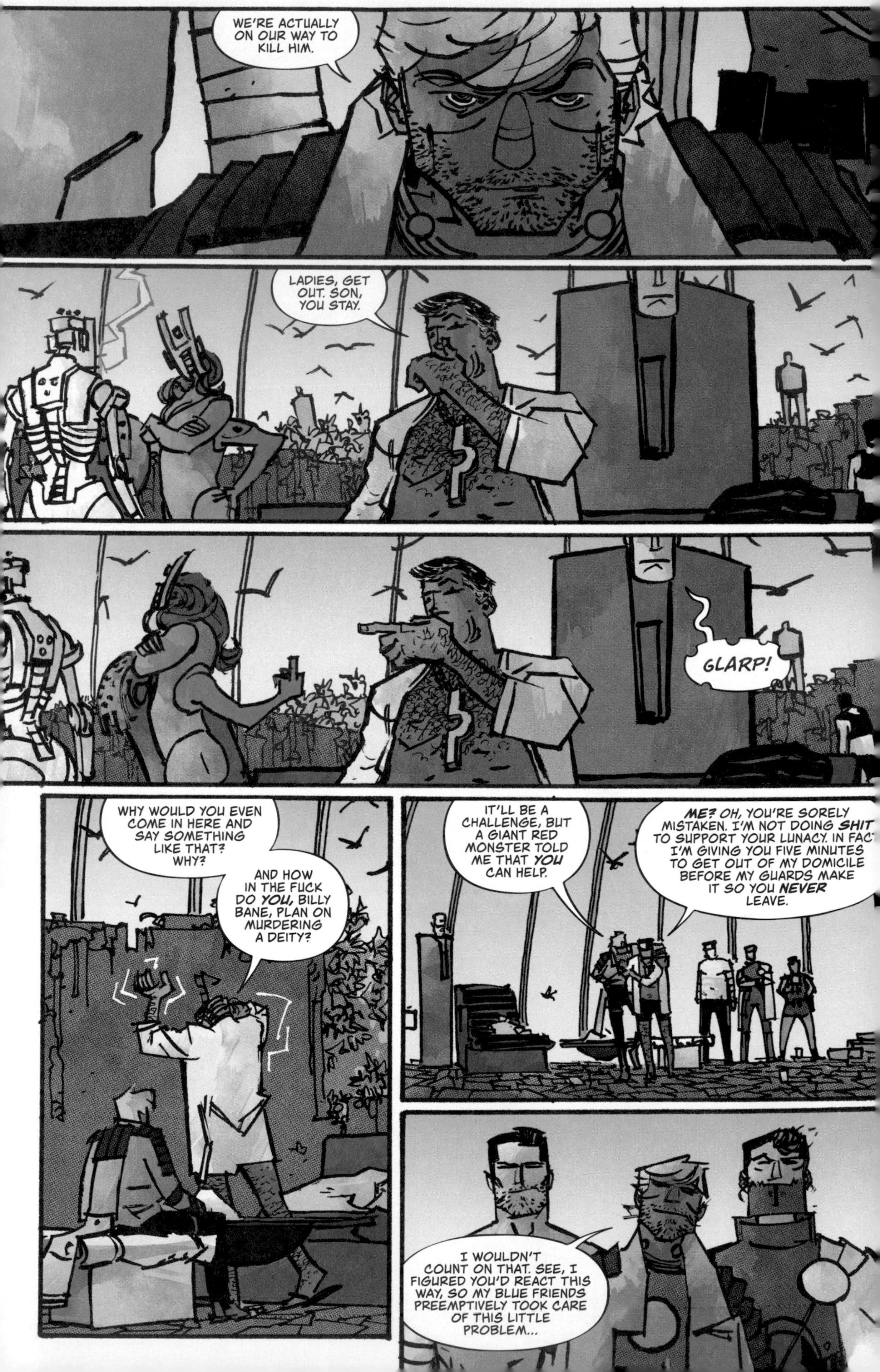
WE'RE ACTUALLY ON OUR WAY TO KILL HIM.
LADIES, GET OUT. SON, YOU STAY.
GLARP!
WHY WOULD YOU EVEN COME IN HERE AND SAY SOMETHING LIKE THAT? WHY?
AND HOW IN THE FUCK DO YOU, BILLY BANE, PLAN ON MURDERING A DEITY?
IT'LL BE A CHALLENGE, BUT A GIANT RED MONSTER TOLD ME THAT YOU CAN HELP.
ME? OH, YOU'RE SORELY MISTAKEN. I'M NOT DOING SHIT TO SUPPORT YOUR LUNACY. IN FACT I'M GIVING YOU FIVE MINUTES TO GET OUT OF MY DOMICILE BEFORE MY GUARDS MAKE IT SO YOU NEVER LEAVE.
I WOULDN'T COUNT ON THAT. SEE, I FIGURED YOU'D REACT THIS WAY, SO MY BLUE FRIENDS PREEMPTIVELY TOOK CARE OF THIS LITTLE PROBLEM...

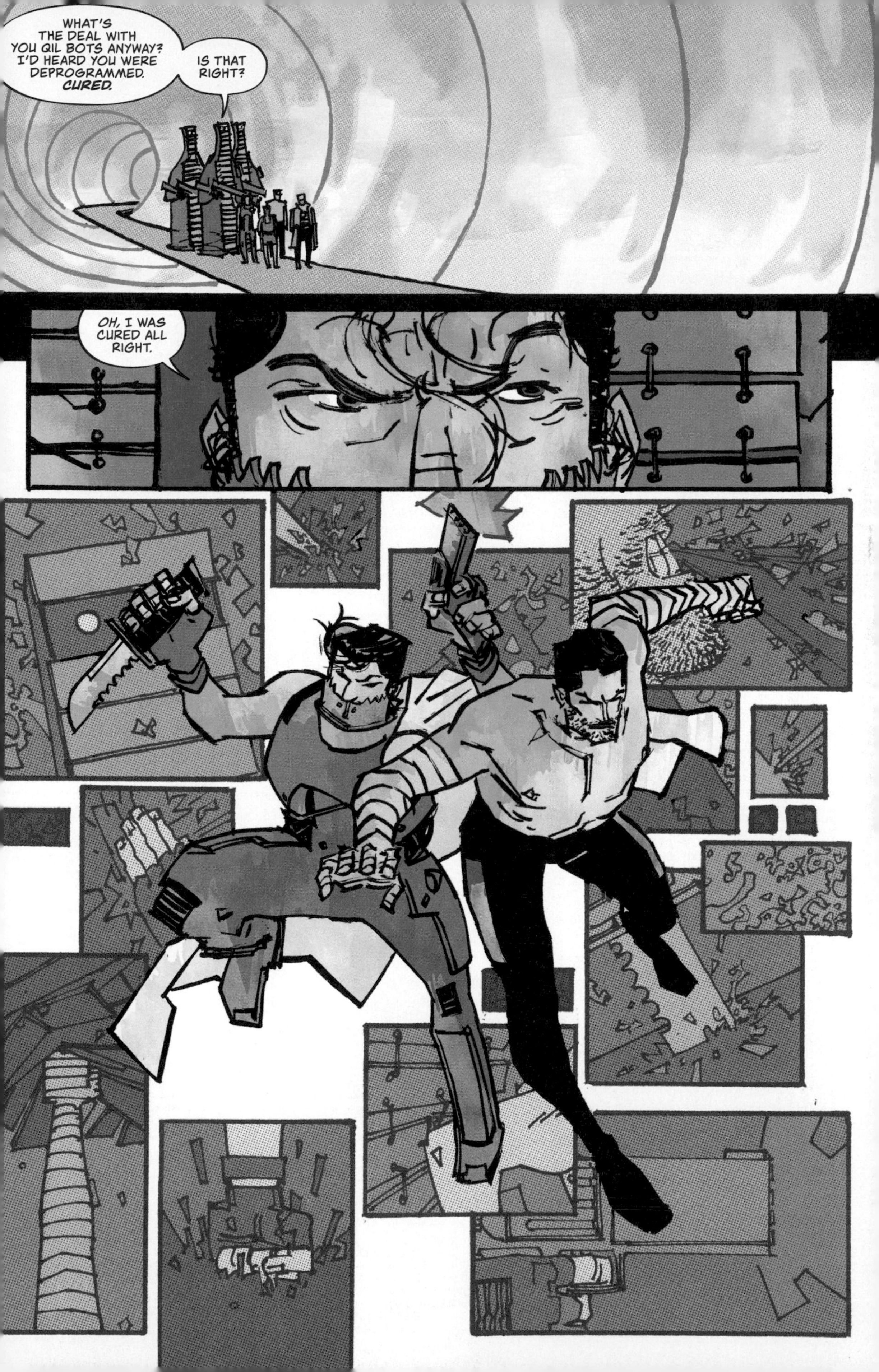
WHAT'S THE DEAL WITH YOU QIL BOTS ANYWAY? I'D HEARD YOU WERE DEPROGRAMMED. CURED.
IS THAT RIGHT?
OH, I WAS CURED ALL RIGHT.

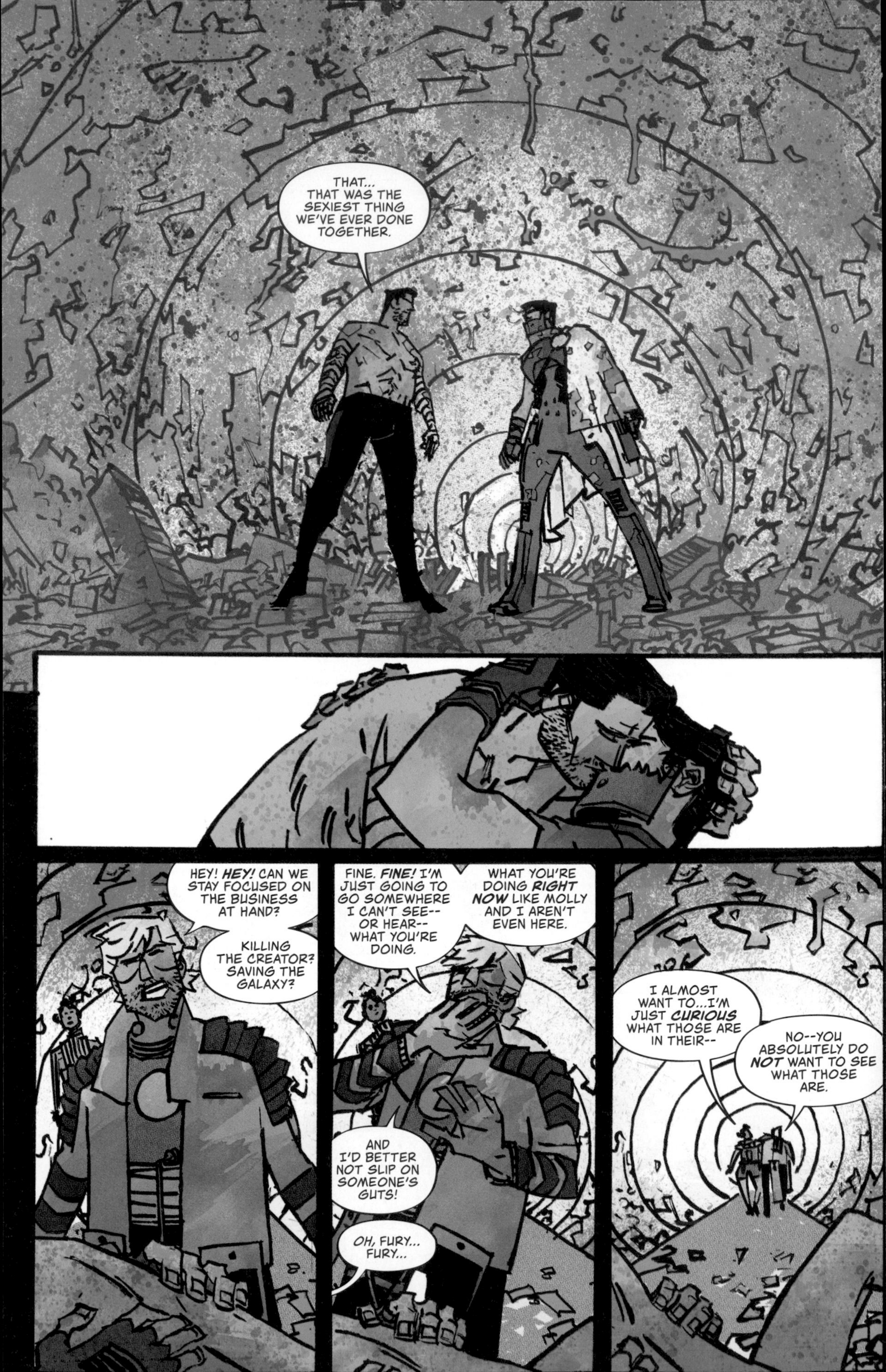
THAT... THAT WAS THE SEXIEST THING WE'VE EVER DONE TOGETHER.
HEY! HEY! CAN WE STAY FOCUSED ON THE BUSINESS AT HAND?
KILLING THE CREATOR? SAVING THE GALAXY?
FINE. FINE! I'M JUST GOING TO GO SOMEWHERE I CAN'T SEE-- OR HEAR-- WHAT YOU'RE DOING.
WHAT YOU'RE DOING RIGHT NOW LIKE MOLLY AND I AREN'T EVEN HERE.
AND I'D BETTER NOT SLIP ON SOMEONE'S GUTS!
OH, FURY... FURY...
I ALMOST WANT TO...I'M JUST CURIOUS WHAT THOSE ARE IN THEIR--
NO--YOU ABSOLUTELY DO NOT WANT TO SEE WHAT THOSE ARE.

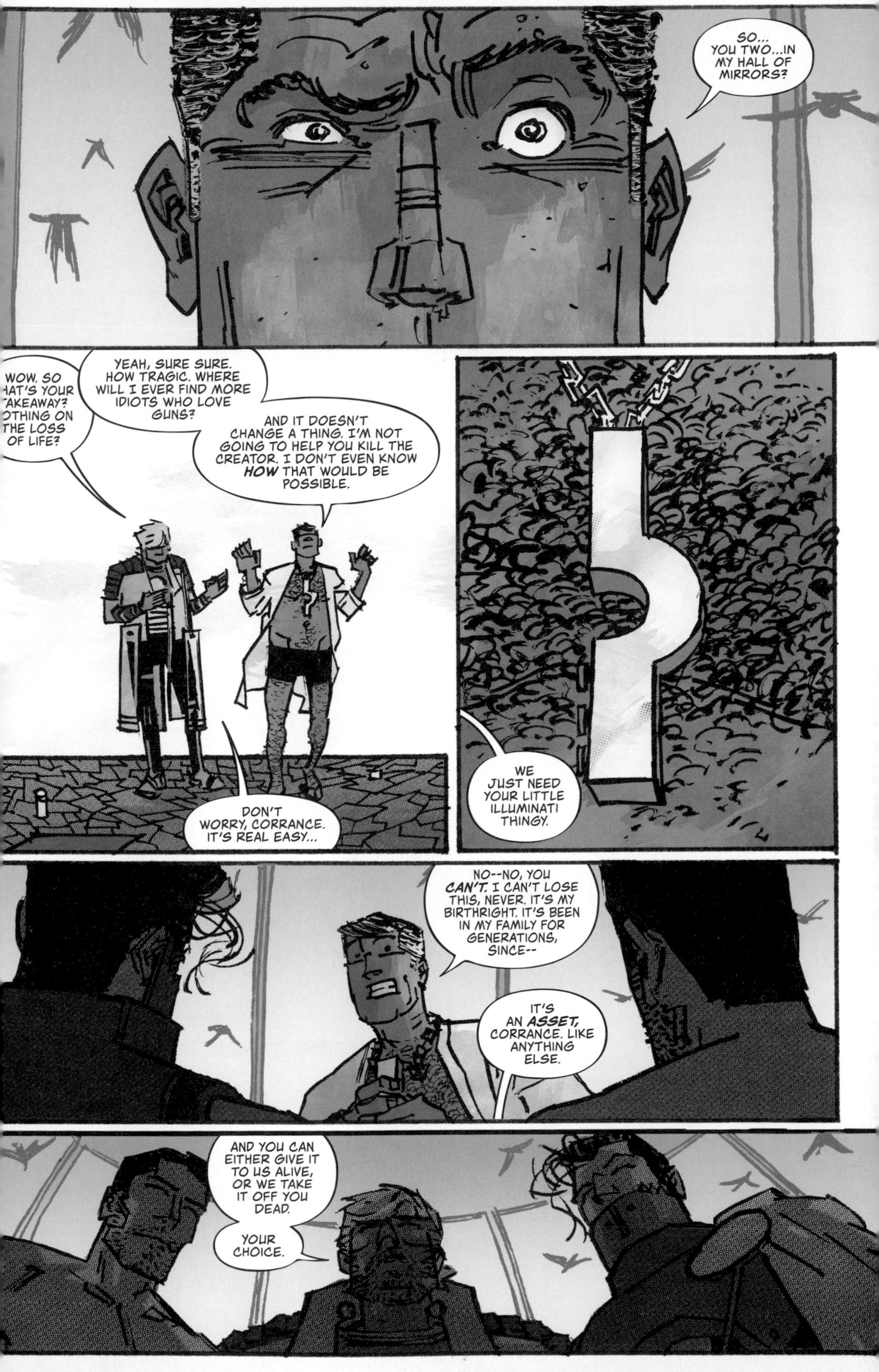
SO... YOU TWO...IN MY HALL OF MIRRORS?
WOW. SO HAT'S YOUR TAKEAWAY? OTHING ON THE LOSS OF LIFE?
YEAH, SURE SURE. HOW TRAGIC. WHERE WILL I EVER FIND MORE IDIOTS WHO LOVE GUNS?
AND IT DOESN'T CHANGE A THING. I'M NOT GOING TO HELP YOU KILL THE CREATOR. I DON'T EVEN KNOW HOW THAT WOULD BE POSSIBLE.
DON'T WORRY, CORRANCE. IT'S REAL EASY...
WE JUST NEED YOUR LITTLE ILLUMINATI THINGY.
NO--NO, YOU CAN'T. I CAN'T LOSE THIS, NEVER. IT'S MY BIRTHRIGHT. IT'S BEEN IN MY FAMILY FOR GENERATIONS, SINCE--
IT'S AN ASSET, CORRANCE. LIKE ANYTHING ELSE.
AND YOU CAN EITHER GIVE IT TO US ALIVE, OR WE TAKE IT OFF YOU DEAD.
YOUR CHOICE.

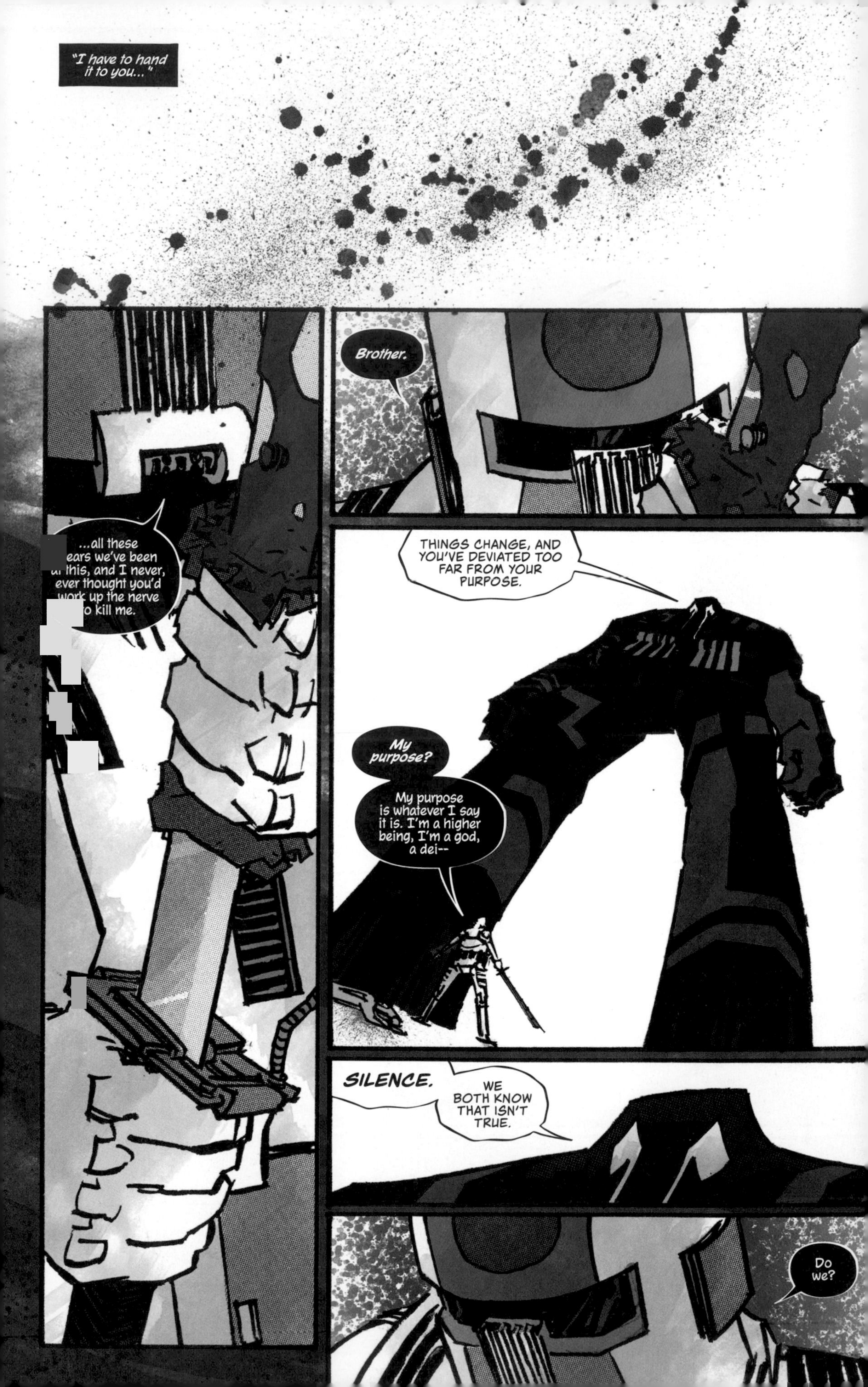
"I have to hand it to you..."
...all these years we've been at this, and I never, ever thought you'd work up the nerve to kill me.
Brother.
THINGS CHANGE, AND YOU'VE DEVIATED TOO FAR FROM YOUR PURPOSE.
My purpose?
My purpose is whatever I say it is. I'm a higher being, I'm a god, a dei--
SILENCE.
WE BOTH KNOW THAT ISN'T TRUE.
Do we?

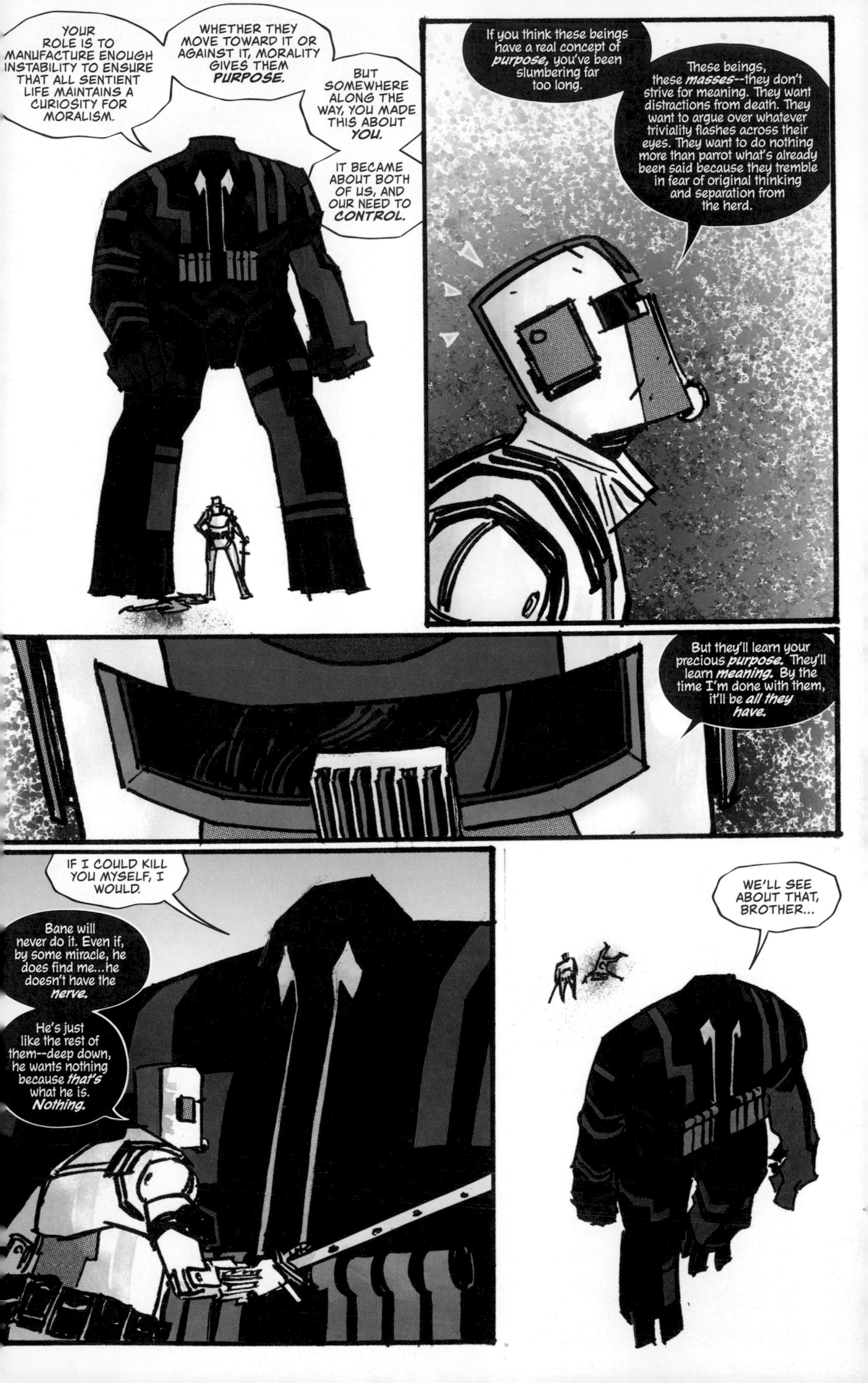
YOUR ROLE IS TO MANUFACTURE ENOUGH INSTABILITY TO ENSURE THAT ALL SENTIENT LIFE MAINTAINS A CURIOSITY FOR MORALISM.
WHETHER THEY MOVE TOWARD IT OR AGAINST IT, MORALITY GIVES THEM *PURPOSE.*
BUT SOMEWHERE ALONG THE WAY, YOU MADE THIS ABOUT *YOU.*
IT BECAME ABOUT BOTH OF US, AND OUR NEED TO *CONTROL.*
If you think these beings have a real concept of *purpose,* you've been slumbering far too long.
These beings, these *masses*--they don't strive for meaning. They want distractions from death. They want to argue over whatever triviality flashes across their eyes. They want to do nothing more than parrot what's already been said because they tremble in fear of original thinking and separation from the herd.
But they'll learn your precious *purpose.* They'll learn *meaning.* By the time I'm done with them, it'll be *all they have.*
IF I COULD KILL YOU MYSELF, I WOULD.
Bane will never do it. Even if, by some miracle, he does find me...he doesn't have the *nerve.*
He's just like the rest of them--deep down, he wants nothing because *that's* what he is. *Nothing.*
WE'LL SEE ABOUT THAT, BROTHER...

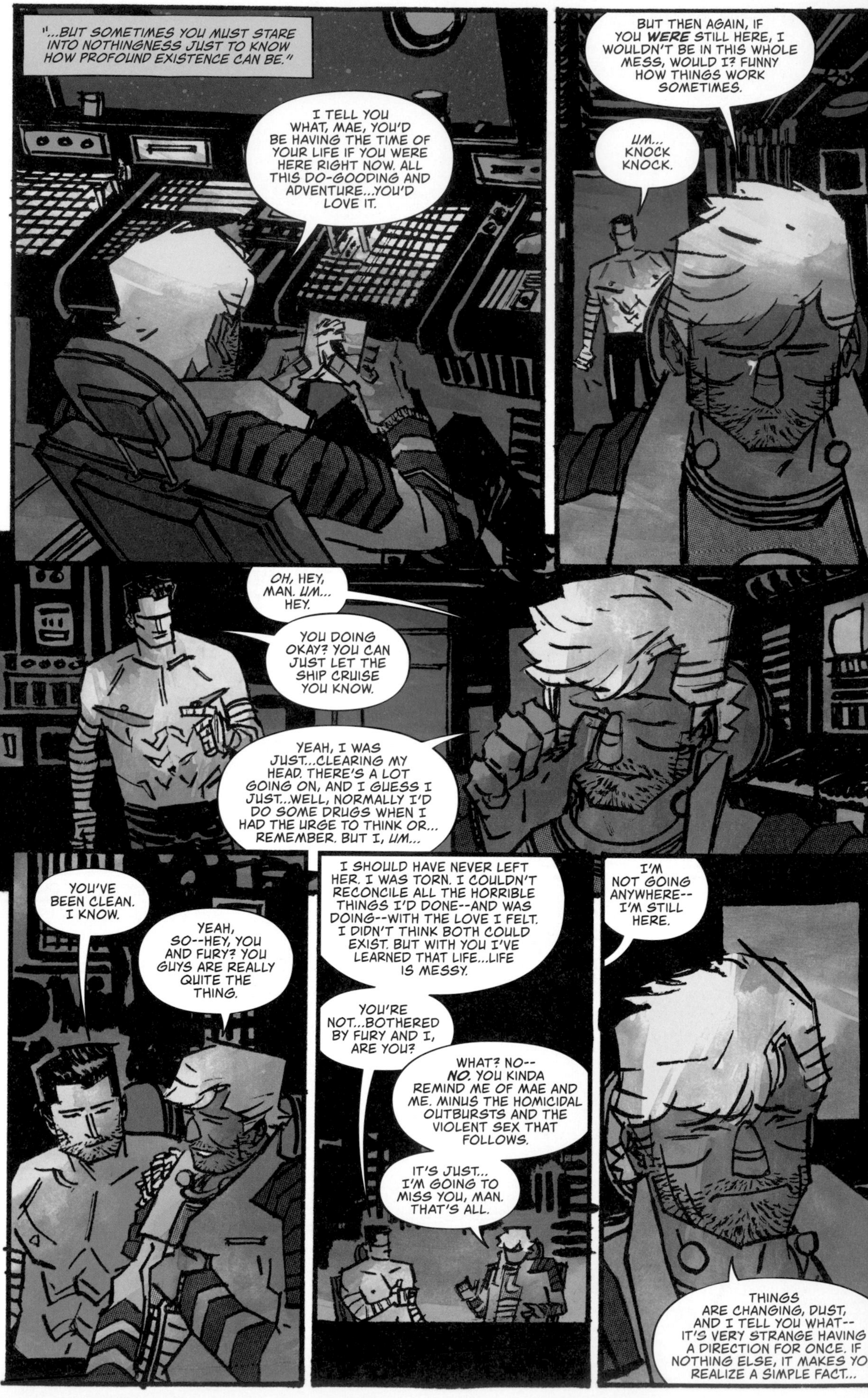
"...BUT SOMETIMES YOU MUST STARE INTO NOTHINGNESS JUST TO KNOW HOW PROFOUND EXISTENCE CAN BE."
I TELL YOU WHAT, MAE, YOU'D BE HAVING THE TIME OF YOUR LIFE IF YOU WERE HERE RIGHT NOW. ALL THIS DO-GOODING AND ADVENTURE...YOU'D LOVE IT.
BUT THEN AGAIN, IF YOU WERE STILL HERE, I WOULDN'T BE IN THIS WHOLE MESS, WOULD I? FUNNY HOW THINGS WORK SOMETIMES.
UM... KNOCK KNOCK.
OH, HEY, MAN. UM... HEY.
YOU DOING OKAY? YOU CAN JUST LET THE SHIP CRUISE YOU KNOW.
YEAH, I WAS JUST...CLEARING MY HEAD. THERE'S A LOT GOING ON, AND I GUESS I JUST...WELL, NORMALLY I'D DO SOME DRUGS WHEN I HAD THE URGE TO THINK OR... REMEMBER. BUT I, UM...
YOU'VE BEEN CLEAN. I KNOW.
YEAH, SO--HEY, YOU AND FURY? YOU GUYS ARE REALLY QUITE THE THING.
I SHOULD HAVE NEVER LEFT HER. I WAS TORN. I COULDN'T RECONCILE ALL THE HORRIBLE THINGS I'D DONE--AND WAS DOING--WITH THE LOVE I FELT. I DIDN'T THINK BOTH COULD EXIST. BUT WITH YOU I'VE LEARNED THAT LIFE...LIFE IS MESSY.
YOU'RE NOT...BOTHERED BY FURY AND I, ARE YOU?
WHAT? NO-- NO. YOU KINDA REMIND ME OF MAE AND ME. MINUS THE HOMICIDAL OUTBURSTS AND THE VIOLENT SEX THAT FOLLOWS.
IT'S JUST... I'M GOING TO MISS YOU, MAN. THAT'S ALL.
I'M NOT GOING ANYWHERE-- I'M STILL HERE.
THINGS ARE CHANGING, DUST, AND I TELL YOU WHAT-- IT'S VERY STRANGE HAVING A DIRECTION FOR ONCE. IF NOTHING ELSE, IT MAKES YOU REALIZE A SIMPLE FACT...

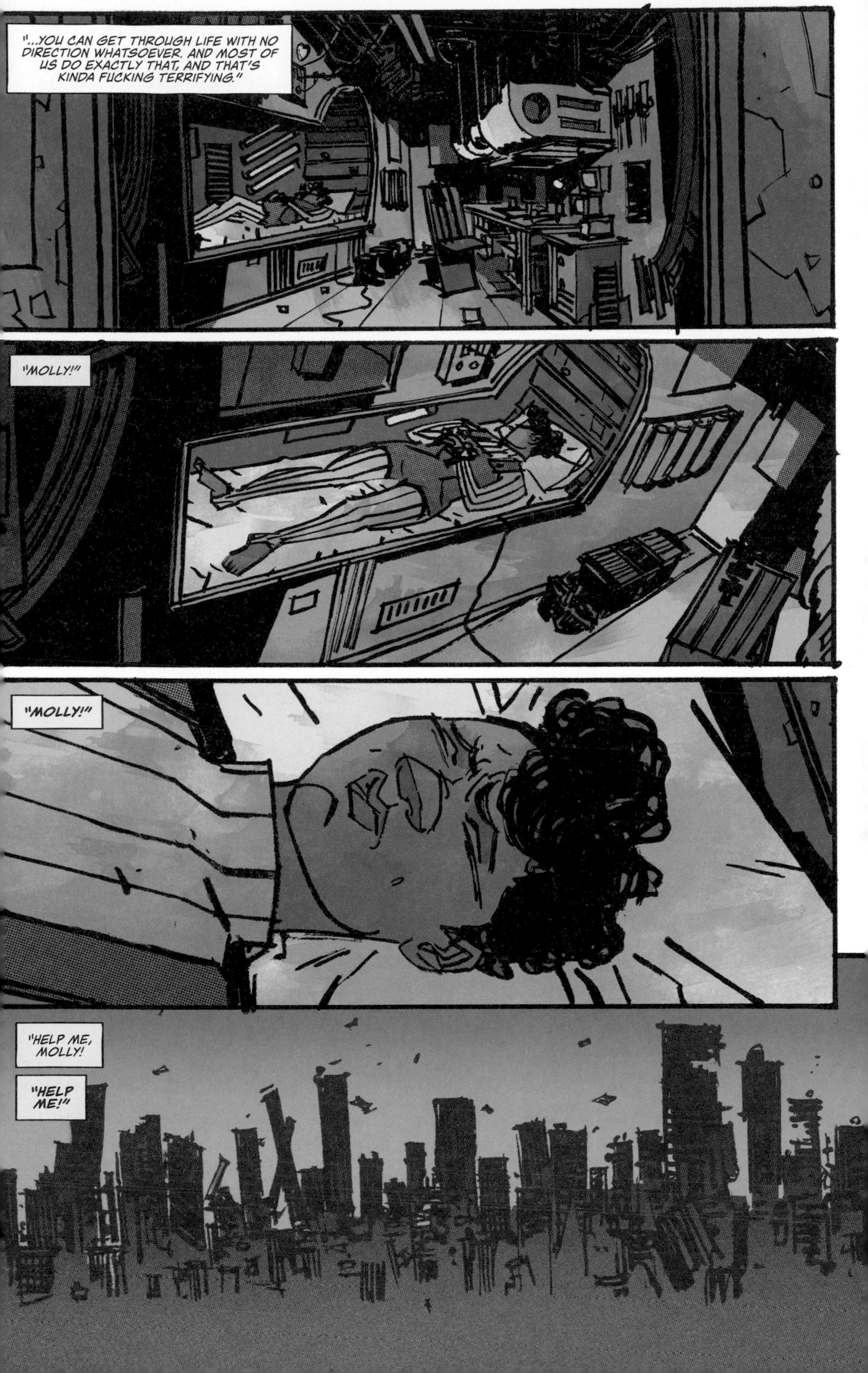
"...YOU CAN GET THROUGH LIFE WITH NO DIRECTION WHATSOEVER. AND MOST OF US DO EXACTLY THAT, AND THAT'S KINDA FUCKING TERRIFYING."
"MOLLY!"
"MOLLY!"
"HELP ME, MOLLY!
"HELP ME!"

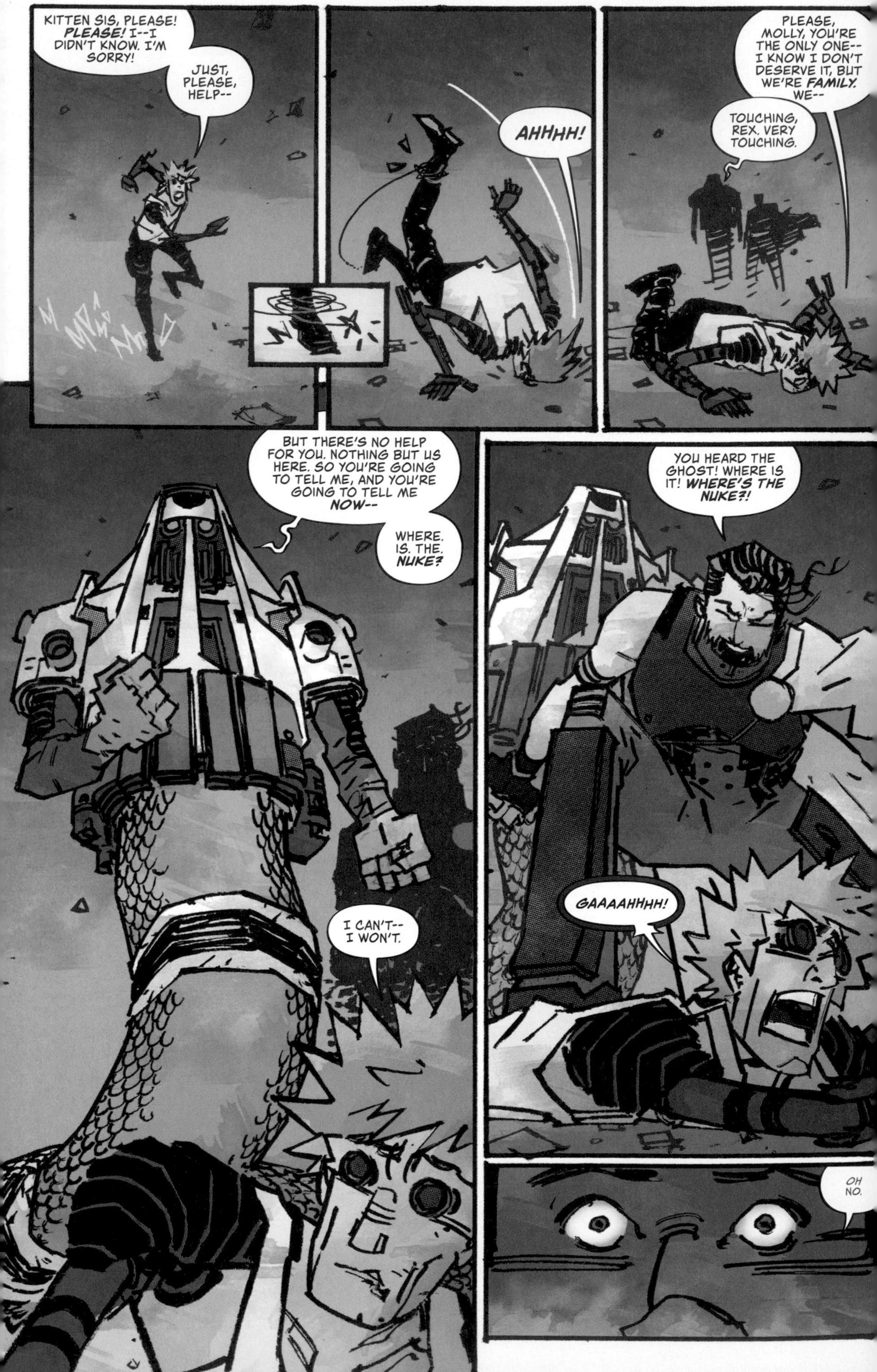
KITTEN SIS, PLEASE! PLEASE! I--I DIDN'T KNOW. I'M SORRY!
JUST, PLEASE, HELP--
AHHHH!
PLEASE, MOLLY, YOU'RE THE ONLY ONE-- I KNOW I DON'T DESERVE IT, BUT WE'RE FAMILY. WE--
TOUCHING, REX. VERY TOUCHING.
BUT THERE'S NO HELP FOR YOU. NOTHING BUT US HERE. SO YOU'RE GOING TO TELL ME, AND YOU'RE GOING TO TELL ME NOW--
WHERE. IS. THE. NUKE?
I CAN'T-- I WON'T.
YOU HEARD THE GHOST! WHERE IS IT! WHERE'S THE NUKE?!
GAAAAHHHH!
OH NO.

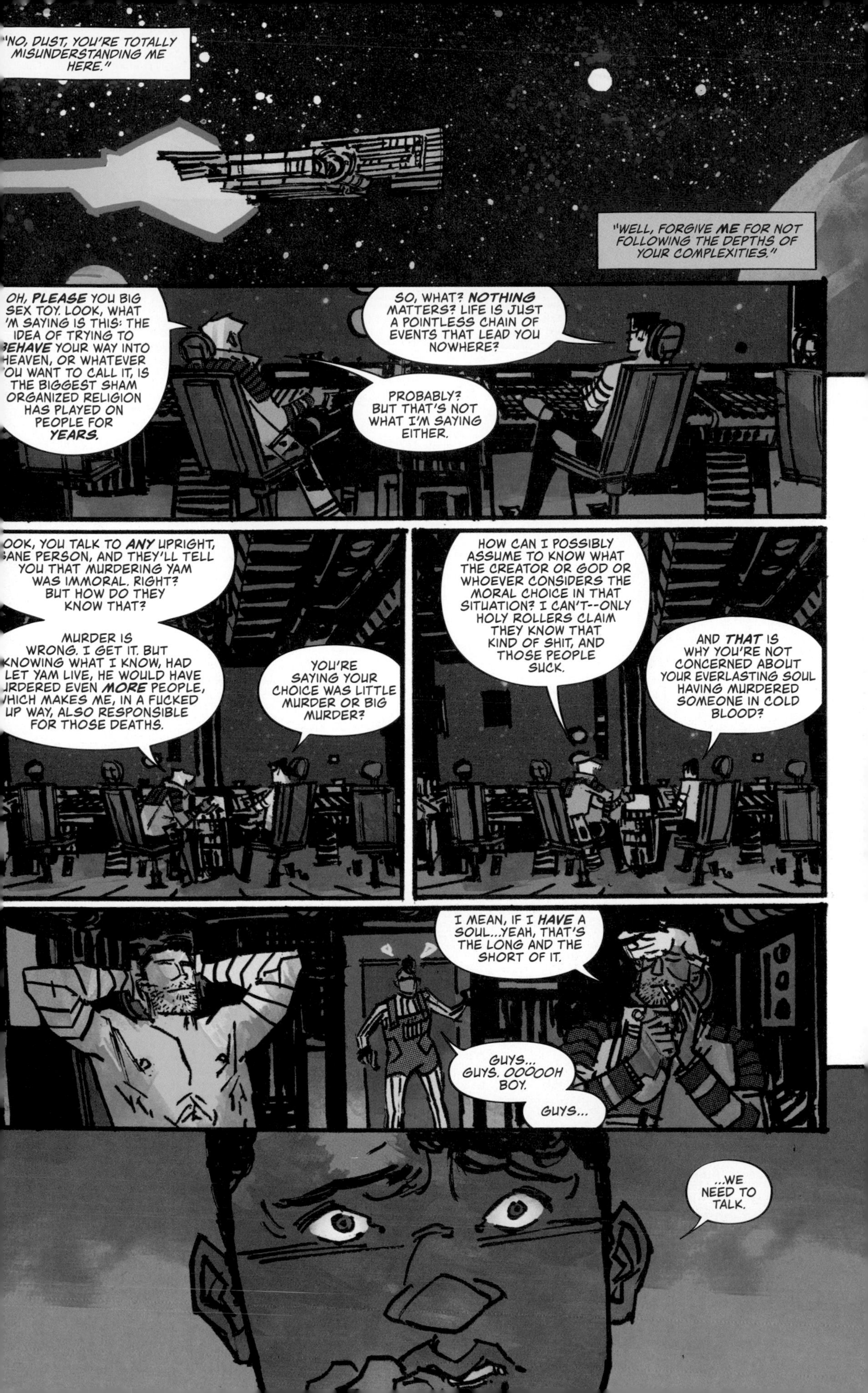
"NO, DUST, YOU'RE TOTALLY MISUNDERSTANDING ME HERE."
"WELL, FORGIVE ME FOR NOT FOLLOWING THE DEPTHS OF YOUR COMPLEXITIES."
OH, PLEASE YOU BIG SEX TOY. LOOK, WHAT I'M SAYING IS THIS: THE IDEA OF TRYING TO BEHAVE YOUR WAY INTO HEAVEN, OR WHATEVER YOU WANT TO CALL IT, IS THE BIGGEST SHAM ORGANIZED RELIGION HAS PLAYED ON PEOPLE FOR YEARS.
SO, WHAT? NOTHING MATTERS? LIFE IS JUST A POINTLESS CHAIN OF EVENTS THAT LEAD YOU NOWHERE?
PROBABLY? BUT THAT'S NOT WHAT I'M SAYING EITHER.
LOOK, YOU TALK TO ANY UPRIGHT, SANE PERSON, AND THEY'LL TELL YOU THAT MURDERING YAM WAS IMMORAL. RIGHT? BUT HOW DO THEY KNOW THAT?
MURDER IS WRONG. I GET IT. BUT KNOWING WHAT I KNOW, HAD I LET YAM LIVE, HE WOULD HAVE MURDERED EVEN MORE PEOPLE, WHICH MAKES ME, IN A FUCKED UP WAY, ALSO RESPONSIBLE FOR THOSE DEATHS.
YOU'RE SAYING YOUR CHOICE WAS LITTLE MURDER OR BIG MURDER?
HOW CAN I POSSIBLY ASSUME TO KNOW WHAT THE CREATOR OR GOD OR WHOEVER CONSIDERS THE MORAL CHOICE IN THAT SITUATION? I CAN'T--ONLY HOLY ROLLERS CLAIM THEY KNOW THAT KIND OF SHIT, AND THOSE PEOPLE SUCK.
AND THAT IS WHY YOU'RE NOT CONCERNED ABOUT YOUR EVERLASTING SOUL HAVING MURDERED SOMEONE IN COLD BLOOD?
I MEAN, IF I HAVE A SOUL...YEAH, THAT'S THE LONG AND THE SHORT OF IT.
GUYS... GUYS. OOOOOH BOY.
GUYS...
...WE NEED TO TALK.

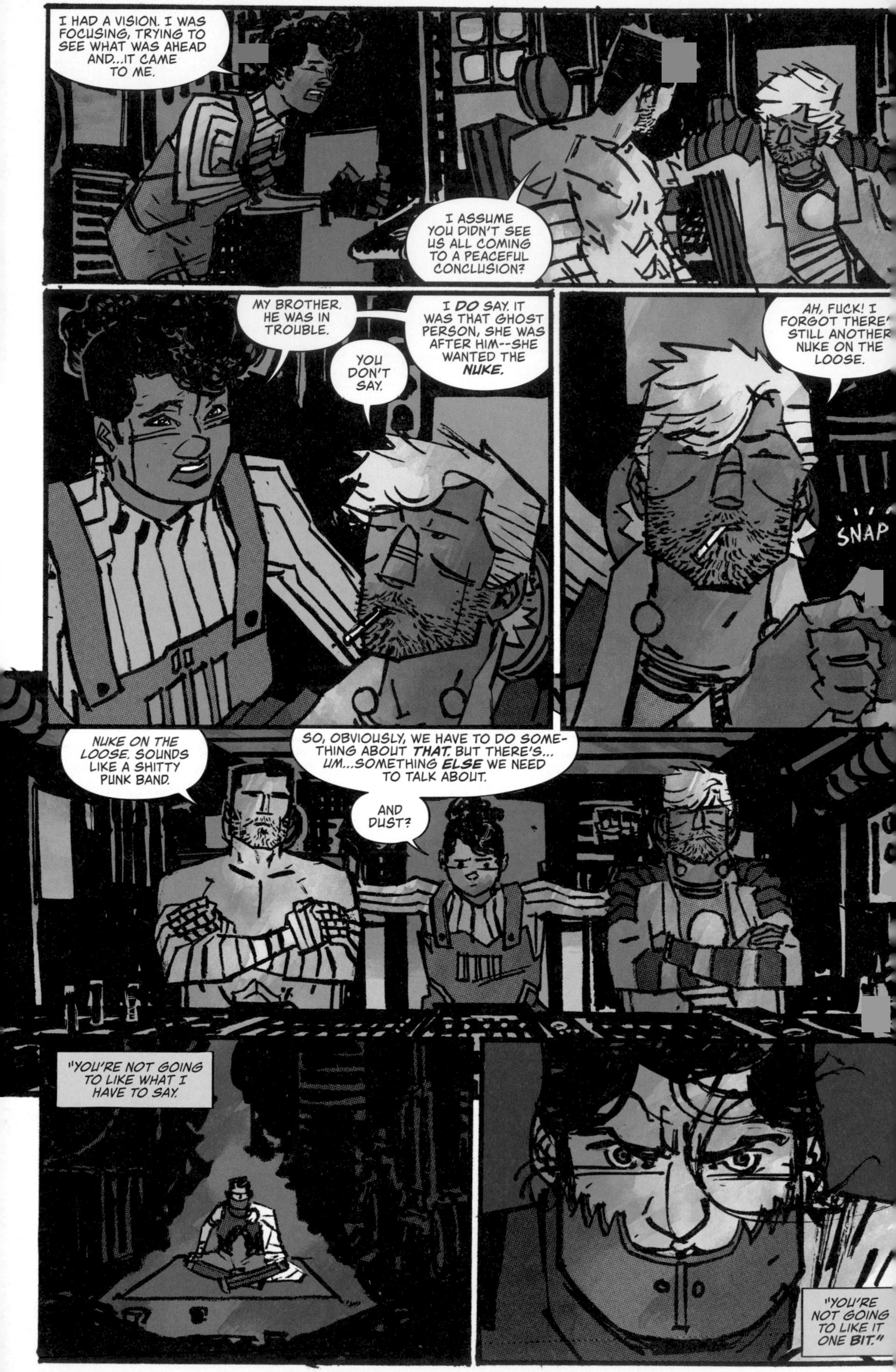
I HAD A VISION. I WAS FOCUSING, TRYING TO SEE WHAT WAS AHEAD AND...IT CAME TO ME.
I ASSUME YOU DIDN'T SEE US ALL COMING TO A PEACEFUL CONCLUSION?
MY BROTHER. HE WAS IN TROUBLE.
I DO SAY. IT WAS THAT GHOST PERSON, SHE WAS AFTER HIM--SHE WANTED THE NUKE.
YOU DON'T SAY.
AH, FUCK! I FORGOT THERE'S STILL ANOTHER NUKE ON THE LOOSE.
SNAP
NUKE ON THE LOOSE. SOUNDS LIKE A SHITTY PUNK BAND.
SO, OBVIOUSLY, WE HAVE TO DO SOMETHING ABOUT THAT. BUT THERE'S... UM...SOMETHING ELSE WE NEED TO TALK ABOUT.
AND DUST?
"YOU'RE NOT GOING TO LIKE WHAT I HAVE TO SAY.
"YOU'RE NOT GOING TO LIKE IT ONE BIT."

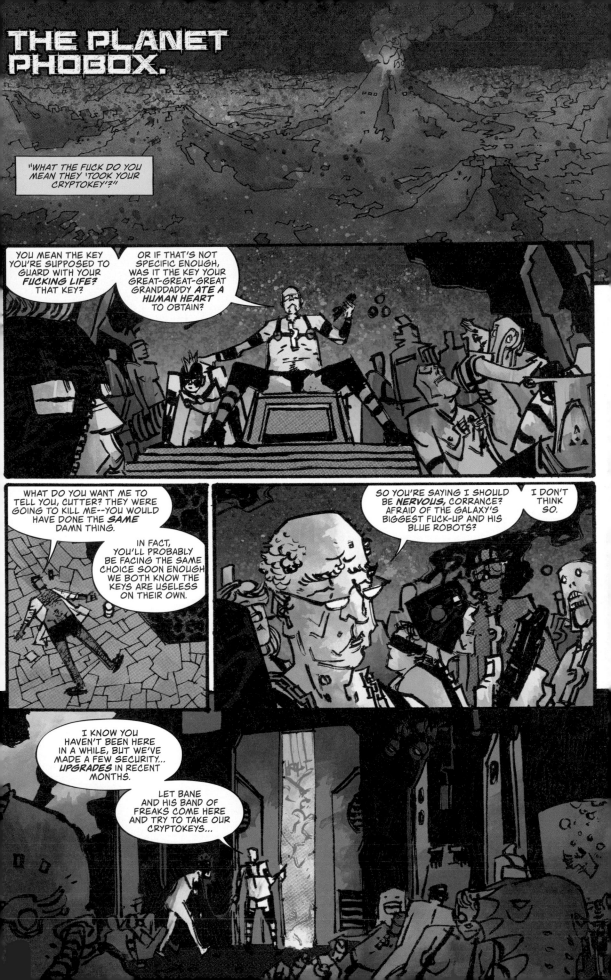

THE PLANET PHOBOX.

"WHAT THE FUCK DO YOU MEAN THEY 'TOOK YOUR CRYPTOKEY'?"

YOU MEAN THE KEY YOU'RE SUPPOSED TO GUARD WITH YOUR *FUCKING LIFE?* THAT KEY?

OR IF THAT'S NOT SPECIFIC ENOUGH, WAS IT THE KEY YOUR GREAT-GREAT-GREAT GRANDDADDY *ATE A HUMAN HEART* TO OBTAIN?

WHAT DO YOU WANT ME TO TELL YOU, CUTTER? THEY WERE GOING TO KILL ME--YOU WOULD HAVE DONE THE *SAME* DAMN THING.

IN FACT, YOU'LL PROBABLY BE FACING THE SAME CHOICE SOON ENOUGH WE BOTH KNOW THE KEYS ARE USELESS ON THEIR OWN.

SO YOU'RE SAYING I SHOULD BE *NERVOUS*, CORRANCE? AFRAID OF THE GALAXY'S BIGGEST FUCK-UP AND HIS BLUE ROBOTS?

I DON'T THINK SO.

I KNOW YOU HAVEN'T BEEN HERE IN A WHILE, BUT WE'VE MADE A FEW SECURITY... *UPGRADES* IN RECENT MONTHS.

AND BANE AND HIS BAND OF FREAKS COME HERE AND TRY TO TAKE OUR CRYPTOKEYS...

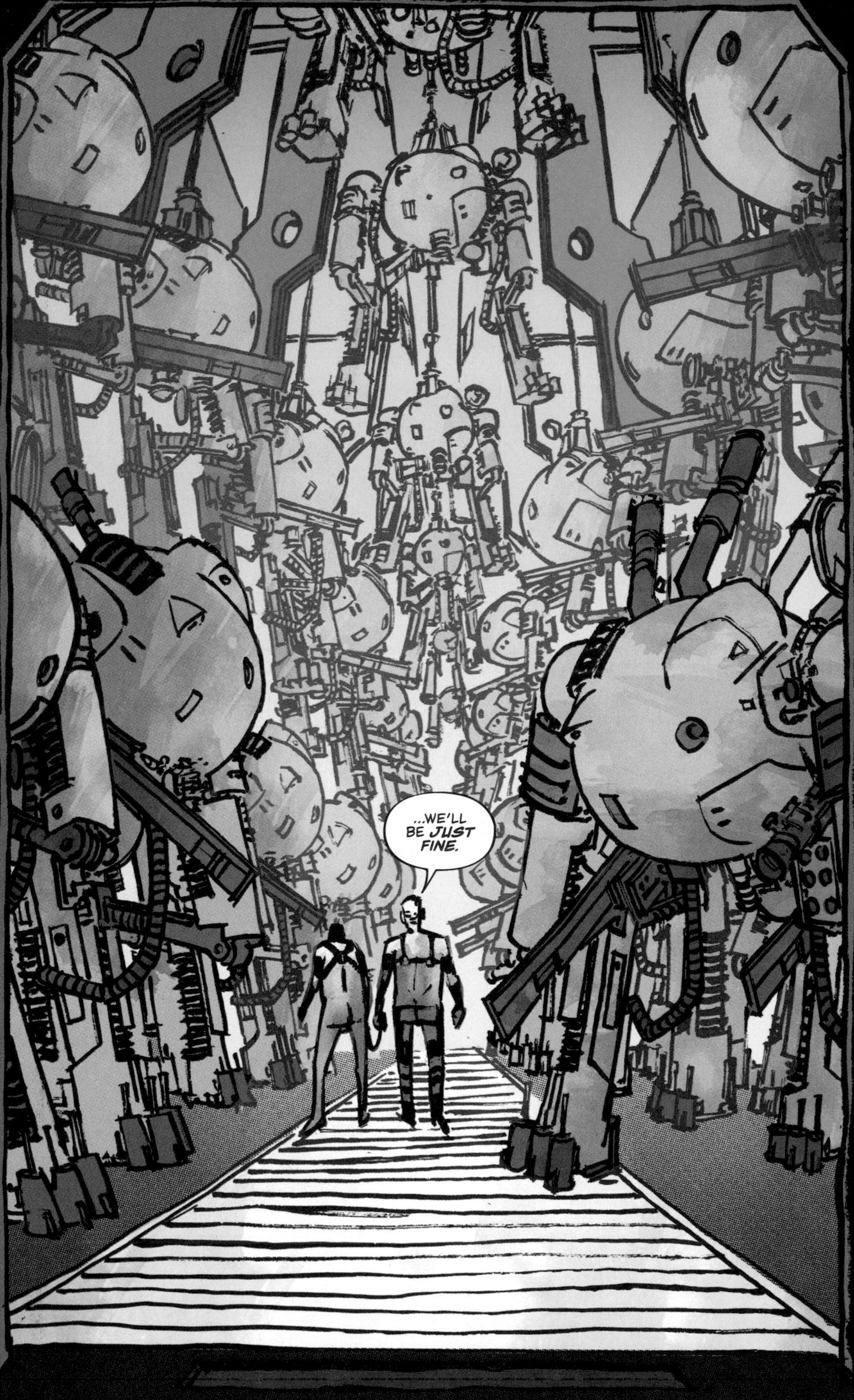
...WE'LL BE JUST FINE.

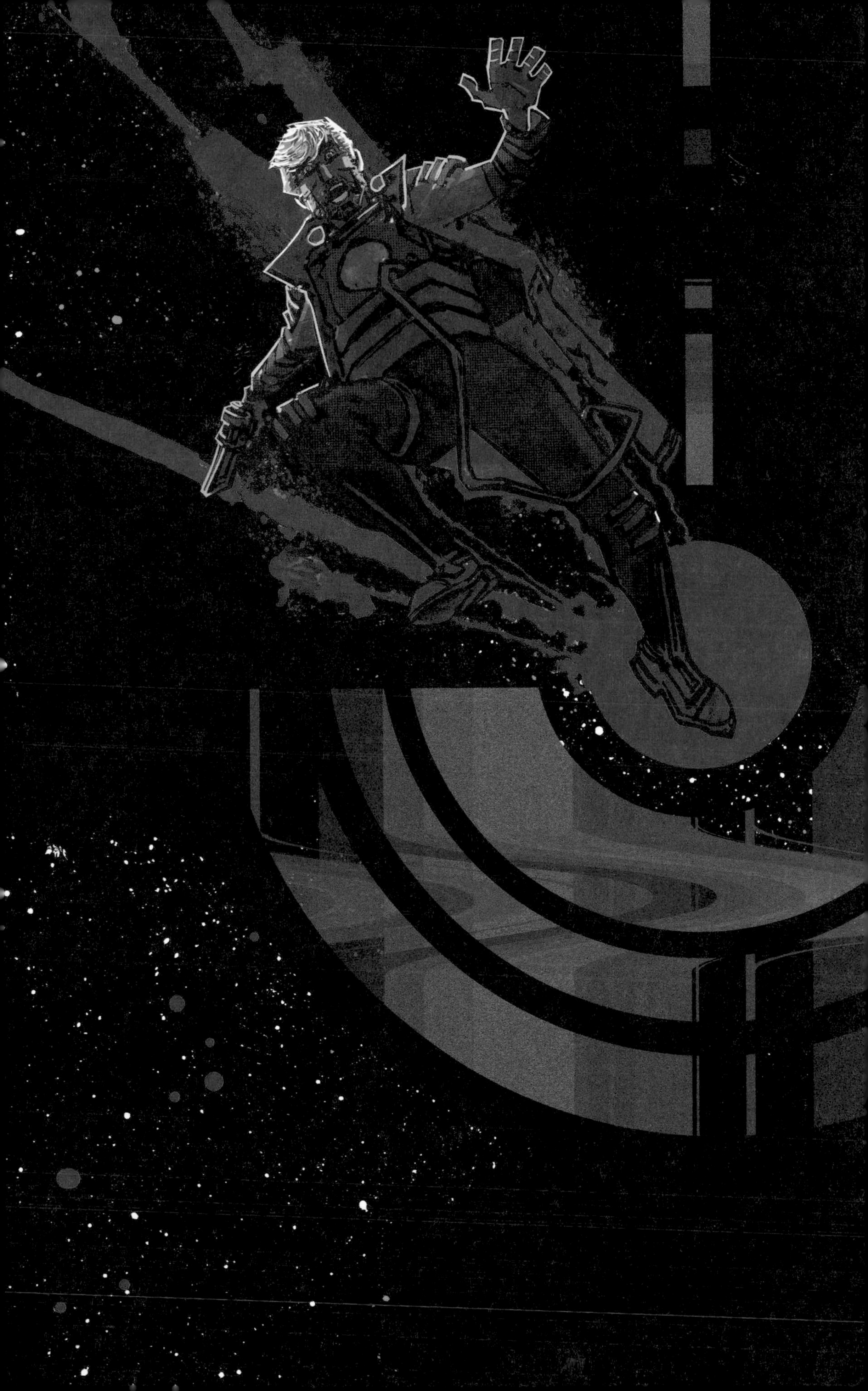

CHAPTER **SEVEN**

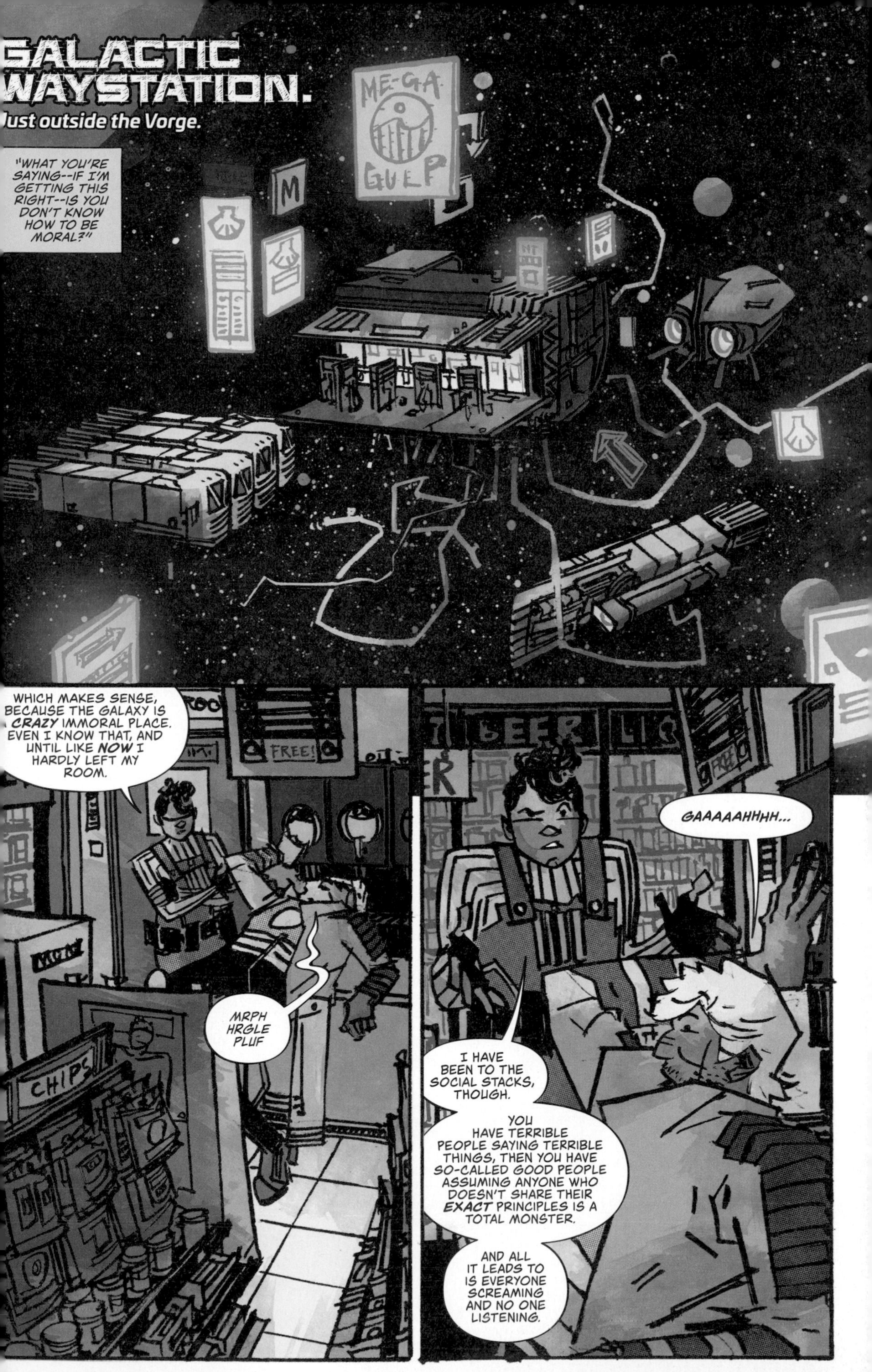
GALACTIC WAYSTATION.
Just outside the Vorge.
"WHAT YOU'RE SAYING--IF I'M GETTING THIS RIGHT--IS YOU DON'T KNOW HOW TO BE MORAL?"
ME-GA GULP
M
WHICH MAKES SENSE, BECAUSE THE GALAXY IS CRAZY IMMORAL PLACE. EVEN I KNOW THAT, AND UNTIL LIKE NOW I HARDLY LEFT MY ROOM.
FREE!
MRPH HRGLE PLUF
CHIPS
BEER
GAAAAAHHHH...
I HAVE BEEN TO THE SOCIAL STACKS, THOUGH.
YOU HAVE TERRIBLE PEOPLE SAYING TERRIBLE THINGS, THEN YOU HAVE SO-CALLED GOOD PEOPLE ASSUMING ANYONE WHO DOESN'T SHARE THEIR EXACT PRINCIPLES IS A TOTAL MONSTER.
AND ALL IT LEADS TO IS EVERYONE SCREAMING AND NO ONE LISTENING.

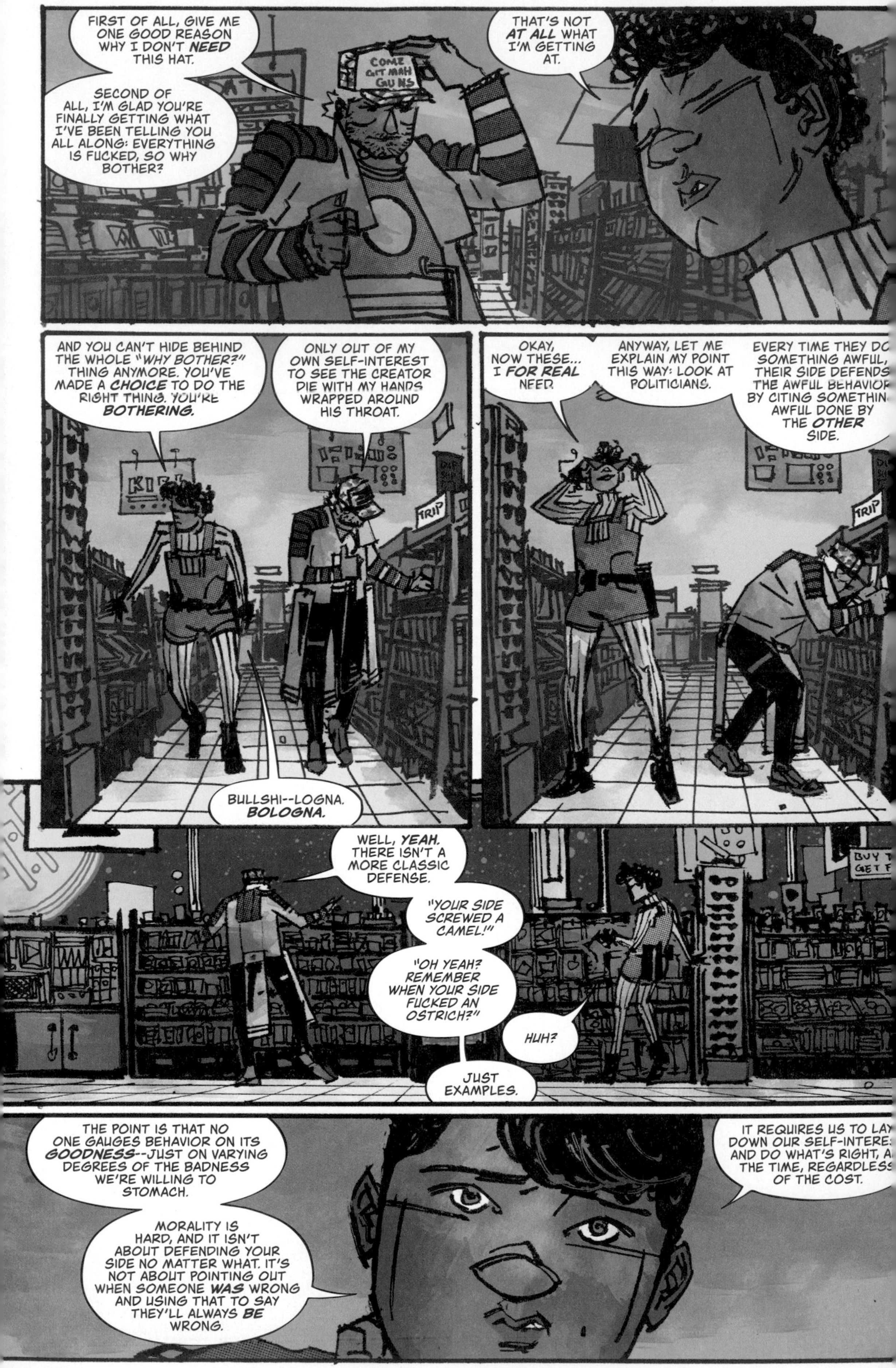
FIRST OF ALL, GIVE ME ONE GOOD REASON WHY I DON'T NEED THIS HAT.
SECOND OF ALL, I'M GLAD YOU'RE FINALLY GETTING WHAT I'VE BEEN TELLING YOU ALL ALONG: EVERYTHING IS FUCKED, SO WHY BOTHER?
THAT'S NOT AT ALL WHAT I'M GETTING AT.
AND YOU CAN'T HIDE BEHIND THE WHOLE "WHY BOTHER?" THING ANYMORE. YOU'VE MADE A CHOICE TO DO THE RIGHT THING. YOU'RE BOTHERING.
ONLY OUT OF MY OWN SELF-INTEREST TO SEE THE CREATOR DIE WITH MY HANDS WRAPPED AROUND HIS THROAT.
BULLSHI--LOGNA. BOLOGNA.
OKAY, NOW THESE... I FOR REAL NEED.
ANYWAY, LET ME EXPLAIN MY POINT THIS WAY: LOOK AT POLITICIANS.
EVERY TIME THEY DO SOMETHING AWFUL, THEIR SIDE DEFENDS THE AWFUL BEHAVIOR BY CITING SOMETHIN AWFUL DONE BY THE OTHER SIDE.
WELL, YEAH. THERE ISN'T A MORE CLASSIC DEFENSE.
"YOUR SIDE SCREWED A CAMEL!"
"OH YEAH? REMEMBER WHEN YOUR SIDE FUCKED AN OSTRICH?"
HUH?
JUST EXAMPLES.
THE POINT IS THAT NO ONE GAUGES BEHAVIOR ON ITS GOODNESS--JUST ON VARYING DEGREES OF THE BADNESS WE'RE WILLING TO STOMACH.
MORALITY IS HARD, AND IT ISN'T ABOUT DEFENDING YOUR SIDE NO MATTER WHAT. IT'S NOT ABOUT POINTING OUT WHEN SOMEONE WAS WRONG AND USING THAT TO SAY THEY'LL ALWAYS BE WRONG.
IT REQUIRES US TO LAY DOWN OUR SELF-INTERES AND DO WHAT'S RIGHT, A THE TIME, REGARDLESS OF THE COST.

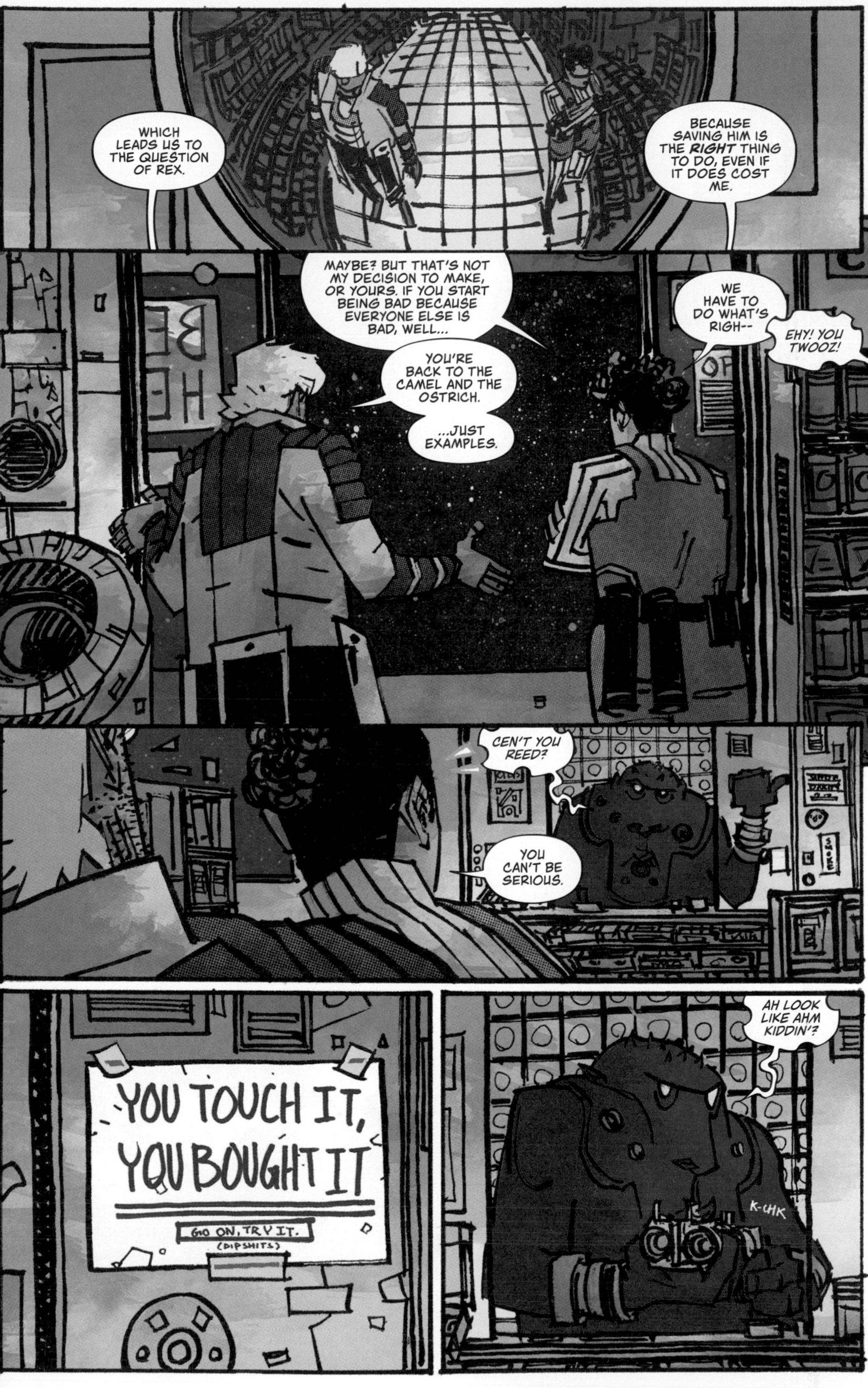
WHICH LEADS US TO THE QUESTION OF REX.
BECAUSE SAVING HIM IS THE *RIGHT* THING TO DO, EVEN IF IT DOES COST ME.
MAYBE? BUT THAT'S NOT MY DECISION TO MAKE, OR YOURS. IF YOU START BEING BAD BECAUSE EVERYONE ELSE IS BAD, WELL...
YOU'RE BACK TO THE CAMEL AND THE OSTRICH.
...JUST EXAMPLES.
WE HAVE TO DO WHAT'S RIGH--
EHY! YOU TWOOZ!
CEN'T YOU REED?
YOU CAN'T BE SERIOUS.
YOU TOUCH IT, YOU BOUGHT IT
GO ON, TRY IT.
(DIPSHITS)
AH LOOK LIKE AHM KIDDIN'?
K-CHK

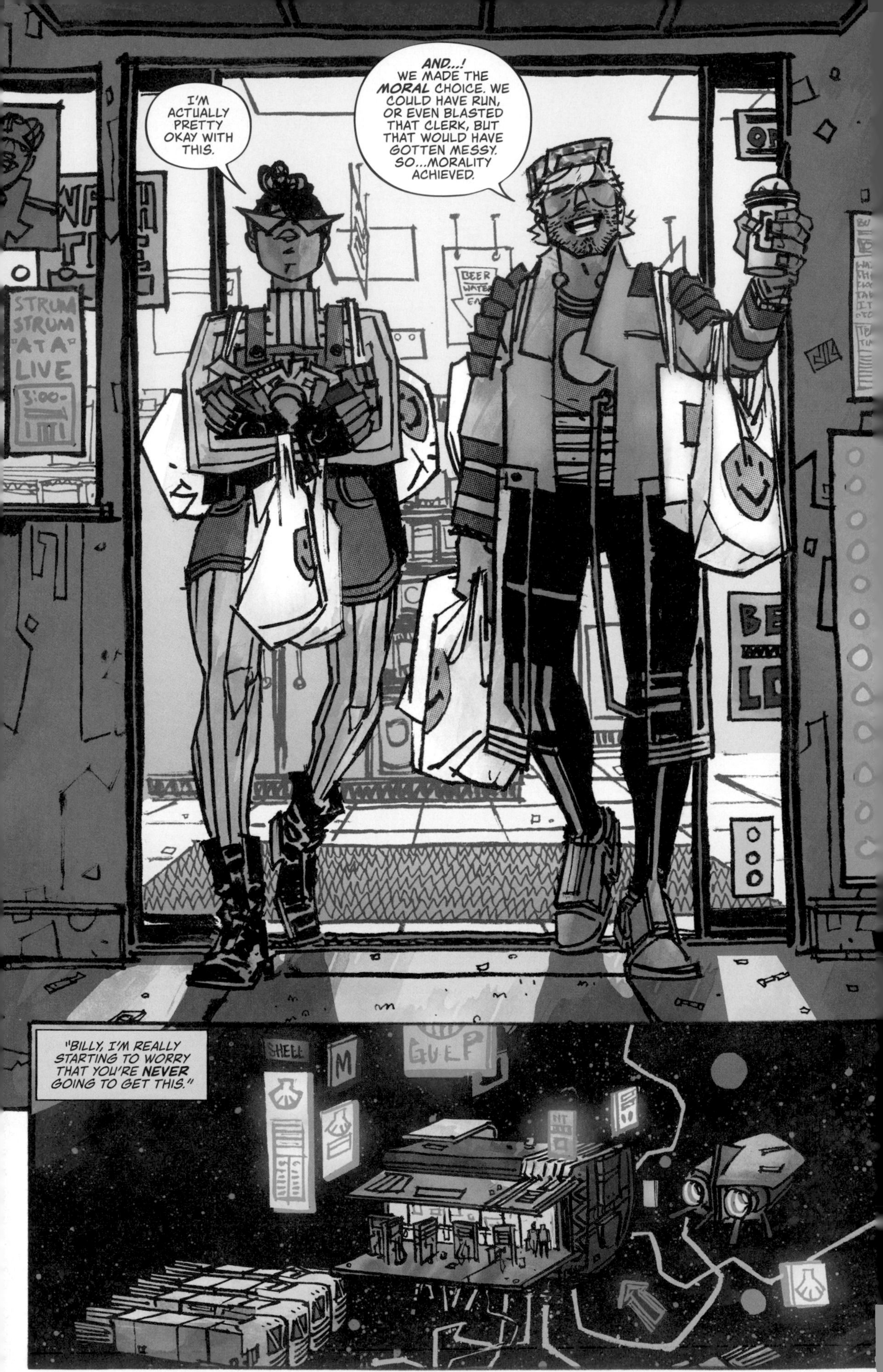
I'M ACTUALLY PRETTY OKAY WITH THIS.
AND...! WE MADE THE MORAL CHOICE. WE COULD HAVE RUN, OR EVEN BLASTED THAT CLERK, BUT THAT WOULD HAVE GOTTEN MESSY. SO...MORALITY ACHIEVED.
STRUM STRUM "ATA" LIVE 3:00-
BEER WATER
"BILLY, I'M REALLY STARTING TO WORRY THAT YOU'RE NEVER GOING TO GET THIS."
SHELL
M
GULP

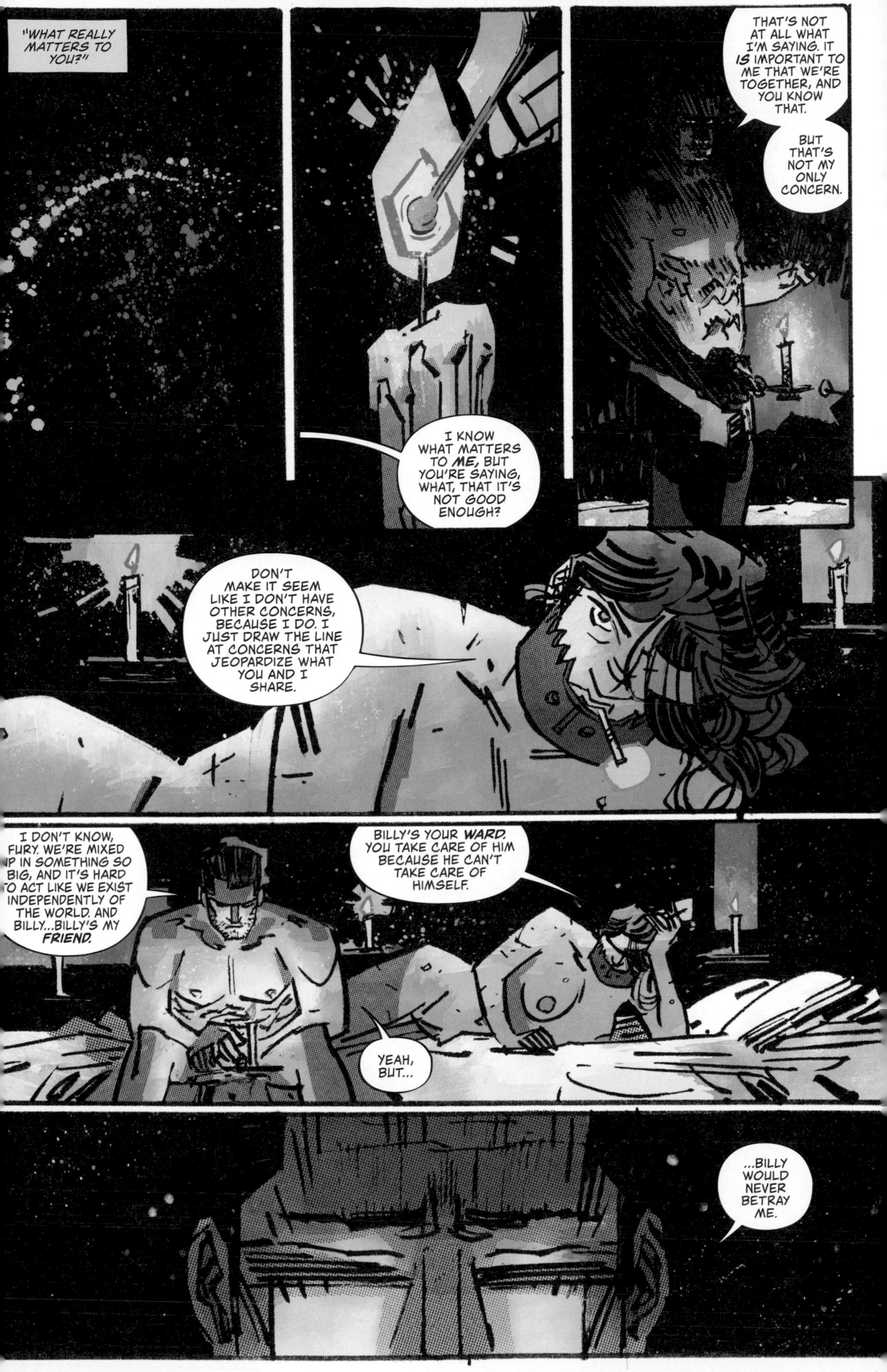
"WHAT REALLY MATTERS TO YOU?"
I KNOW WHAT MATTERS TO ME, BUT YOU'RE SAYING, WHAT, THAT IT'S NOT GOOD ENOUGH?
THAT'S NOT AT ALL WHAT I'M SAYING. IT IS IMPORTANT TO ME THAT WE'RE TOGETHER, AND YOU KNOW THAT.
BUT THAT'S NOT MY ONLY CONCERN.
DON'T MAKE IT SEEM LIKE I DON'T HAVE OTHER CONCERNS, BECAUSE I DO. I JUST DRAW THE LINE AT CONCERNS THAT JEOPARDIZE WHAT YOU AND I SHARE.
I DON'T KNOW, FURY. WE'RE MIXED UP IN SOMETHING SO BIG, AND IT'S HARD TO ACT LIKE WE EXIST INDEPENDENTLY OF THE WORLD. AND BILLY...BILLY'S MY FRIEND.
BILLY'S YOUR WARD. YOU TAKE CARE OF HIM BECAUSE HE CAN'T TAKE CARE OF HIMSELF.
YEAH, BUT...
...BILLY WOULD NEVER BETRAY ME.

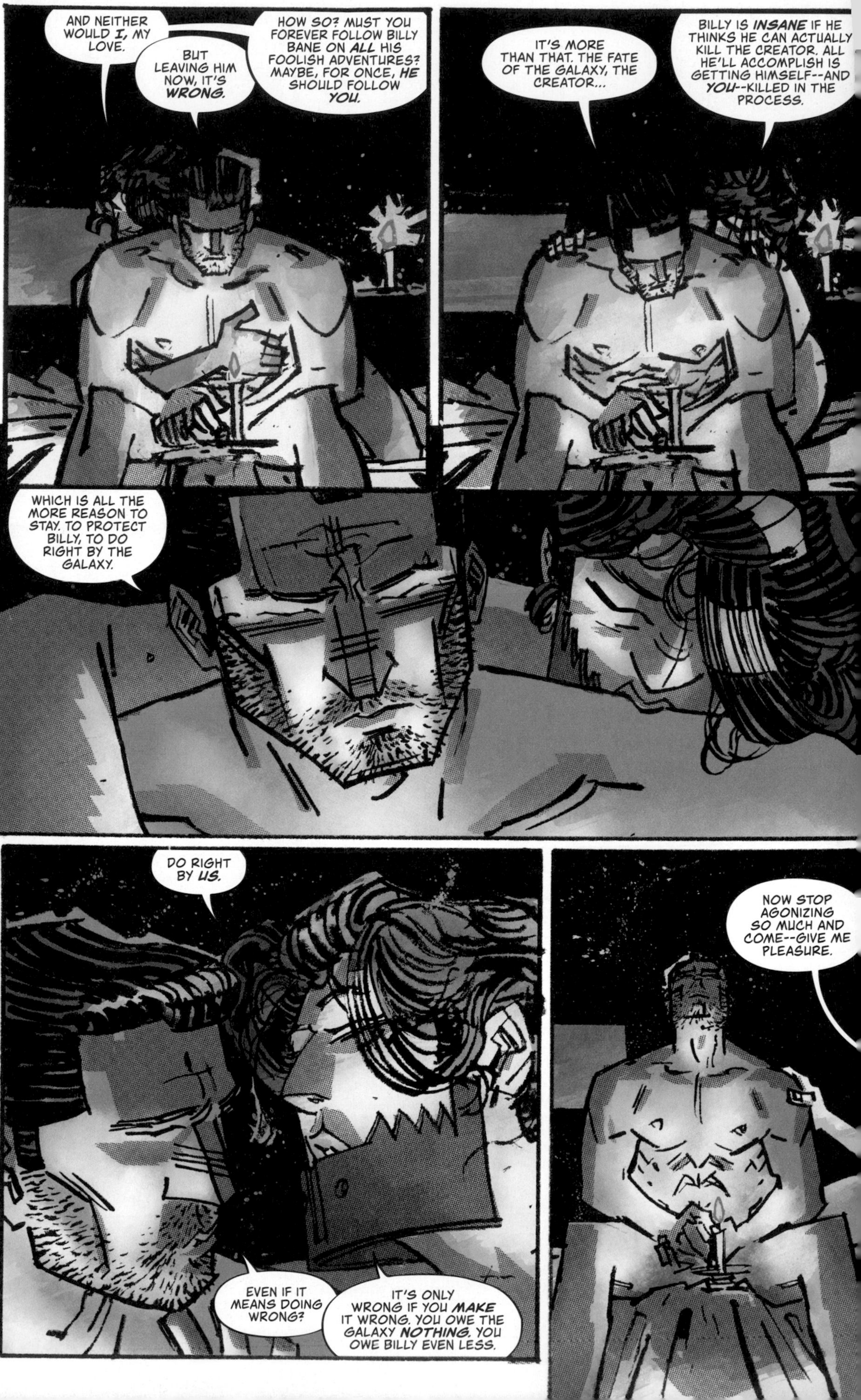
AND NEITHER WOULD *I*, MY LOVE.
BUT LEAVING HIM NOW, IT'S *WRONG.*
HOW SO? MUST YOU FOREVER FOLLOW BILLY BANE ON *ALL* HIS FOOLISH ADVENTURES? MAYBE, FOR ONCE, *HE* SHOULD FOLLOW *YOU.*
IT'S MORE THAN THAT. THE FATE OF THE GALAXY, THE CREATOR...
BILLY IS *INSANE* IF HE THINKS HE CAN ACTUALLY KILL THE CREATOR. ALL HE'LL ACCOMPLISH IS GETTING HIMSELF--AND *YOU*--KILLED IN THE PROCESS.
WHICH IS ALL THE MORE REASON TO STAY. TO PROTECT BILLY, TO DO RIGHT BY THE GALAXY.
DO RIGHT BY *US.*
EVEN IF IT MEANS DOING WRONG?
IT'S ONLY WRONG IF YOU *MAKE* IT WRONG. YOU OWE THE GALAXY *NOTHING.* YOU OWE BILLY EVEN LESS.
NOW STOP AGONIZING SO MUCH AND COME--GIVE ME PLEASURE.

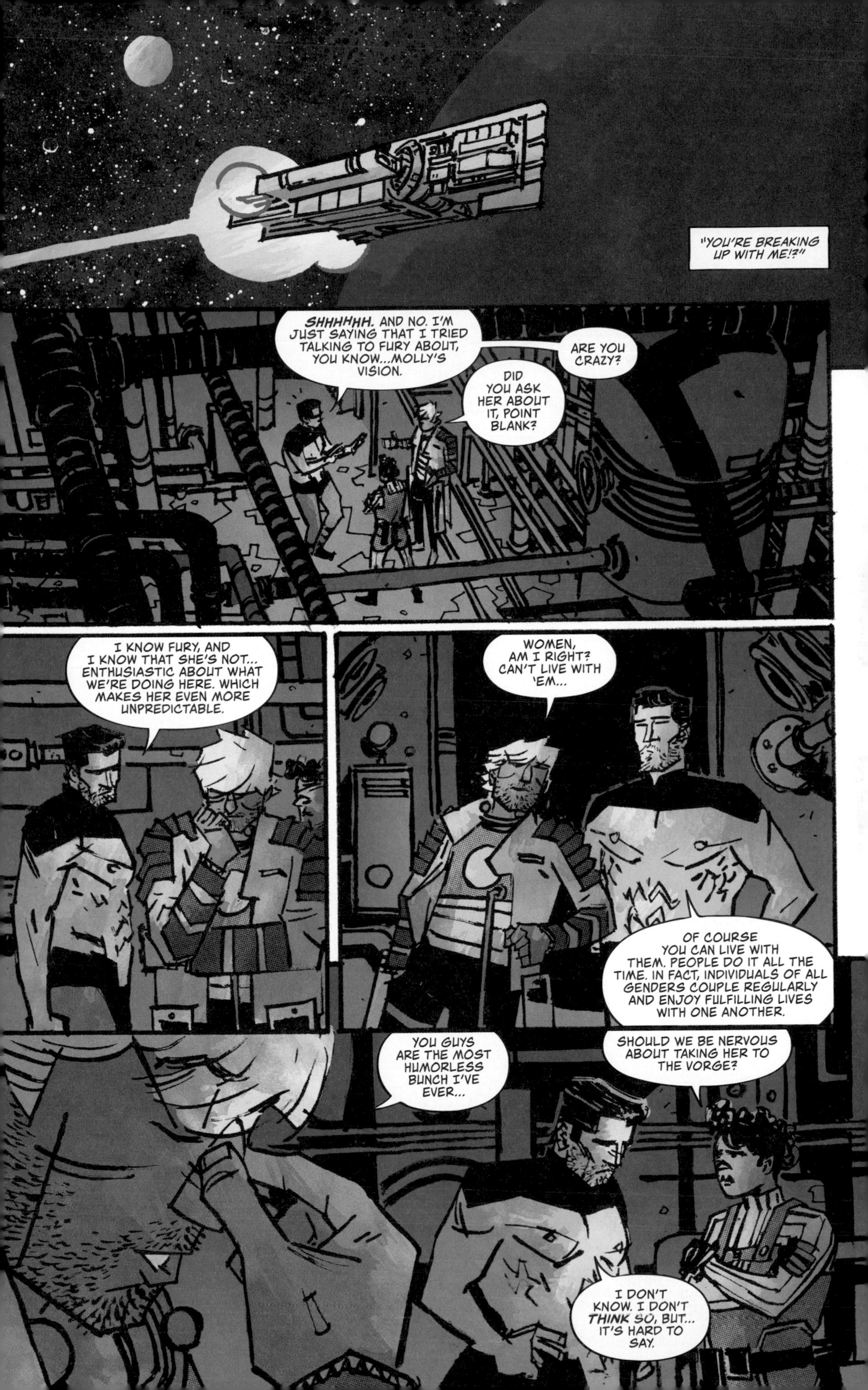
"YOU'RE BREAKING UP WITH ME!?"
SHHHHHH. AND NO. I'M JUST SAYING THAT I TRIED TALKING TO FURY ABOUT, YOU KNOW...MOLLY'S VISION.
ARE YOU CRAZY?
DID YOU ASK HER ABOUT IT, POINT BLANK?
I KNOW FURY, AND I KNOW THAT SHE'S NOT... ENTHUSIASTIC ABOUT WHAT WE'RE DOING HERE. WHICH MAKES HER EVEN MORE UNPREDICTABLE.
WOMEN, AM I RIGHT? CAN'T LIVE WITH 'EM...
OF COURSE YOU CAN LIVE WITH THEM. PEOPLE DO IT ALL THE TIME. IN FACT, INDIVIDUALS OF ALL GENDERS COUPLE REGULARLY AND ENJOY FULFILLING LIVES WITH ONE ANOTHER.
YOU GUYS ARE THE MOST HUMORLESS BUNCH I'VE EVER...
SHOULD WE BE NERVOUS ABOUT TAKING HER TO THE VORGE?
I DON'T KNOW. I DON'T THINK SO, BUT... IT'S HARD TO SAY.

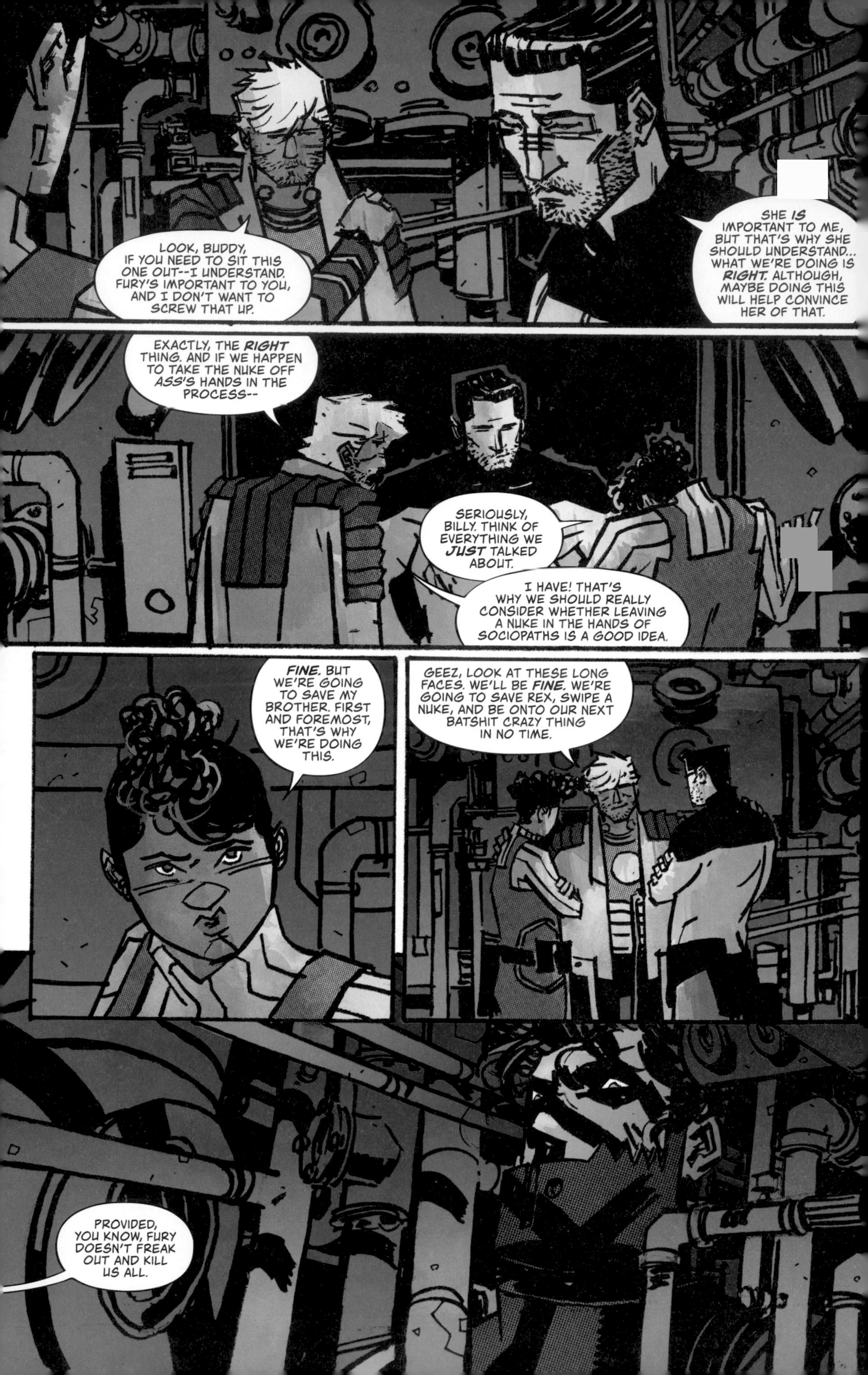
LOOK, BUDDY, IF YOU NEED TO SIT THIS ONE OUT--I UNDERSTAND. FURY'S IMPORTANT TO YOU, AND I DON'T WANT TO SCREW THAT UP.
SHE IS IMPORTANT TO ME, BUT THAT'S WHY SHE SHOULD UNDERSTAND... WHAT WE'RE DOING IS RIGHT. ALTHOUGH, MAYBE DOING THIS WILL HELP CONVINCE HER OF THAT.
EXACTLY, THE RIGHT THING. AND IF WE HAPPEN TO TAKE THE NUKE OFF ASS'S HANDS IN THE PROCESS--
SERIOUSLY, BILLY. THINK OF EVERYTHING WE JUST TALKED ABOUT.
I HAVE! THAT'S WHY WE SHOULD REALLY CONSIDER WHETHER LEAVING A NUKE IN THE HANDS OF SOCIOPATHS IS A GOOD IDEA.
FINE. BUT WE'RE GOING TO SAVE MY BROTHER. FIRST AND FOREMOST, THAT'S WHY WE'RE DOING THIS.
GEEZ, LOOK AT THESE LONG FACES. WE'LL BE FINE. WE'RE GOING TO SAVE REX, SWIPE A NUKE, AND BE ONTO OUR NEXT BATSHIT CRAZY THING IN NO TIME.
PROVIDED, YOU KNOW, FURY DOESN'T FREAK OUT AND KILL US ALL.

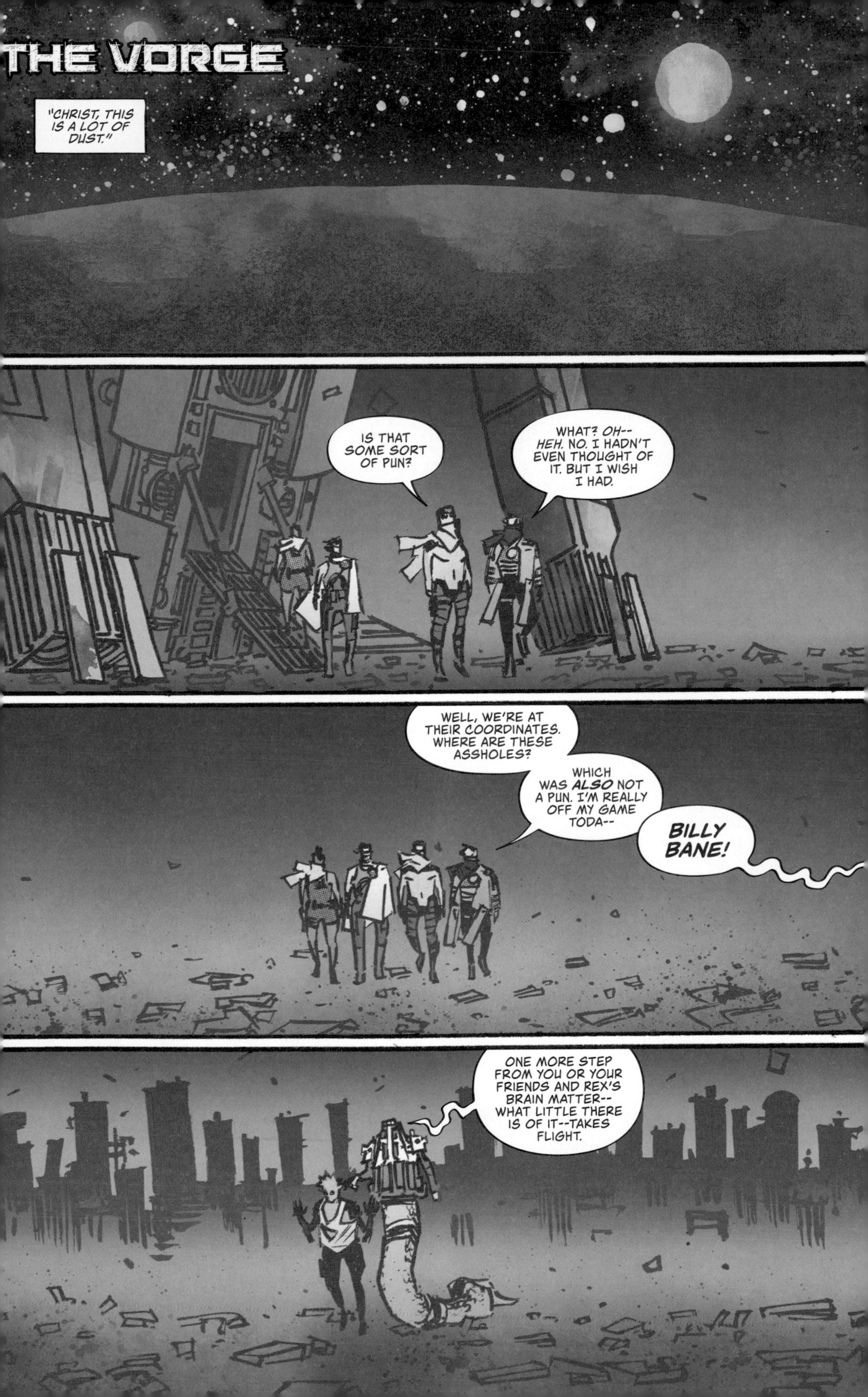
THE VORGE
"CHRIST, THIS IS A LOT OF DUST."
IS THAT SOME SORT OF PUN?
WHAT? *OH-- HEH.* NO. I HADN'T EVEN THOUGHT OF IT. BUT I WISH I HAD.
WELL, WE'RE AT THEIR COORDINATES. WHERE ARE THESE ASSHOLES?
WHICH WAS **ALSO** NOT A PUN. I'M REALLY OFF MY GAME TODA--
BILLY BANE!
ONE MORE STEP FROM YOU OR YOUR FRIENDS AND REX'S BRAIN MATTER-- WHAT LITTLE THERE IS OF IT--TAKES FLIGHT.

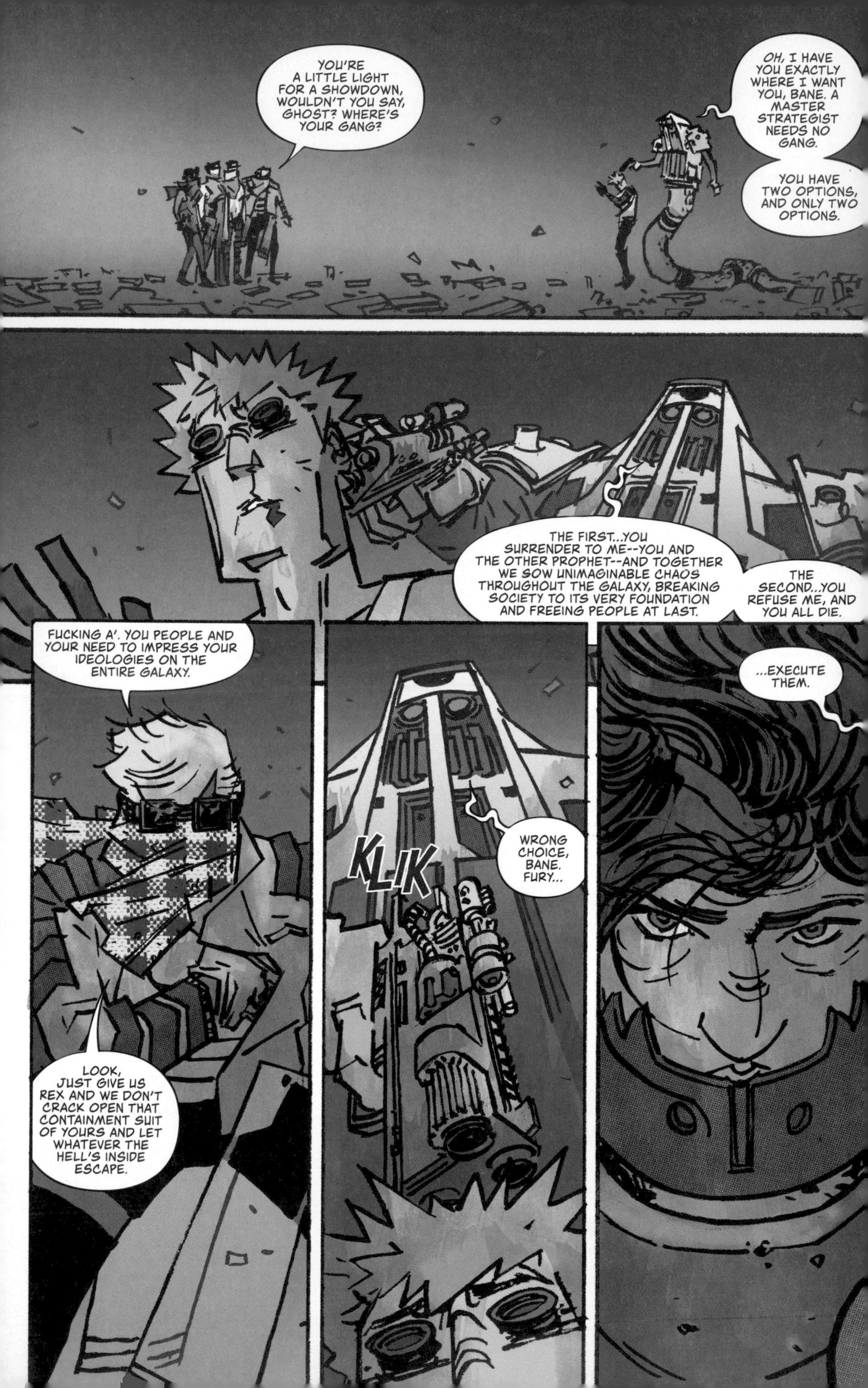
YOU'RE A LITTLE LIGHT FOR A SHOWDOWN, WOULDN'T YOU SAY, GHOST? WHERE'S YOUR GANG?
OH, I HAVE YOU EXACTLY WHERE I WANT YOU, BANE. A MASTER STRATEGIST NEEDS NO GANG.
YOU HAVE TWO OPTIONS, AND ONLY TWO OPTIONS.
THE FIRST...YOU SURRENDER TO ME--YOU AND THE OTHER PROPHET--AND TOGETHER WE SOW UNIMAGINABLE CHAOS THROUGHOUT THE GALAXY, BREAKING SOCIETY TO ITS VERY FOUNDATION AND FREEING PEOPLE AT LAST.
THE SECOND...YOU REFUSE ME, AND YOU ALL DIE.
FUCKING A'. YOU PEOPLE AND YOUR NEED TO IMPRESS YOUR IDEOLOGIES ON THE ENTIRE GALAXY.
LOOK, JUST GIVE US REX AND WE DON'T CRACK OPEN THAT CONTAINMENT SUIT OF YOURS AND LET WHATEVER THE HELL'S INSIDE ESCAPE.
KLIK
WRONG CHOICE, BANE. FURY...
...EXECUTE THEM.

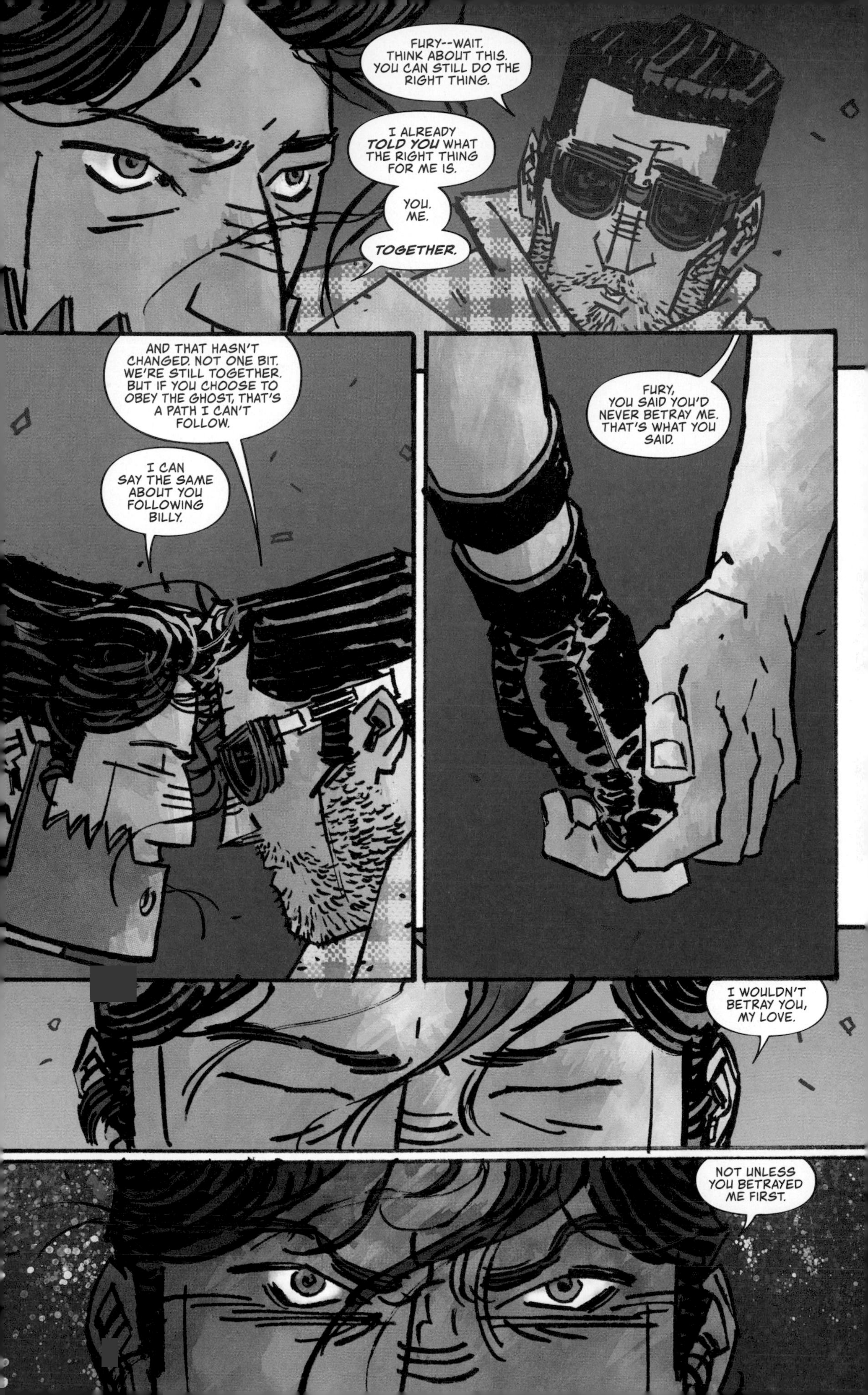
FURY--WAIT. THINK ABOUT THIS. YOU CAN STILL DO THE RIGHT THING.
I ALREADY *TOLD YOU* WHAT THE RIGHT THING FOR ME IS.
YOU. ME.
TOGETHER.
AND THAT HASN'T CHANGED. NOT ONE BIT. WE'RE STILL TOGETHER. BUT IF YOU CHOOSE TO OBEY THE GHOST, THAT'S A PATH I CAN'T FOLLOW.
I CAN SAY THE SAME ABOUT YOU FOLLOWING BILLY.
FURY, YOU SAID YOU'D NEVER BETRAY ME. THAT'S WHAT YOU SAID.
I WOULDN'T BETRAY YOU, MY LOVE.
NOT UNLESS YOU BETRAYED ME FIRST.

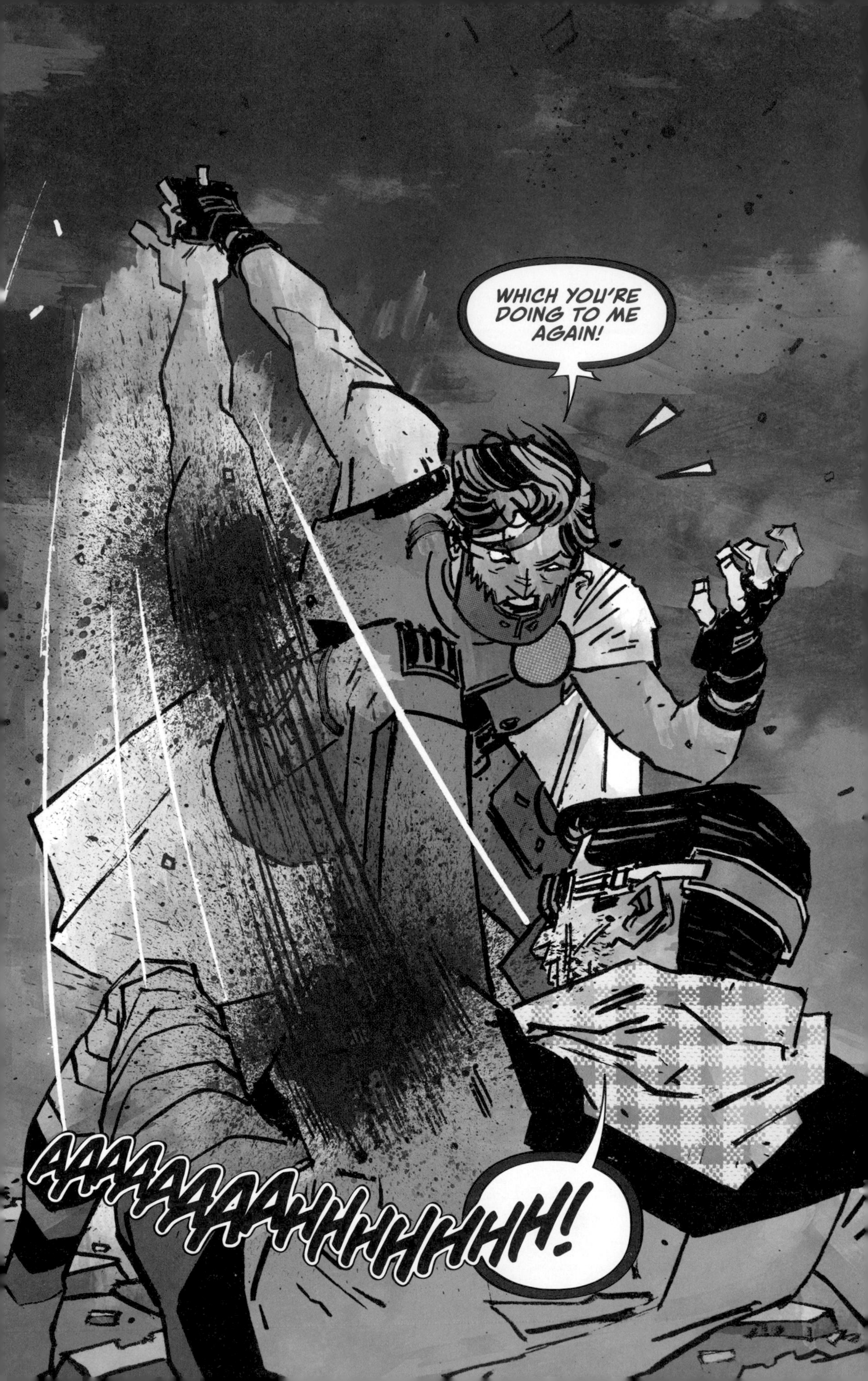
WHICH YOU'RE DOING TO ME AGAIN!
AAAAAAAAHHHHHHHH!

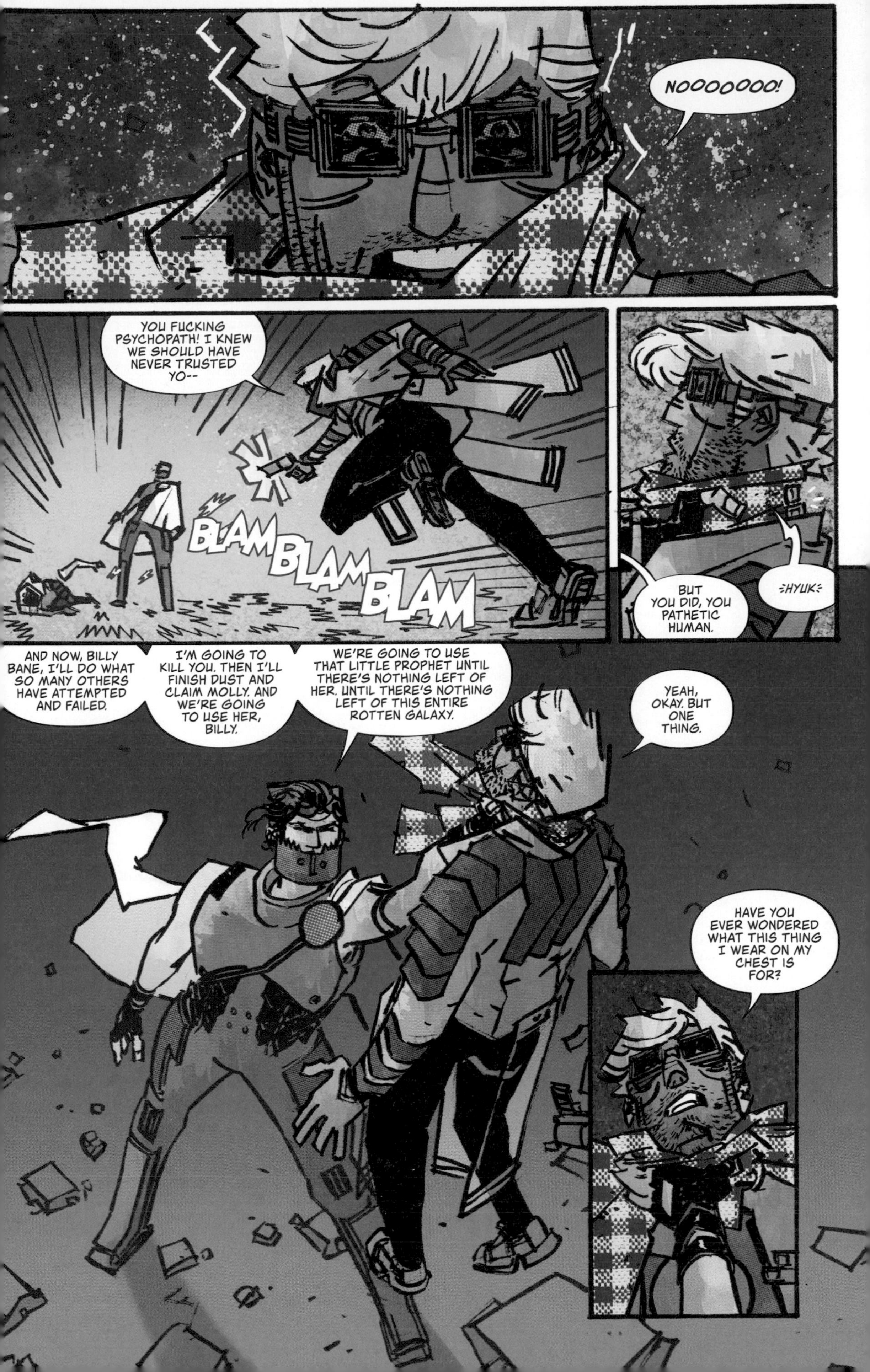
NOOOOOOO!
YOU FUCKING PSYCHOPATH! I KNEW WE SHOULD HAVE NEVER TRUSTED YO--
BLAM BLAM BLAM
=HYUK=
BUT YOU DID, YOU PATHETIC HUMAN.
AND NOW, BILLY BANE, I'LL DO WHAT SO MANY OTHERS HAVE ATTEMPTED AND FAILED.
I'M GOING TO KILL YOU. THEN I'LL FINISH DUST AND CLAIM MOLLY. AND WE'RE GOING TO USE HER, BILLY.
WE'RE GOING TO USE THAT LITTLE PROPHET UNTIL THERE'S NOTHING LEFT OF HER. UNTIL THERE'S NOTHING LEFT OF THIS ENTIRE ROTTEN GALAXY.
YEAH, OKAY. BUT ONE THING.
HAVE YOU EVER WONDERED WHAT THIS THING I WEAR ON MY CHEST IS FOR?

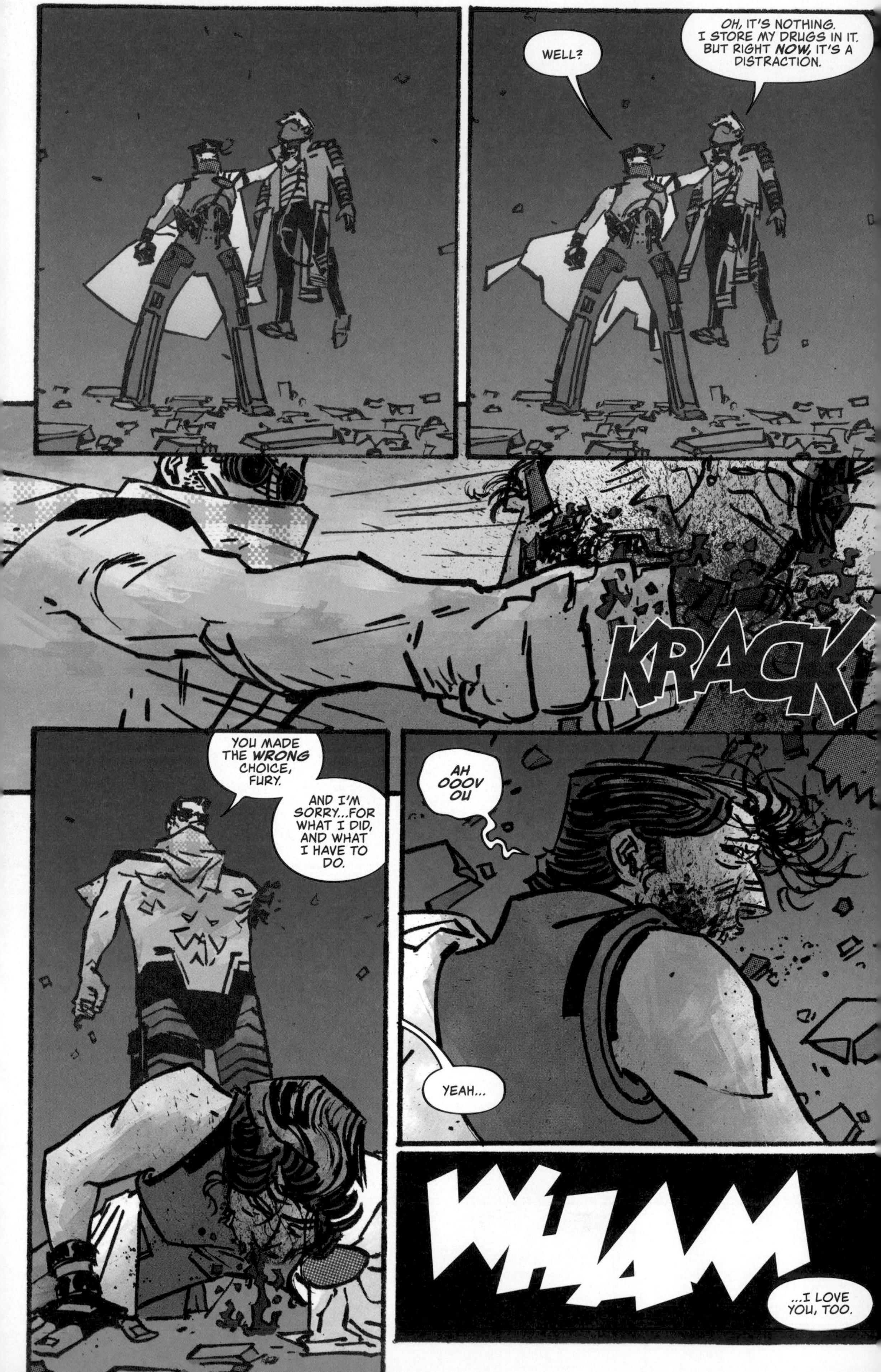
WELL?
OH, IT'S NOTHING. I STORE MY DRUGS IN IT. BUT RIGHT NOW, IT'S A DISTRACTION.
KRACK
YOU MADE THE WRONG CHOICE, FURY.
AND I'M SORRY...FOR WHAT I DID, AND WHAT I HAVE TO DO.
AH OOOV OU
YEAH...
WHAM
...I LOVE YOU, TOO.

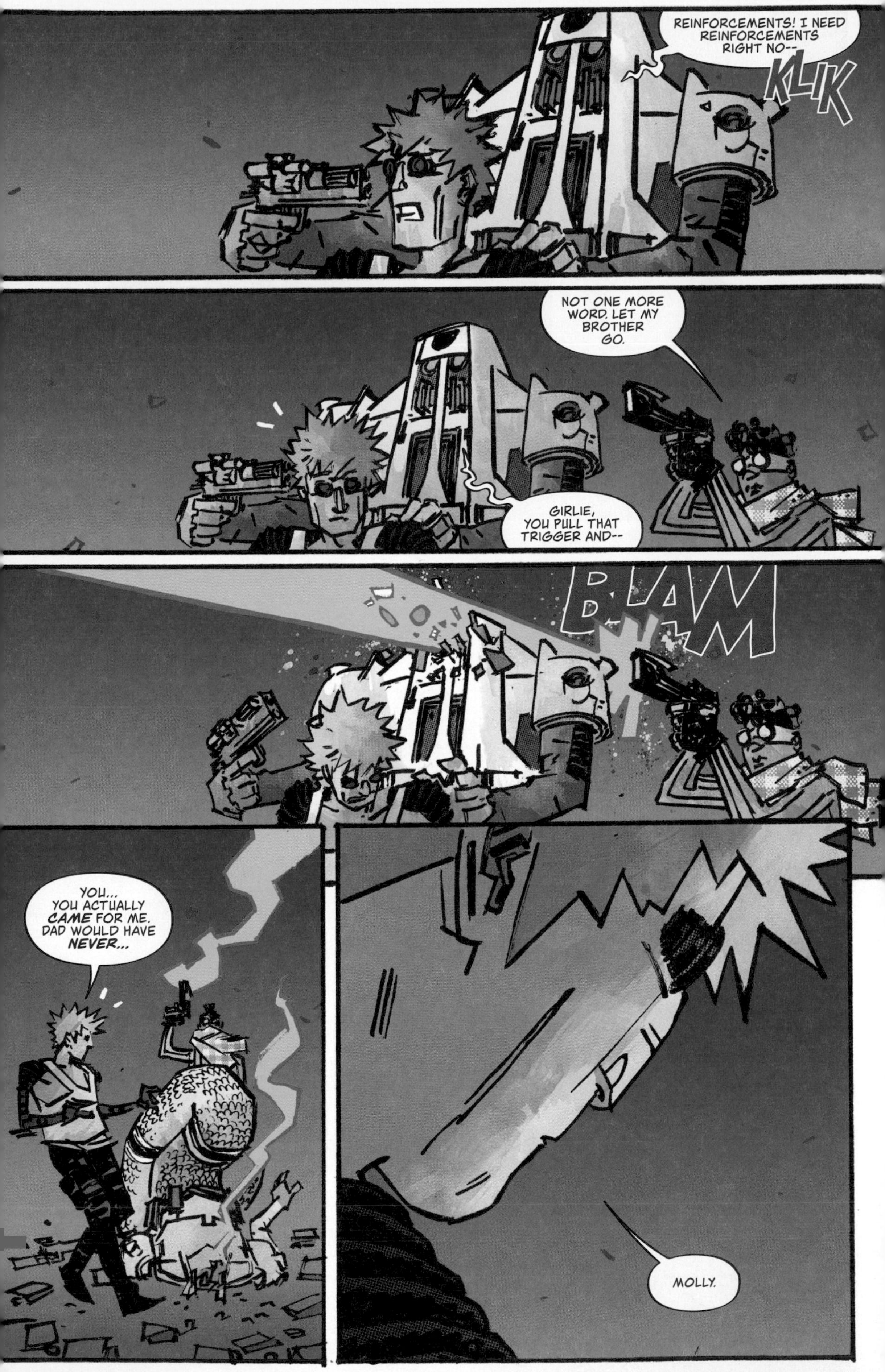
REINFORCEMENTS! I NEED REINFORCEMENTS RIGHT NO--
KLIK
NOT ONE MORE WORD. LET MY BROTHER GO.
GIRLIE, YOU PULL THAT TRIGGER AND--
BLAM
YOU... YOU ACTUALLY CAME FOR ME. DAD WOULD HAVE NEVER...
MOLLY.

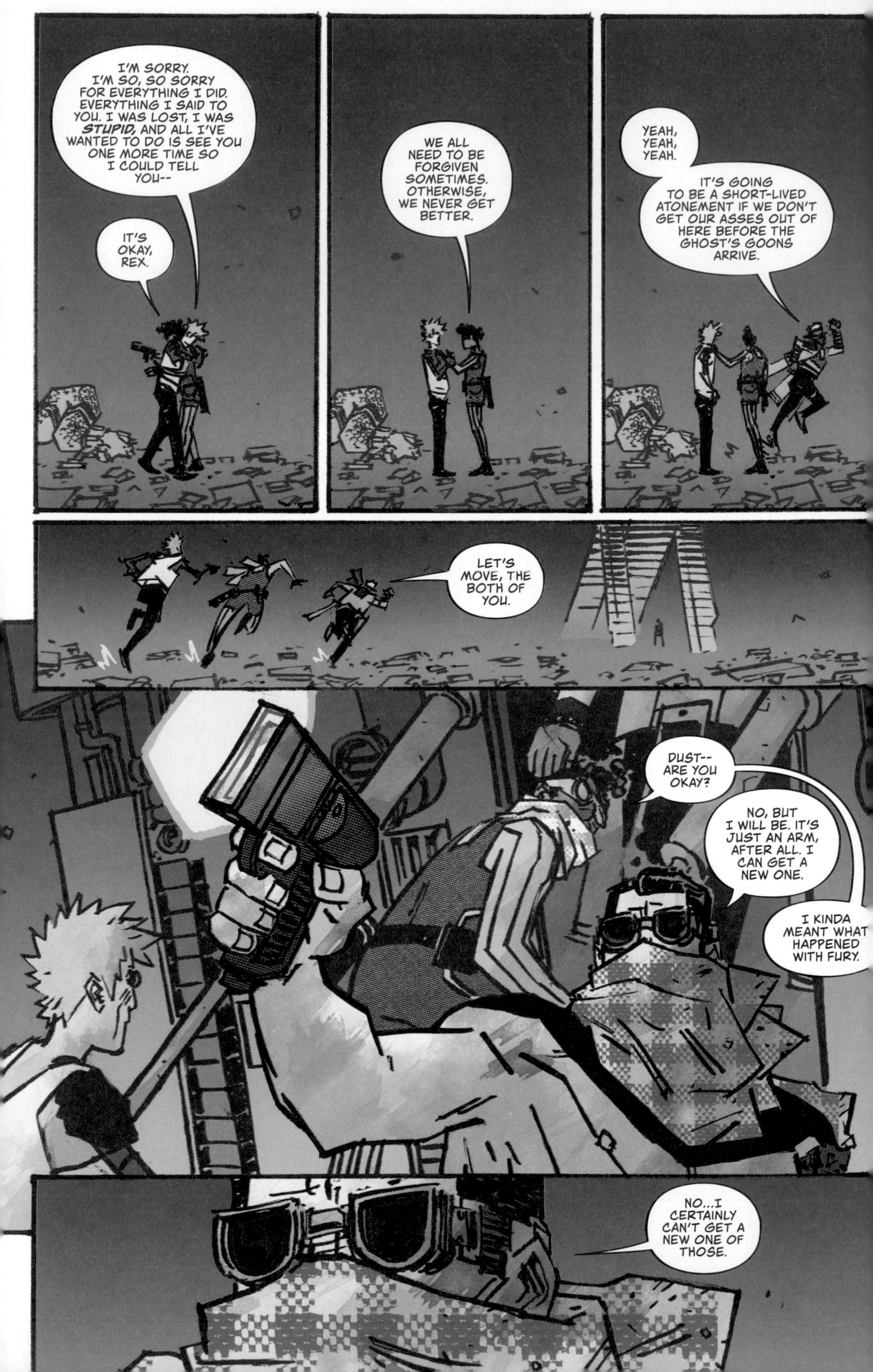
I'M SORRY. I'M SO, SO SORRY FOR EVERYTHING I DID. EVERYTHING I SAID TO YOU. I WAS LOST, I WAS STUPID, AND ALL I'VE WANTED TO DO IS SEE YOU ONE MORE TIME SO I COULD TELL YOU--
IT'S OKAY, REX.
WE ALL NEED TO BE FORGIVEN SOMETIMES. OTHERWISE, WE NEVER GET BETTER.
YEAH, YEAH, YEAH.
IT'S GOING TO BE A SHORT-LIVED ATONEMENT IF WE DON'T GET OUR ASSES OUT OF HERE BEFORE THE GHOST'S GOONS ARRIVE.
LET'S MOVE, THE BOTH OF YOU.
DUST-- ARE YOU OKAY?
NO, BUT I WILL BE. IT'S JUST AN ARM, AFTER ALL. I CAN GET A NEW ONE.
I KINDA MEANT WHAT HAPPENED WITH FURY.
NO...I CERTAINLY CAN'T GET A NEW ONE OF THOSE.

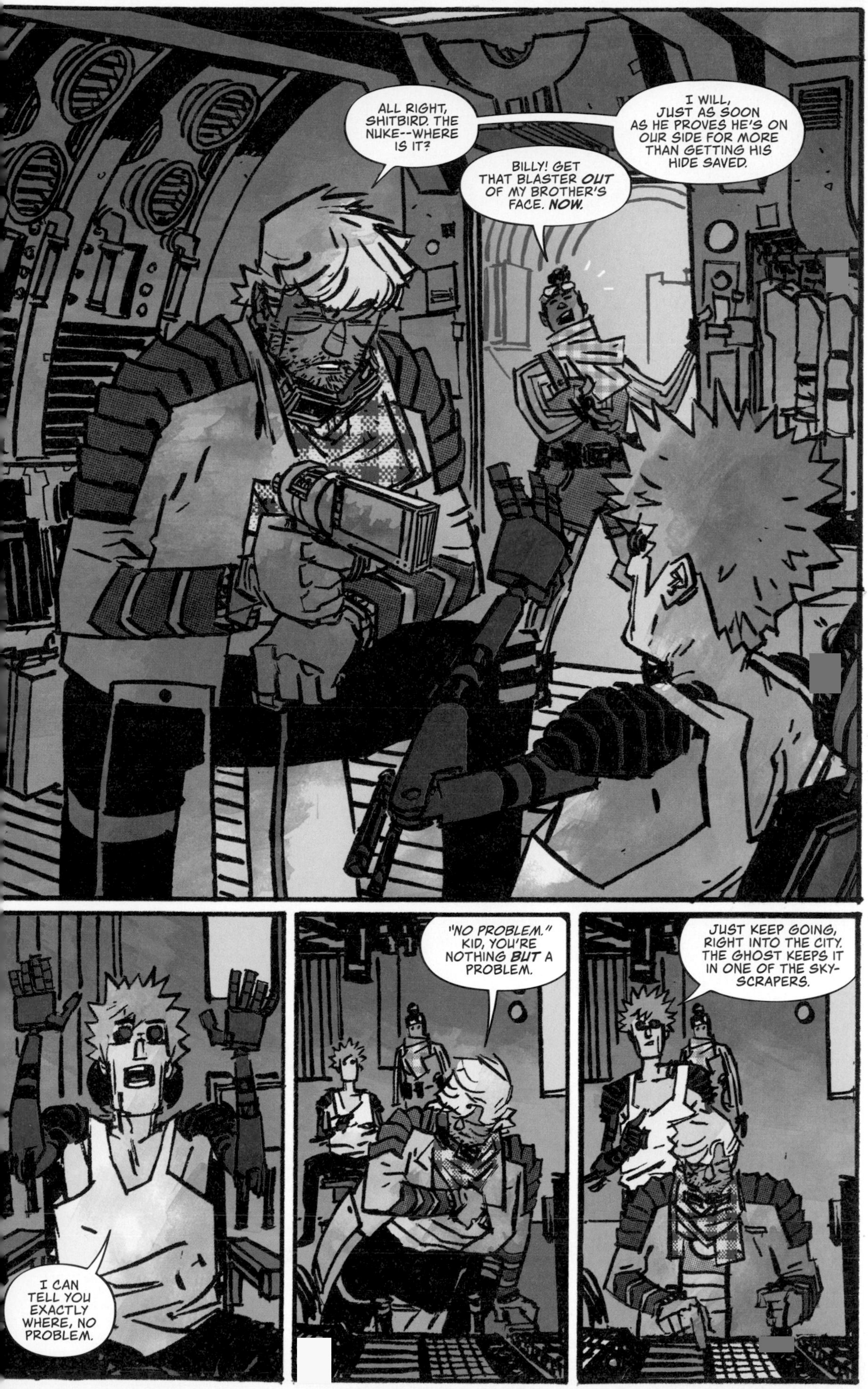
ALL RIGHT, SHITBIRD. THE NUKE--WHERE IS IT?
BILLY! GET THAT BLASTER OUT OF MY BROTHER'S FACE. NOW.
I WILL, JUST AS SOON AS HE PROVES HE'S ON OUR SIDE FOR MORE THAN GETTING HIS HIDE SAVED.
I CAN TELL YOU EXACTLY WHERE, NO PROBLEM.
"NO PROBLEM." KID, YOU'RE NOTHING BUT A PROBLEM.
JUST KEEP GOING, RIGHT INTO THE CITY. THE GHOST KEEPS IT IN ONE OF THE SKY-SCRAPERS.

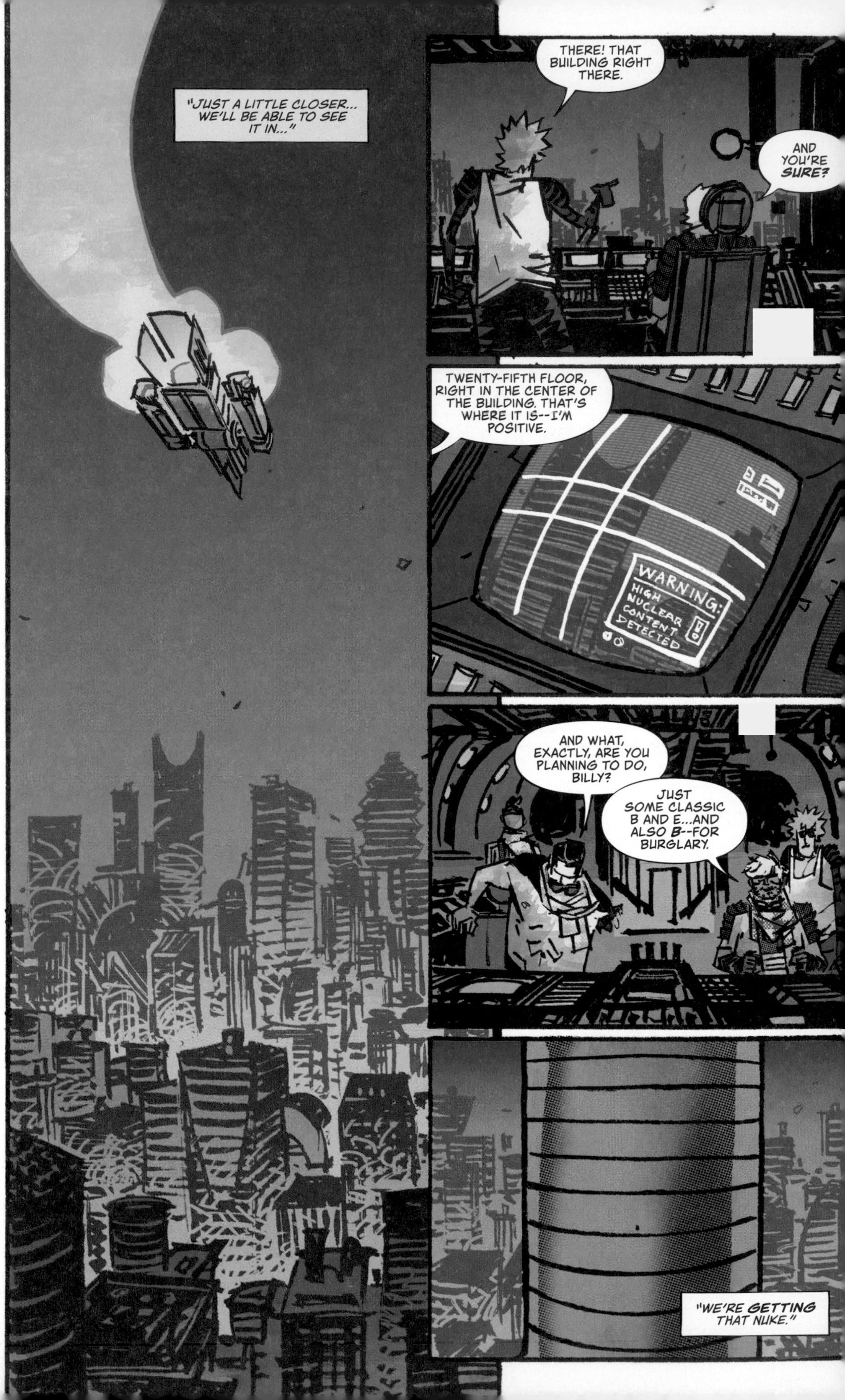
"JUST A LITTLE CLOSER... WE'LL BE ABLE TO SEE IT IN..."
THERE! THAT BUILDING RIGHT THERE.
AND YOU'RE SURE?
TWENTY-FIFTH FLOOR, RIGHT IN THE CENTER OF THE BUILDING. THAT'S WHERE IT IS--I'M POSITIVE.
WARNING: HIGH NUCLEAR CONTENT DETECTED
AND WHAT, EXACTLY, ARE YOU PLANNING TO DO, BILLY?
JUST SOME CLASSIC B AND E...AND ALSO B--FOR BURGLARY.
"WE'RE GETTING THAT NUKE."

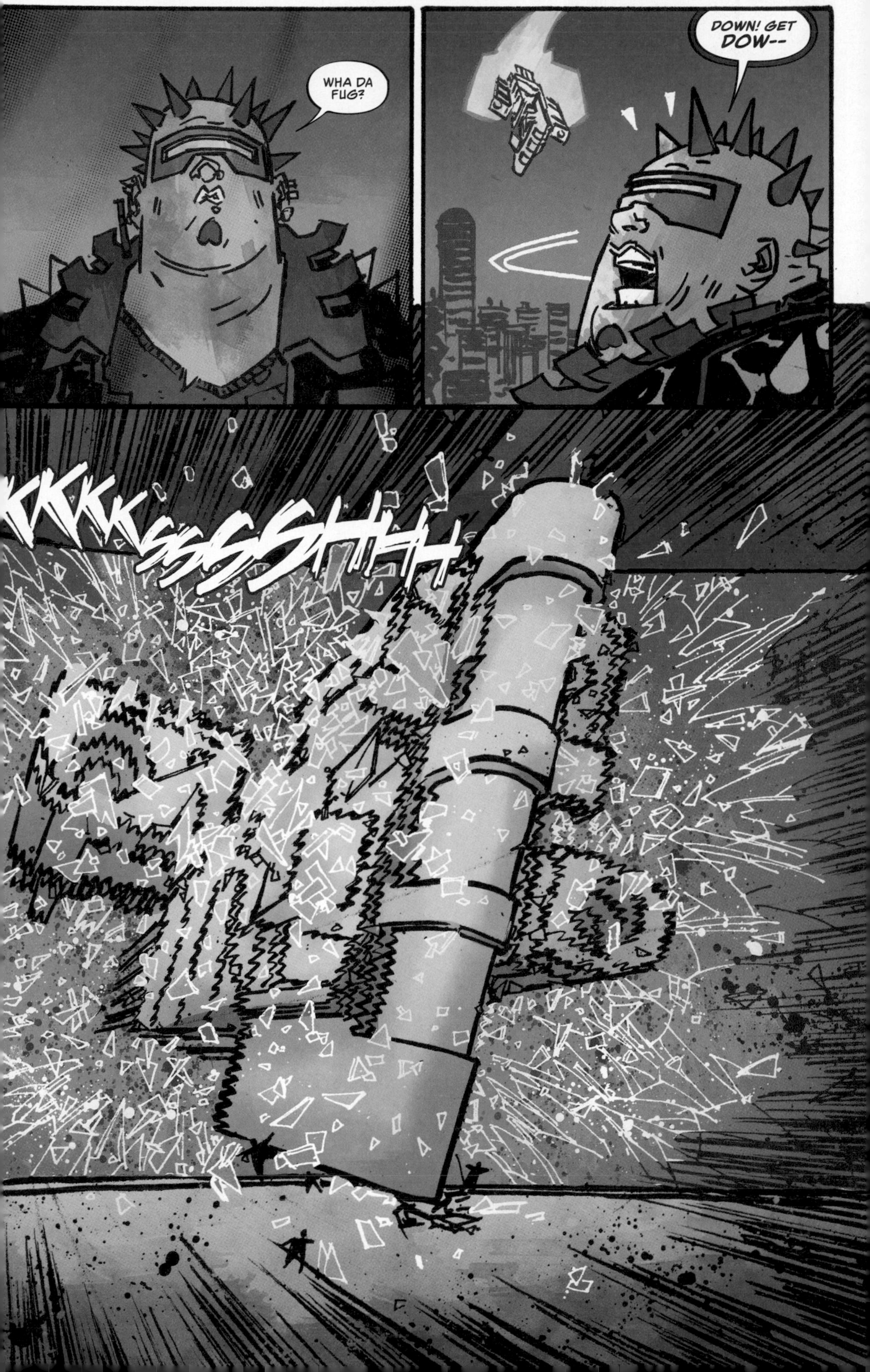
WHA DA FUG?
DOWN! GET DOW--
KKKKSSSSSHHHH

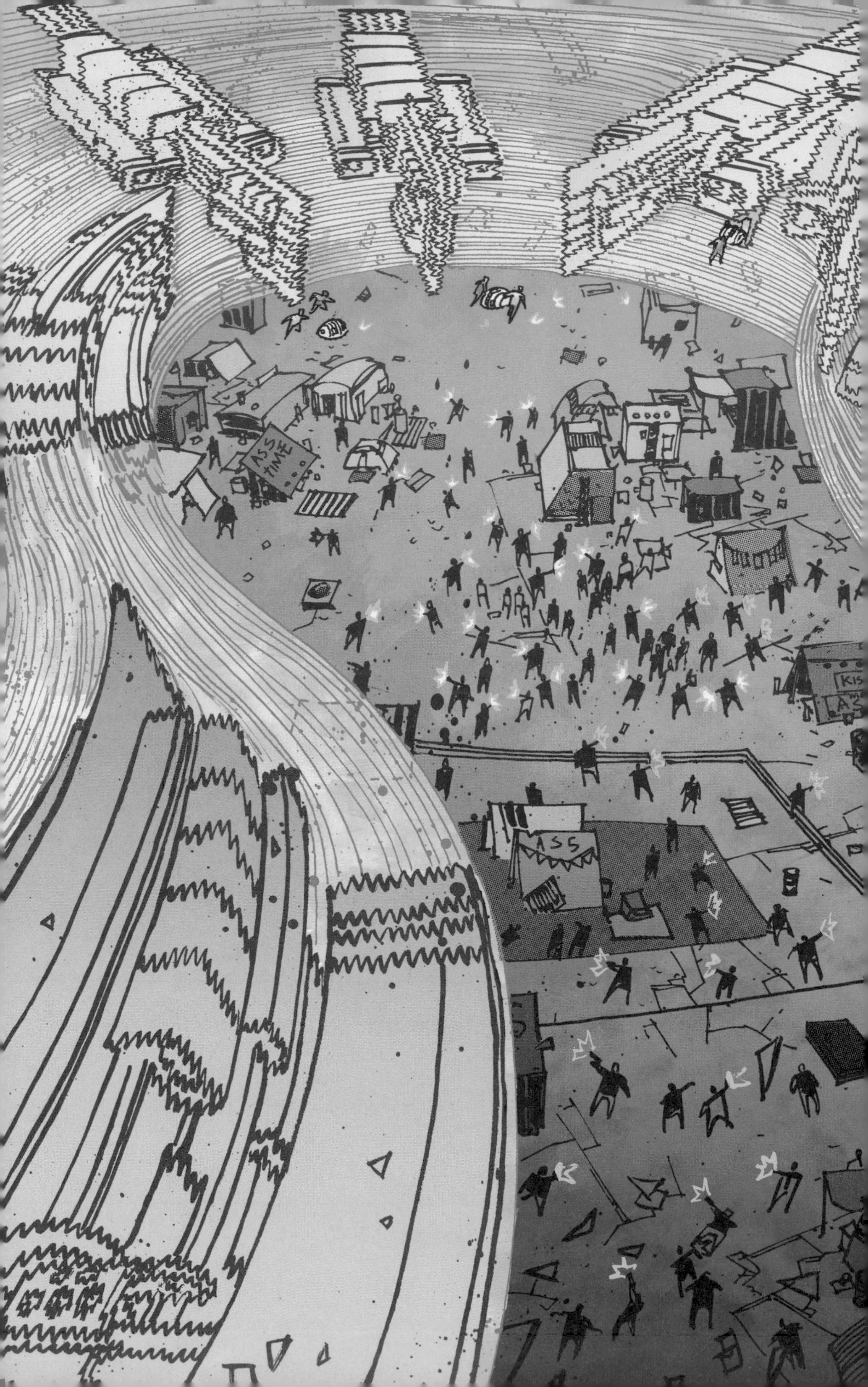
ASS time
ASS

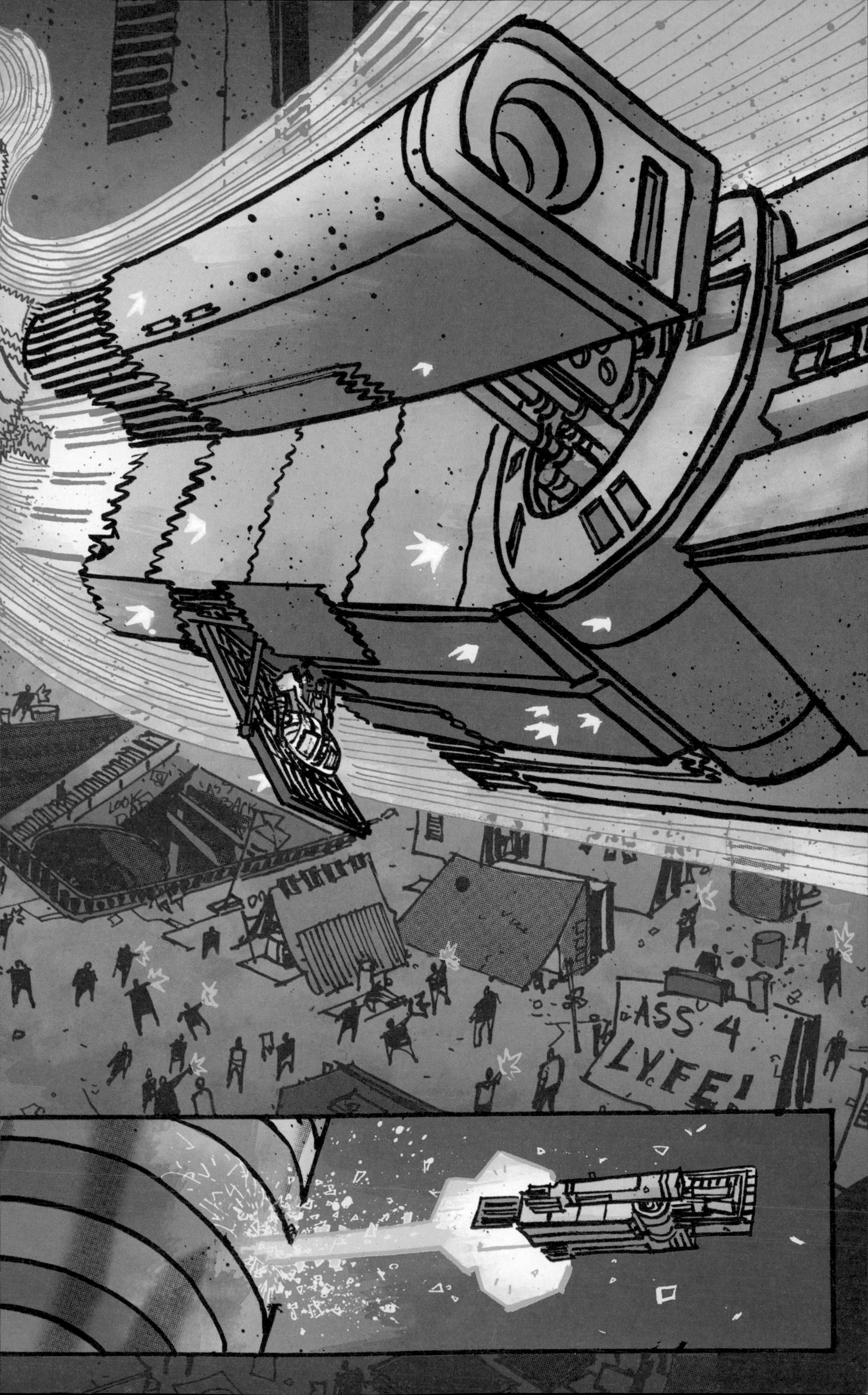
ASS 4 LYFE!

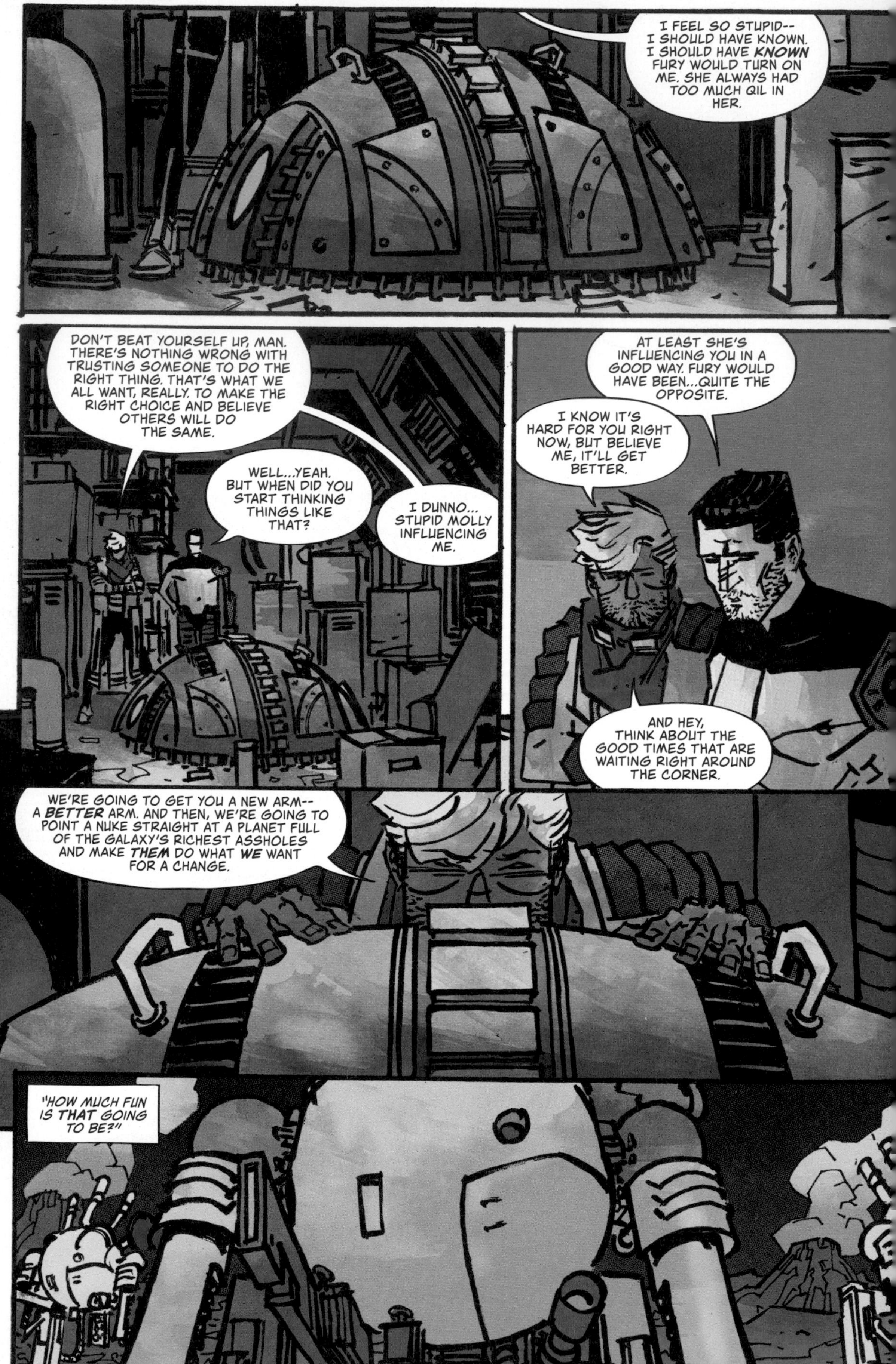
I FEEL SO STUPID-- I SHOULD HAVE KNOWN. I SHOULD HAVE **KNOWN** FURY WOULD TURN ON ME. SHE ALWAYS HAD TOO MUCH QIL IN HER.
DON'T BEAT YOURSELF UP, MAN. THERE'S NOTHING WRONG WITH TRUSTING SOMEONE TO DO THE RIGHT THING. THAT'S WHAT WE ALL WANT, REALLY. TO MAKE THE RIGHT CHOICE AND BELIEVE OTHERS WILL DO THE SAME.
WELL...YEAH. BUT WHEN DID YOU START THINKING THINGS LIKE THAT?
I DUNNO... STUPID MOLLY INFLUENCING ME.
AT LEAST SHE'S INFLUENCING YOU IN A GOOD WAY. FURY WOULD HAVE BEEN...QUITE THE OPPOSITE.
I KNOW IT'S HARD FOR YOU RIGHT NOW, BUT BELIEVE ME, IT'LL GET BETTER.
AND HEY, THINK ABOUT THE GOOD TIMES THAT ARE WAITING RIGHT AROUND THE CORNER.
WE'RE GOING TO GET YOU A NEW ARM-- A **BETTER** ARM. AND THEN, WE'RE GOING TO POINT A NUKE STRAIGHT AT A PLANET FULL OF THE GALAXY'S RICHEST ASSHOLES AND MAKE **THEM** DO WHAT **WE** WANT FOR A CHANGE.
"HOW MUCH FUN IS **THAT** GOING TO BE?"

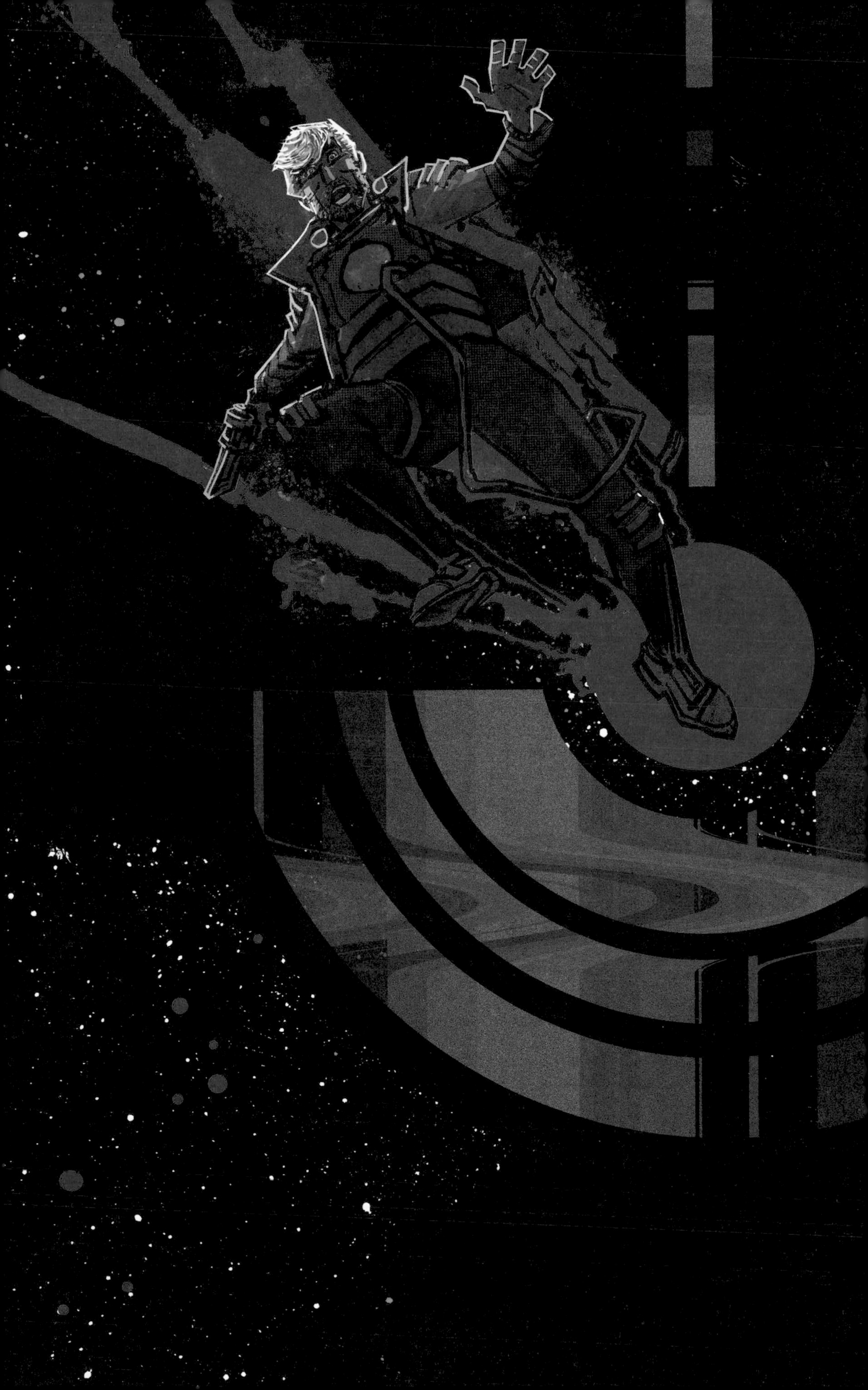

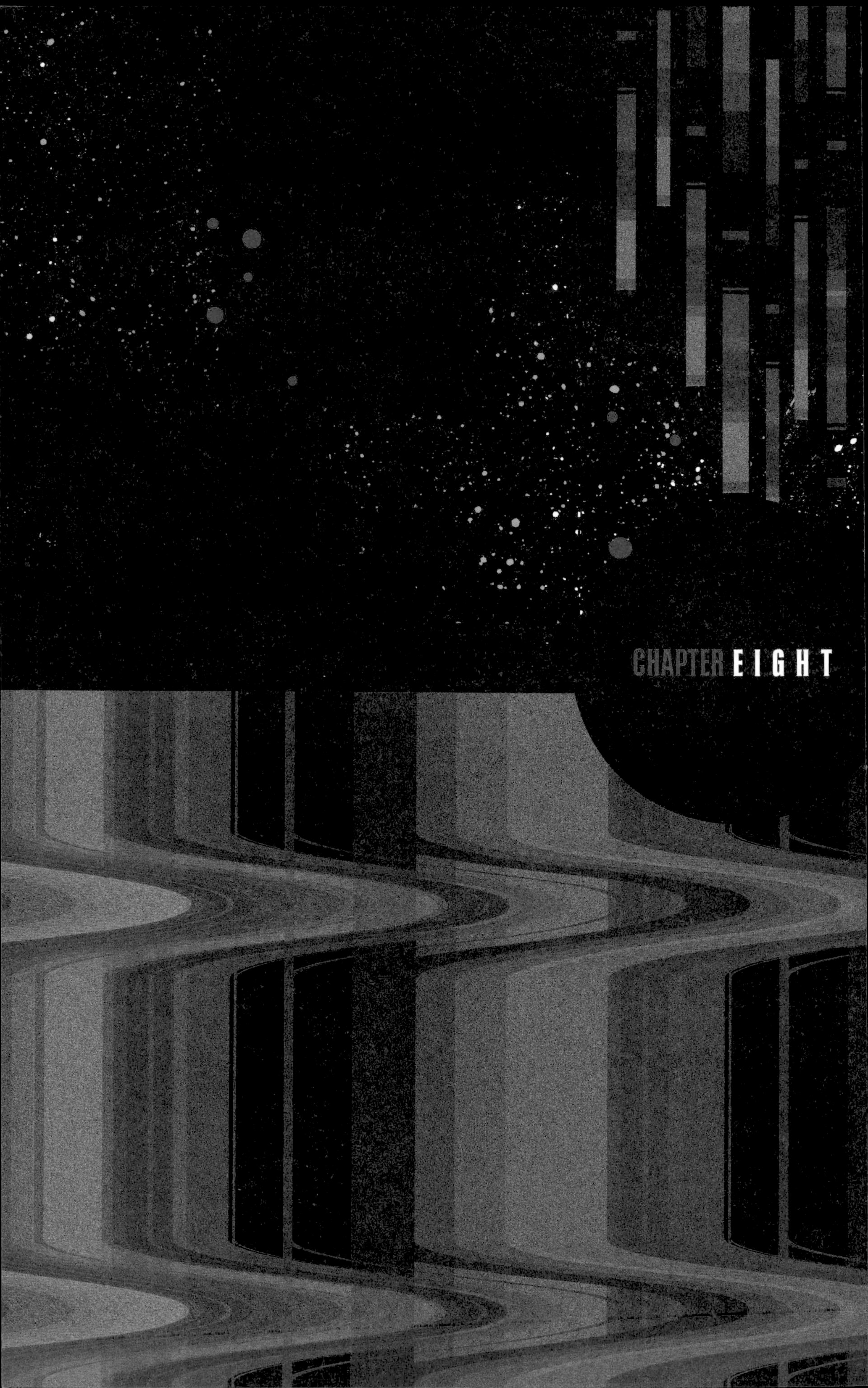

CHAPTER **EIGHT**

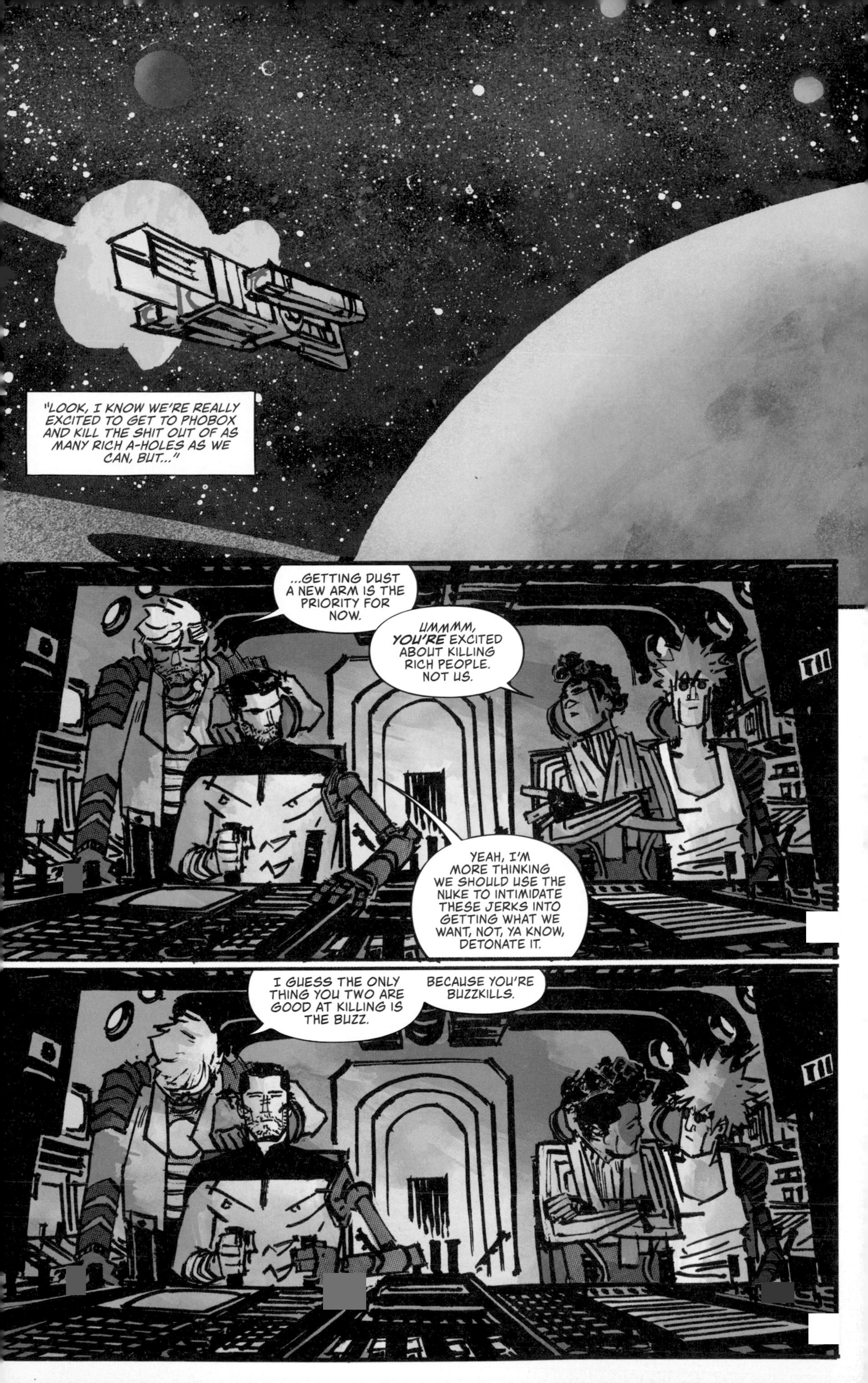
"LOOK, I KNOW WE'RE REALLY EXCITED TO GET TO PHOBOX AND KILL THE SHIT OUT OF AS MANY RICH A-HOLES AS WE CAN, BUT..."
...GETTING DUST A NEW ARM IS THE PRIORITY FOR NOW.
UMMMM, YOU'RE EXCITED ABOUT KILLING RICH PEOPLE. NOT US.
YEAH, I'M MORE THINKING WE SHOULD USE THE NUKE TO INTIMIDATE THESE JERKS INTO GETTING WHAT WE WANT, NOT, YA KNOW, DETONATE IT.
I GUESS THE ONLY THING YOU TWO ARE GOOD AT KILLING IS THE BUZZ.
BECAUSE YOU'RE BUZZKILLS.

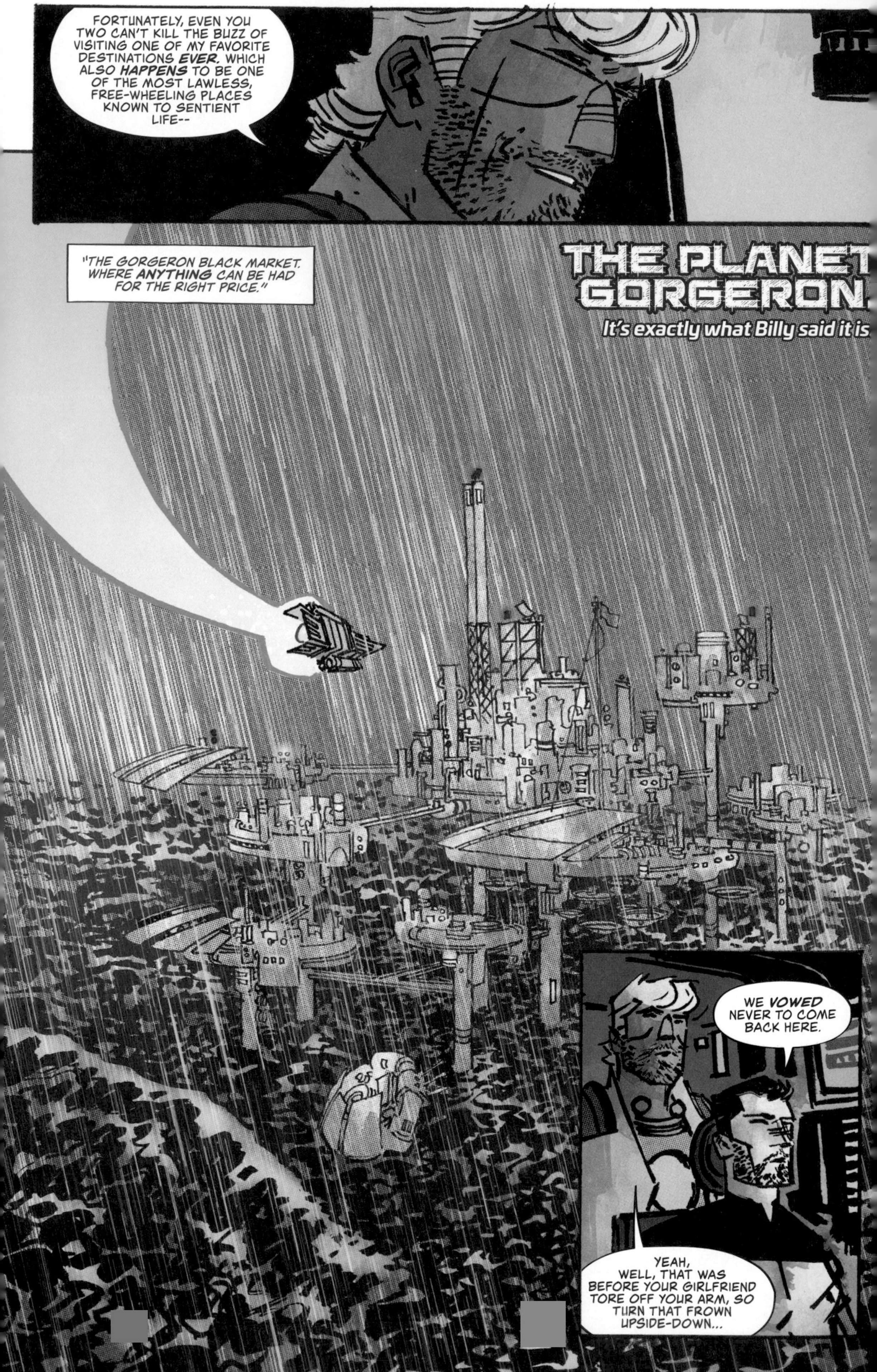
FORTUNATELY, EVEN YOU TWO CAN'T KILL THE BUZZ OF VISITING ONE OF MY FAVORITE DESTINATIONS EVER. WHICH ALSO HAPPENS TO BE ONE OF THE MOST LAWLESS, FREE-WHEELING PLACES KNOWN TO SENTIENT LIFE--
"THE GORGERON BLACK MARKET. WHERE ANYTHING CAN BE HAD FOR THE RIGHT PRICE."
THE PLANET GORGERON.
It's exactly what Billy said it is.
WE VOWED NEVER TO COME BACK HERE.
YEAH, WELL, THAT WAS BEFORE YOUR GIRLFRIEND TORE OFF YOUR ARM, SO TURN THAT FROWN UPSIDE-DOWN...

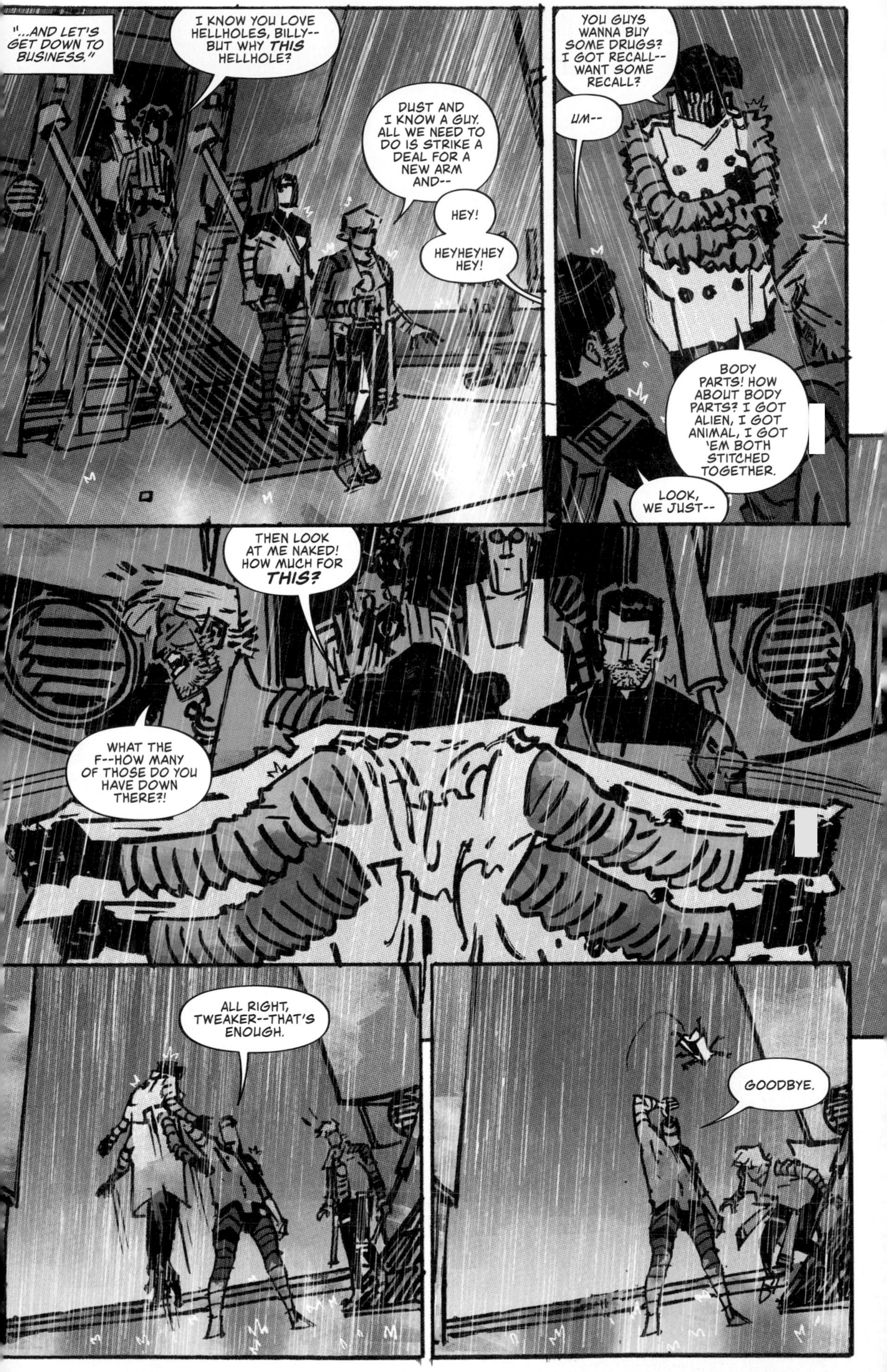
"...AND LET'S GET DOWN TO BUSINESS."
I KNOW YOU LOVE HELLHOLES, BILLY--BUT WHY THIS HELLHOLE?
DUST AND I KNOW A GUY. ALL WE NEED TO DO IS STRIKE A DEAL FOR A NEW ARM AND--
HEY!
HEYHEYHEY HEY!
YOU GUYS WANNA BUY SOME DRUGS? I GOT RECALL--WANT SOME RECALL?
UM--
BODY PARTS! HOW ABOUT BODY PARTS? I GOT ALIEN, I GOT ANIMAL, I GOT 'EM BOTH STITCHED TOGETHER.
LOOK, WE JUST--
THEN LOOK AT ME NAKED! HOW MUCH FOR THIS?
WHAT THE F--HOW MANY OF THOSE DO YOU HAVE DOWN THERE?!
ALL RIGHT, TWEAKER--THAT'S ENOUGH.
GOODBYE.

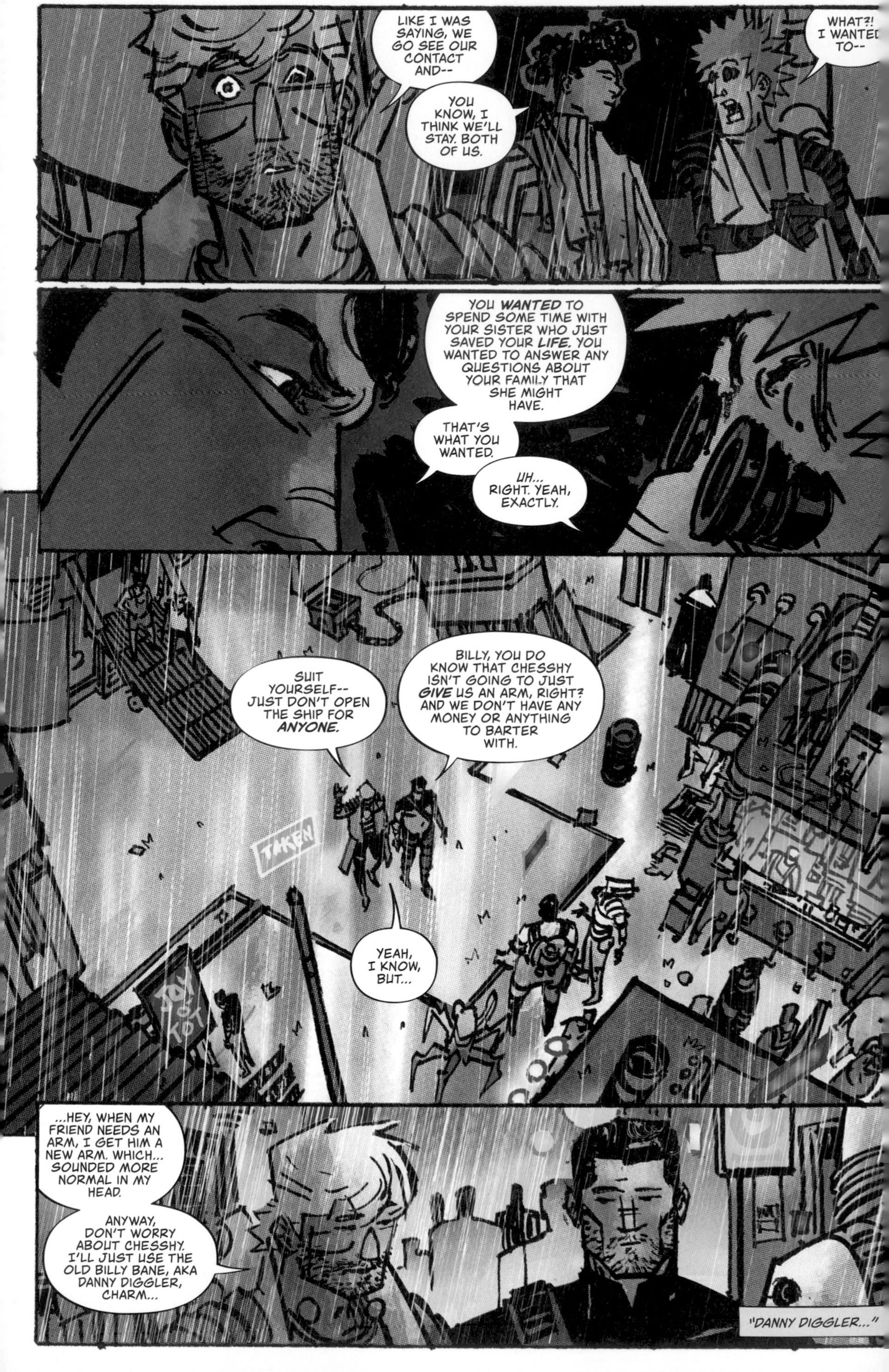

LIKE I WAS SAYING, WE GO SEE OUR CONTACT AND--
YOU KNOW, I THINK WE'LL STAY. BOTH OF US.
WHAT?! I WANTED TO--
YOU WANTED TO SPEND SOME TIME WITH YOUR SISTER WHO JUST SAVED YOUR LIFE. YOU WANTED TO ANSWER ANY QUESTIONS ABOUT YOUR FAMILY THAT SHE MIGHT HAVE.
THAT'S WHAT YOU WANTED.
UH... RIGHT. YEAH, EXACTLY.
SUIT YOURSELF-- JUST DON'T OPEN THE SHIP FOR ANYONE.
BILLY, YOU DO KNOW THAT CHESSHY ISN'T GOING TO JUST GIVE US AN ARM, RIGHT? AND WE DON'T HAVE ANY MONEY OR ANYTHING TO BARTER WITH.
TAKEN
YEAH, I KNOW, BUT...
...HEY, WHEN MY FRIEND NEEDS AN ARM, I GET HIM A NEW ARM. WHICH... SOUNDED MORE NORMAL IN MY HEAD.
ANYWAY, DON'T WORRY ABOUT CHESSHY. I'LL JUST USE THE OLD BILLY BANE, AKA DANNY DIGGLER, CHARM...
"DANNY DIGGLER..."

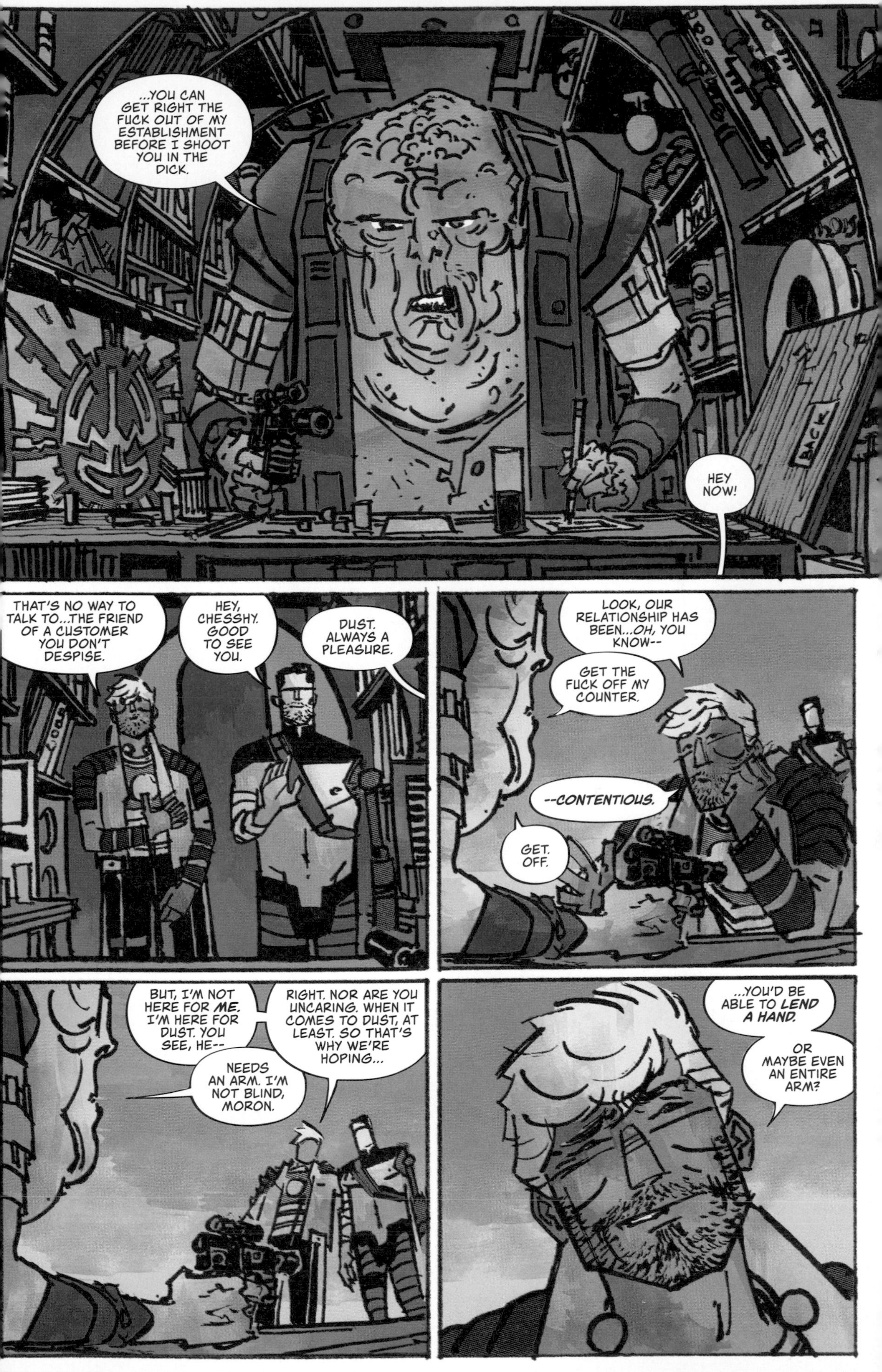
...YOU CAN GET RIGHT THE FUCK OUT OF MY ESTABLISHMENT BEFORE I SHOOT YOU IN THE DICK.
BACK
HEY NOW!
THAT'S NO WAY TO TALK TO...THE FRIEND OF A CUSTOMER YOU DON'T DESPISE.
HEY, CHESSHY. GOOD TO SEE YOU.
DUST. ALWAYS A PLEASURE.
LOOK, OUR RELATIONSHIP HAS BEEN...OH, YOU KNOW--
GET THE FUCK OFF MY COUNTER.
--CONTENTIOUS.
GET. OFF.
BUT, I'M NOT HERE FOR ME. I'M HERE FOR DUST. YOU SEE, HE--
NEEDS AN ARM. I'M NOT BLIND, MORON.
RIGHT. NOR ARE YOU UNCARING. WHEN IT COMES TO DUST, AT LEAST. SO THAT'S WHY WE'RE HOPING...
...YOU'D BE ABLE TO LEND A HAND.
OR MAYBE EVEN AN ENTIRE ARM?

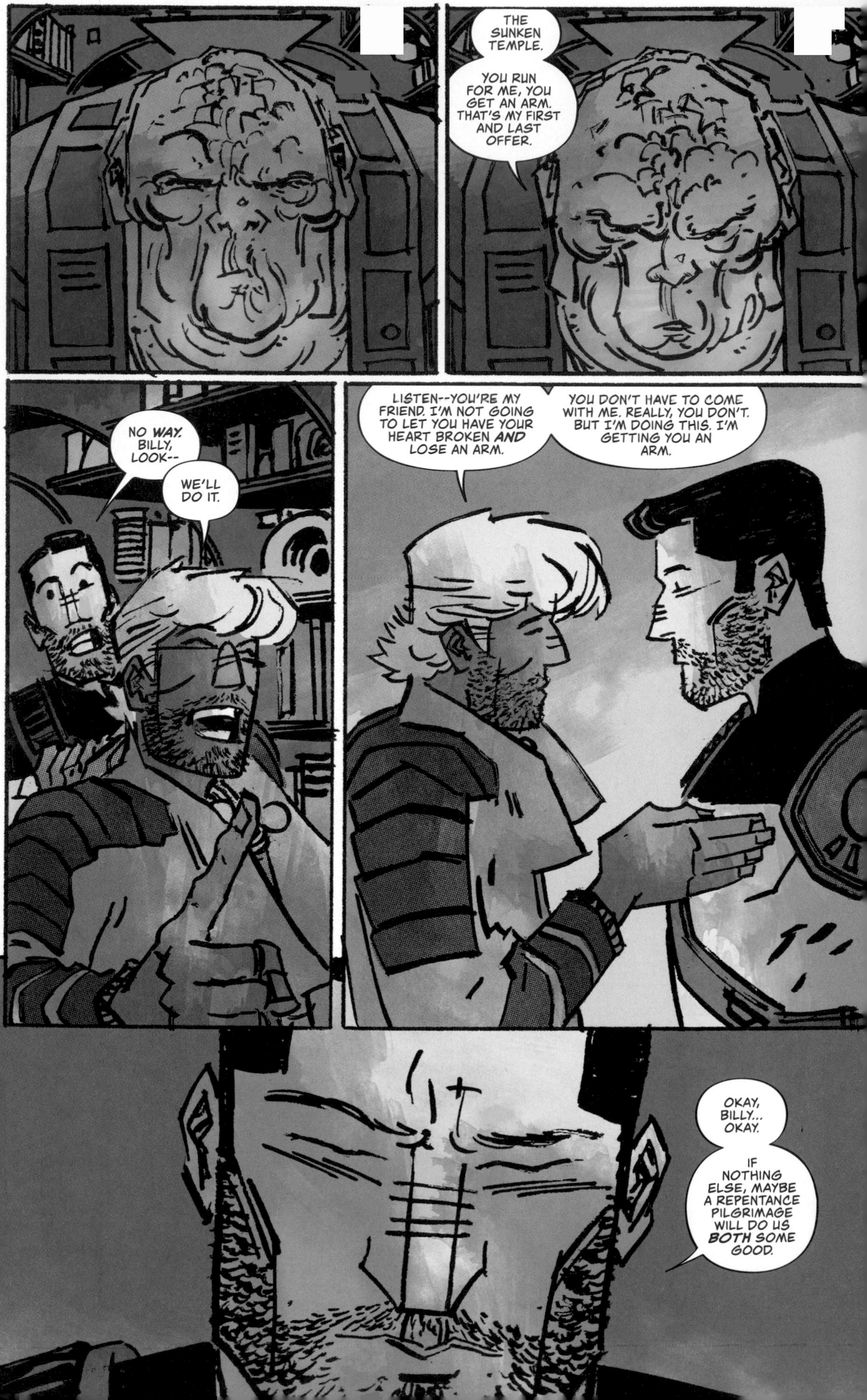
THE SUNKEN TEMPLE.
YOU RUN FOR ME, YOU GET AN ARM. THAT'S MY FIRST AND LAST OFFER.
NO **WAY.** BILLY, LOOK--
WE'LL DO IT.
LISTEN--YOU'RE MY FRIEND. I'M NOT GOING TO LET YOU HAVE YOUR HEART BROKEN **AND** LOSE AN ARM.
YOU DON'T HAVE TO COME WITH ME. REALLY, YOU DON'T. BUT I'M DOING THIS. I'M GETTING YOU AN ARM.
OKAY, BILLY... OKAY.
IF NOTHING ELSE, MAYBE A REPENTANCE PILGRIMAGE WILL DO US **BOTH** SOME GOOD.

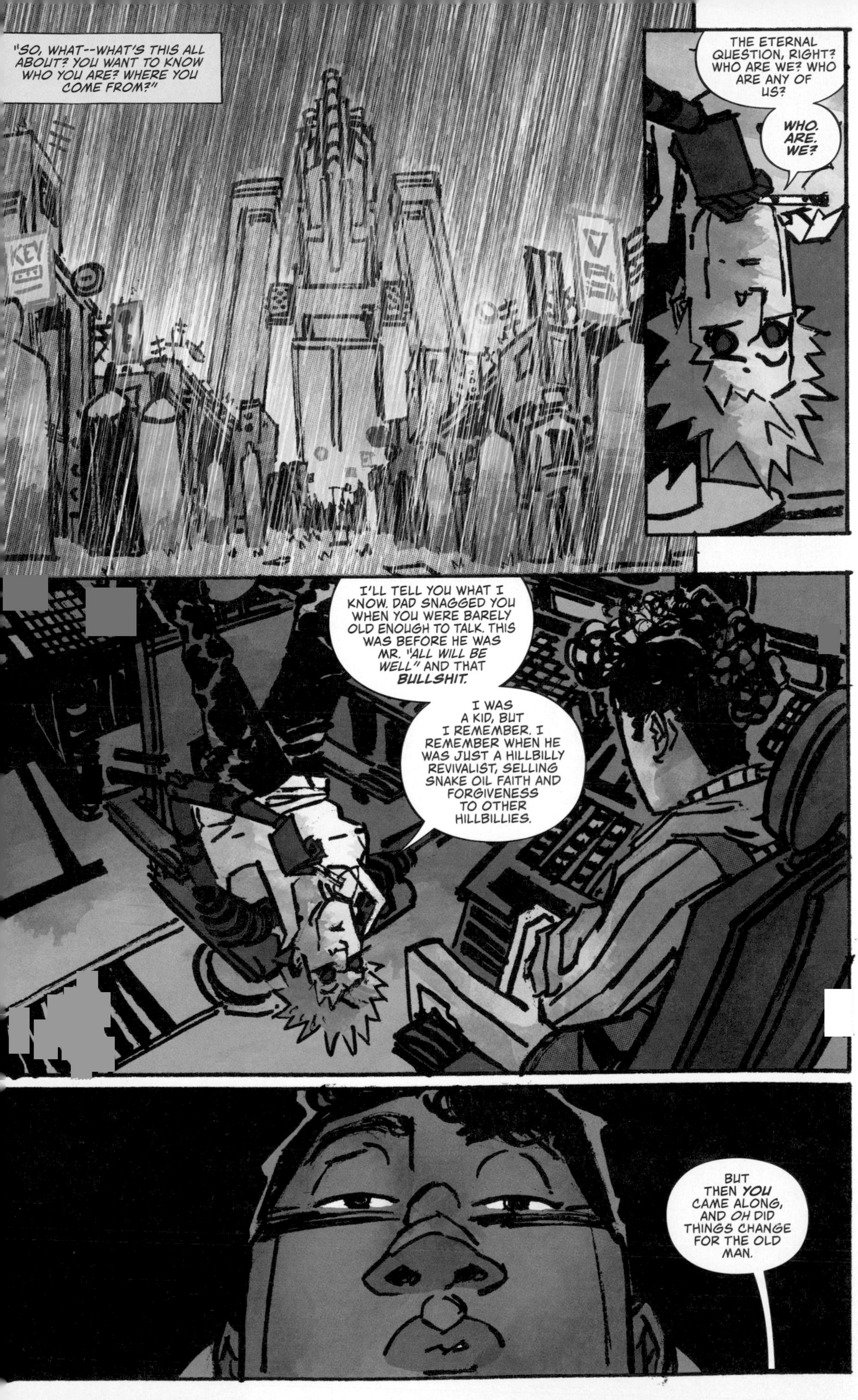
"SO, WHAT--WHAT'S THIS ALL ABOUT? YOU WANT TO KNOW WHO YOU ARE? WHERE YOU COME FROM?"
THE ETERNAL QUESTION, RIGHT? WHO ARE WE? WHO ARE ANY OF US?
WHO. ARE. WE?
I'LL TELL YOU WHAT I KNOW. DAD SNAGGED YOU WHEN YOU WERE BARELY OLD ENOUGH TO TALK. THIS WAS BEFORE HE WAS MR. "ALL WILL BE WELL" AND THAT BULLSHIT.
I WAS A KID, BUT I REMEMBER. I REMEMBER WHEN HE WAS JUST A HILLBILLY REVIVALIST, SELLING SNAKE OIL FAITH AND FORGIVENESS TO OTHER HILLBILLIES.
BUT THEN YOU CAME ALONG, AND OH DID THINGS CHANGE FOR THE OLD MAN.

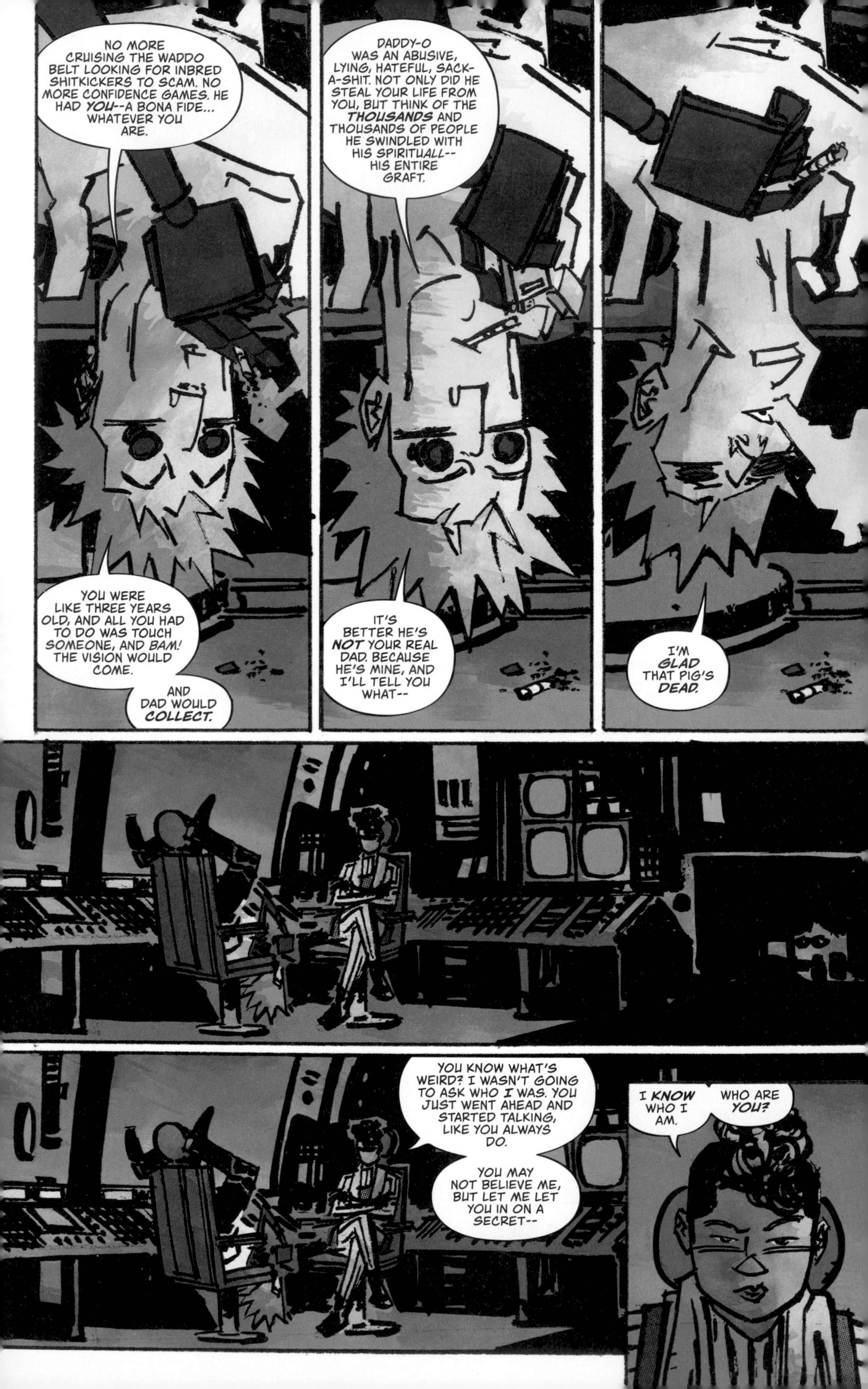
NO MORE CRUISING THE WADDO BELT LOOKING FOR INBRED SHITKICKERS TO SCAM. NO MORE CONFIDENCE GAMES. HE HAD YOU--A BONA FIDE... WHATEVER YOU ARE.
YOU WERE LIKE THREE YEARS OLD, AND ALL YOU HAD TO DO WAS TOUCH SOMEONE, AND BAM! THE VISION WOULD COME.
AND DAD WOULD COLLECT.
DADDY-O WAS AN ABUSIVE, LYING, HATEFUL, SACK-A-SHIT. NOT ONLY DID HE STEAL YOUR LIFE FROM YOU, BUT THINK OF THE THOUSANDS AND THOUSANDS OF PEOPLE HE SWINDLED WITH HIS SPIRITUALL-- HIS ENTIRE GRAFT.
IT'S BETTER HE'S NOT YOUR REAL DAD. BECAUSE HE'S MINE, AND I'LL TELL YOU WHAT--
I'M GLAD THAT PIG'S DEAD.
YOU KNOW WHAT'S WEIRD? I WASN'T GOING TO ASK WHO I WAS. YOU JUST WENT AHEAD AND STARTED TALKING, LIKE YOU ALWAYS DO.
YOU MAY NOT BELIEVE ME, BUT LET ME LET YOU IN ON A SECRET--
I KNOW WHO I AM.
WHO ARE YOU?

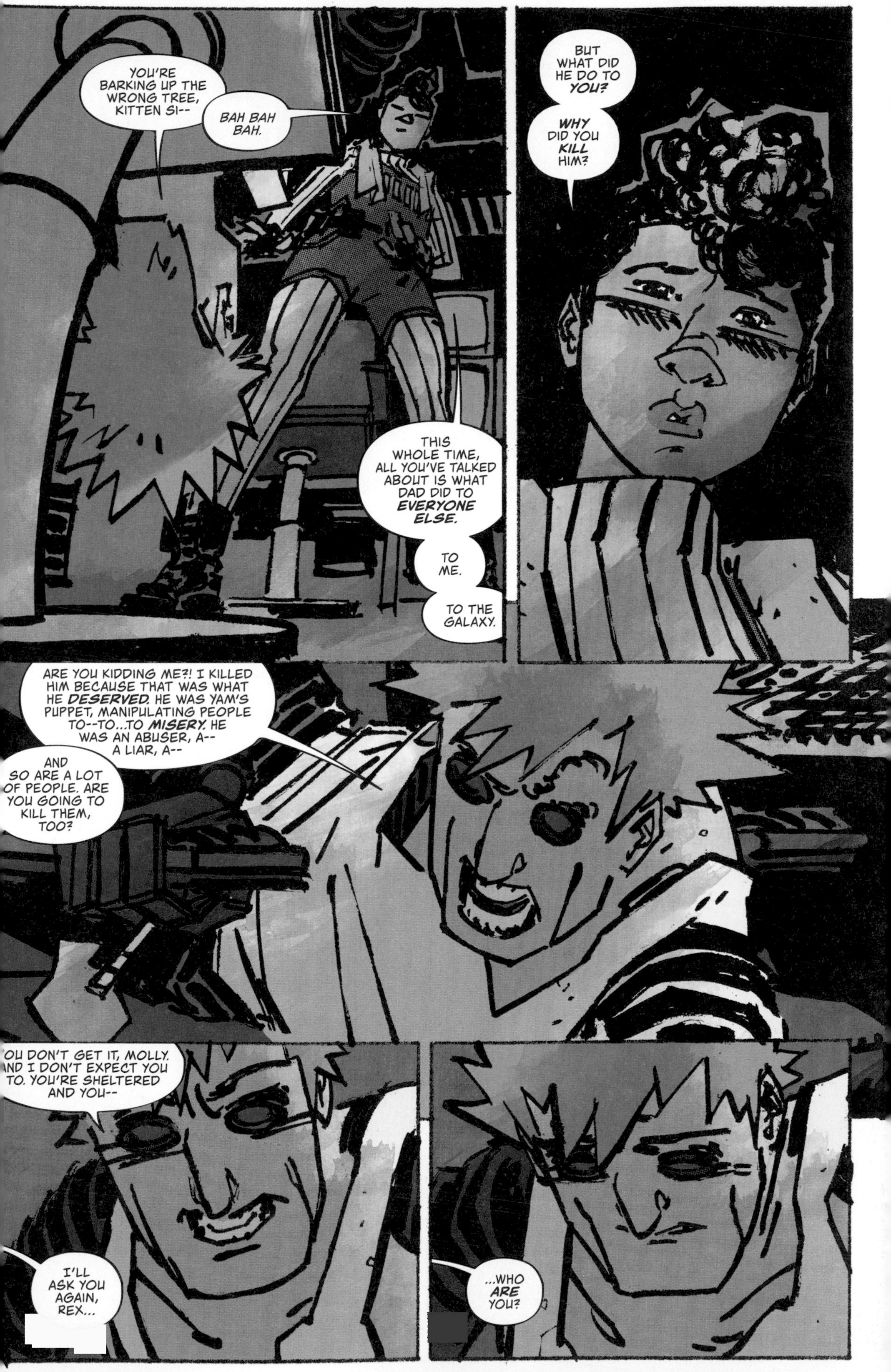
YOU'RE BARKING UP THE WRONG TREE, KITTEN SI--
BAH BAH BAH.
THIS WHOLE TIME, ALL YOU'VE TALKED ABOUT IS WHAT DAD DID TO **EVERYONE ELSE.**
TO ME.
TO THE GALAXY.
BUT WHAT DID HE DO TO **YOU?**
WHY DID YOU **KILL** HIM?
ARE YOU KIDDING ME?! I KILLED HIM BECAUSE THAT WAS WHAT HE **DESERVED.** HE WAS YAM'S PUPPET, MANIPULATING PEOPLE TO--TO...TO **MISERY.** HE WAS AN ABUSER, A-- A LIAR, A--
AND SO ARE A LOT OF PEOPLE. ARE YOU GOING TO KILL THEM, TOO?
YOU DON'T GET IT, MOLLY. AND I DON'T EXPECT YOU TO. YOU'RE SHELTERED AND YOU--
I'LL ASK YOU AGAIN, REX...
...WHO **ARE** YOU?

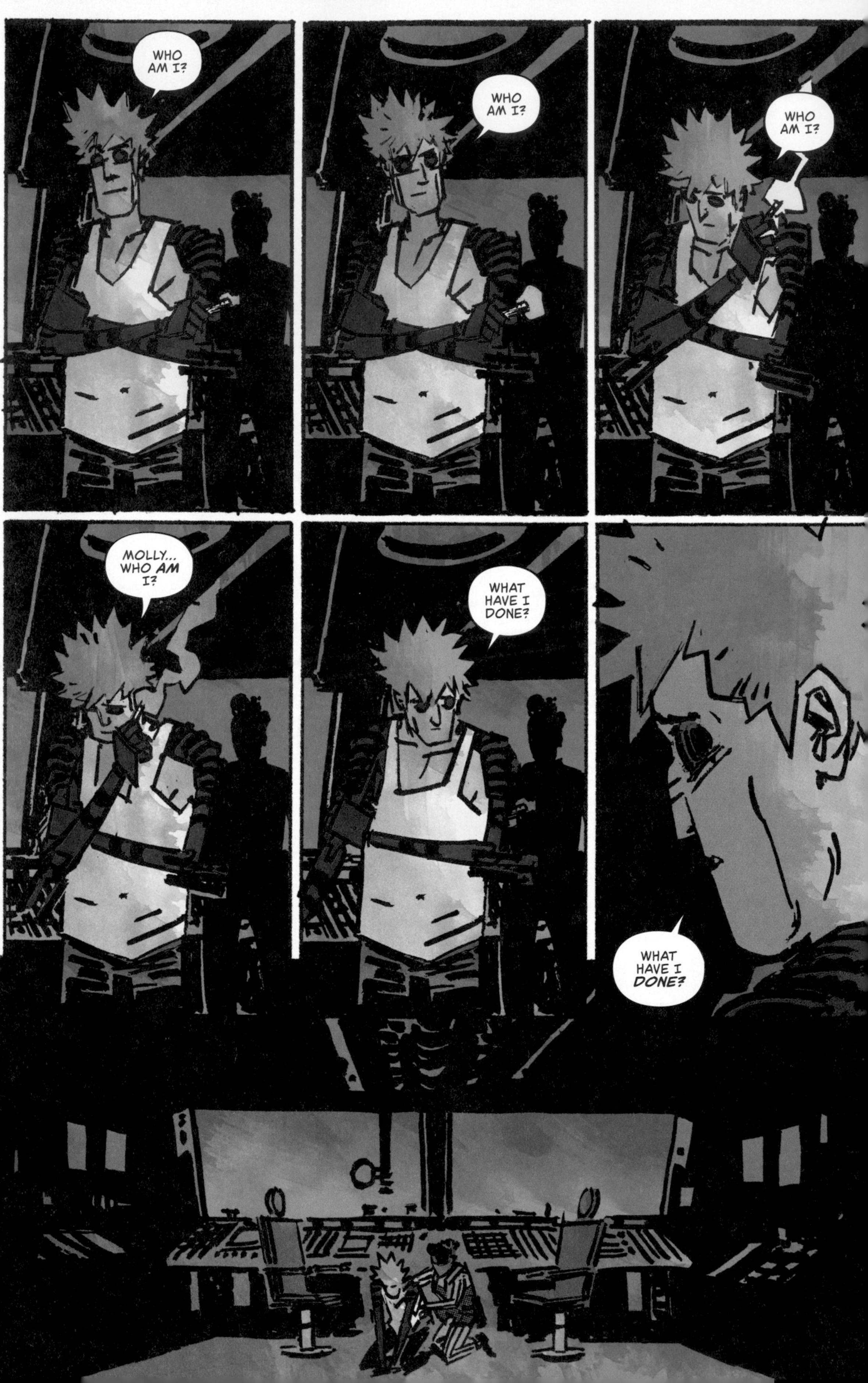
WHO AM I?
WHO AM I?
WHO AM I?
MOLLY... WHO AM I?
WHAT HAVE I DONE?
WHAT HAVE I DONE?

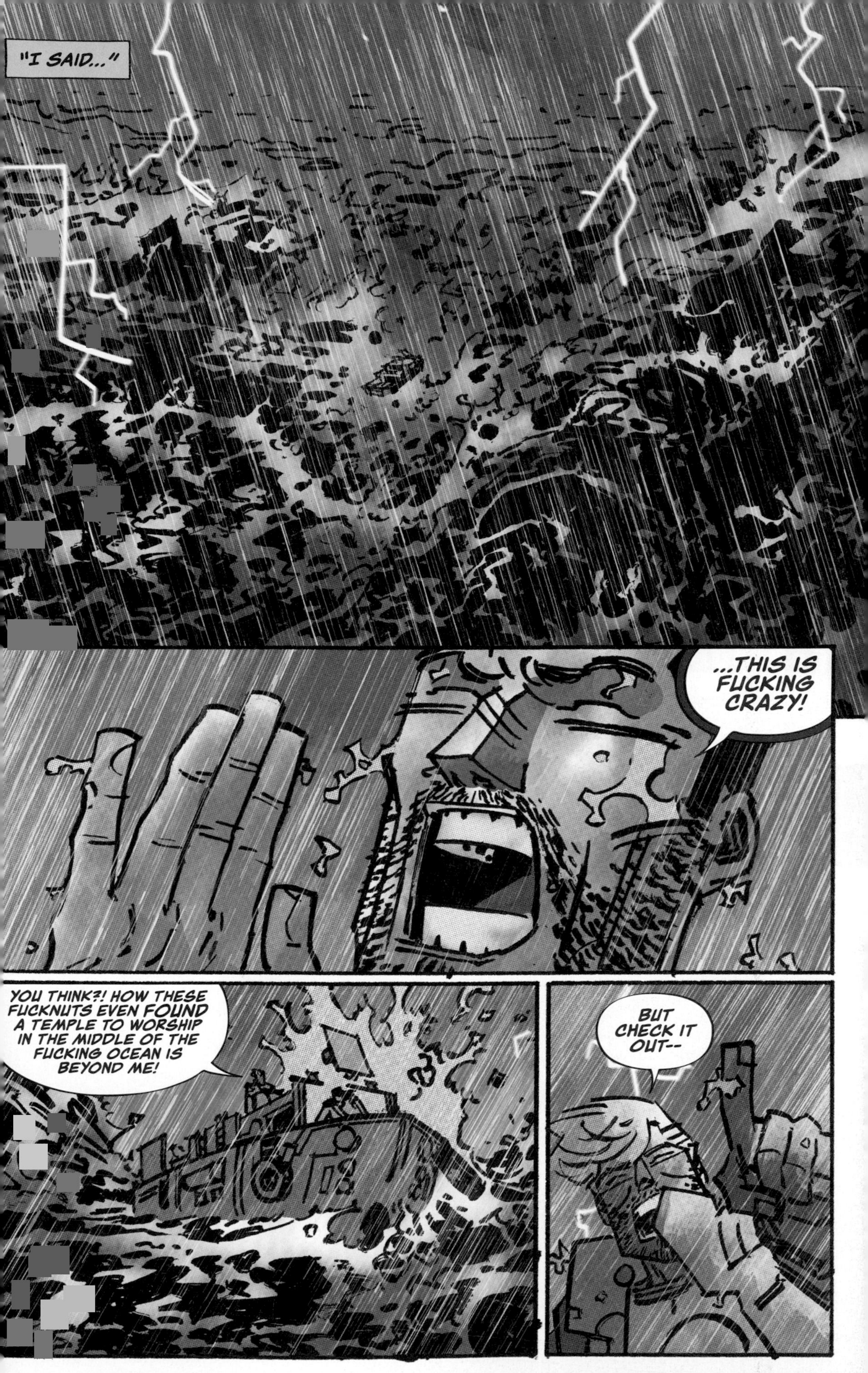
"I SAID..."
...THIS IS FUCKING CRAZY!
YOU THINK?! HOW THESE FUCKNUTS EVEN FOUND A TEMPLE TO WORSHIP IN THE MIDDLE OF THE FUCKING OCEAN IS BEYOND ME!
BUT CHECK IT OUT--

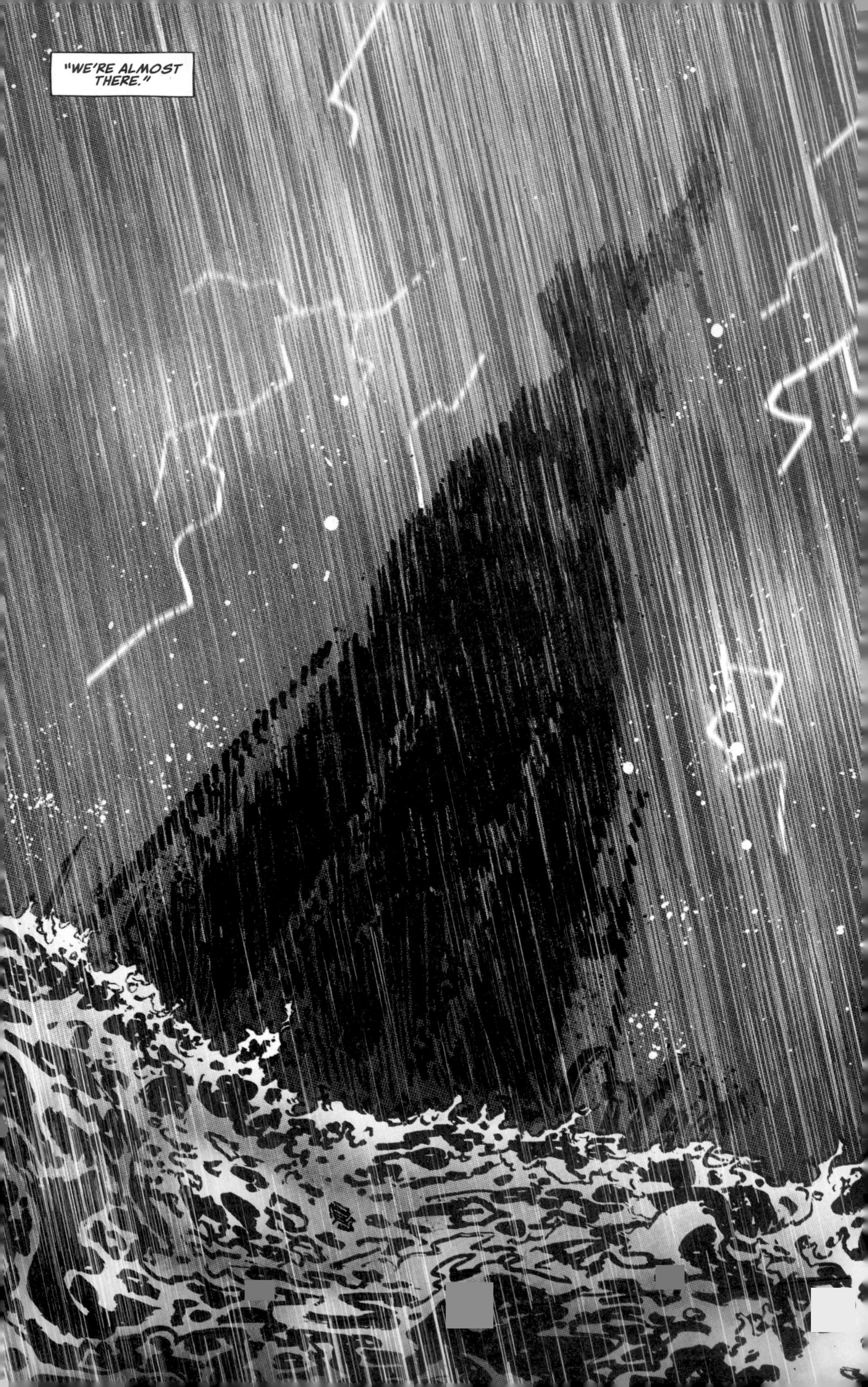
"WE'RE ALMOST THERE."

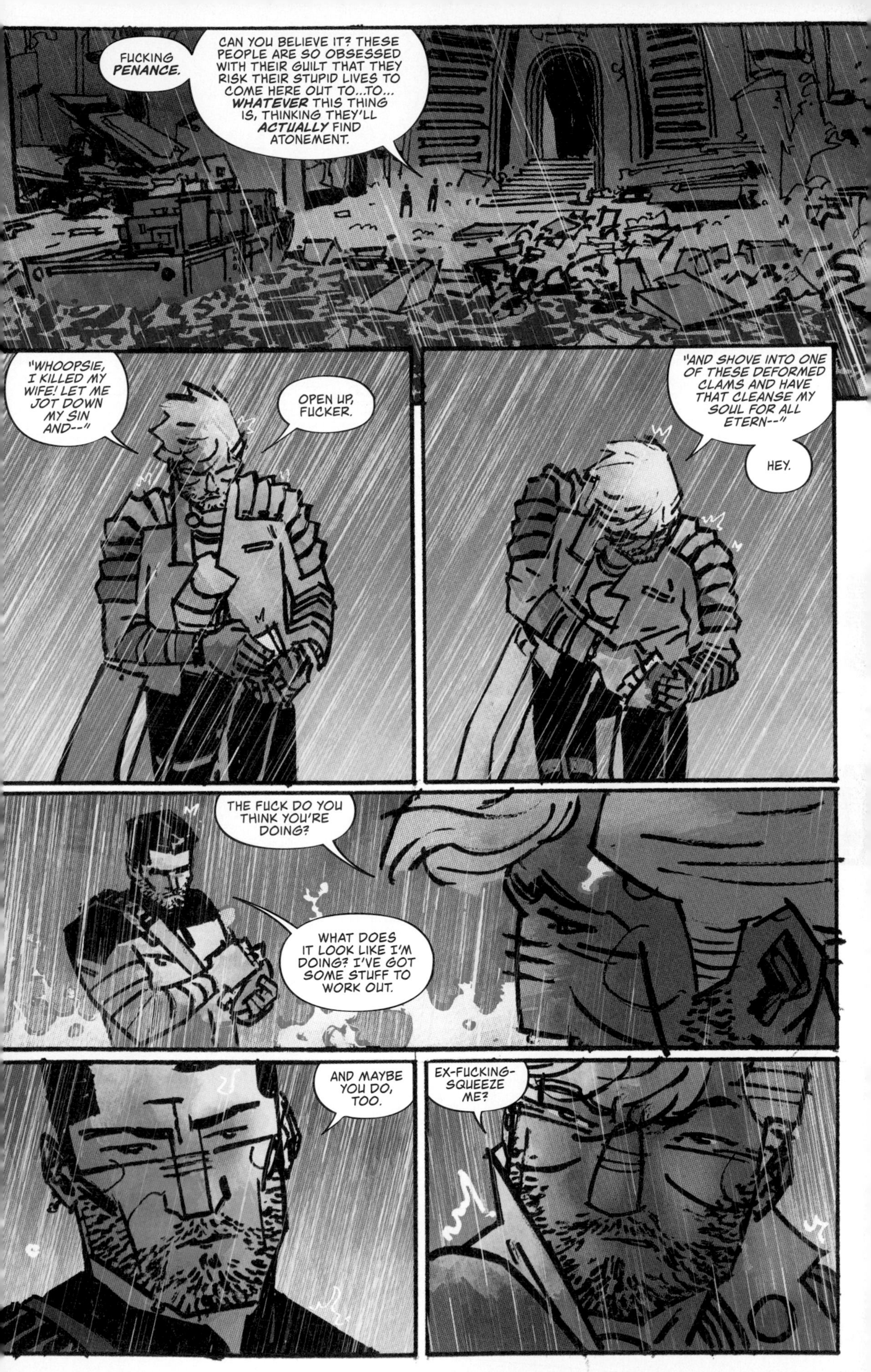
FUCKING PENANCE.
CAN YOU BELIEVE IT? THESE PEOPLE ARE SO OBSESSED WITH THEIR GUILT THAT THEY RISK THEIR STUPID LIVES TO COME HERE OUT TO...TO... WHATEVER THIS THING IS, THINKING THEY'LL ACTUALLY FIND ATONEMENT.
"WHOOPSIE, I KILLED MY WIFE! LET ME JOT DOWN MY SIN AND--"
OPEN UP, FUCKER.
"AND SHOVE INTO ONE OF THESE DEFORMED CLAMS AND HAVE THAT CLEANSE MY SOUL FOR ALL ETERN--"
HEY.
THE FUCK DO YOU THINK YOU'RE DOING?
WHAT DOES IT LOOK LIKE I'M DOING? I'VE GOT SOME STUFF TO WORK OUT.
AND MAYBE YOU DO, TOO.
EX-FUCKING-SQUEEZE ME?

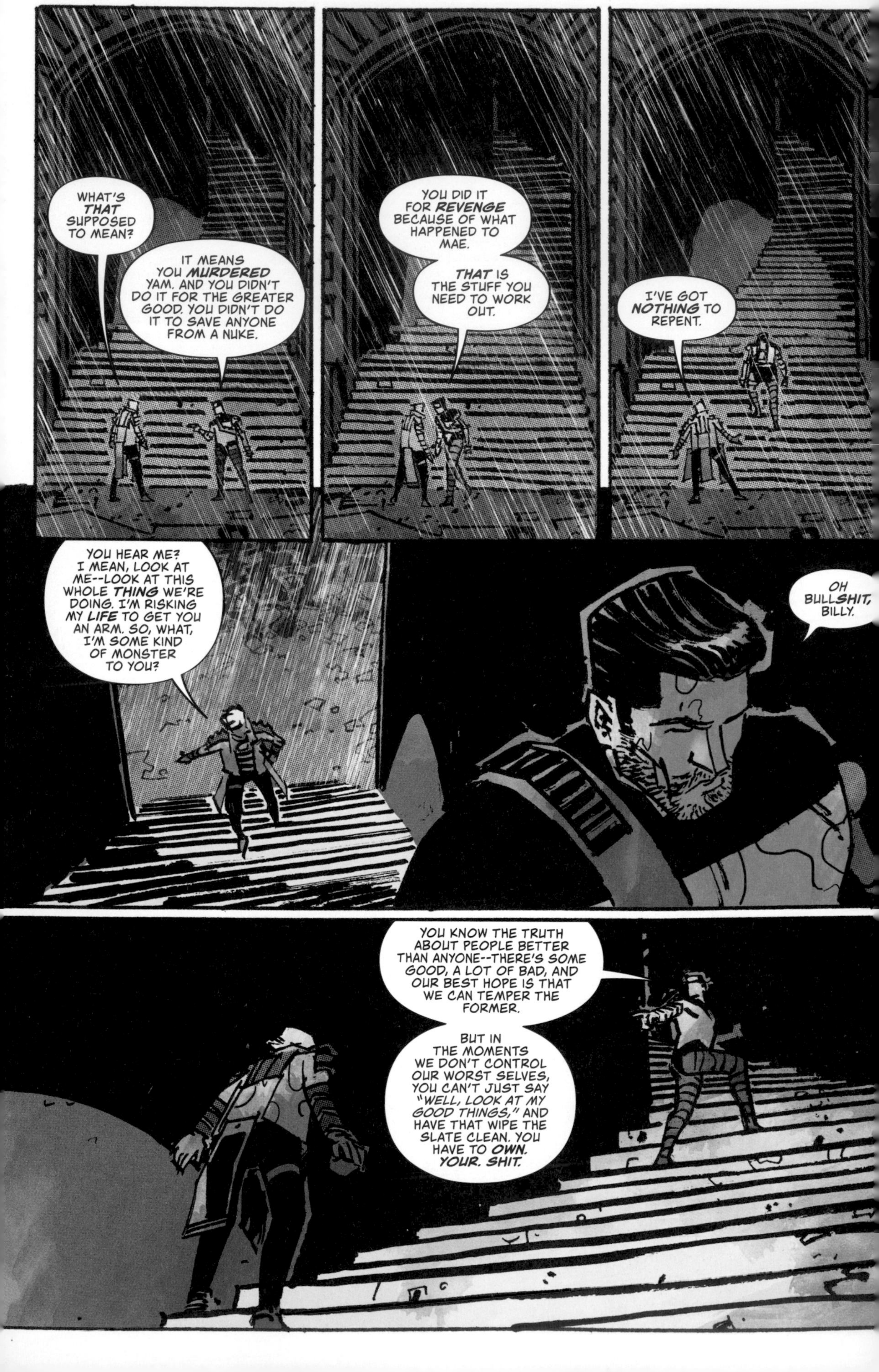
WHAT'S THAT SUPPOSED TO MEAN?
IT MEANS YOU MURDERED YAM. AND YOU DIDN'T DO IT FOR THE GREATER GOOD. YOU DIDN'T DO IT TO SAVE ANYONE FROM A NUKE.
YOU DID IT FOR REVENGE BECAUSE OF WHAT HAPPENED TO MAE.
THAT IS THE STUFF YOU NEED TO WORK OUT.
I'VE GOT NOTHING TO REPENT.
YOU HEAR ME? I MEAN, LOOK AT ME--LOOK AT THIS WHOLE THING WE'RE DOING. I'M RISKING MY LIFE TO GET YOU AN ARM. SO, WHAT, I'M SOME KIND OF MONSTER TO YOU?
OH BULLSHIT, BILLY.
YOU KNOW THE TRUTH ABOUT PEOPLE BETTER THAN ANYONE--THERE'S SOME GOOD, A LOT OF BAD, AND OUR BEST HOPE IS THAT WE CAN TEMPER THE FORMER.
BUT IN THE MOMENTS WE DON'T CONTROL OUR WORST SELVES, YOU CAN'T JUST SAY "WELL, LOOK AT MY GOOD THINGS," AND HAVE THAT WIPE THE SLATE CLEAN. YOU HAVE TO OWN. YOUR. SHIT.

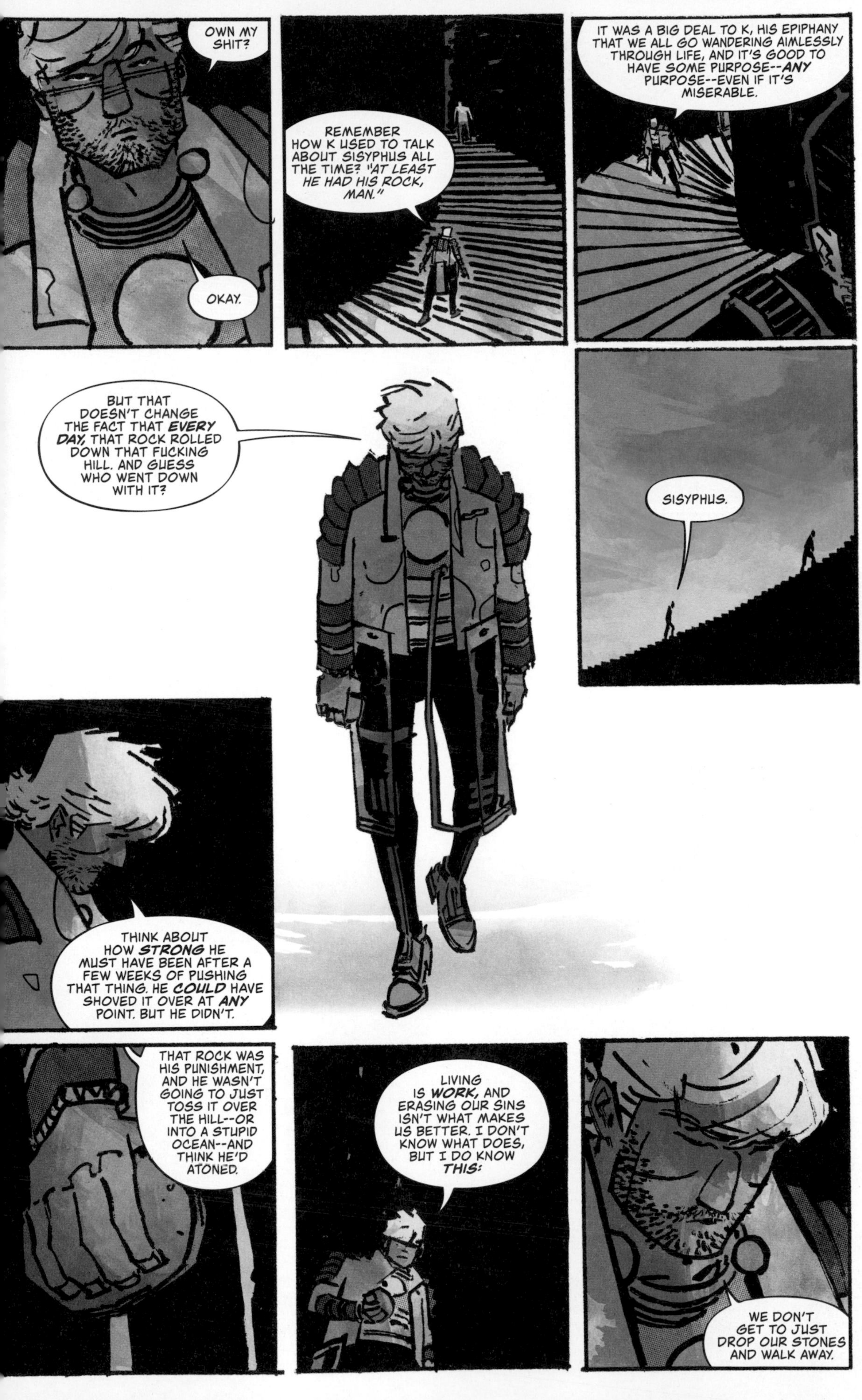
OWN MY SHIT?
OKAY.
REMEMBER HOW K USED TO TALK ABOUT SISYPHUS ALL THE TIME? "AT LEAST HE HAD HIS ROCK, MAN."
IT WAS A BIG DEAL TO K, HIS EPIPHANY THAT WE ALL GO WANDERING AIMLESSLY THROUGH LIFE, AND IT'S GOOD TO HAVE SOME PURPOSE--ANY PURPOSE--EVEN IF IT'S MISERABLE.
BUT THAT DOESN'T CHANGE THE FACT THAT EVERY DAY, THAT ROCK ROLLED DOWN THAT FUCKING HILL. AND GUESS WHO WENT DOWN WITH IT?
SISYPHUS.
THINK ABOUT HOW STRONG HE MUST HAVE BEEN AFTER A FEW WEEKS OF PUSHING THAT THING. HE COULD HAVE SHOVED IT OVER AT ANY POINT. BUT HE DIDN'T.
THAT ROCK WAS HIS PUNISHMENT, AND HE WASN'T GOING TO JUST TOSS IT OVER THE HILL--OR INTO A STUPID OCEAN--AND THINK HE'D ATONED.
LIVING IS WORK, AND ERASING OUR SINS ISN'T WHAT MAKES US BETTER. I DON'T KNOW WHAT DOES, BUT I DO KNOW THIS:
WE DON'T GET TO JUST DROP OUR STONES AND WALK AWAY.

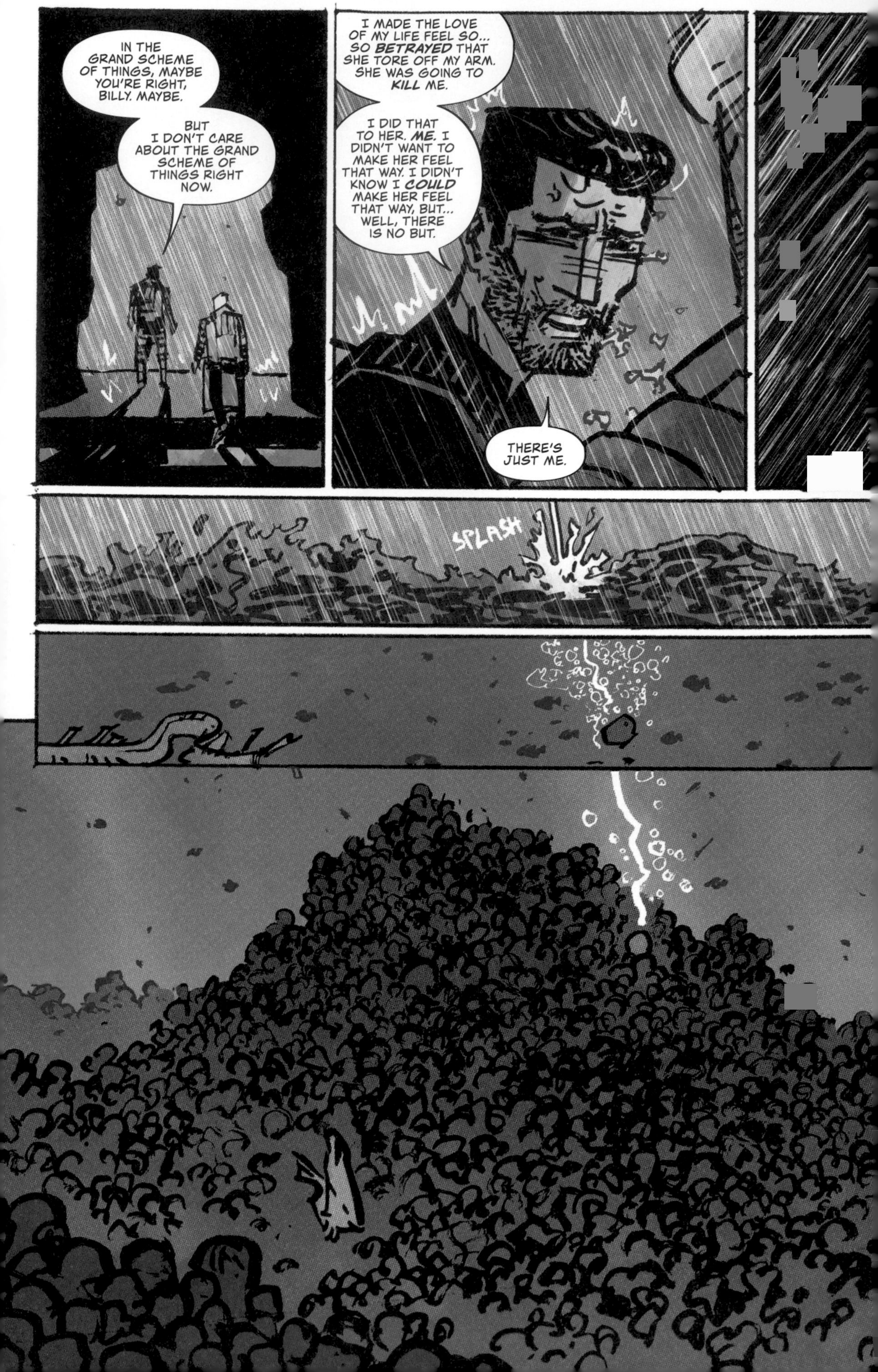

IN THE GRAND SCHEME OF THINGS, MAYBE YOU'RE RIGHT, BILLY. MAYBE.
BUT I DON'T CARE ABOUT THE GRAND SCHEME OF THINGS RIGHT NOW.
I MADE THE LOVE OF MY LIFE FEEL SO... SO BETRAYED THAT SHE TORE OFF MY ARM. SHE WAS GOING TO KILL ME.
I DID THAT TO HER. ME. I DIDN'T WANT TO MAKE HER FEEL THAT WAY. I DIDN'T KNOW I COULD MAKE HER FEEL THAT WAY, BUT... WELL, THERE IS NO BUT.
THERE'S JUST ME.
SPLASH

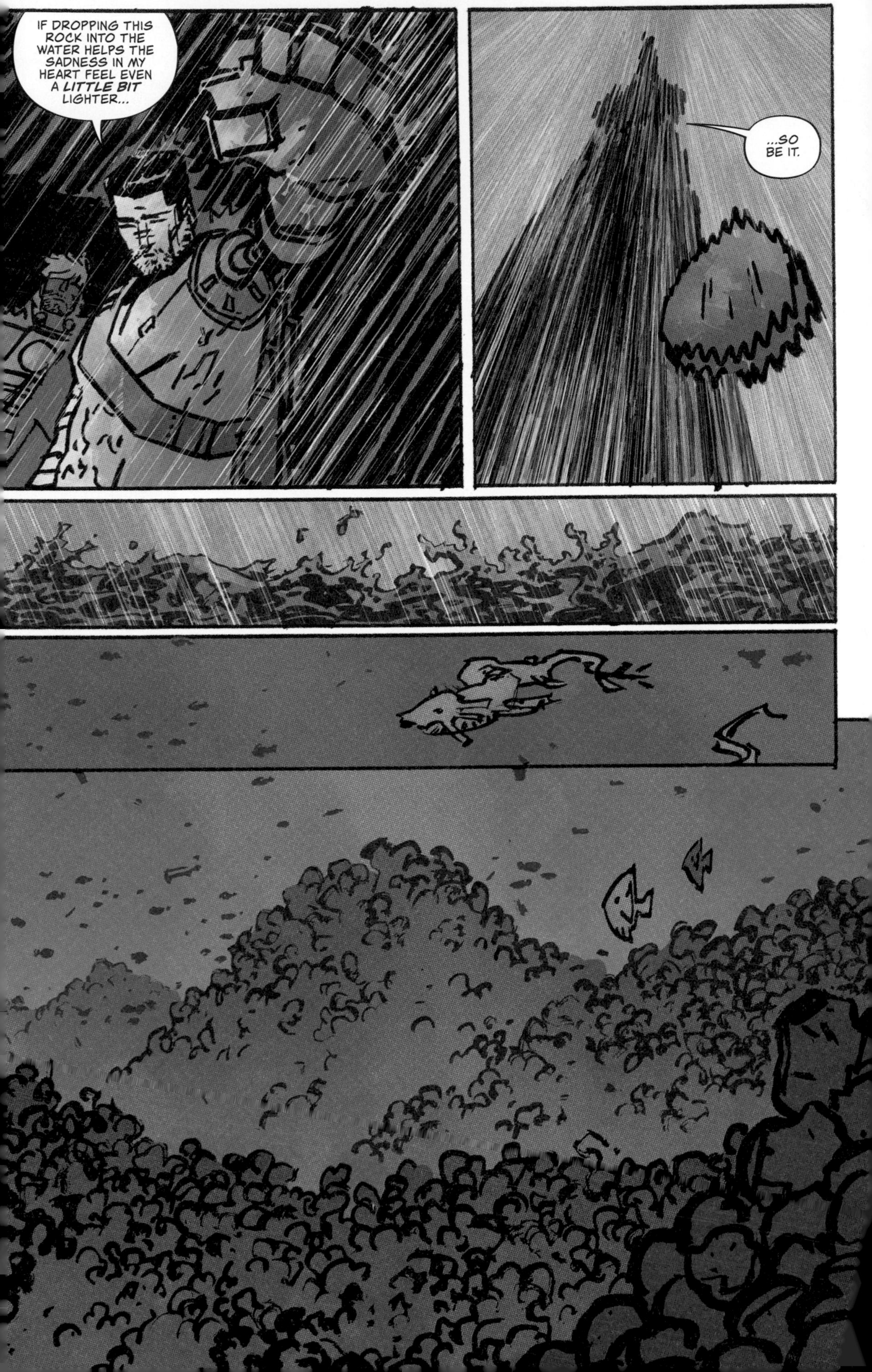
IF DROPPING THIS ROCK INTO THE WATER HELPS THE SADNESS IN MY HEART FEEL EVEN A *LITTLE BIT* LIGHTER...
...SO BE IT.

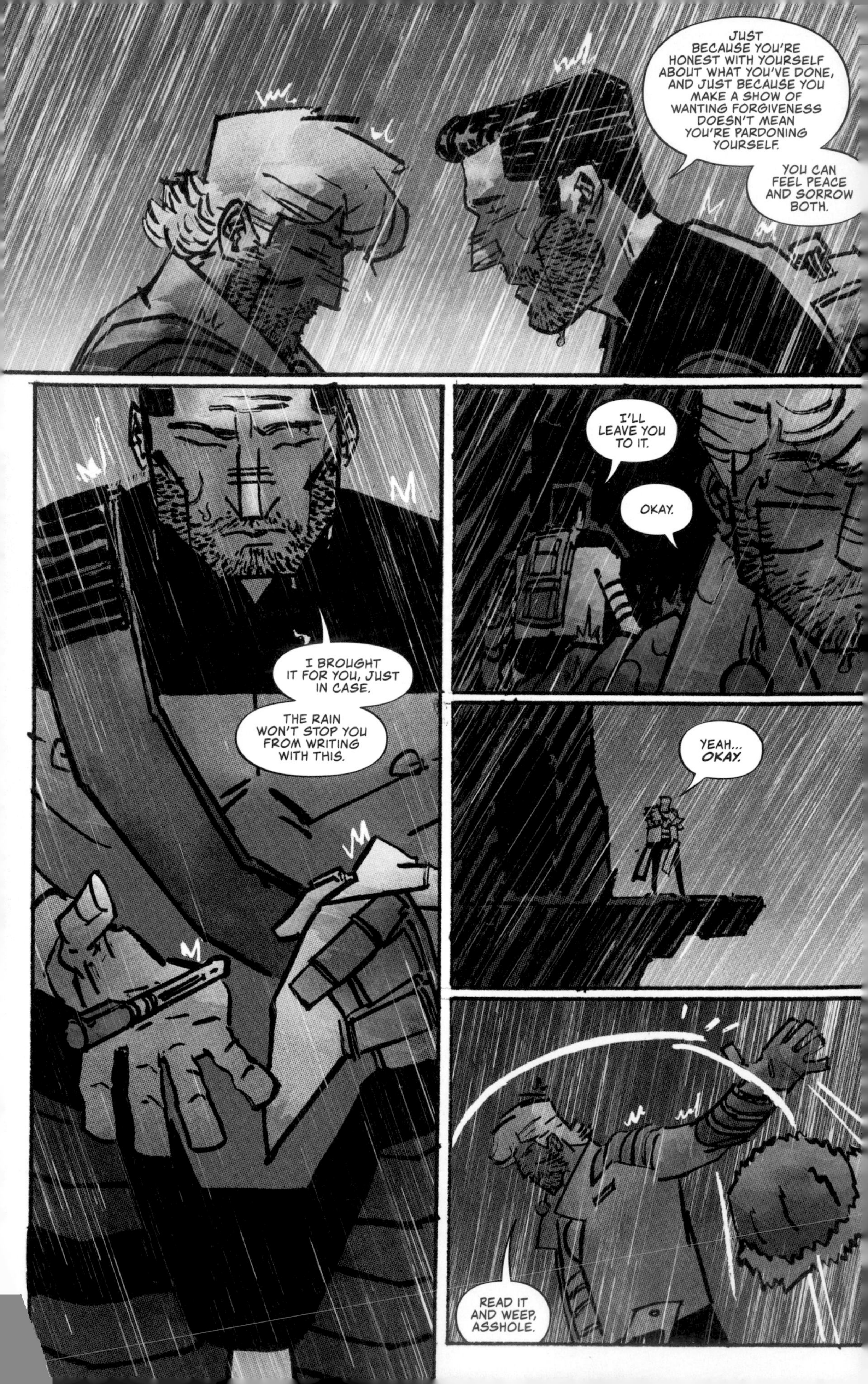
JUST BECAUSE YOU'RE HONEST WITH YOURSELF ABOUT WHAT YOU'VE DONE, AND JUST BECAUSE YOU MAKE A SHOW OF WANTING FORGIVENESS DOESN'T MEAN YOU'RE PARDONING YOURSELF.
YOU CAN FEEL PEACE AND SORROW BOTH.
I BROUGHT IT FOR YOU, JUST IN CASE.
THE RAIN WON'T STOP YOU FROM WRITING WITH THIS.
I'LL LEAVE YOU TO IT.
OKAY.
YEAH... **OKAY.**
READ IT AND WEEP, ASSHOLE.

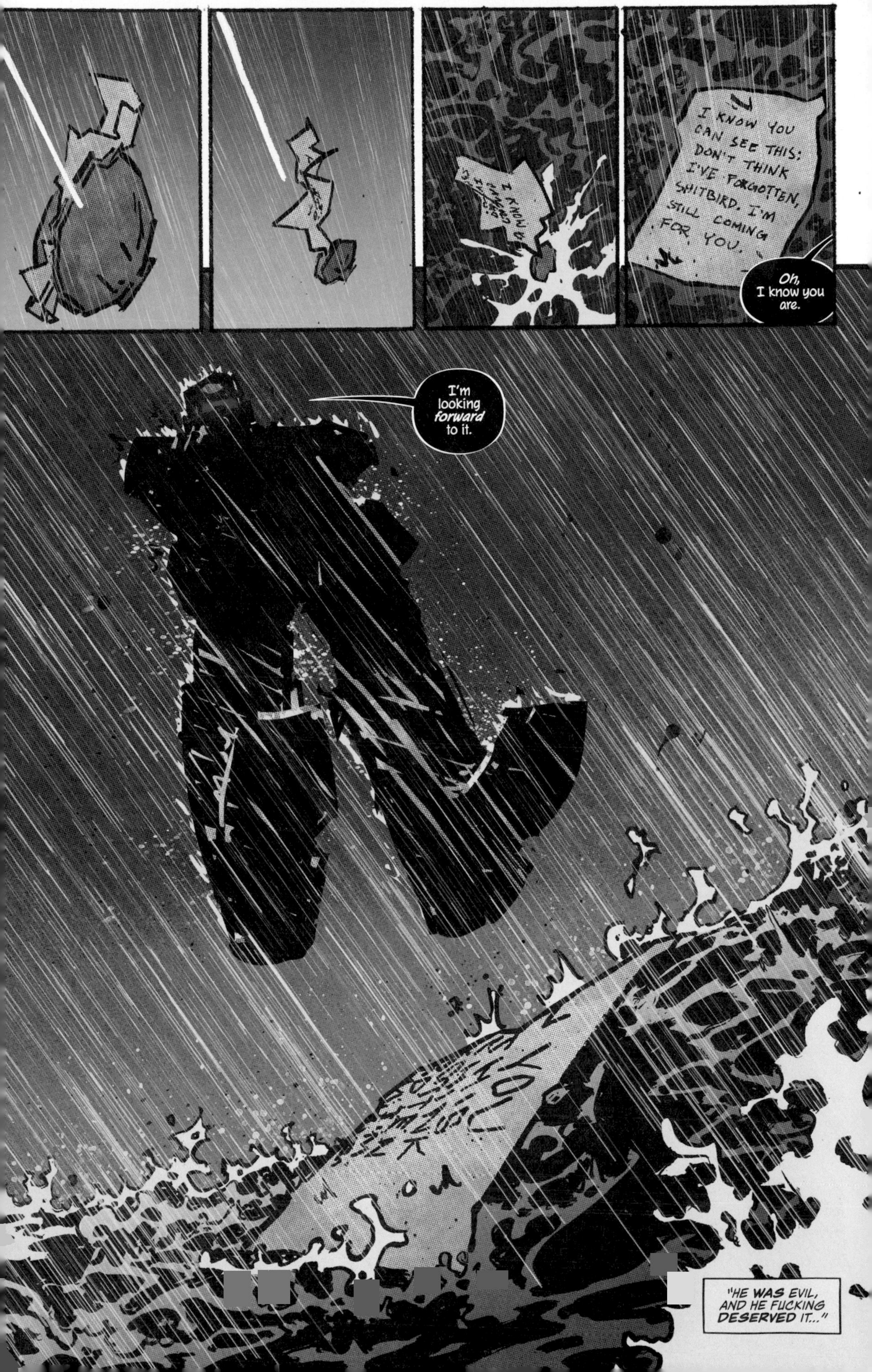
I KNOW YOU CAN SEE THIS: DON'T THINK I'VE FORGOTTEN, SHITBIRD. I'M STILL COMING FOR YOU.
Oh, I know you are.
I'm looking *forward* to it.
"HE **WAS** EVIL, AND HE FUCKING **DESERVED** IT..."

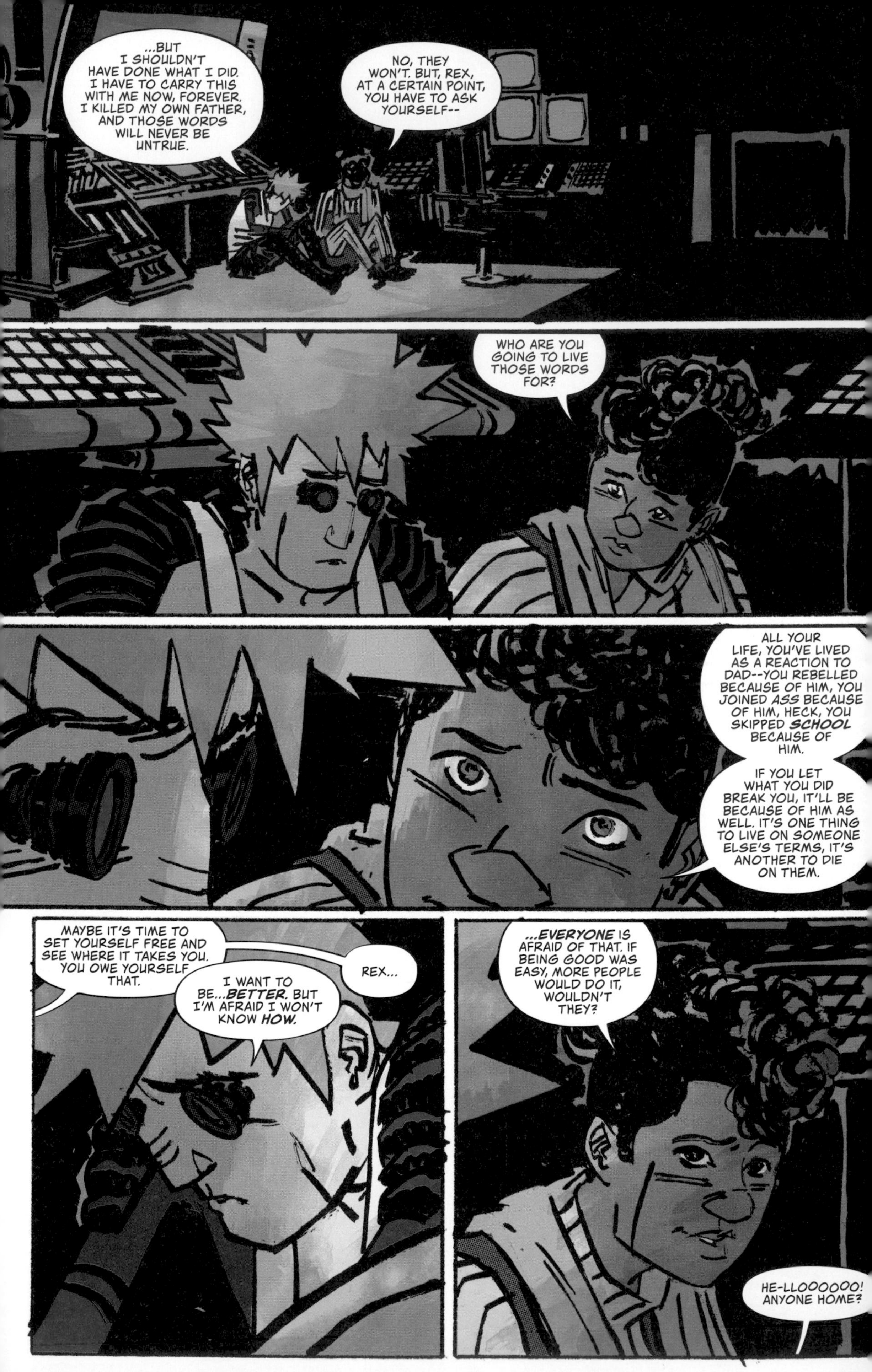
...BUT I SHOULDN'T HAVE DONE WHAT I DID. I HAVE TO CARRY THIS WITH ME NOW, FOREVER. I KILLED MY OWN FATHER, AND THOSE WORDS WILL NEVER BE UNTRUE.
NO, THEY WON'T. BUT, REX, AT A CERTAIN POINT, YOU HAVE TO ASK YOURSELF--
WHO ARE YOU GOING TO LIVE THOSE WORDS FOR?
ALL YOUR LIFE, YOU'VE LIVED AS A REACTION TO DAD--YOU REBELLED BECAUSE OF HIM, YOU JOINED ASS BECAUSE OF HIM, HECK, YOU SKIPPED SCHOOL BECAUSE OF HIM.
IF YOU LET WHAT YOU DID BREAK YOU, IT'LL BE BECAUSE OF HIM AS WELL. IT'S ONE THING TO LIVE ON SOMEONE ELSE'S TERMS, IT'S ANOTHER TO DIE ON THEM.
MAYBE IT'S TIME TO SET YOURSELF FREE AND SEE WHERE IT TAKES YOU. YOU OWE YOURSELF THAT.
REX...
I WANT TO BE...BETTER. BUT I'M AFRAID I WON'T KNOW HOW.
...EVERYONE IS AFRAID OF THAT. IF BEING GOOD WAS EASY, MORE PEOPLE WOULD DO IT, WOULDN'T THEY?
HE-LLOOOOOO! ANYONE HOME?

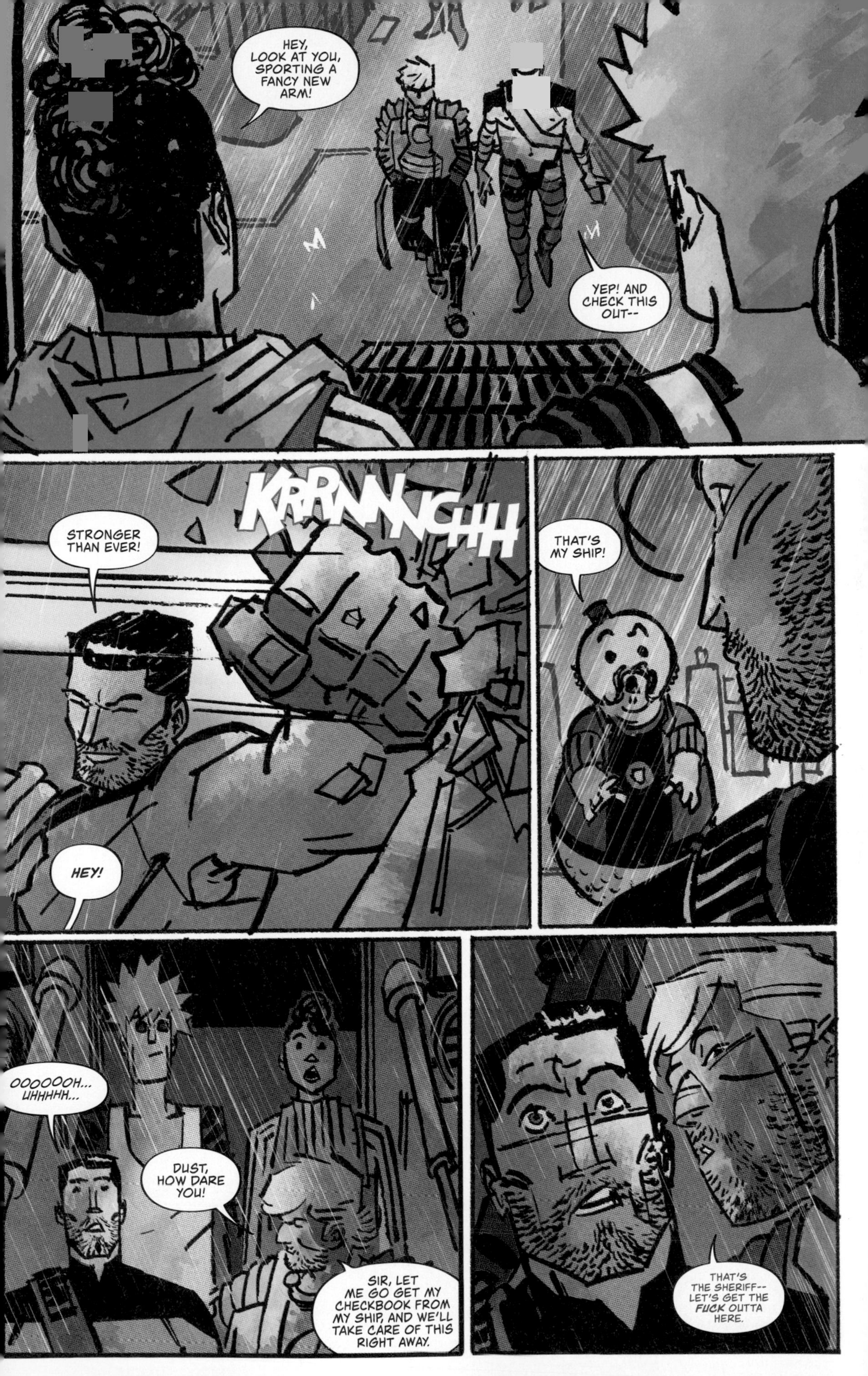
HEY, LOOK AT YOU, SPORTING A FANCY NEW ARM!
YEP! AND CHECK THIS OUT--
KRRNNNGHH
STRONGER THAN EVER!
HEY!
THAT'S MY SHIP!
OOOOOOH... UHHHHH...
DUST, HOW DARE YOU!
SIR, LET ME GO GET MY CHECKBOOK FROM MY SHIP, AND WE'LL TAKE CARE OF THIS RIGHT AWAY.
THAT'S THE SHERIFF-- LET'S GET THE *FUCK* OUTTA HERE.

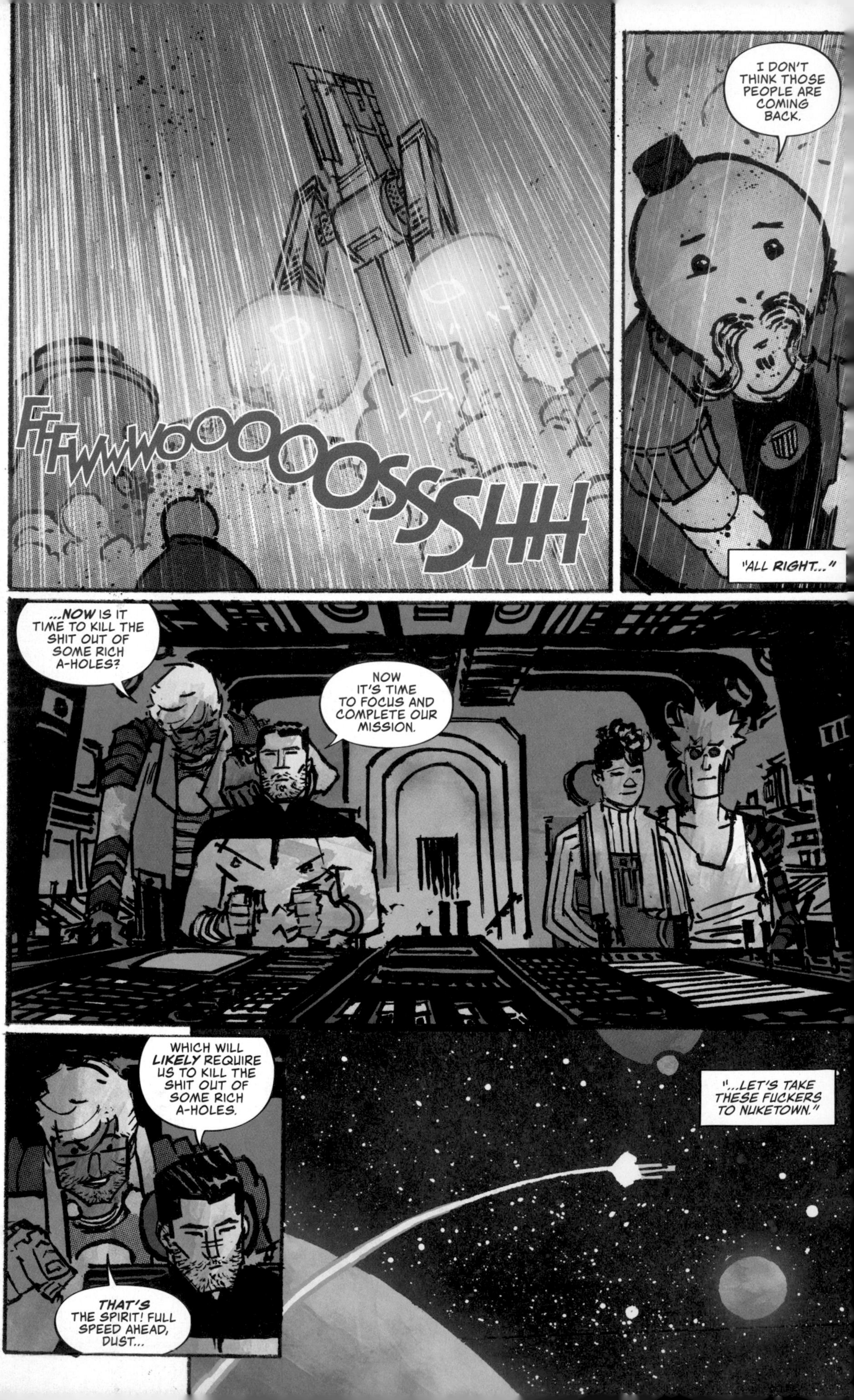
FFFWWWOOOOOOOSSSSHH
I DON'T THINK THOSE PEOPLE ARE COMING BACK.
"ALL RIGHT..."
...NOW IS IT TIME TO KILL THE SHIT OUT OF SOME RICH A-HOLES?
NOW IT'S TIME TO FOCUS AND COMPLETE OUR MISSION.
WHICH WILL LIKELY REQUIRE US TO KILL THE SHIT OUT OF SOME RICH A-HOLES.
THAT'S THE SPIRIT! FULL SPEED AHEAD, DUST...
"...LET'S TAKE THESE FUCKERS TO NUKETOWN."

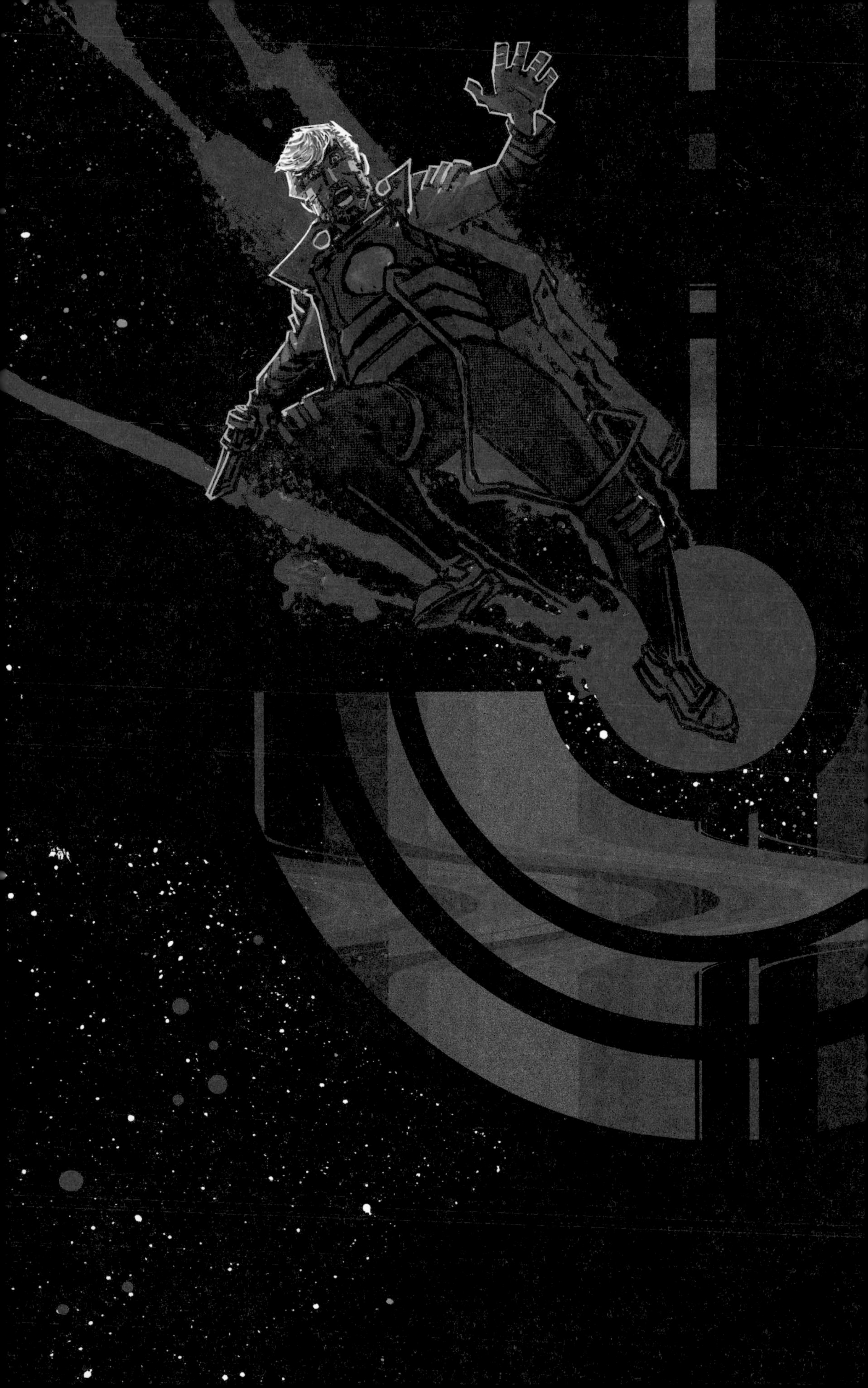

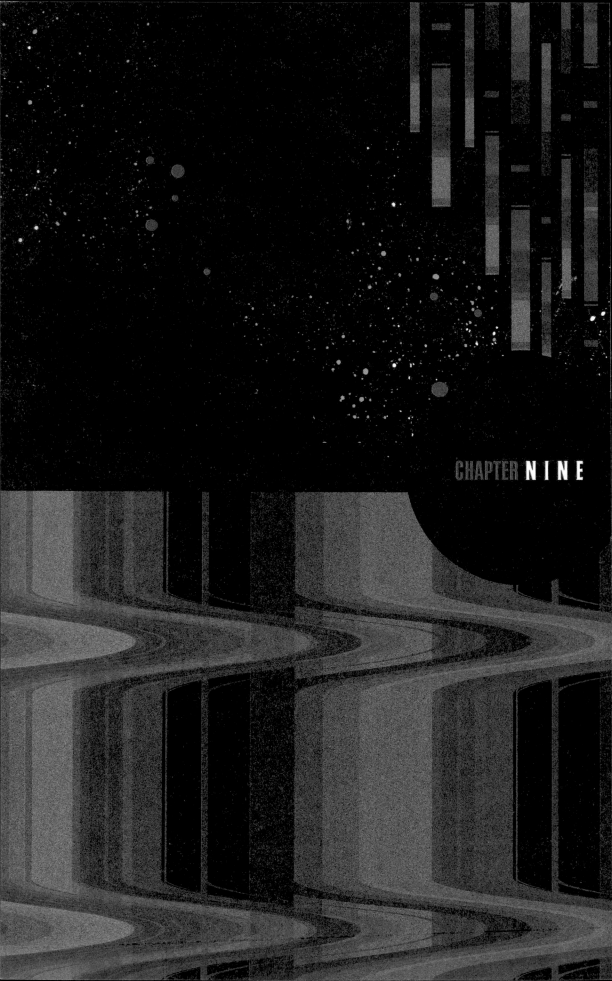

CHAPTER **N I N E**

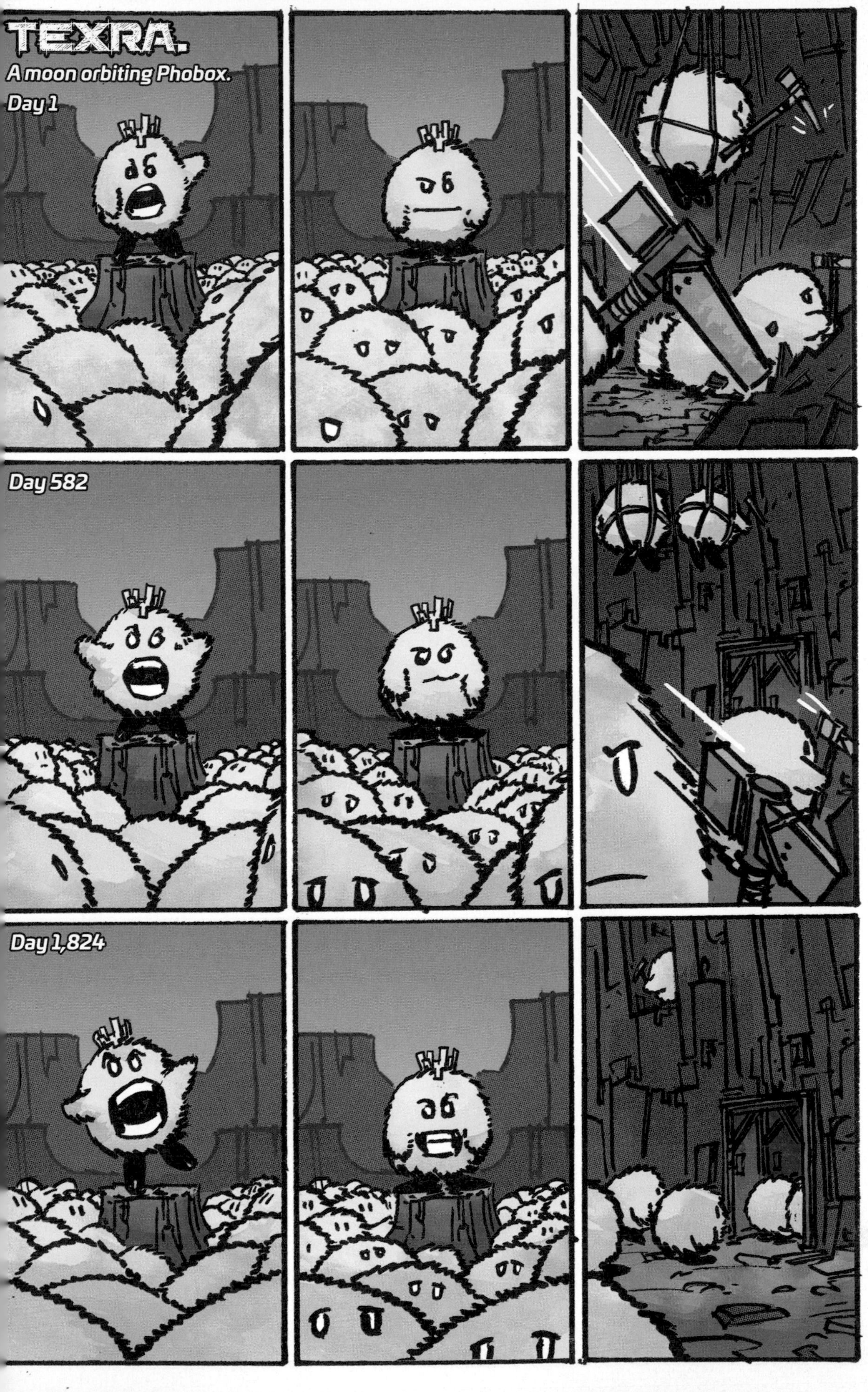
TEXRA.
A moon orbiting Phobox.
Day 1
Day 582
Day 1,824

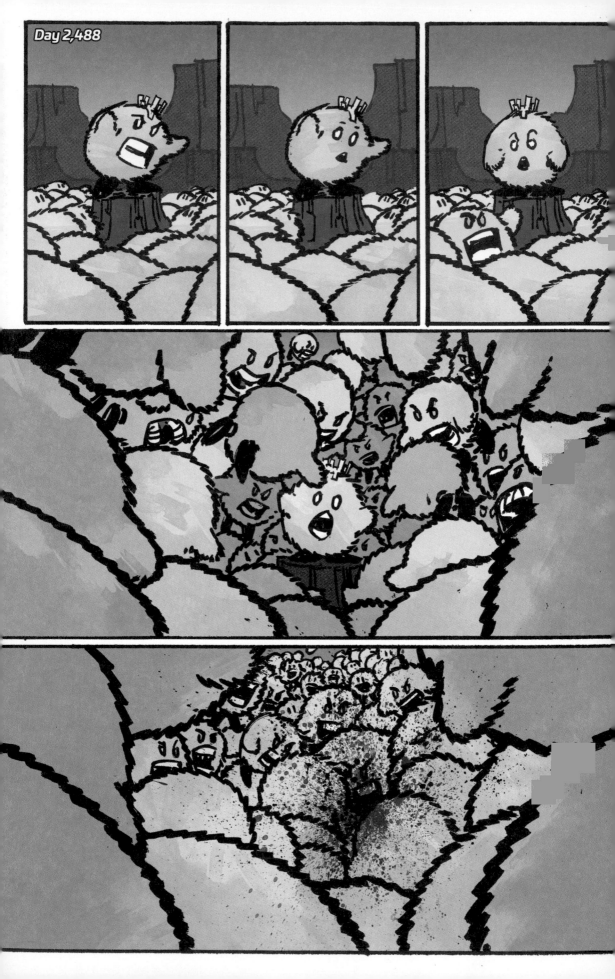

Day 2,488

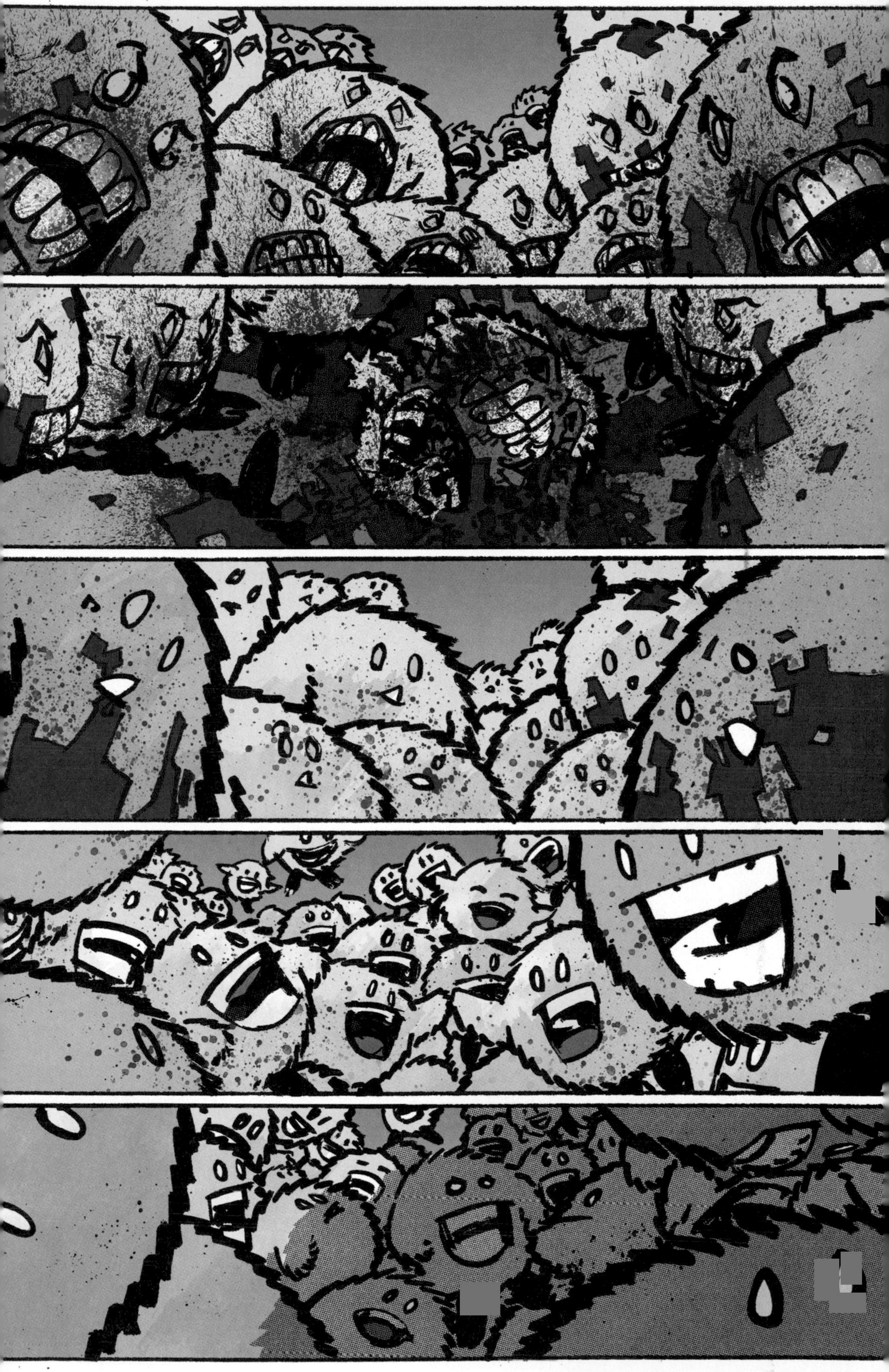

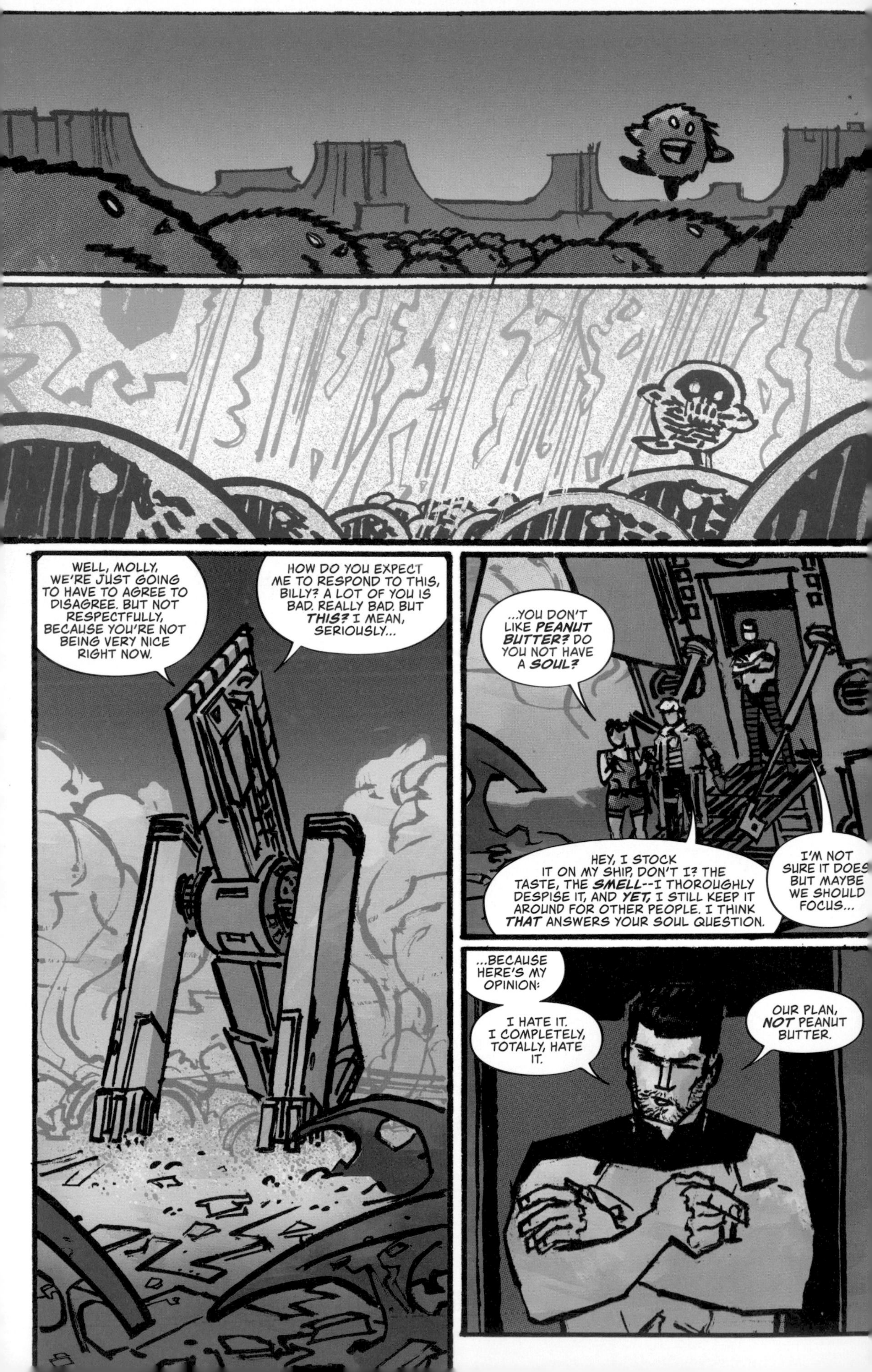
WELL, MOLLY, WE'RE JUST GOING TO HAVE TO AGREE TO DISAGREE. BUT NOT RESPECTFULLY, BECAUSE YOU'RE NOT BEING VERY NICE RIGHT NOW.
HOW DO YOU EXPECT ME TO RESPOND TO THIS, BILLY? A LOT OF YOU IS BAD. REALLY BAD. BUT THIS? I MEAN, SERIOUSLY...
...YOU DON'T LIKE PEANUT BUTTER? DO YOU NOT HAVE A SOUL?
HEY, I STOCK IT ON MY SHIP, DON'T I? THE TASTE, THE SMELL--I THOROUGHLY DESPISE IT, AND YET, I STILL KEEP IT AROUND FOR OTHER PEOPLE. I THINK THAT ANSWERS YOUR SOUL QUESTION.
I'M NOT SURE IT DOES BUT MAYBE WE SHOULD FOCUS...
...BECAUSE HERE'S MY OPINION:
I HATE IT. I COMPLETELY, TOTALLY, HATE IT.
OUR PLAN, NOT PEANUT BUTTER.

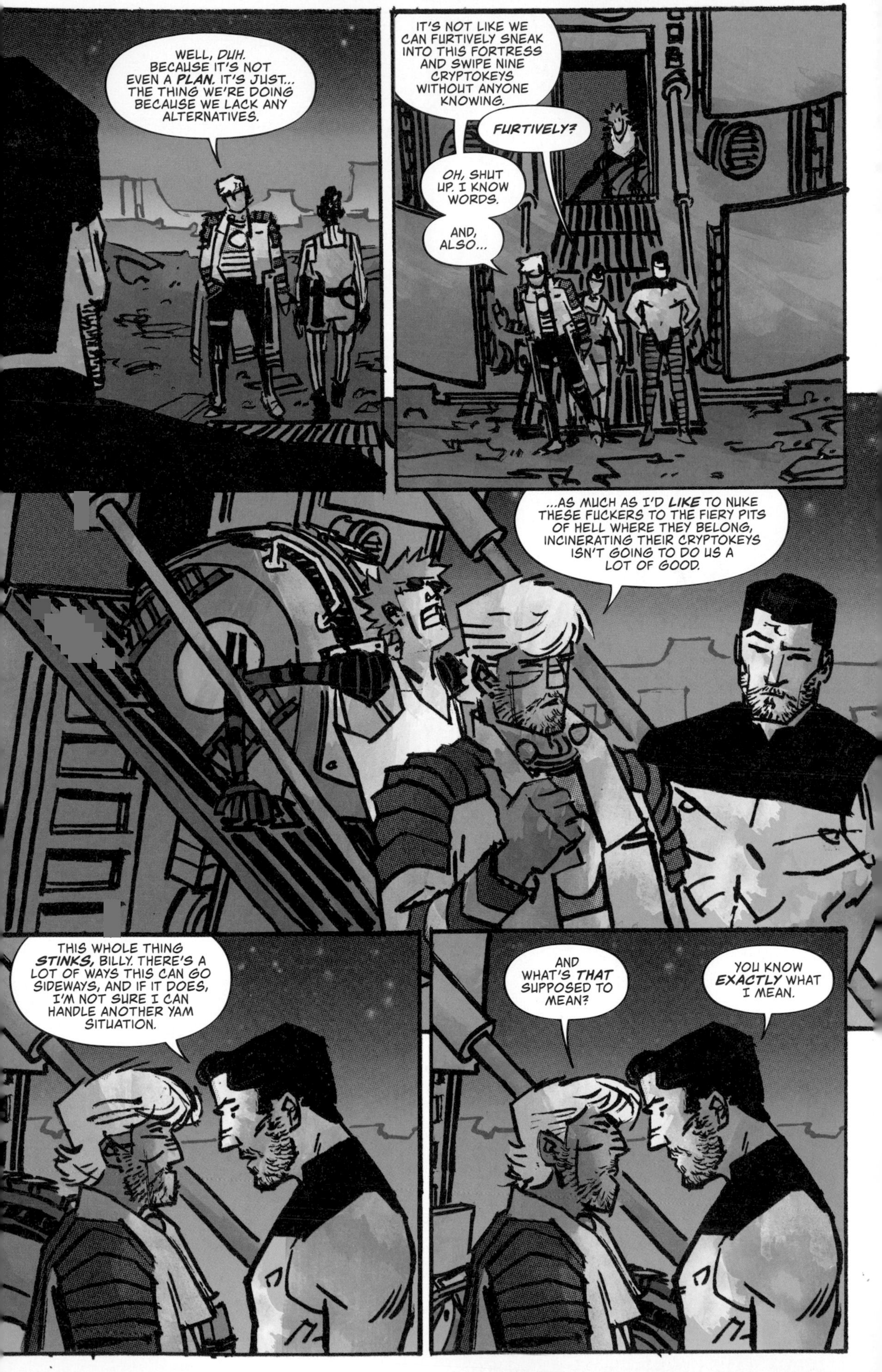
WELL, DUH. BECAUSE IT'S NOT EVEN A PLAN. IT'S JUST... THE THING WE'RE DOING BECAUSE WE LACK ANY ALTERNATIVES.
IT'S NOT LIKE WE CAN FURTIVELY SNEAK INTO THIS FORTRESS AND SWIPE NINE CRYPTOKEYS WITHOUT ANYONE KNOWING.
FURTIVELY?
OH, SHUT UP. I KNOW WORDS.
AND, ALSO...
...AS MUCH AS I'D LIKE TO NUKE THESE FUCKERS TO THE FIERY PITS OF HELL WHERE THEY BELONG, INCINERATING THEIR CRYPTOKEYS ISN'T GOING TO DO US A LOT OF GOOD.
THIS WHOLE THING STINKS, BILLY. THERE'S A LOT OF WAYS THIS CAN GO SIDEWAYS, AND IF IT DOES, I'M NOT SURE I CAN HANDLE ANOTHER YAM SITUATION.
AND WHAT'S THAT SUPPOSED TO MEAN?
YOU KNOW EXACTLY WHAT I MEAN.

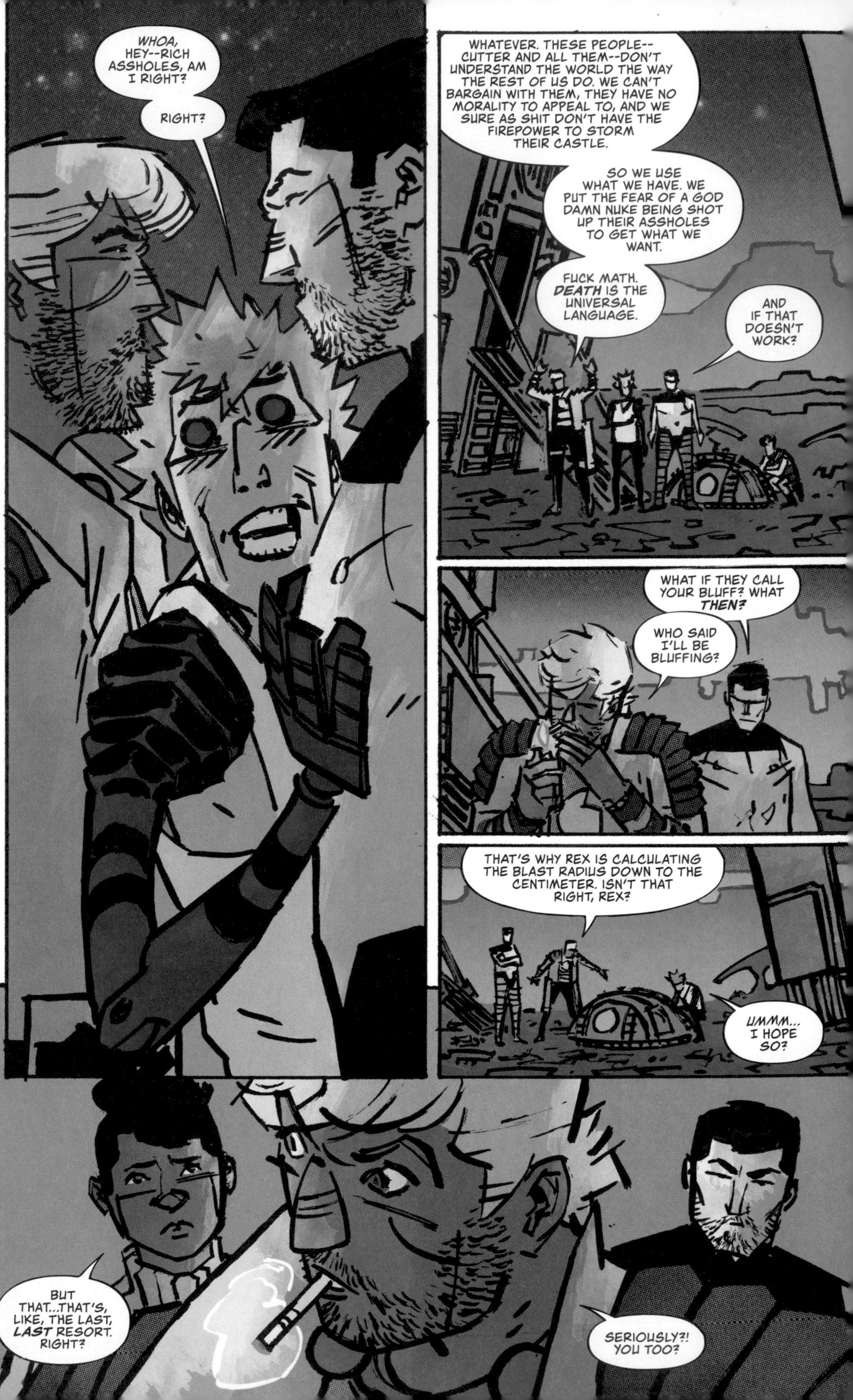
WHOA, HEY--RICH ASSHOLES, AM I RIGHT?
RIGHT?
WHATEVER. THESE PEOPLE--CUTTER AND ALL THEM--DON'T UNDERSTAND THE WORLD THE WAY THE REST OF US DO. WE CAN'T BARGAIN WITH THEM, THEY HAVE NO MORALITY TO APPEAL TO, AND WE SURE AS SHIT DON'T HAVE THE FIREPOWER TO STORM THEIR CASTLE.
SO WE USE WHAT WE HAVE. WE PUT THE FEAR OF A GOD DAMN NUKE BEING SHOT UP THEIR ASSHOLES TO GET WHAT WE WANT.
FUCK MATH. DEATH IS THE UNIVERSAL LANGUAGE.
AND IF THAT DOESN'T WORK?
WHAT IF THEY CALL YOUR BLUFF? WHAT THEN?
WHO SAID I'LL BE BLUFFING?
THAT'S WHY REX IS CALCULATING THE BLAST RADIUS DOWN TO THE CENTIMETER. ISN'T THAT RIGHT, REX?
UMMM... I HOPE SO?
BUT THAT...THAT'S, LIKE, THE LAST, LAST RESORT. RIGHT?
SERIOUSLY?! YOU TOO?

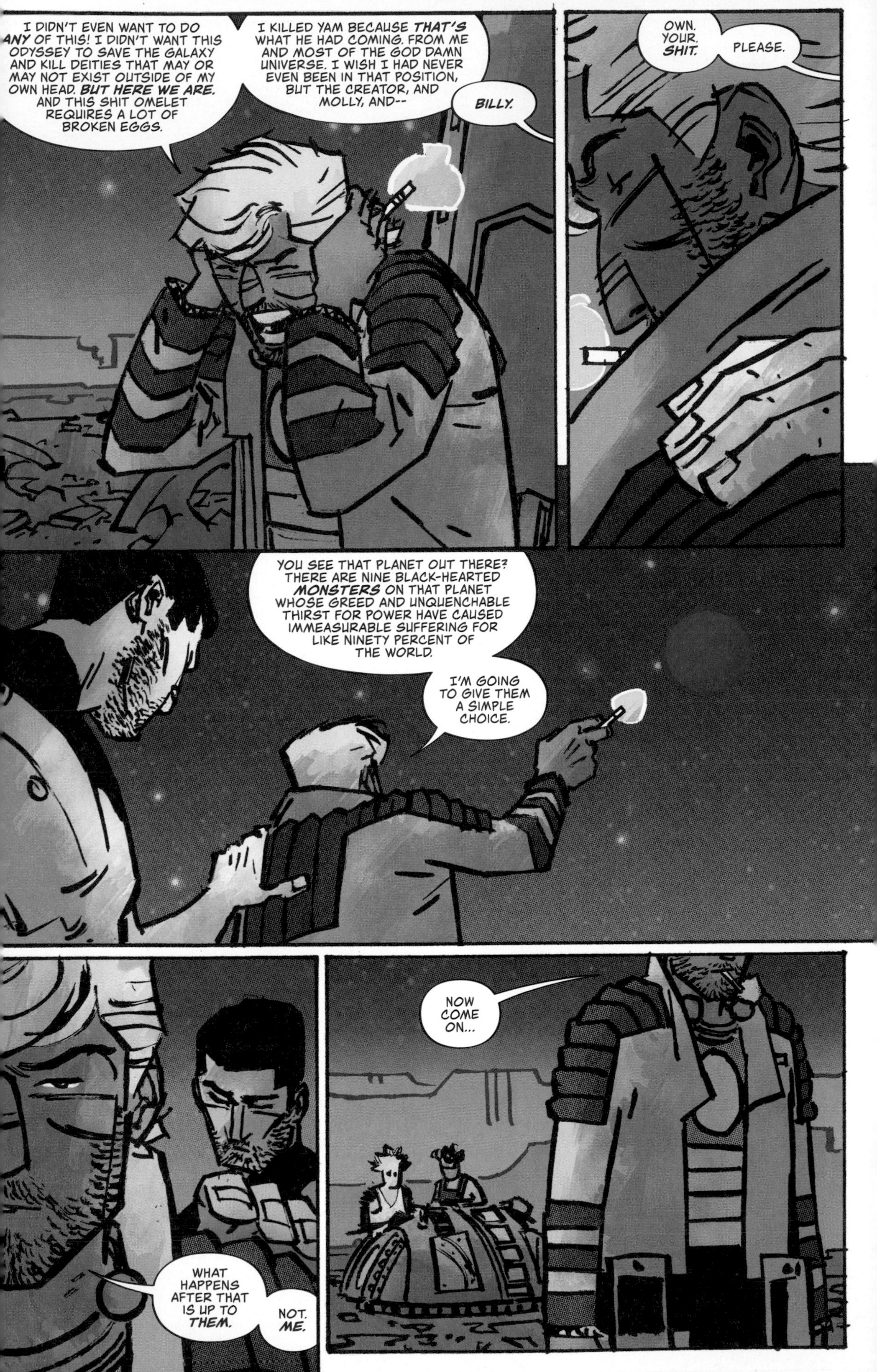
I DIDN'T EVEN WANT TO DO ANY OF THIS! I DIDN'T WANT THIS ODYSSEY TO SAVE THE GALAXY AND KILL DEITIES THAT MAY OR MAY NOT EXIST OUTSIDE OF MY OWN HEAD. BUT HERE WE ARE. AND THIS SHIT OMELET REQUIRES A LOT OF BROKEN EGGS.
I KILLED YAM BECAUSE THAT'S WHAT HE HAD COMING. FROM ME AND MOST OF THE GOD DAMN UNIVERSE. I WISH I HAD NEVER EVEN BEEN IN THAT POSITION, BUT THE CREATOR, AND MOLLY, AND--
BILLY.
OWN. YOUR. SHIT.
PLEASE.
YOU SEE THAT PLANET OUT THERE? THERE ARE NINE BLACK-HEARTED MONSTERS ON THAT PLANET WHOSE GREED AND UNQUENCHABLE THIRST FOR POWER HAVE CAUSED IMMEASURABLE SUFFERING FOR LIKE NINETY PERCENT OF THE WORLD.
I'M GOING TO GIVE THEM A SIMPLE CHOICE.
WHAT HAPPENS AFTER THAT IS UP TO THEM.
NOT. ME.
NOW COME ON...

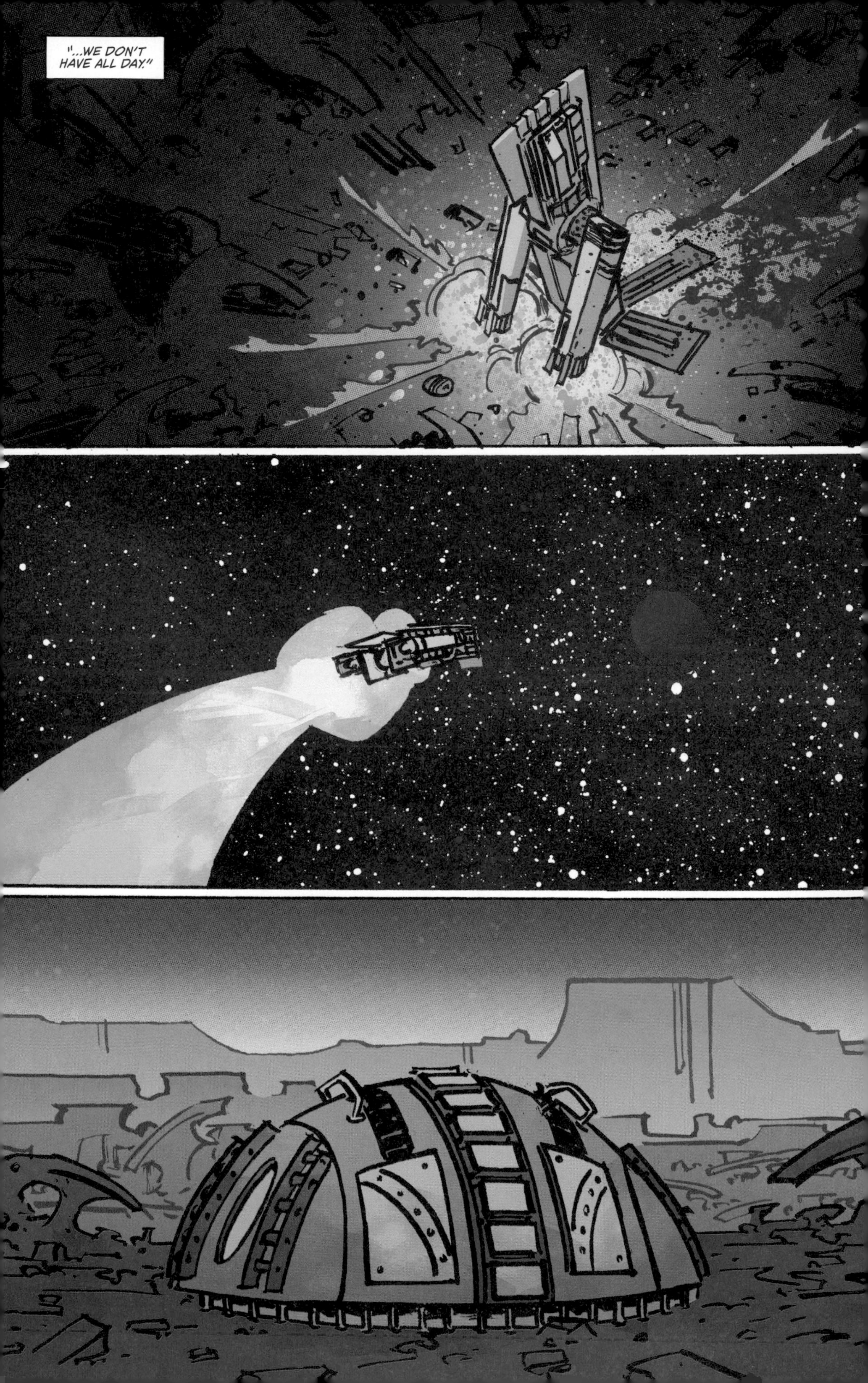
"...WE DON'T HAVE ALL DAY."

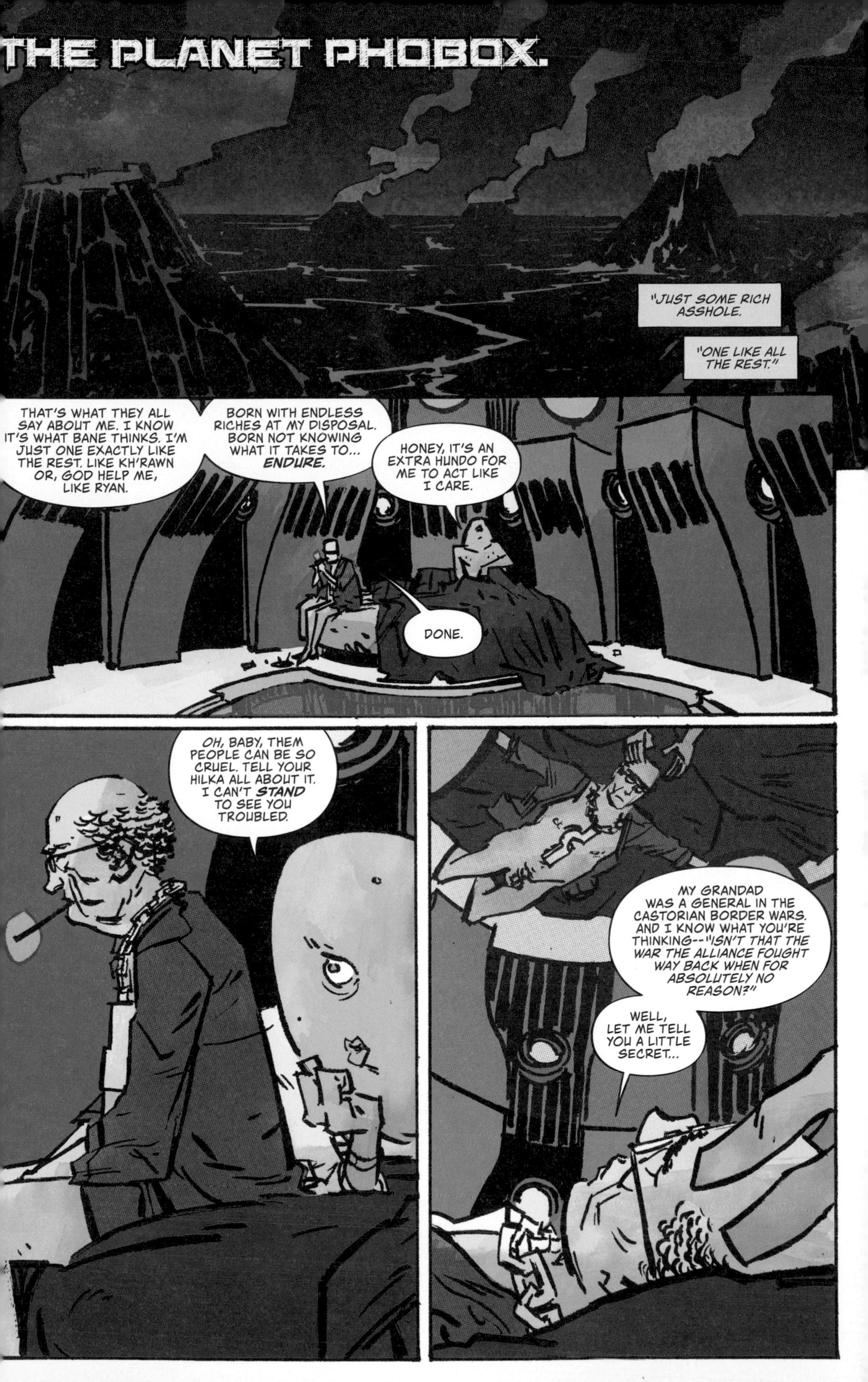
THE PLANET PHOBOX.
"JUST SOME RICH ASSHOLE.
"ONE LIKE ALL THE REST."
THAT'S WHAT THEY ALL SAY ABOUT ME. I KNOW IT'S WHAT BANE THINKS. I'M JUST ONE EXACTLY LIKE THE REST. LIKE KH'RAWN OR, GOD HELP ME, LIKE RYAN.
BORN WITH ENDLESS RICHES AT MY DISPOSAL. BORN NOT KNOWING WHAT IT TAKES TO... ENDURE.
HONEY, IT'S AN EXTRA HUNDO FOR ME TO ACT LIKE I CARE.
DONE.
OH, BABY, THEM PEOPLE CAN BE SO CRUEL. TELL YOUR HILKA ALL ABOUT IT. I CAN'T STAND TO SEE YOU TROUBLED.
MY GRANDAD WAS A GENERAL IN THE CASTORIAN BORDER WARS. AND I KNOW WHAT YOU'RE THINKING--"ISN'T THAT THE WAR THE ALLIANCE FOUGHT WAY BACK WHEN FOR ABSOLUTELY NO REASON?"
WELL, LET ME TELL YOU A LITTLE SECRET...

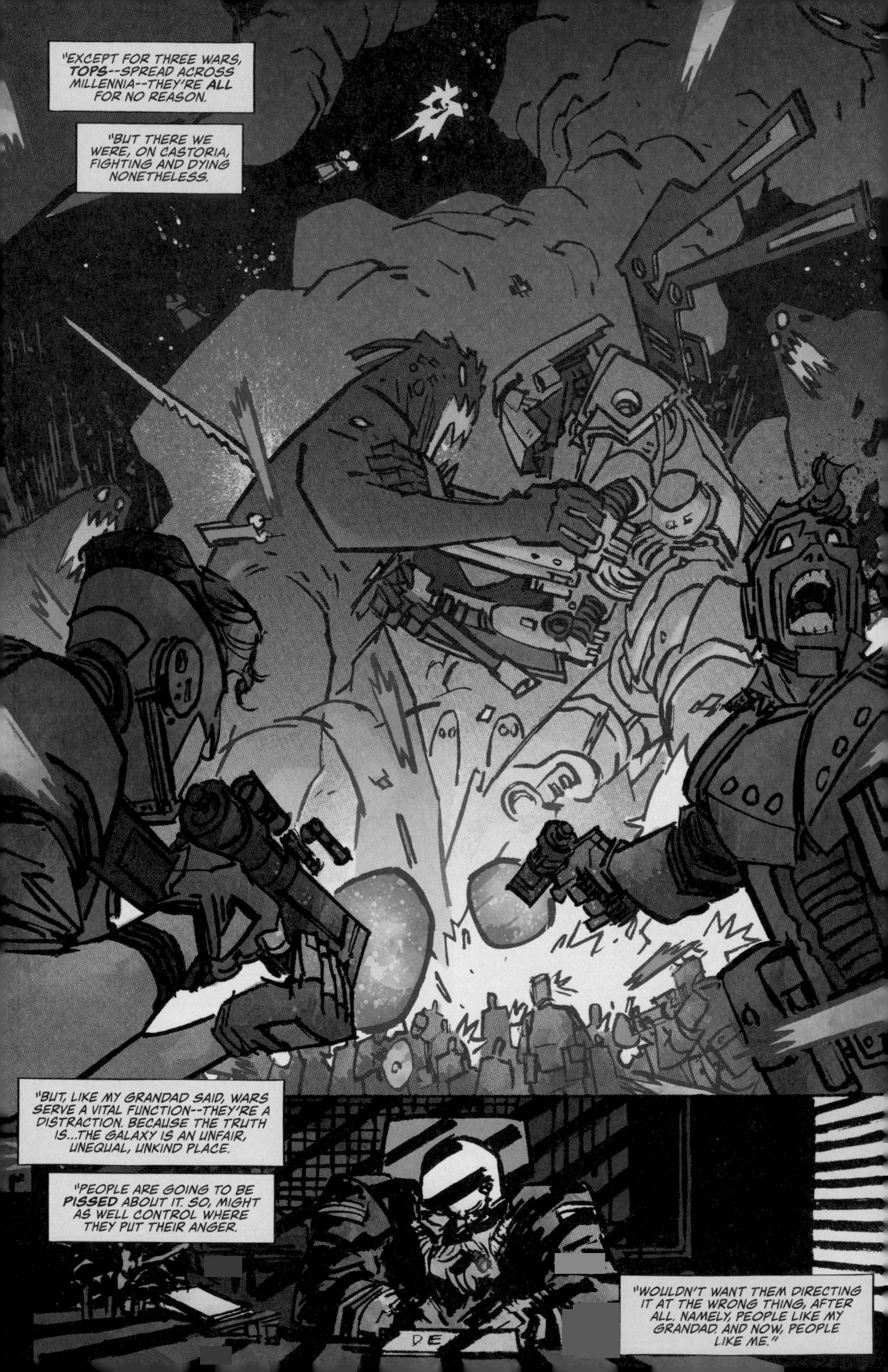
"EXCEPT FOR THREE WARS, **TOPS**--SPREAD ACROSS MILLENNIA--THEY'RE **ALL** FOR NO REASON.
"BUT THERE WE WERE, ON CASTORIA, FIGHTING AND DYING NONETHELESS.
"BUT, LIKE MY GRANDAD SAID, WARS SERVE A VITAL FUNCTION--THEY'RE A DISTRACTION. BECAUSE THE TRUTH IS...THE GALAXY IS AN UNFAIR, UNEQUAL, UNKIND PLACE.
"PEOPLE ARE GOING TO BE **PISSED** ABOUT IT. SO, MIGHT AS WELL CONTROL WHERE THEY PUT THEIR ANGER.
"WOULDN'T WANT THEM DIRECTING IT AT THE WRONG THING, AFTER ALL. NAMELY, PEOPLE LIKE MY GRANDAD. AND NOW, PEOPLE LIKE ME."

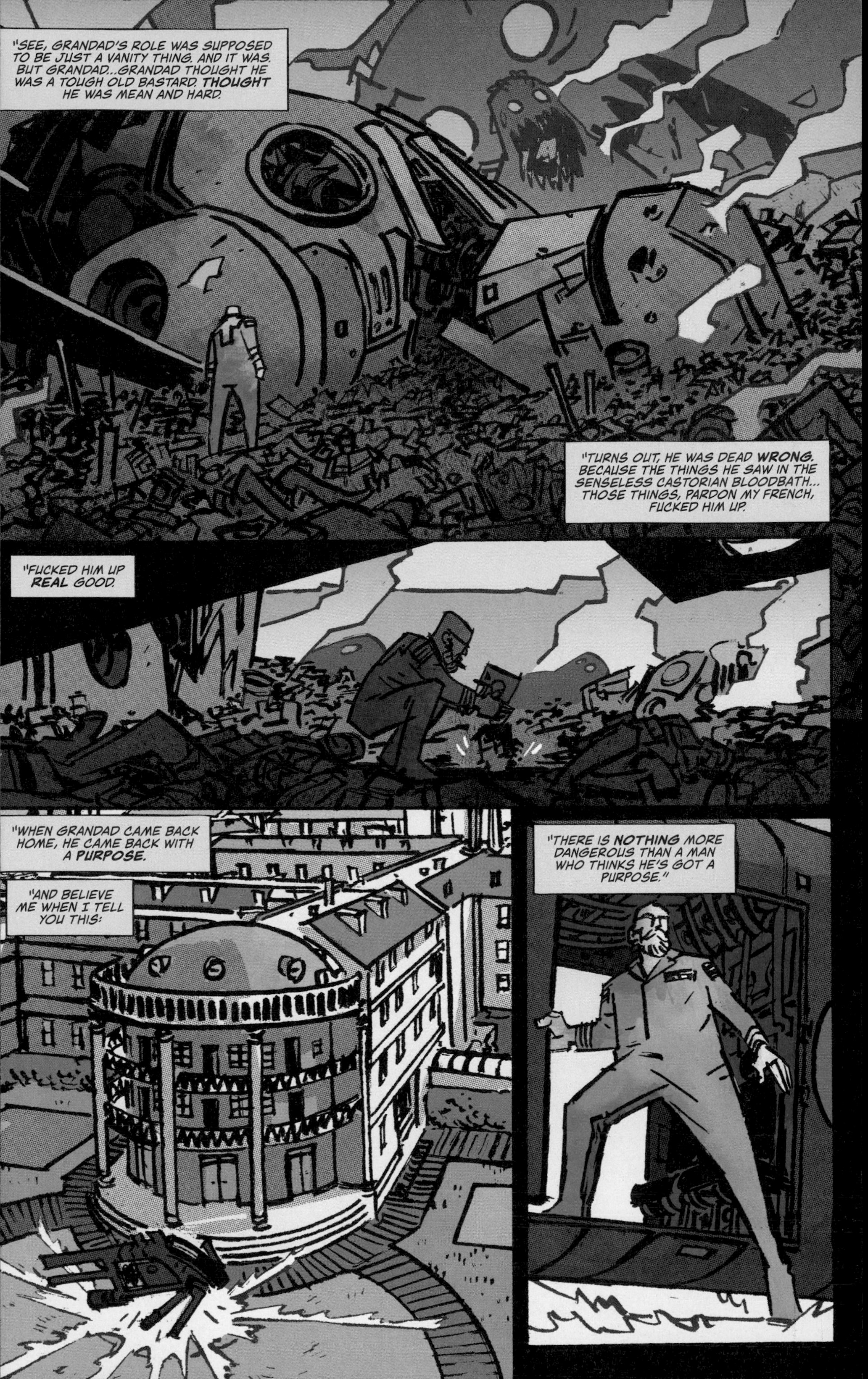
"SEE, GRANDAD'S ROLE WAS SUPPOSED TO BE JUST A VANITY THING. AND IT WAS. BUT GRANDAD...GRANDAD THOUGHT HE WAS A TOUGH OLD BASTARD. THOUGHT HE WAS MEAN AND HARD.
"TURNS OUT, HE WAS DEAD WRONG. BECAUSE THE THINGS HE SAW IN THE SENSELESS CASTORIAN BLOODBATH... THOSE THINGS, PARDON MY FRENCH, FUCKED HIM UP.
"FUCKED HIM UP REAL GOOD.
"WHEN GRANDAD CAME BACK HOME, HE CAME BACK WITH A PURPOSE.
"AND BELIEVE ME WHEN I TELL YOU THIS:
"THERE IS NOTHING MORE DANGEROUS THAN A MAN WHO THINKS HE'S GOT A PURPOSE."

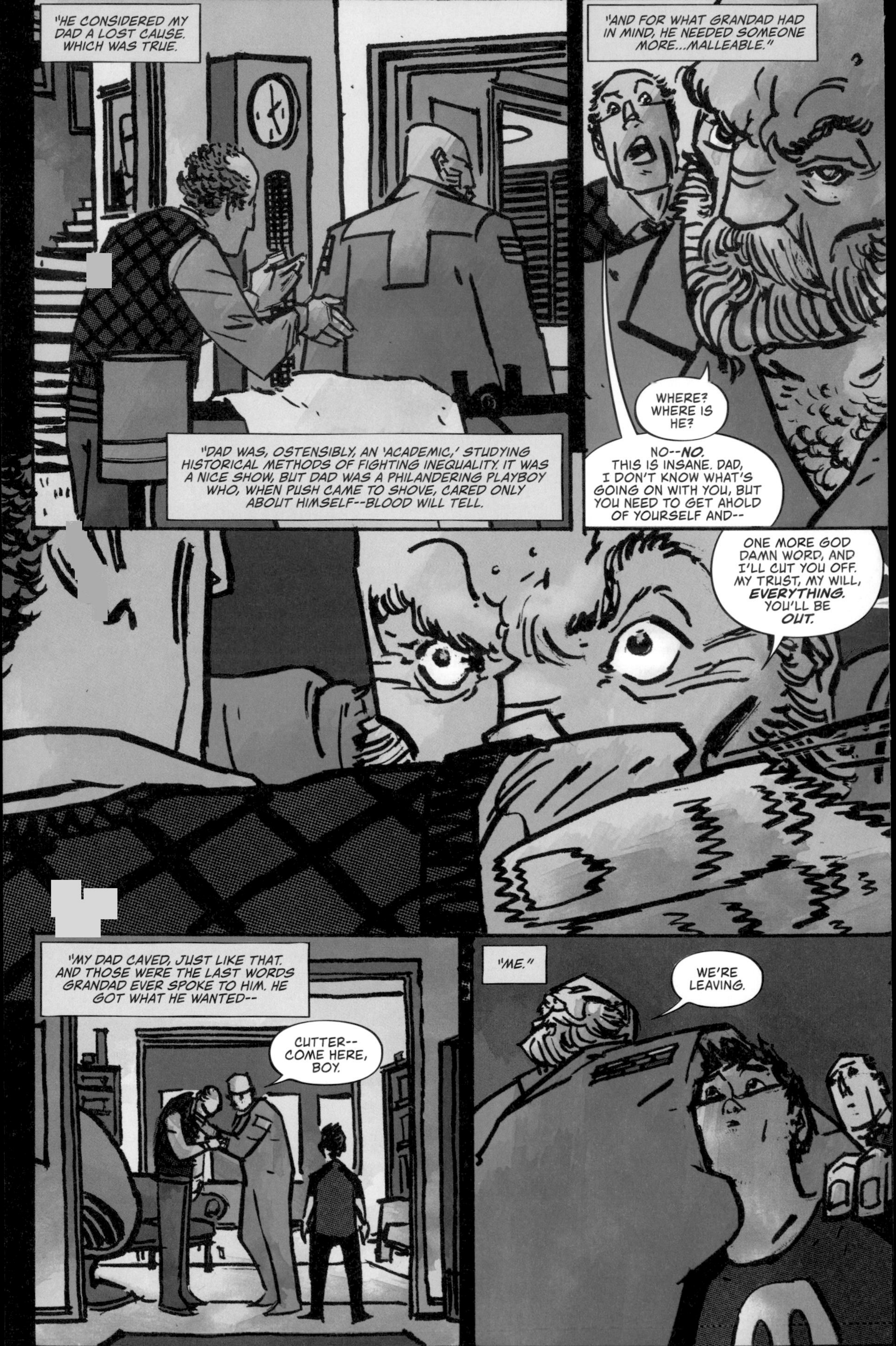
"HE CONSIDERED MY DAD A LOST CAUSE. WHICH WAS TRUE.
"DAD WAS, OSTENSIBLY, AN 'ACADEMIC,' STUDYING HISTORICAL METHODS OF FIGHTING INEQUALITY. IT WAS A NICE SHOW, BUT DAD WAS A PHILANDERING PLAYBOY WHO, WHEN PUSH CAME TO SHOVE, CARED ONLY ABOUT HIMSELF--BLOOD WILL TELL.
"AND FOR WHAT GRANDAD HAD IN MIND, HE NEEDED SOMEONE MORE...MALLEABLE."
WHERE? WHERE IS HE?
NO--NO. THIS IS INSANE. DAD, I DON'T KNOW WHAT'S GOING ON WITH YOU, BUT YOU NEED TO GET AHOLD OF YOURSELF AND--
ONE MORE GOD DAMN WORD, AND I'LL CUT YOU OFF. MY TRUST, MY WILL, EVERYTHING. YOU'LL BE OUT.
"MY DAD CAVED, JUST LIKE THAT. AND THOSE WERE THE LAST WORDS GRANDAD EVER SPOKE TO HIM. HE GOT WHAT HE WANTED--
CUTTER--COME HERE, BOY.
"ME."
WE'RE LEAVING.

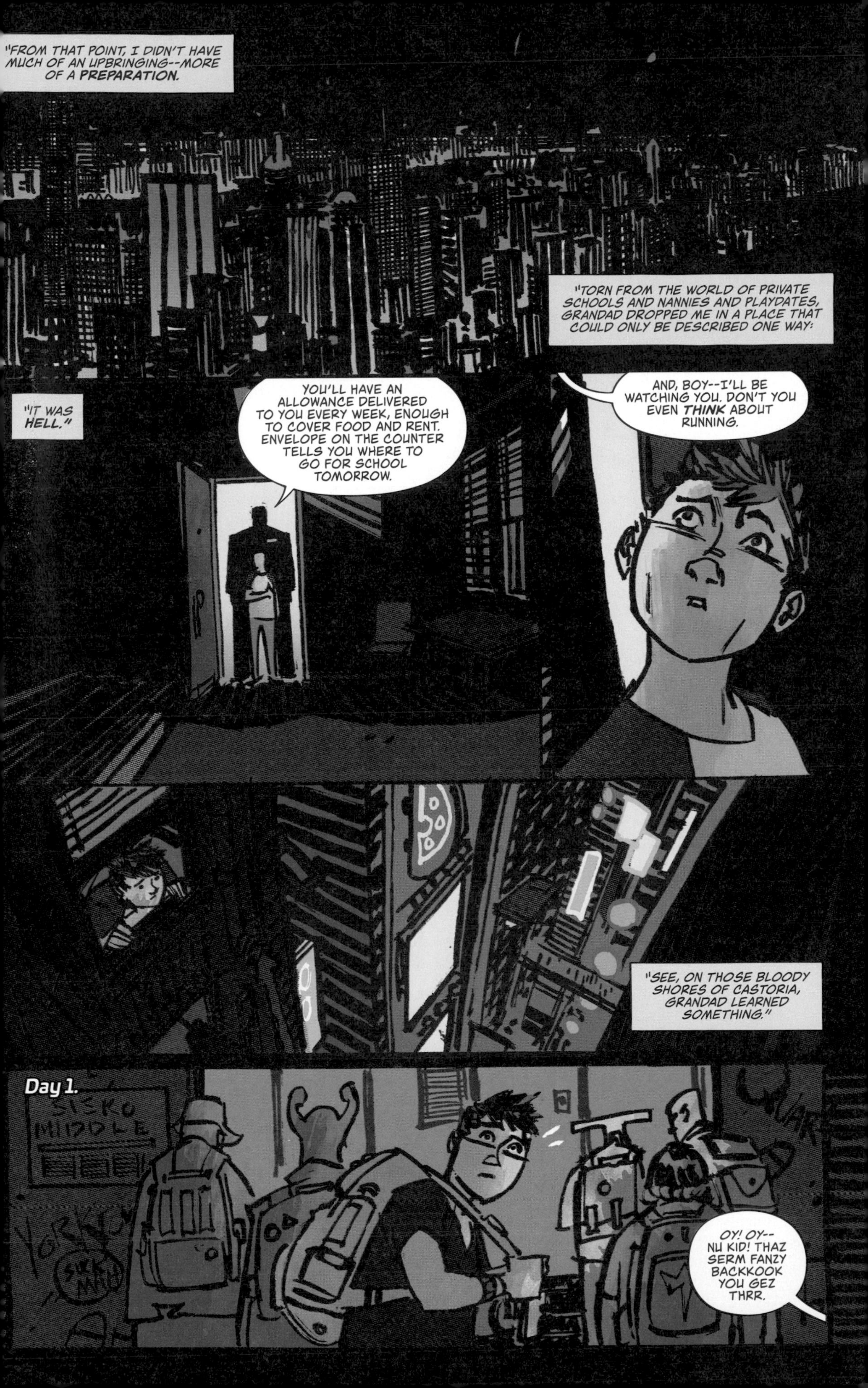
"FROM THAT POINT, I DIDN'T HAVE MUCH OF AN UPBRINGING--MORE OF A PREPARATION.
"TORN FROM THE WORLD OF PRIVATE SCHOOLS AND NANNIES AND PLAYDATES, GRANDAD DROPPED ME IN A PLACE THAT COULD ONLY BE DESCRIBED ONE WAY:
"IT WAS HELL."
YOU'LL HAVE AN ALLOWANCE DELIVERED TO YOU EVERY WEEK, ENOUGH TO COVER FOOD AND RENT. ENVELOPE ON THE COUNTER TELLS YOU WHERE TO GO FOR SCHOOL TOMORROW.
AND, BOY--I'LL BE WATCHING YOU. DON'T YOU EVEN THINK ABOUT RUNNING.
"SEE, ON THOSE BLOODY SHORES OF CASTORIA, GRANDAD LEARNED SOMETHING."
Day 1.
SISKO MIDDLE
OY! OY--NU KID! THAZ SERM FANZY BACKKOOK YOU GEZ THRR.

I NEVER SAW MY GRANDAD AGAIN. BUT THE DAY HE DIED...HE DIDN'T LEAVE HIS CRYPTOKEY TO MY DAD. HE--

EXCUSE ME, SIR?

BILLY BANE'S SHIP IS ABOUT TO MAKE LANDFALL. THE OTHERS HAVE EXPRESSED CONCERNS OVER--

THE OTHERS WILL FOLLOW MY PLAN TO THE *WORD*.

THEY'RE WORRIED, SIR, ABOUT THE NUKE. RECONNAISSANCE HAS LEARNED THAT IT IS INDEED ARMED AND READY TO BE LAUNCHED FROM THE SURFACE OF TEXRA.

WE'LL ACQUIRE THE NUKE SOON ENOUGH. YOU GO AND TELL THOSE BEDWETTERS TO TRUST ME. OR *ELSE*.

AS I WAS SAYING. GRANDAD, HE DIDN'T LEAVE HIS CRYPTOKEY TO MY FATHER.

HE LEFT IT TO *ME*.

AND NOW BILLY BANE THINKS HE CAN COME HERE AND TAKE IT FROM ME.

BECAUSE I'M JUST ANOTHER RICH ASSHOLE.

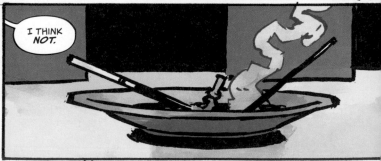

I THINK *NOT*.

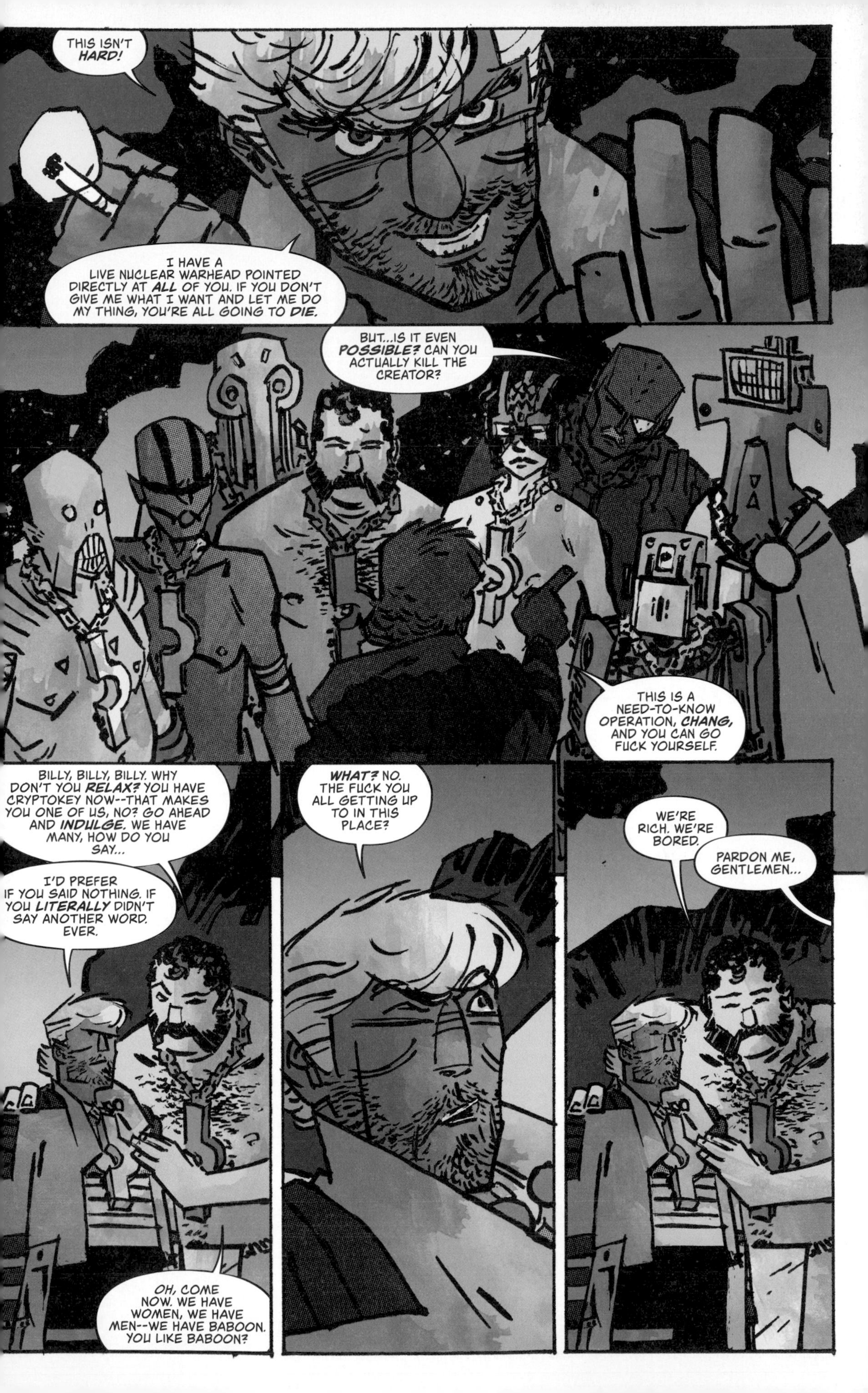
THIS ISN'T HARD!
I HAVE A LIVE NUCLEAR WARHEAD POINTED DIRECTLY AT ALL OF YOU. IF YOU DON'T GIVE ME WHAT I WANT AND LET ME DO MY THING, YOU'RE ALL GOING TO DIE.
BUT...IS IT EVEN POSSIBLE? CAN YOU ACTUALLY KILL THE CREATOR?
THIS IS A NEED-TO-KNOW OPERATION, CHANG, AND YOU CAN GO FUCK YOURSELF.
BILLY, BILLY, BILLY. WHY DON'T YOU RELAX? YOU HAVE CRYPTOKEY NOW--THAT MAKES YOU ONE OF US, NO? GO AHEAD AND INDULGE. WE HAVE MANY, HOW DO YOU SAY...
I'D PREFER IF YOU SAID NOTHING. IF YOU LITERALLY DIDN'T SAY ANOTHER WORD. EVER.
OH, COME NOW. WE HAVE WOMEN, WE HAVE MEN--WE HAVE BABOON. YOU LIKE BABOON?
WHAT? NO. THE FUCK YOU ALL GETTING UP TO IN THIS PLACE?
WE'RE RICH. WE'RE BORED.
PARDON ME, GENTLEMEN...

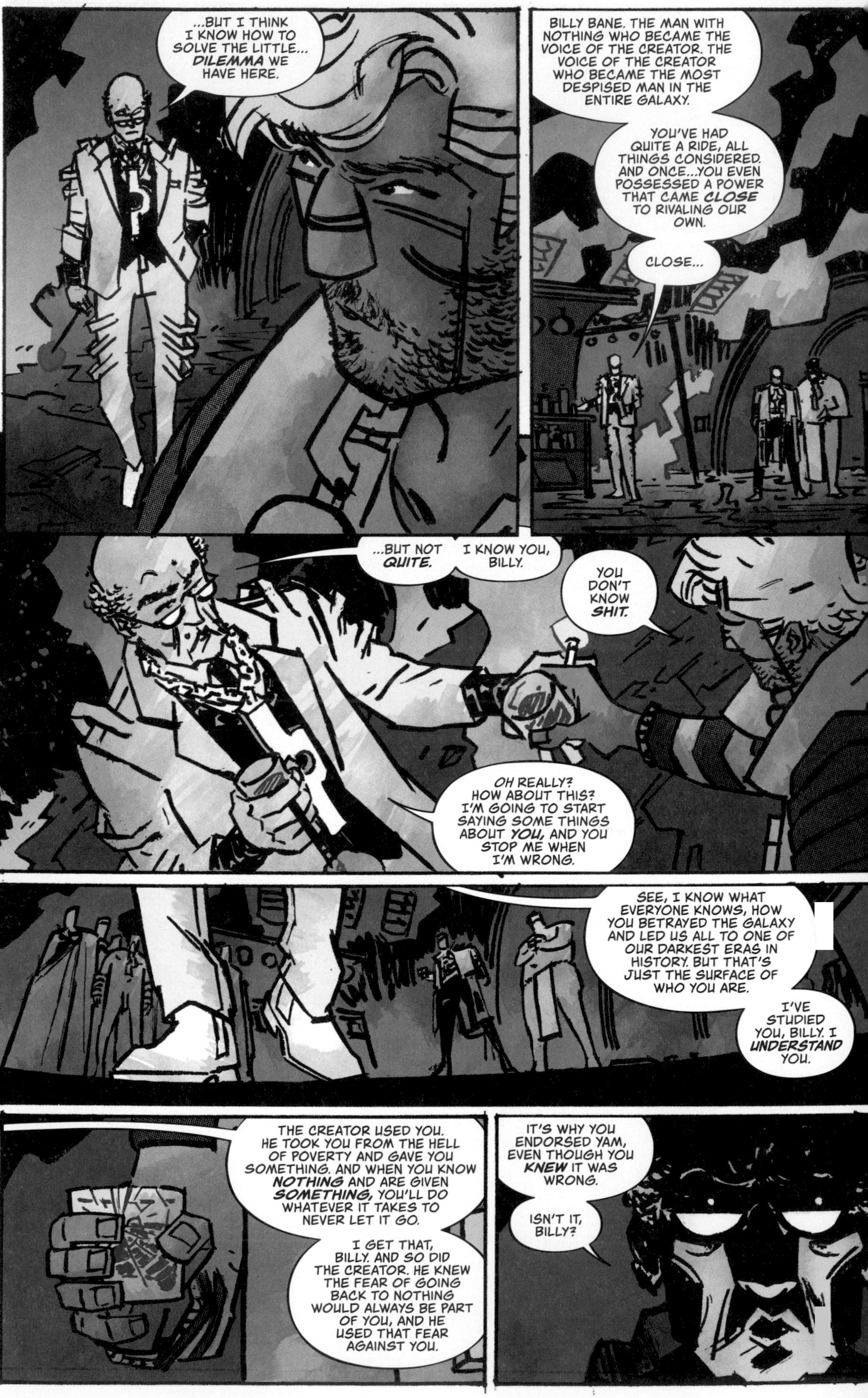
...BUT I THINK I KNOW HOW TO SOLVE THE LITTLE... DILEMMA WE HAVE HERE.
BILLY BANE. THE MAN WITH NOTHING WHO BECAME THE VOICE OF THE CREATOR. THE VOICE OF THE CREATOR WHO BECAME THE MOST DESPISED MAN IN THE ENTIRE GALAXY.
YOU'VE HAD QUITE A RIDE, ALL THINGS CONSIDERED. AND ONCE...YOU EVEN POSSESSED A POWER THAT CAME CLOSE TO RIVALING OUR OWN.
CLOSE...
...BUT NOT QUITE.
I KNOW YOU, BILLY.
YOU DON'T KNOW SHIT.
OH REALLY? HOW ABOUT THIS? I'M GOING TO START SAYING SOME THINGS ABOUT YOU, AND YOU STOP ME WHEN I'M WRONG.
SEE, I KNOW WHAT EVERYONE KNOWS, HOW YOU BETRAYED THE GALAXY AND LED US ALL TO ONE OF OUR DARKEST ERAS IN HISTORY. BUT THAT'S JUST THE SURFACE OF WHO YOU ARE.
I'VE STUDIED YOU, BILLY. I UNDERSTAND YOU.
THE CREATOR USED YOU. HE TOOK YOU FROM THE HELL OF POVERTY AND GAVE YOU SOMETHING. AND WHEN YOU KNOW NOTHING AND ARE GIVEN SOMETHING, YOU'LL DO WHATEVER IT TAKES TO NEVER LET IT GO.
I GET THAT, BILLY. AND SO DID THE CREATOR. HE KNEW THE FEAR OF GOING BACK TO NOTHING WOULD ALWAYS BE PART OF YOU, AND HE USED THAT FEAR AGAINST YOU.
IT'S WHY YOU ENDORSED YAM, EVEN THOUGH YOU KNEW IT WAS WRONG.
ISN'T IT, BILLY?

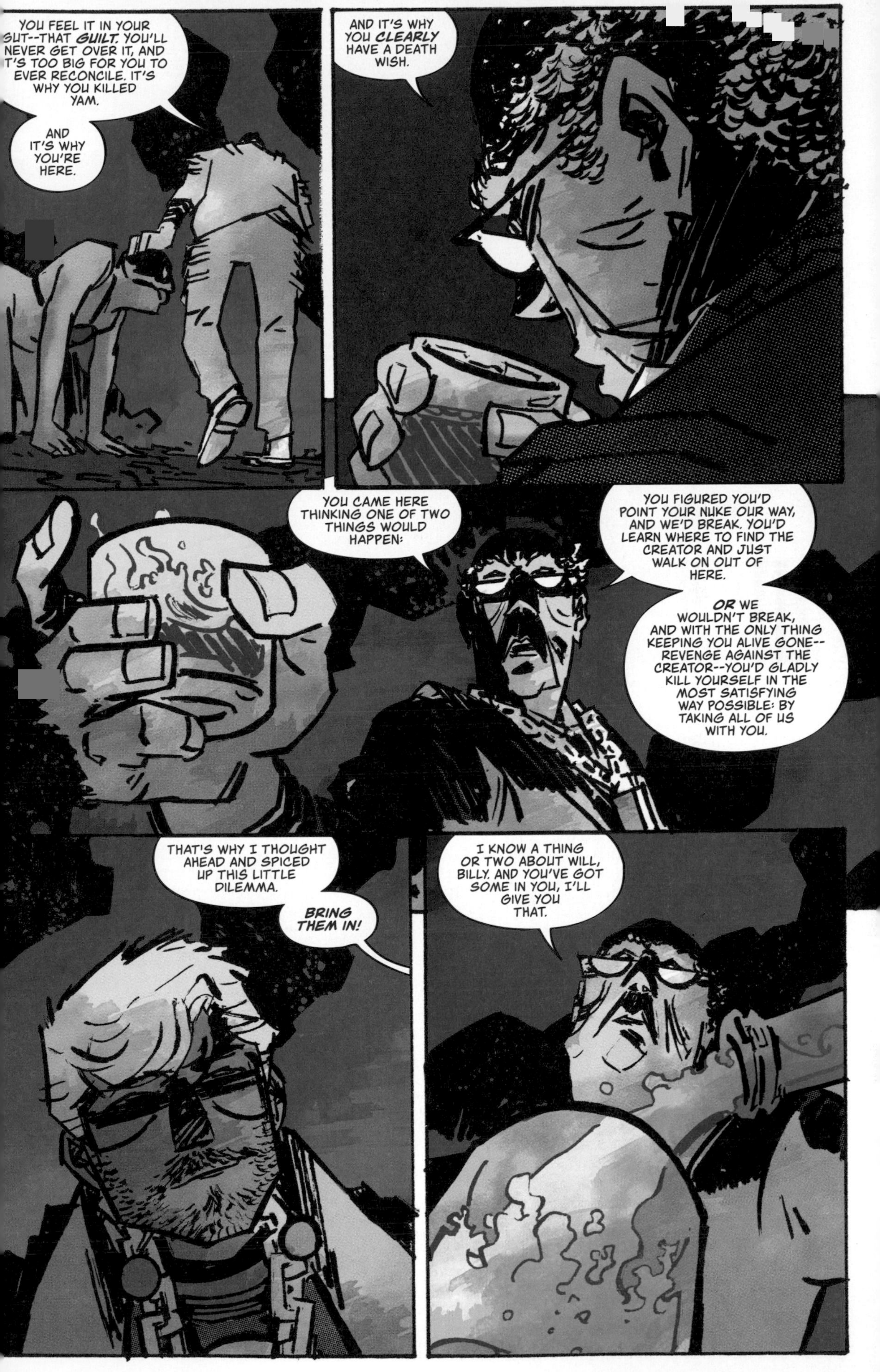
YOU FEEL IT IN YOUR GUT--THAT *GUILT.* YOU'LL NEVER GET OVER IT, AND IT'S TOO BIG FOR YOU TO EVER RECONCILE. IT'S WHY YOU KILLED YAM.
AND IT'S WHY YOU'RE HERE.
AND IT'S WHY YOU *CLEARLY* HAVE A DEATH WISH.
YOU CAME HERE THINKING ONE OF TWO THINGS WOULD HAPPEN:
YOU FIGURED YOU'D POINT YOUR NUKE OUR WAY, AND WE'D BREAK. YOU'D LEARN WHERE TO FIND THE CREATOR AND JUST WALK ON OUT OF HERE.
OR WE WOULDN'T BREAK, AND WITH THE ONLY THING KEEPING YOU ALIVE GONE--REVENGE AGAINST THE CREATOR--YOU'D GLADLY KILL YOURSELF IN THE MOST SATISFYING WAY POSSIBLE: BY TAKING ALL OF US WITH YOU.
THAT'S WHY I THOUGHT AHEAD AND SPICED UP THIS LITTLE DILEMMA.
BRING THEM IN!
I KNOW A THING OR TWO ABOUT WILL, BILLY. AND YOU'VE GOT SOME IN YOU, I'LL GIVE YOU THAT.

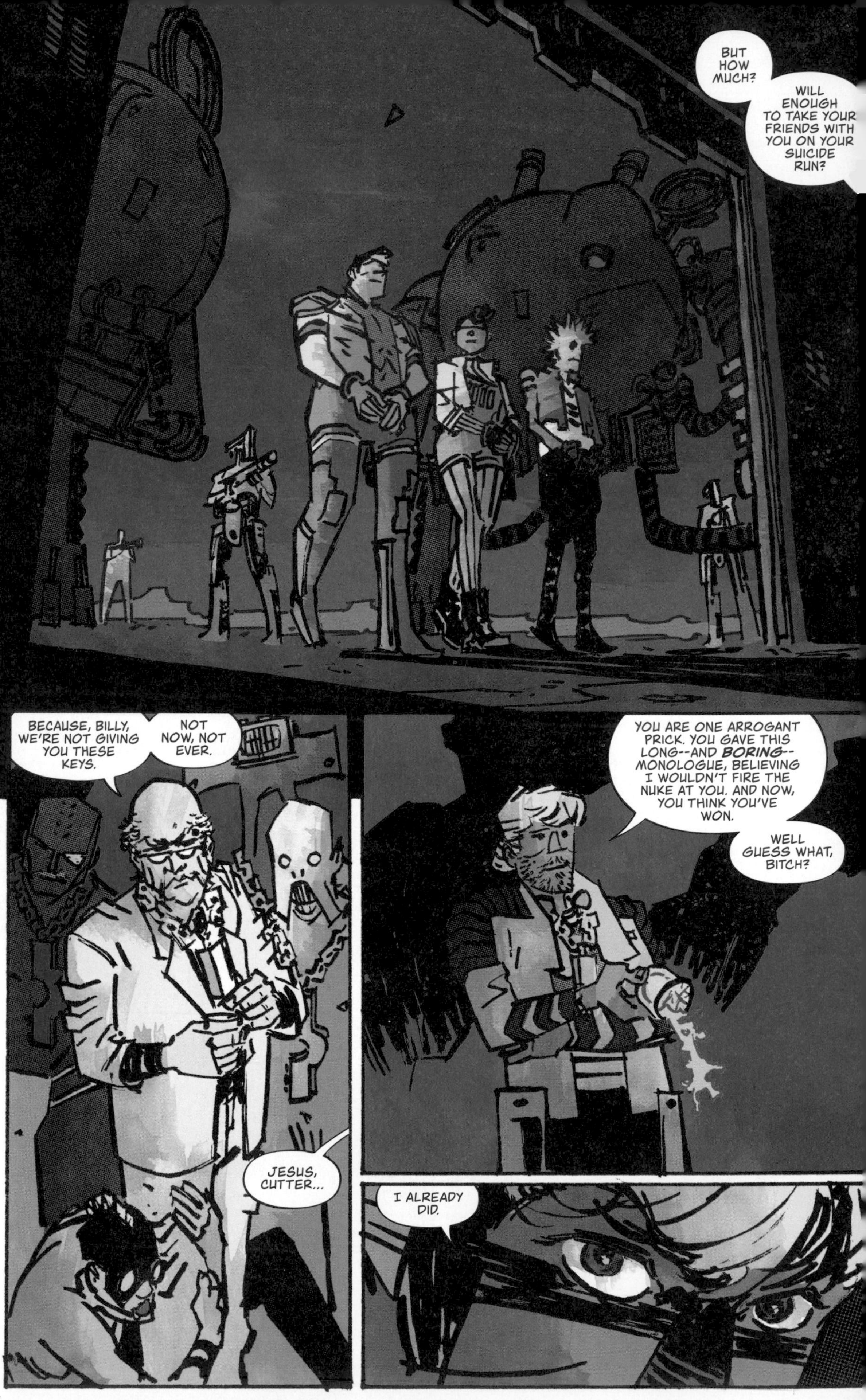
BUT HOW MUCH?
WILL ENOUGH TO TAKE YOUR FRIENDS WITH YOU ON YOUR SUICIDE RUN?
BECAUSE, BILLY, WE'RE NOT GIVING YOU THESE KEYS.
NOT NOW, NOT EVER.
JESUS, CUTTER...
YOU ARE ONE ARROGANT PRICK. YOU GAVE THIS LONG--AND BORING--MONOLOGUE, BELIEVING I WOULDN'T FIRE THE NUKE AT YOU. AND NOW, YOU THINK YOU'VE WON.
WELL GUESS WHAT, BITCH?
I ALREADY DID.

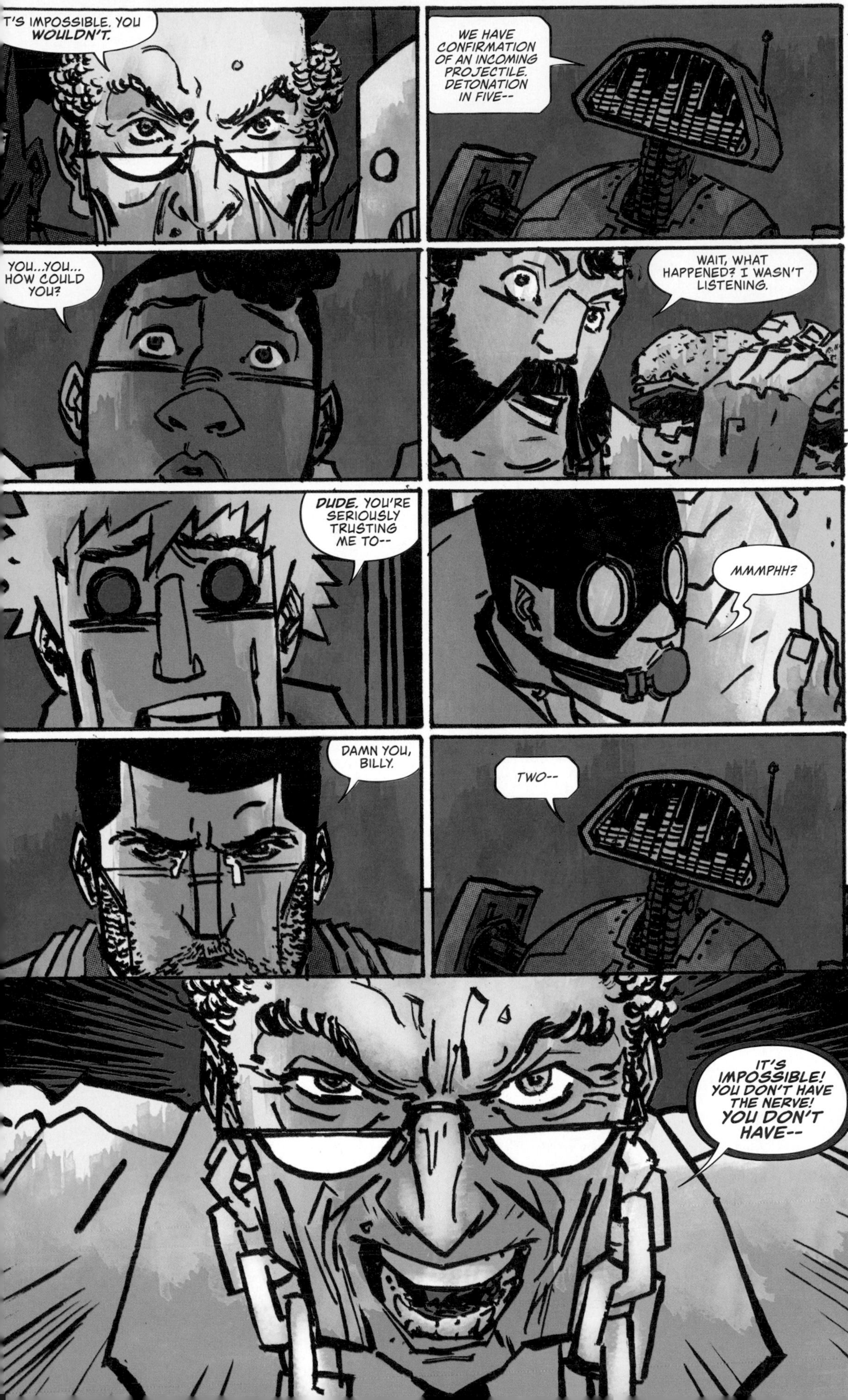
IT'S IMPOSSIBLE. YOU WOULDN'T.
WE HAVE CONFIRMATION OF AN INCOMING PROJECTILE. DETONATION IN FIVE--
YOU...YOU... HOW COULD YOU?
WAIT, WHAT HAPPENED? I WASN'T LISTENING.
DUDE. YOU'RE SERIOUSLY TRUSTING ME TO--
MMMPHH?
DAMN YOU, BILLY.
TWO--
IT'S IMPOSSIBLE! YOU DON'T HAVE THE NERVE! YOU DON'T HAVE--

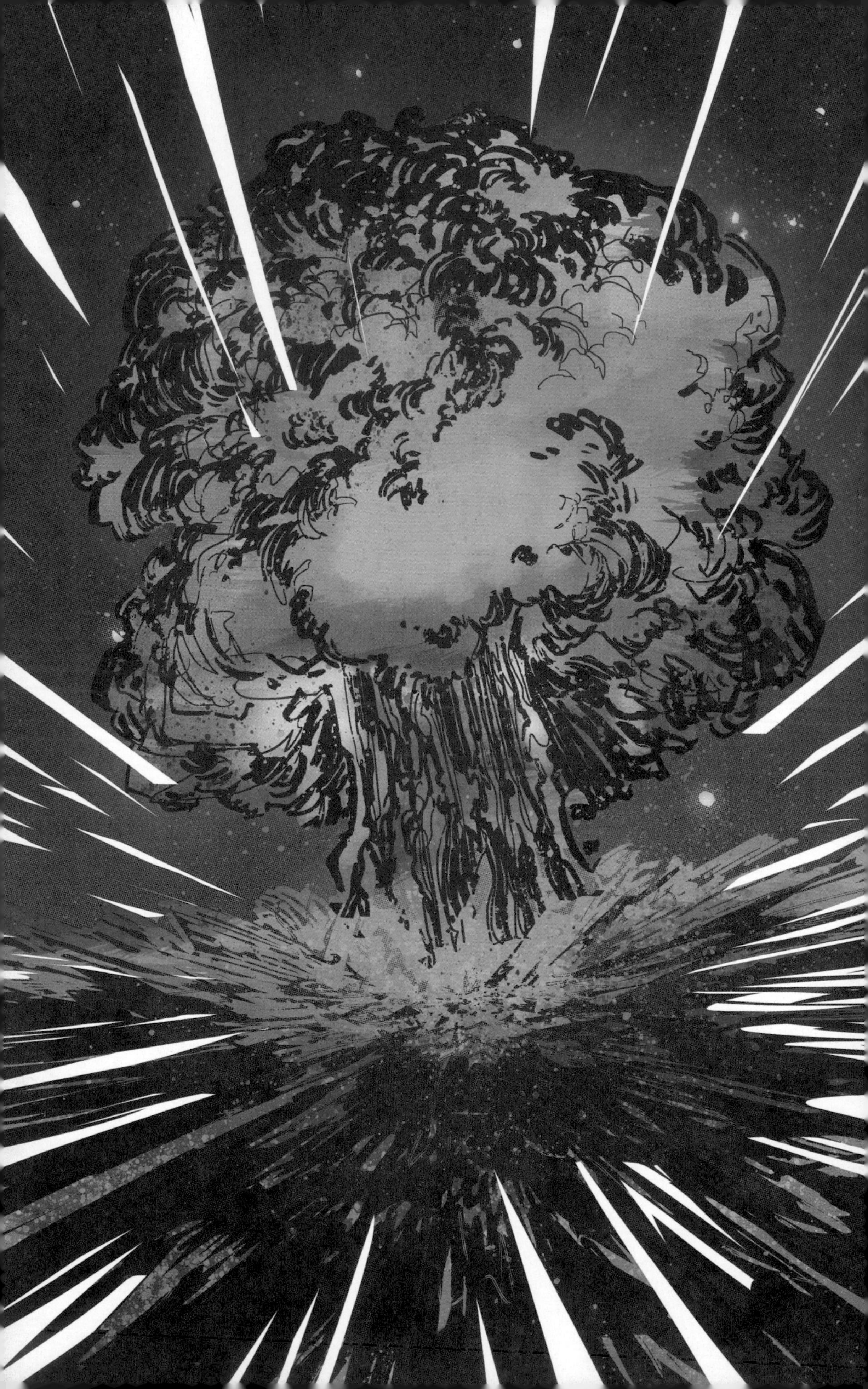

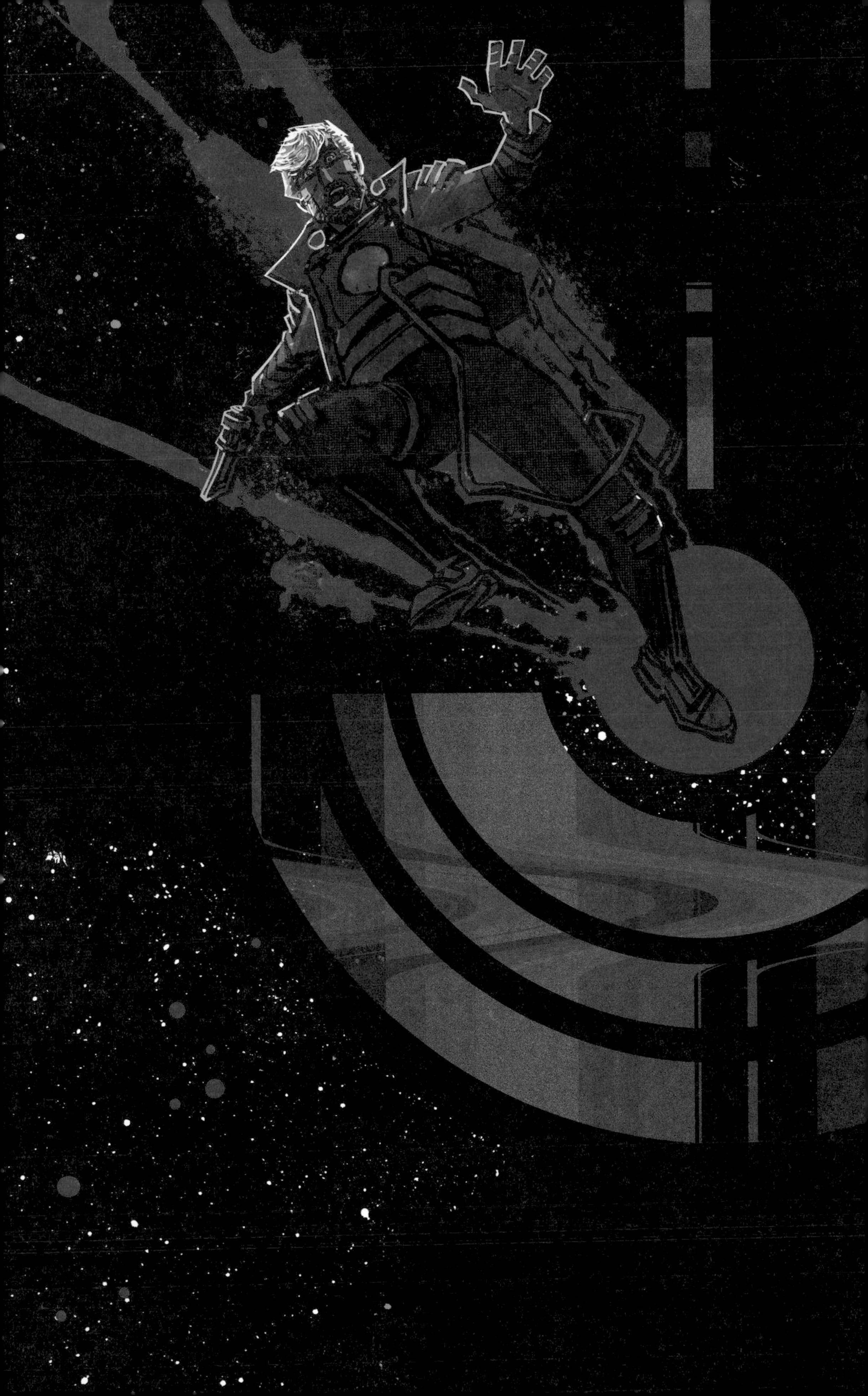

CHAPTER TEN

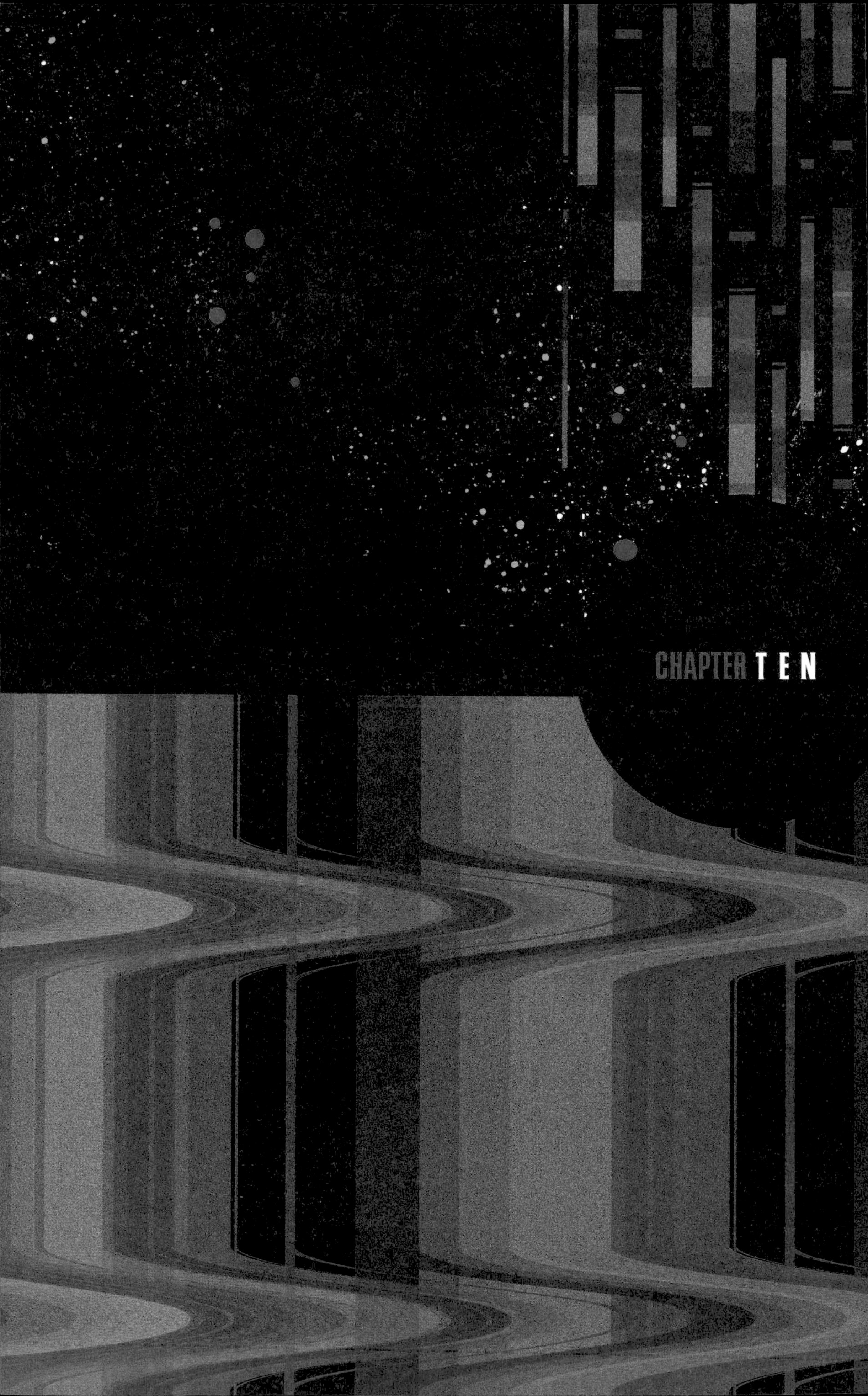

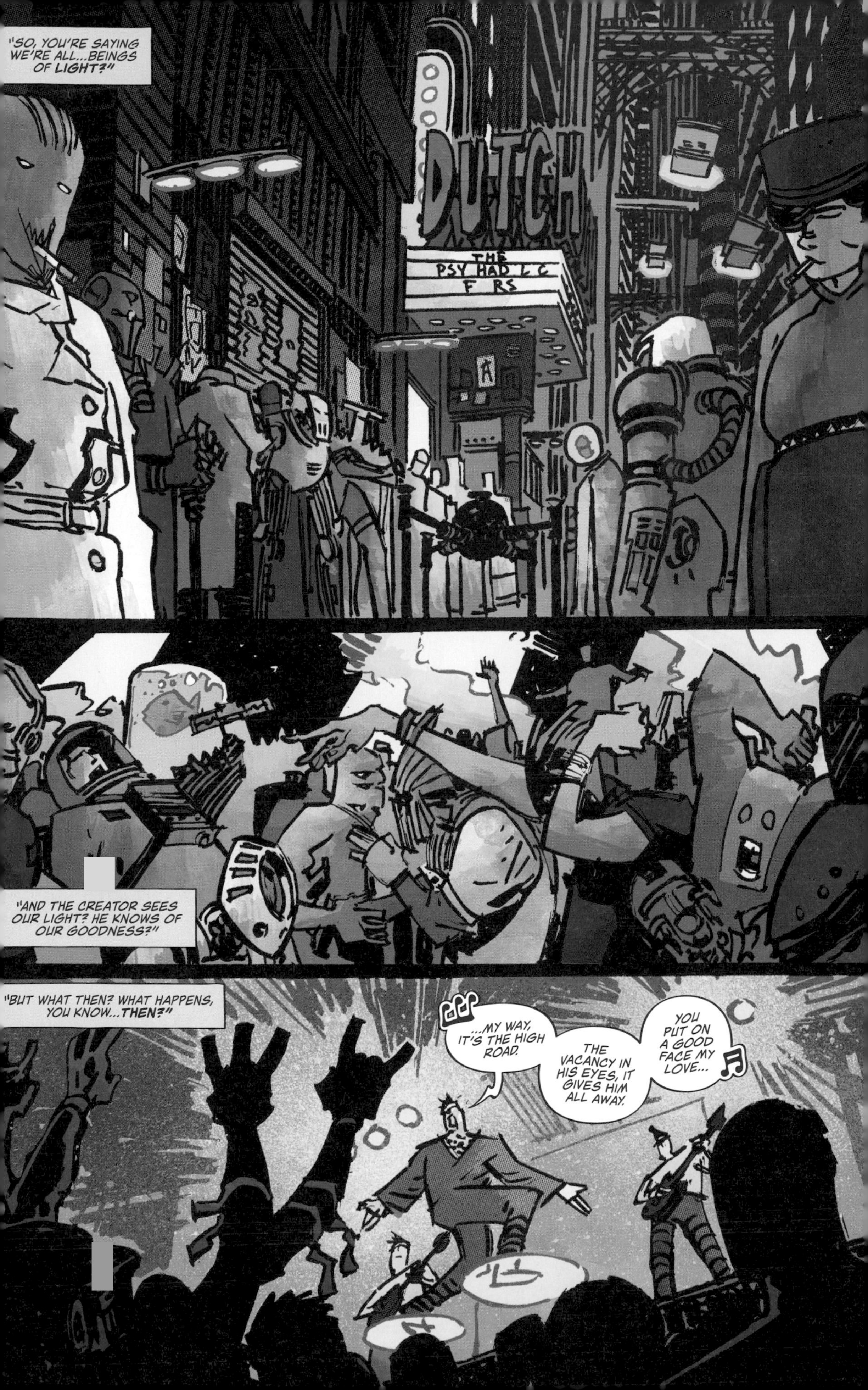
"SO, YOU'RE SAYING WE'RE ALL...BEINGS OF LIGHT?"
DUTCH
THE PSY HAD L C F RS
"AND THE CREATOR SEES OUR LIGHT? HE KNOWS OF OUR GOODNESS?"
"BUT WHAT THEN? WHAT HAPPENS, YOU KNOW...THEN?"
...MY WAY, IT'S THE HIGH ROAD.
THE VACANCY IN HIS EYES, IT GIVES HIM ALL AWAY.
YOU PUT ON A GOOD FACE MY LOVE...

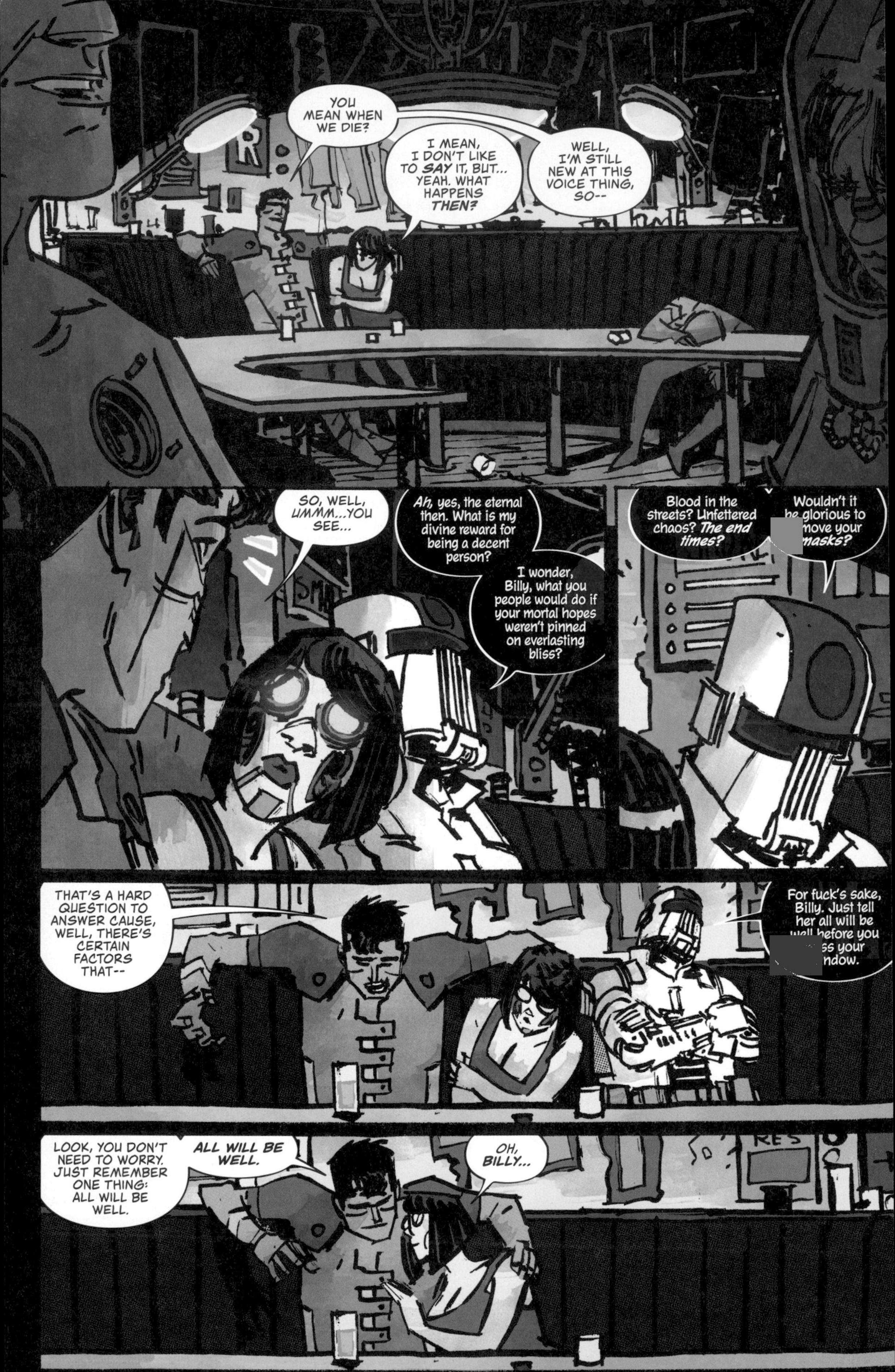

YOU MEAN WHEN WE DIE?
I MEAN, I DON'T LIKE TO *SAY* IT, BUT... YEAH. WHAT HAPPENS *THEN?*
WELL, I'M STILL NEW AT THIS VOICE THING, SO--
SO, WELL, UMMM...YOU SEE...
Ah, yes, the eternal then. What is my divine reward for being a decent person?
I wonder, Billy, what you people would do if your mortal hopes weren't pinned on everlasting bliss?
Blood in the streets? Unfettered chaos? *The end times?*
Wouldn't it glorious to move your *masks?*
THAT'S A HARD QUESTION TO ANSWER CAUSE, WELL, THERE'S CERTAIN FACTORS THAT--
For fuck's sake, Billy. Just tell her all will be well before you ss your ndow.
LOOK, YOU DON'T NEED TO WORRY. JUST REMEMBER ONE THING: ALL WILL BE WELL.
ALL WILL BE WELL.
OH, BILLY...

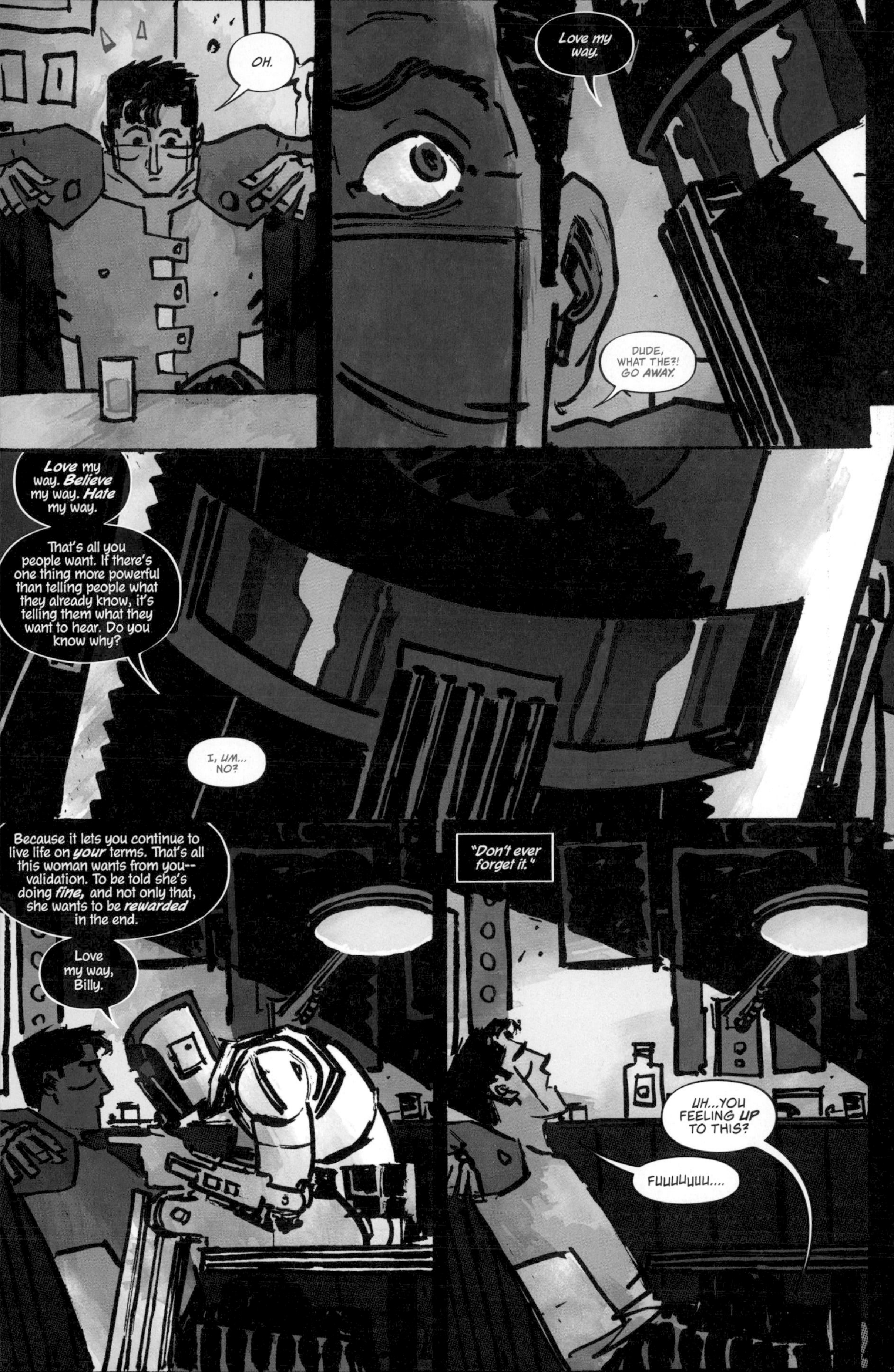

OH.
Love my way.
DUDE, WHAT THE?! GO AWAY.
Love my way. Believe my way. Hate my way.
That's all you people want. If there's one thing more powerful than telling people what they already know, it's telling them what they want to hear. Do you know why?
I, UM... NO?
Because it lets you continue to live life on your terms. That's all this woman wants from you-- validation. To be told she's doing fine, and not only that, she wants to be rewarded in the end.
Love my way, Billy.
"Don't ever forget it."
UH...YOU FEELING UP TO THIS?
FUUUUUUU....

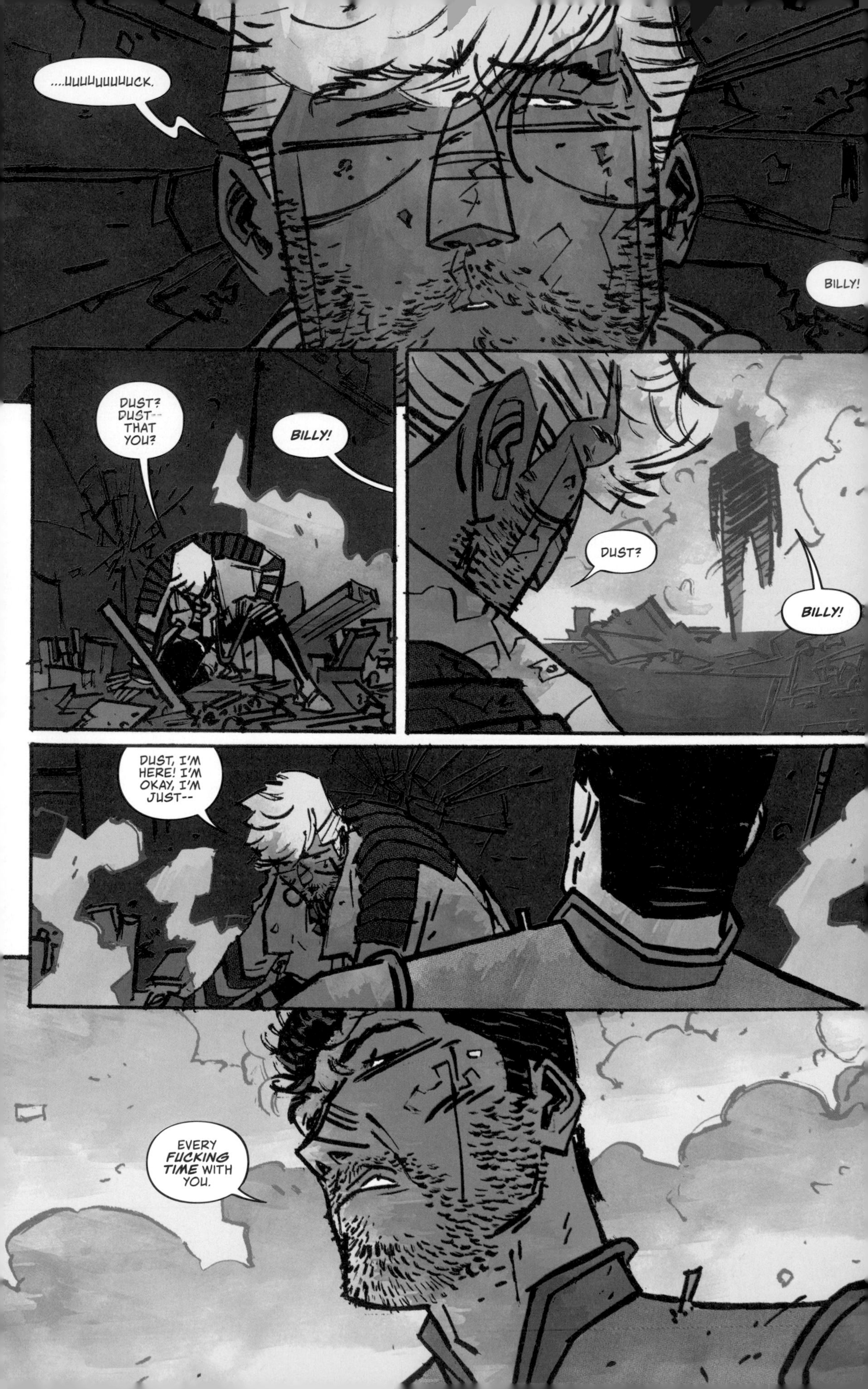
....UUUUUUUUUCK.
BILLY!
DUST? DUST-- THAT YOU?
BILLY!
DUST?
BILLY!
DUST, I'M HERE! I'M OKAY, I'M JUST--
EVERY FUCKING TIME WITH YOU.

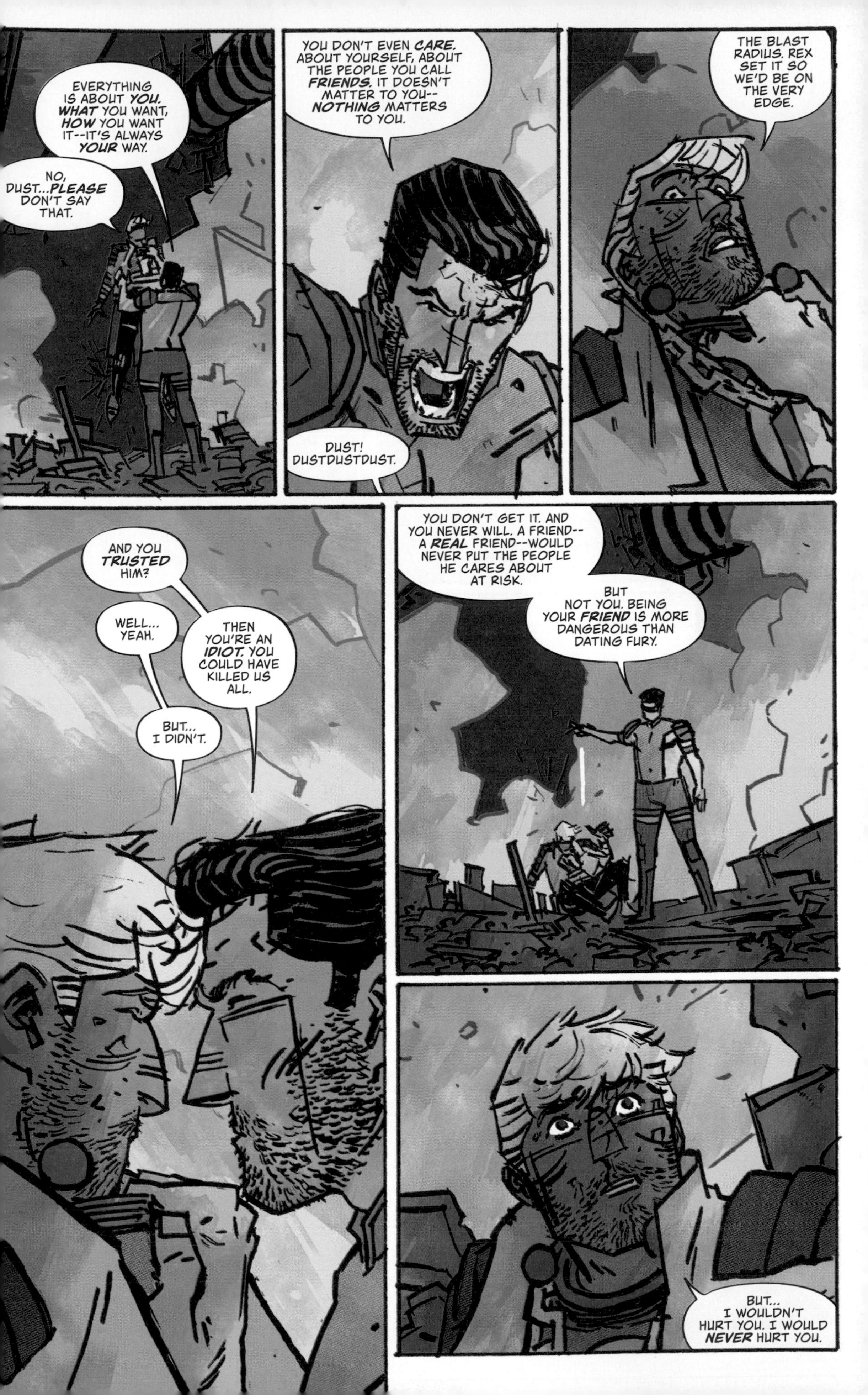
EVERYTHING IS ABOUT YOU. WHAT YOU WANT, HOW YOU WANT IT--IT'S ALWAYS YOUR WAY.
NO, DUST...PLEASE DON'T SAY THAT.
YOU DON'T EVEN CARE. ABOUT YOURSELF, ABOUT THE PEOPLE YOU CALL FRIENDS. IT DOESN'T MATTER TO YOU--NOTHING MATTERS TO YOU.
DUST! DUSTDUSTDUST.
THE BLAST RADIUS. REX SET IT SO WE'D BE ON THE VERY EDGE.
AND YOU TRUSTED HIM?
WELL... YEAH.
THEN YOU'RE AN IDIOT. YOU COULD HAVE KILLED US ALL.
BUT... I DIDN'T.
YOU DON'T GET IT. AND YOU NEVER WILL. A FRIEND--A REAL FRIEND--WOULD NEVER PUT THE PEOPLE HE CARES ABOUT AT RISK.
BUT NOT YOU. BEING YOUR FRIEND IS MORE DANGEROUS THAN DATING FURY.
BUT... I WOULDN'T HURT YOU. I WOULD NEVER HURT YOU.

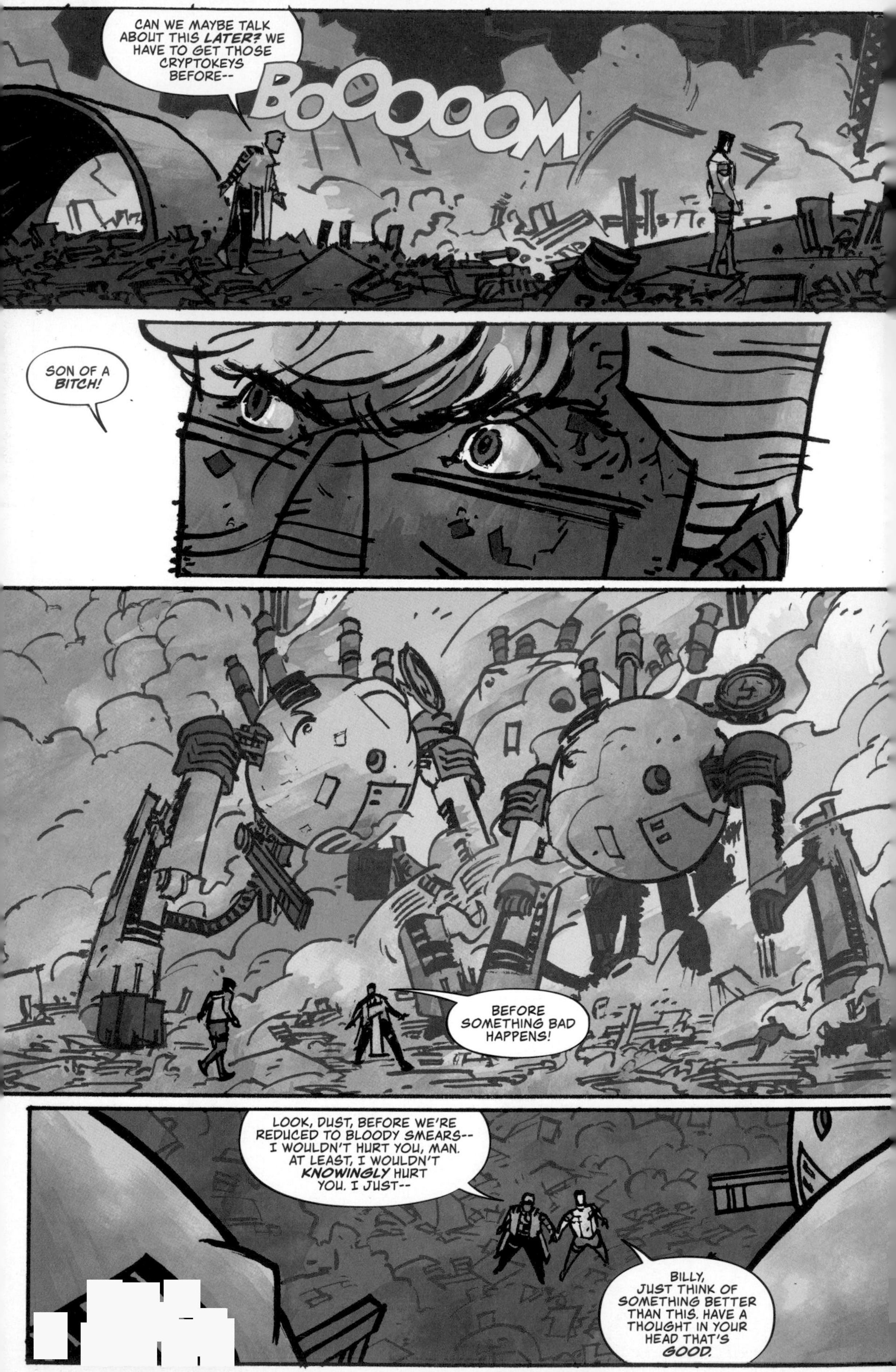

CAN WE MAYBE TALK ABOUT THIS LATER? WE HAVE TO GET THOSE CRYPTOKEYS BEFORE--
BOOOOOOM
SON OF A BITCH!
BEFORE SOMETHING BAD HAPPENS!
LOOK, DUST, BEFORE WE'RE REDUCED TO BLOODY SMEARS-- I WOULDN'T HURT YOU, MAN. AT LEAST, I WOULDN'T KNOWINGLY HURT YOU. I JUST--
BILLY, JUST THINK OF SOMETHING BETTER THAN THIS. HAVE A THOUGHT IN YOUR HEAD THAT'S GOOD.

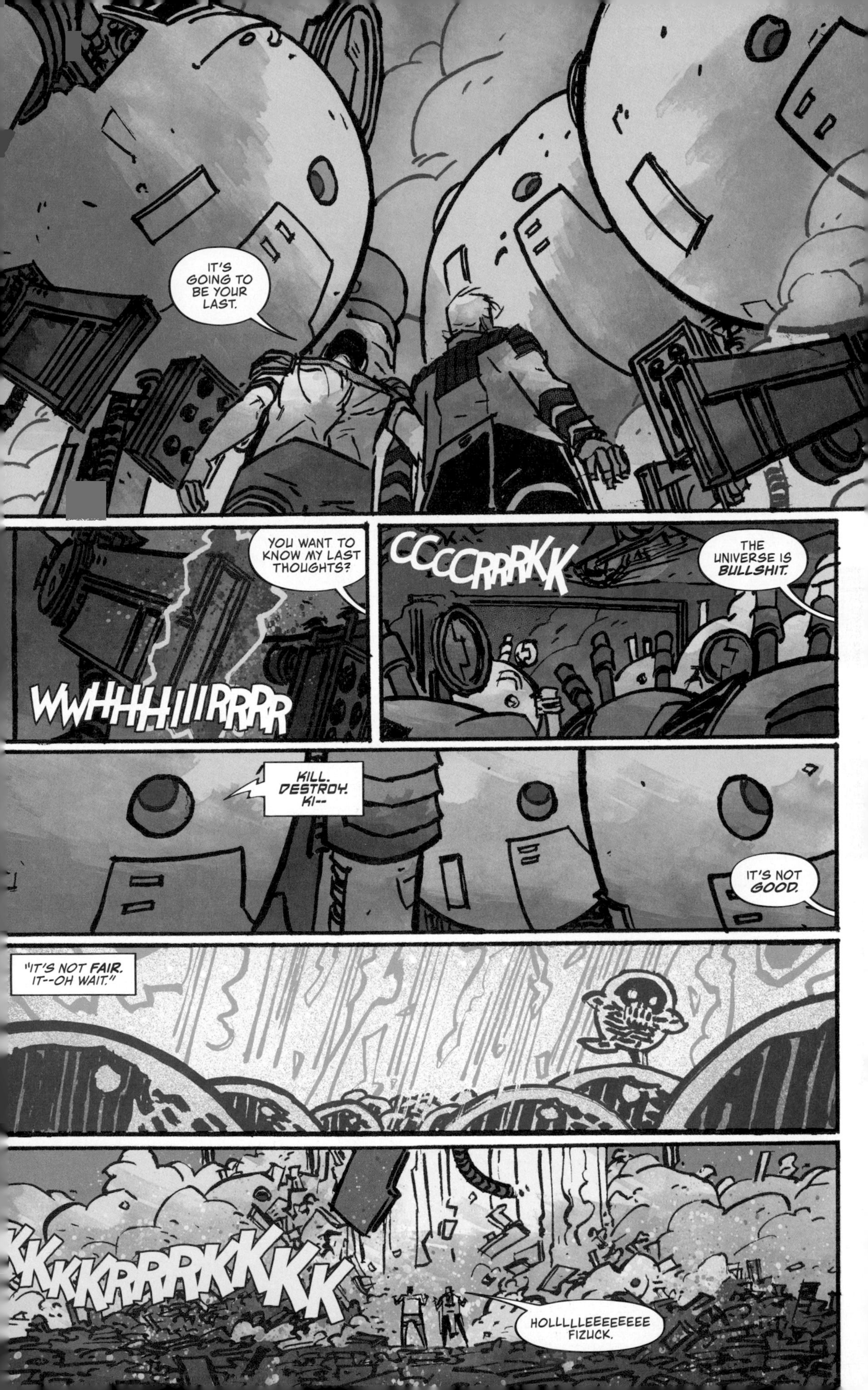
IT'S GOING TO BE YOUR LAST.
YOU WANT TO KNOW MY LAST THOUGHTS?
WWHHHHIIIIRRRR
CCCCCRRRRKK
THE UNIVERSE IS BULLSHIT.
KILL. DESTROY. KI--
IT'S NOT GOOD.
"IT'S NOT FAIR. IT--OH WAIT."
KKKKRRRRKKKKK
HOLLLLLEEEEEEEE FIZUCK.

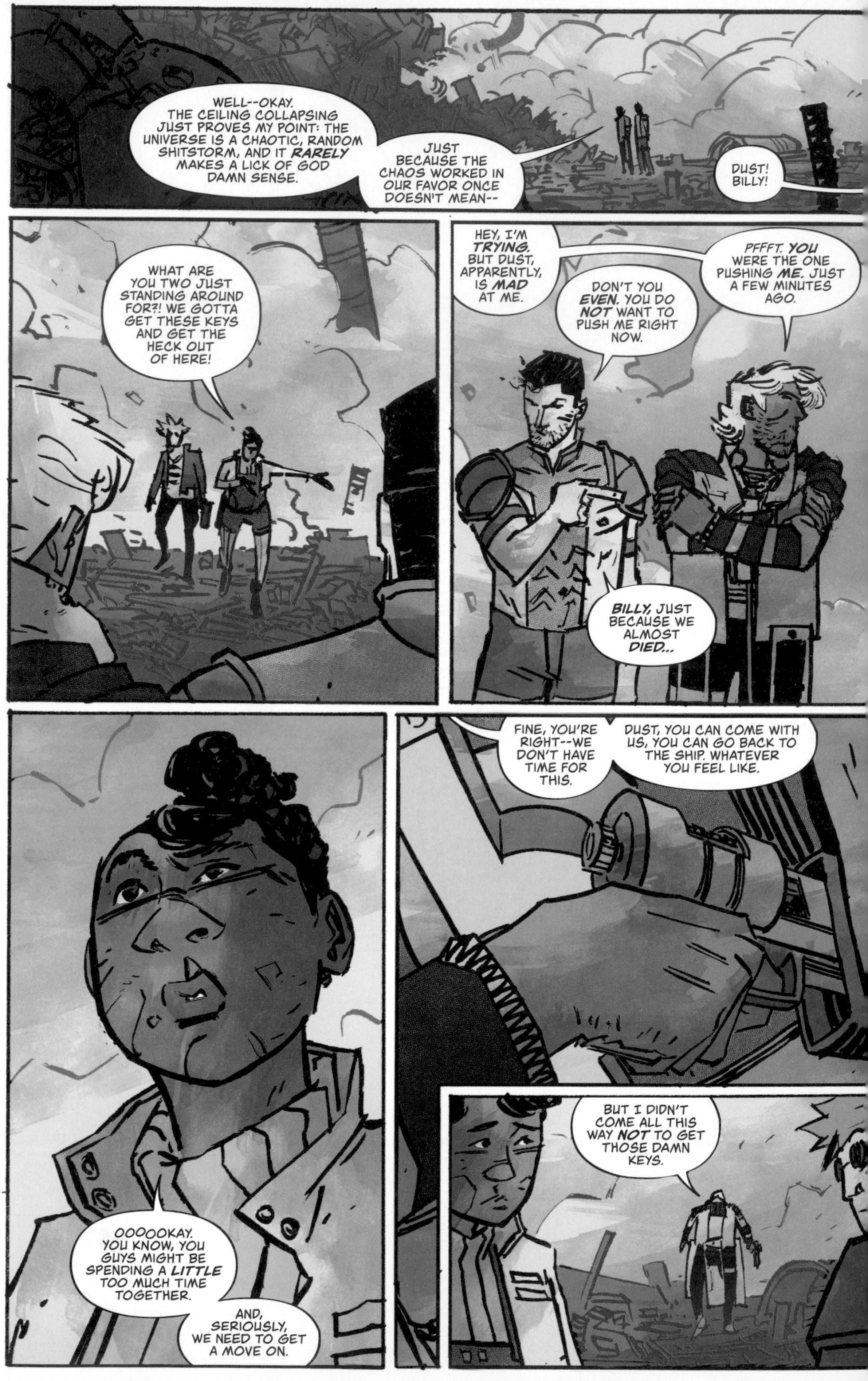
WELL--OKAY. THE CEILING COLLAPSING JUST PROVES MY POINT: THE UNIVERSE IS A CHAOTIC, RANDOM SHITSTORM, AND IT RARELY MAKES A LICK OF GOD DAMN SENSE.
JUST BECAUSE THE CHAOS WORKED IN OUR FAVOR ONCE DOESN'T MEAN--
DUST! BILLY!
WHAT ARE YOU TWO JUST STANDING AROUND FOR?! WE GOTTA GET THESE KEYS AND GET THE HECK OUT OF HERE!
HEY, I'M TRYING. BUT DUST, APPARENTLY, IS MAD AT ME.
PFFFT. YOU WERE THE ONE PUSHING ME. JUST A FEW MINUTES AGO.
DON'T YOU EVEN. YOU DO NOT WANT TO PUSH ME RIGHT NOW.
BILLY, JUST BECAUSE WE ALMOST DIED...
OOOOOKAY. YOU KNOW, YOU GUYS MIGHT BE SPENDING A LITTLE TOO MUCH TIME TOGETHER.
AND, SERIOUSLY, WE NEED TO GET A MOVE ON.
FINE, YOU'RE RIGHT--WE DON'T HAVE TIME FOR THIS.
DUST, YOU CAN COME WITH US, YOU CAN GO BACK TO THE SHIP. WHATEVER YOU FEEL LIKE.
BUT I DIDN'T COME ALL THIS WAY NOT TO GET THOSE DAMN KEYS.

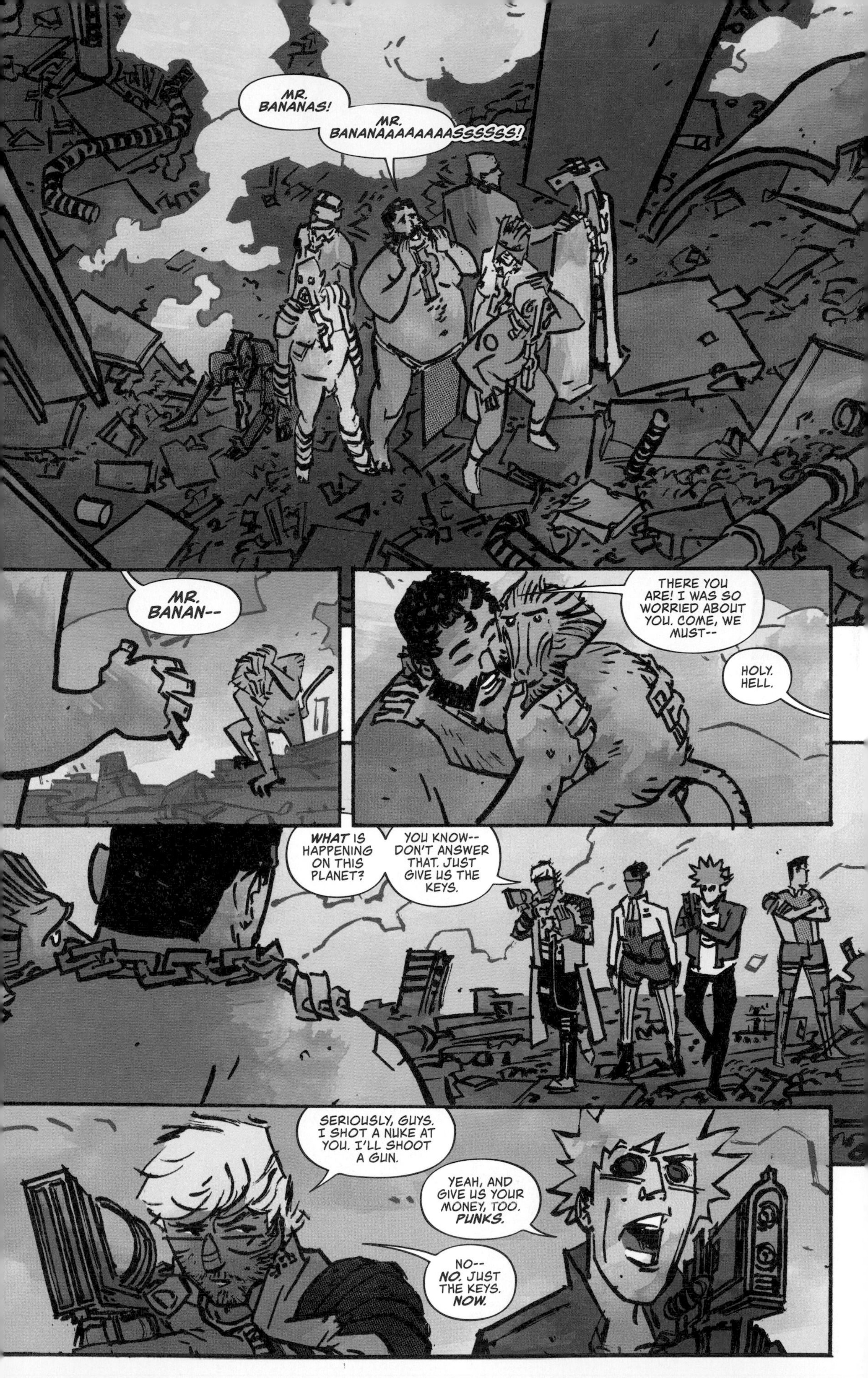
MR. BANANAS!
MR. BANANAAAAAAAASSSSSS!
MR. BANAN--
THERE YOU ARE! I WAS SO WORRIED ABOUT YOU. COME, WE MUST--
HOLY. HELL.
WHAT IS HAPPENING ON THIS PLANET?
YOU KNOW-- DON'T ANSWER THAT. JUST GIVE US THE KEYS.
SERIOUSLY, GUYS. I SHOT A NUKE AT YOU. I'LL SHOOT A GUN.
YEAH, AND GIVE US YOUR MONEY, TOO. PUNKS.
NO-- NO. JUST THE KEYS. NOW.

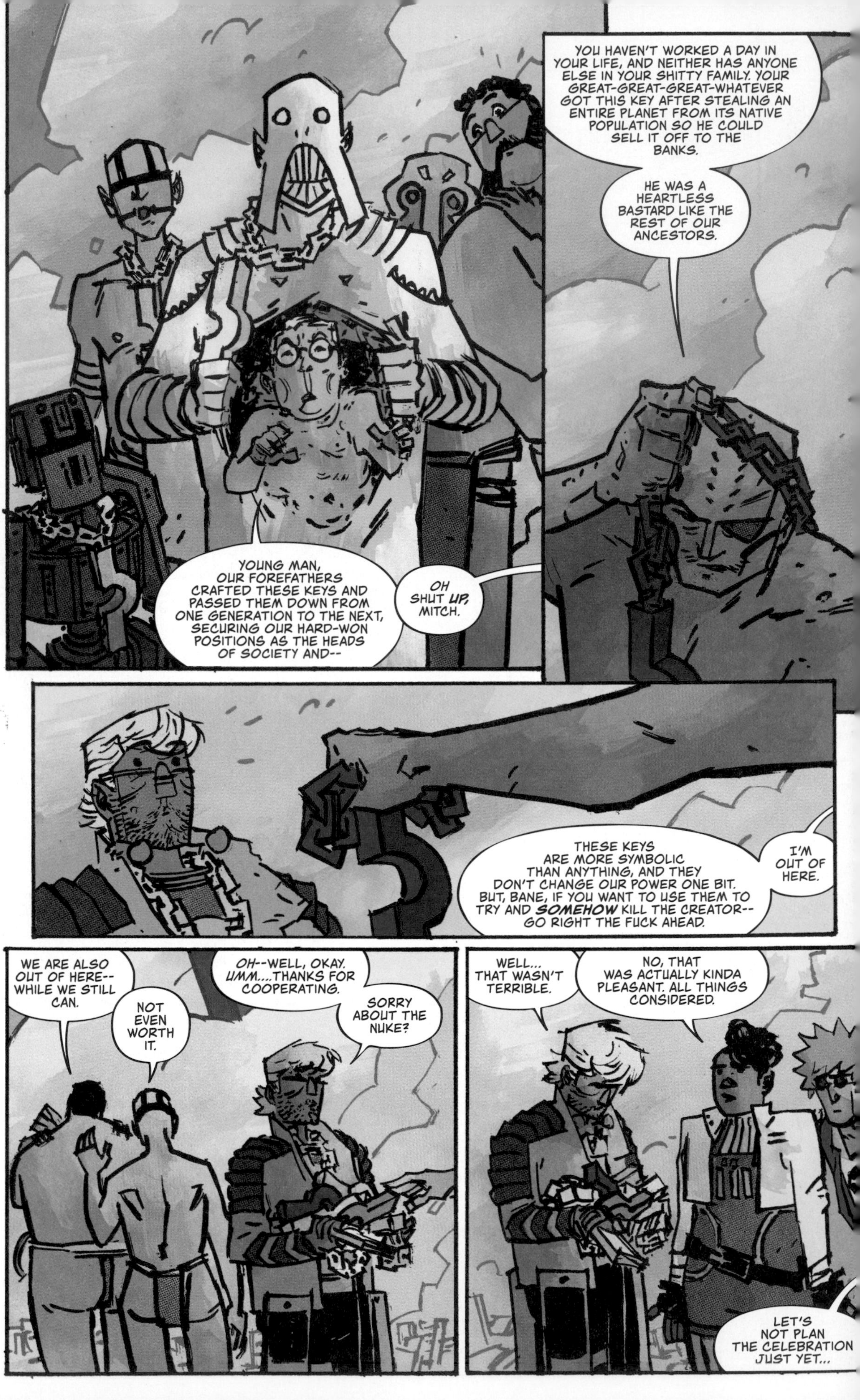
YOUNG MAN, OUR FOREFATHERS CRAFTED THESE KEYS AND PASSED THEM DOWN FROM ONE GENERATION TO THE NEXT, SECURING OUR HARD-WON POSITIONS AS THE HEADS OF SOCIETY AND--
OH SHUT *UP*, MITCH.
YOU HAVEN'T WORKED A DAY IN YOUR LIFE, AND NEITHER HAS ANYONE ELSE IN YOUR SHITTY FAMILY. YOUR GREAT-GREAT-GREAT-WHATEVER GOT THIS KEY AFTER STEALING AN ENTIRE PLANET FROM ITS NATIVE POPULATION SO HE COULD SELL IT OFF TO THE BANKS.
HE WAS A HEARTLESS BASTARD LIKE THE REST OF OUR ANCESTORS.
THESE KEYS ARE MORE SYMBOLIC THAN ANYTHING, AND THEY DON'T CHANGE OUR POWER ONE BIT. BUT, BANE, IF YOU WANT TO USE THEM TO TRY AND ***SOMEHOW*** KILL THE CREATOR-- GO RIGHT THE FUCK AHEAD.
I'M OUT OF HERE.
WE ARE ALSO OUT OF HERE-- WHILE WE STILL CAN.
NOT EVEN WORTH IT.
OH--WELL, OKAY. *UMM*....THANKS FOR COOPERATING.
SORRY ABOUT THE NUKE?
WELL... THAT WASN'T TERRIBLE.
NO, THAT WAS ACTUALLY KINDA PLEASANT. ALL THINGS CONSIDERED.
LET'S NOT PLAN THE CELEBRATION JUST YET...

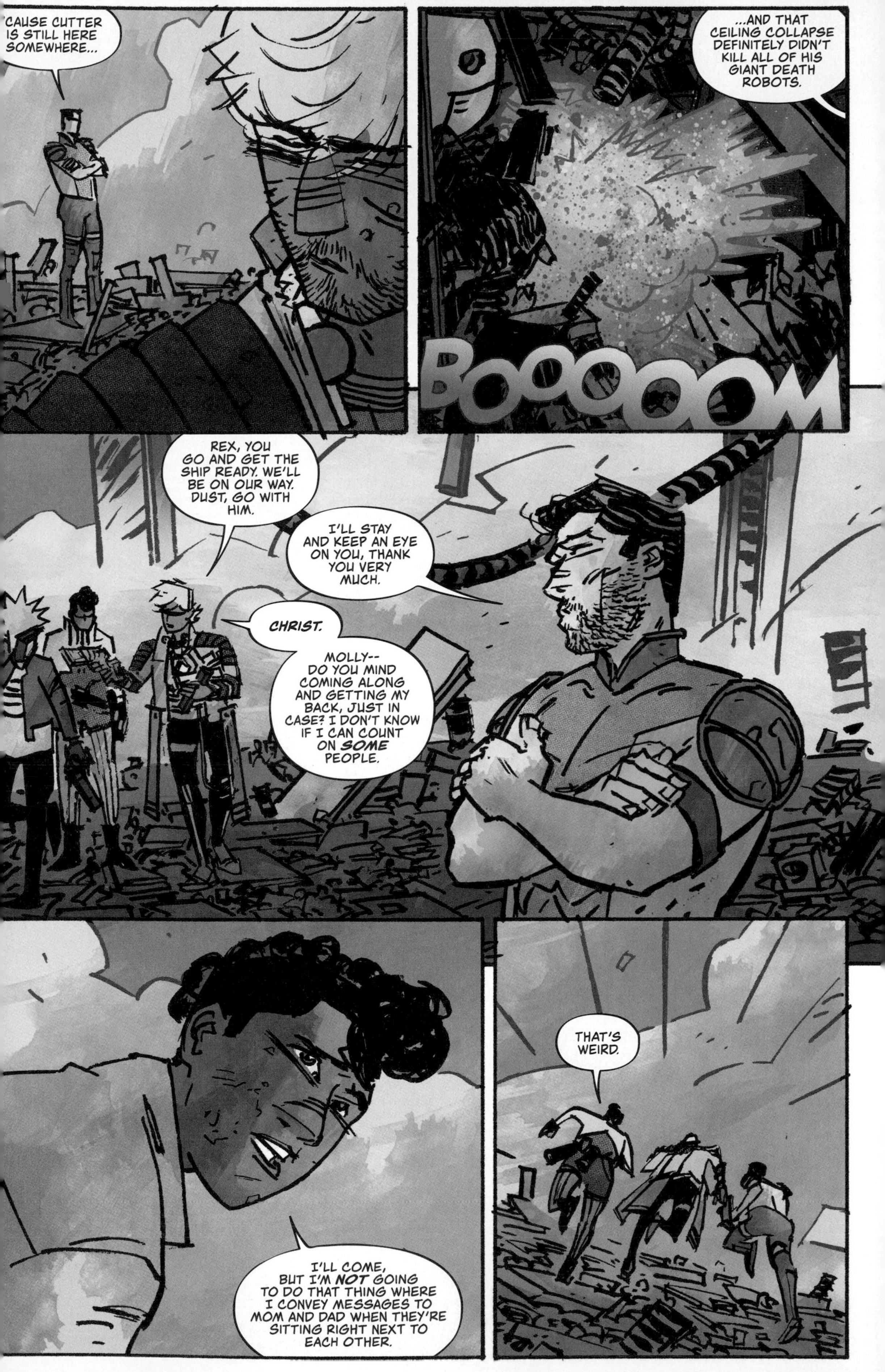
'CAUSE CUTTER IS STILL HERE SOMEWHERE...
...AND THAT CEILING COLLAPSE DEFINITELY DIDN'T KILL ALL OF HIS GIANT DEATH ROBOTS.
BOOOOOOM
REX, YOU GO AND GET THE SHIP READY. WE'LL BE ON OUR WAY. DUST, GO WITH HIM.
I'LL STAY AND KEEP AN EYE ON YOU, THANK YOU VERY MUCH.
CHRIST.
MOLLY-- DO YOU MIND COMING ALONG AND GETTING MY BACK, JUST IN CASE? I DON'T KNOW IF I CAN COUNT ON SOME PEOPLE.
I'LL COME, BUT I'M NOT GOING TO DO THAT THING WHERE I CONVEY MESSAGES TO MOM AND DAD WHEN THEY'RE SITTING RIGHT NEXT TO EACH OTHER.
THAT'S WEIRD.

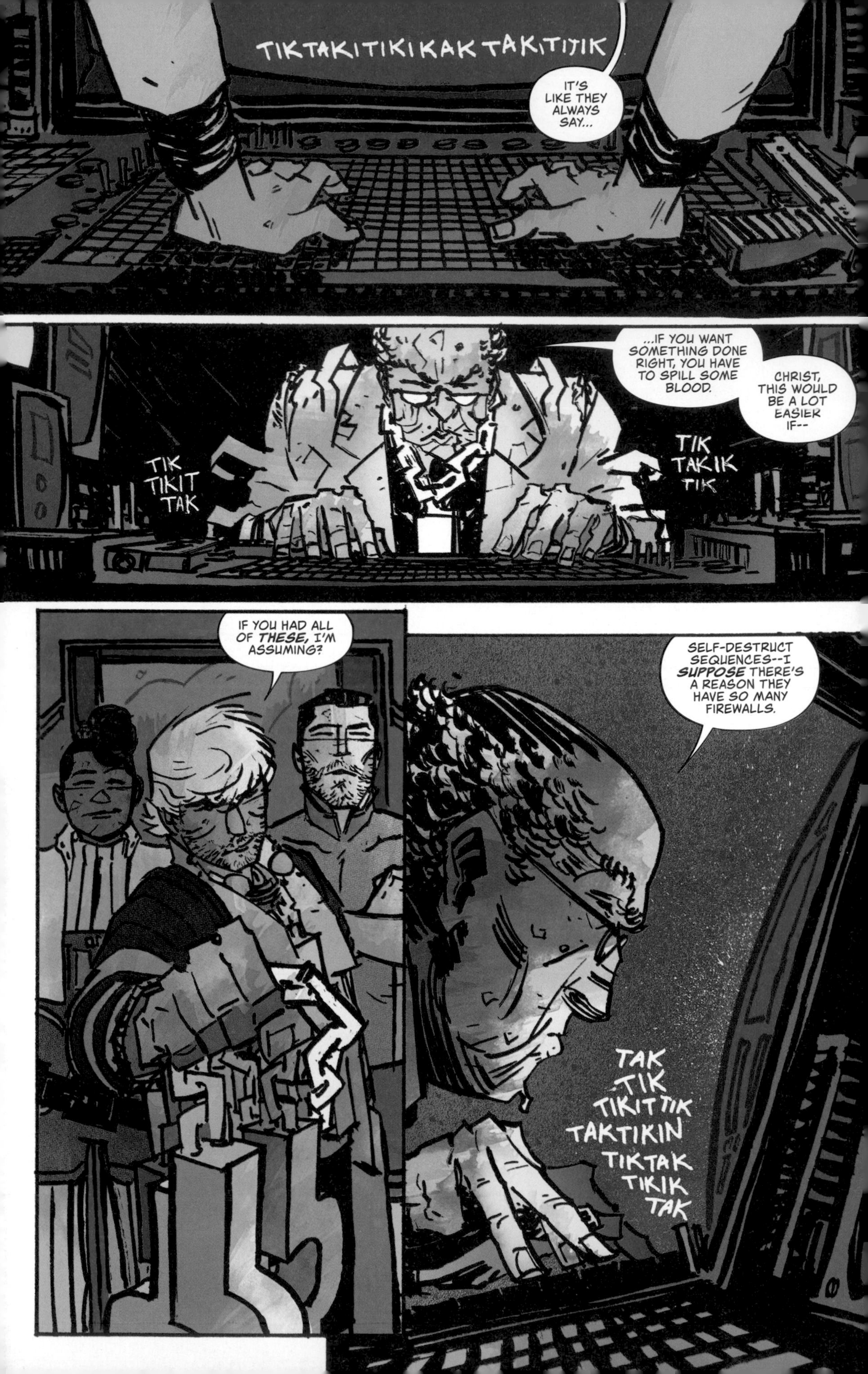
TIKTAKITIKIKAK TAKITIJIK
IT'S LIKE THEY ALWAYS SAY...
...IF YOU WANT SOMETHING DONE RIGHT, YOU HAVE TO SPILL SOME BLOOD.
CHRIST, THIS WOULD BE A LOT EASIER IF--
TIK TIKIT TAK
TIK TAKIK TIK
IF YOU HAD ALL OF *THESE*, I'M ASSUMING?
SELF-DESTRUCT SEQUENCES--I *SUPPOSE* THERE'S A REASON THEY HAVE SO MANY FIREWALLS.
TAK TIK TIKITTIK TAKTIKIN TIKTAK TIKIK TAK

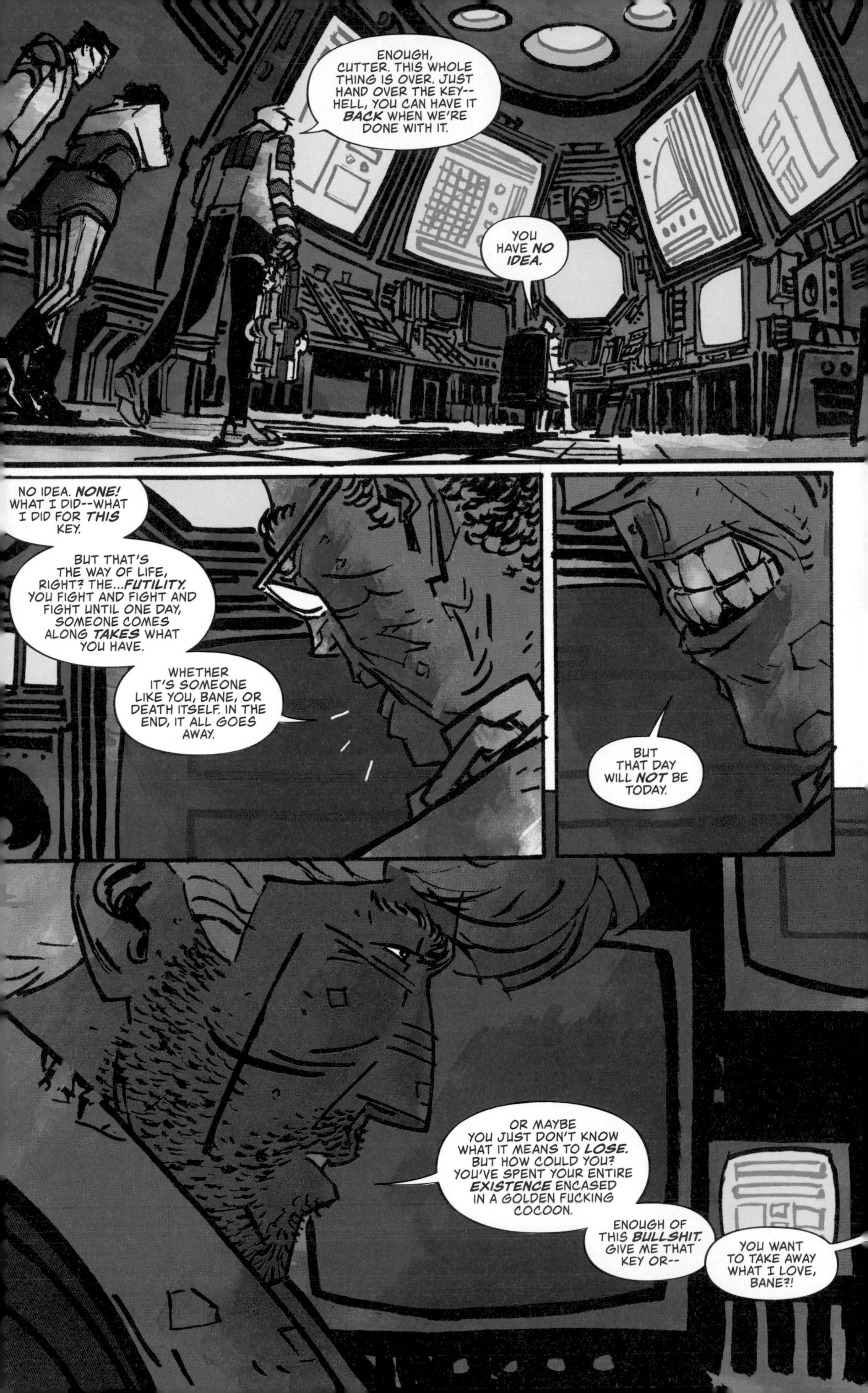
ENOUGH, CUTTER. THIS WHOLE THING IS OVER. JUST HAND OVER THE KEY-- HELL, YOU CAN HAVE IT BACK WHEN WE'RE DONE WITH IT.
YOU HAVE NO IDEA.
NO IDEA. NONE! WHAT I DID--WHAT I DID FOR THIS KEY.
BUT THAT'S THE WAY OF LIFE, RIGHT? THE...FUTILITY. YOU FIGHT AND FIGHT AND FIGHT UNTIL ONE DAY, SOMEONE COMES ALONG TAKES WHAT YOU HAVE.
WHETHER IT'S SOMEONE LIKE YOU, BANE, OR DEATH ITSELF. IN THE END, IT ALL GOES AWAY.
BUT THAT DAY WILL NOT BE TODAY.
OR MAYBE YOU JUST DON'T KNOW WHAT IT MEANS TO LOSE. BUT HOW COULD YOU? YOU'VE SPENT YOUR ENTIRE EXISTENCE ENCASED IN A GOLDEN FUCKING COCOON.
ENOUGH OF THIS BULLSHIT. GIVE ME THAT KEY OR--
YOU WANT TO TAKE AWAY WHAT I LOVE, BANE?!

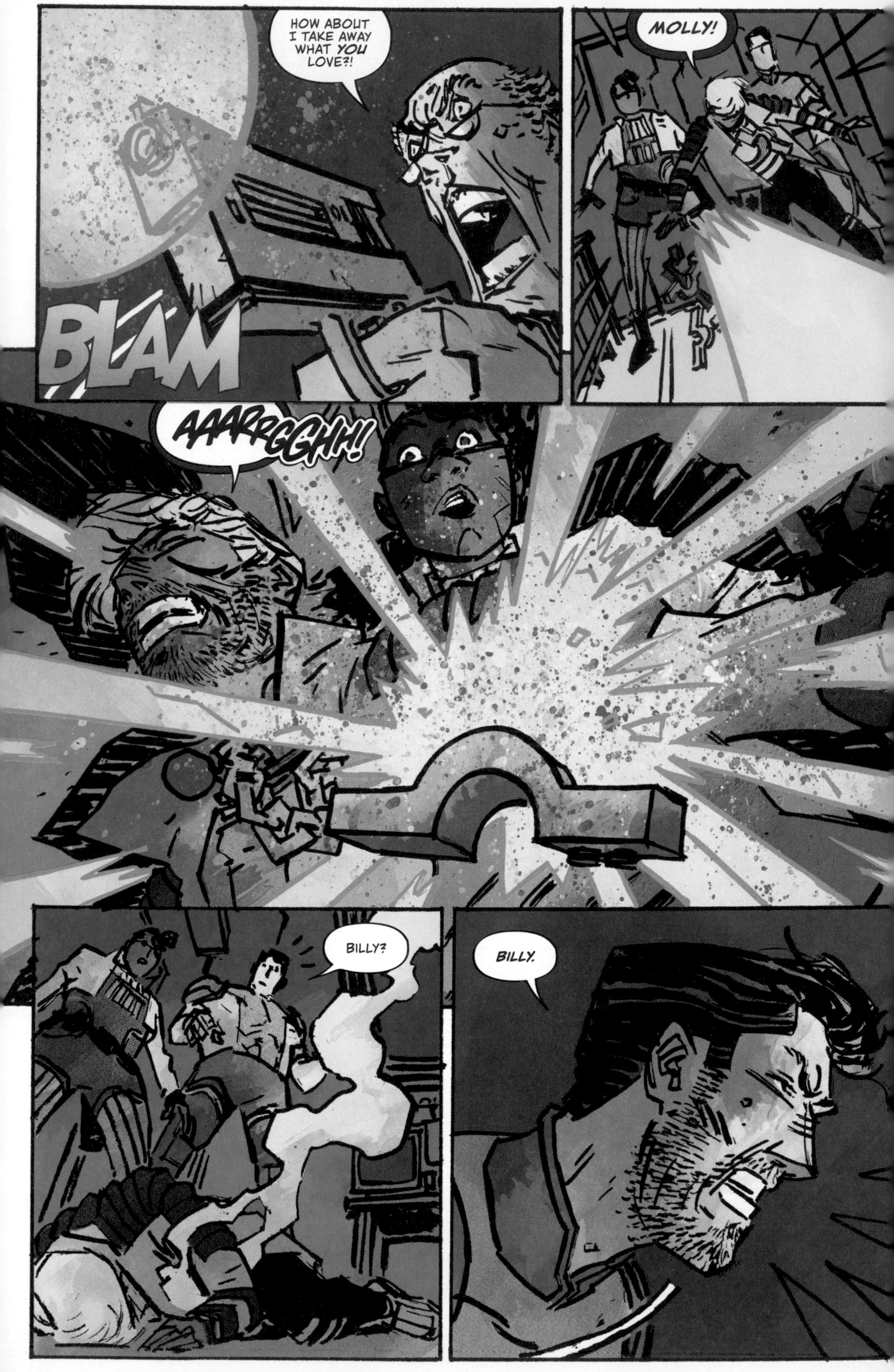
HOW ABOUT I TAKE AWAY WHAT YOU LOVE?!
BLAM
MOLLY!
AAARRGGHH!
BILLY?
BILLY.

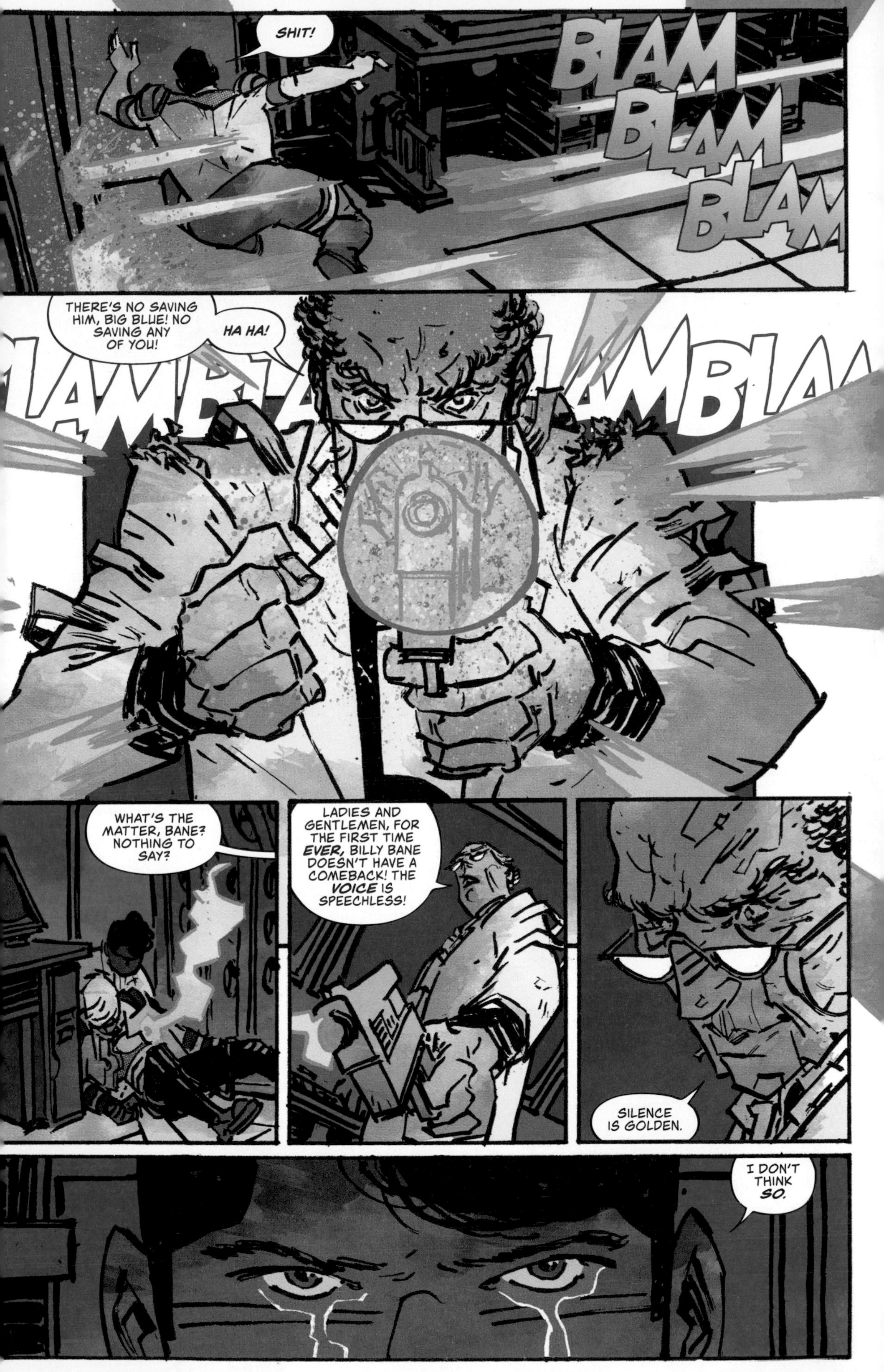
SHIT!
BLAM
BLAM
BLAM
THERE'S NO SAVING HIM, BIG BLUE! NO SAVING ANY OF YOU!
HA HA!
WHAT'S THE MATTER, BANE? NOTHING TO SAY?
LADIES AND GENTLEMEN, FOR THE FIRST TIME EVER, BILLY BANE DOESN'T HAVE A COMEBACK! THE VOICE IS SPEECHLESS!
SILENCE IS GOLDEN.
I DON'T THINK SO.

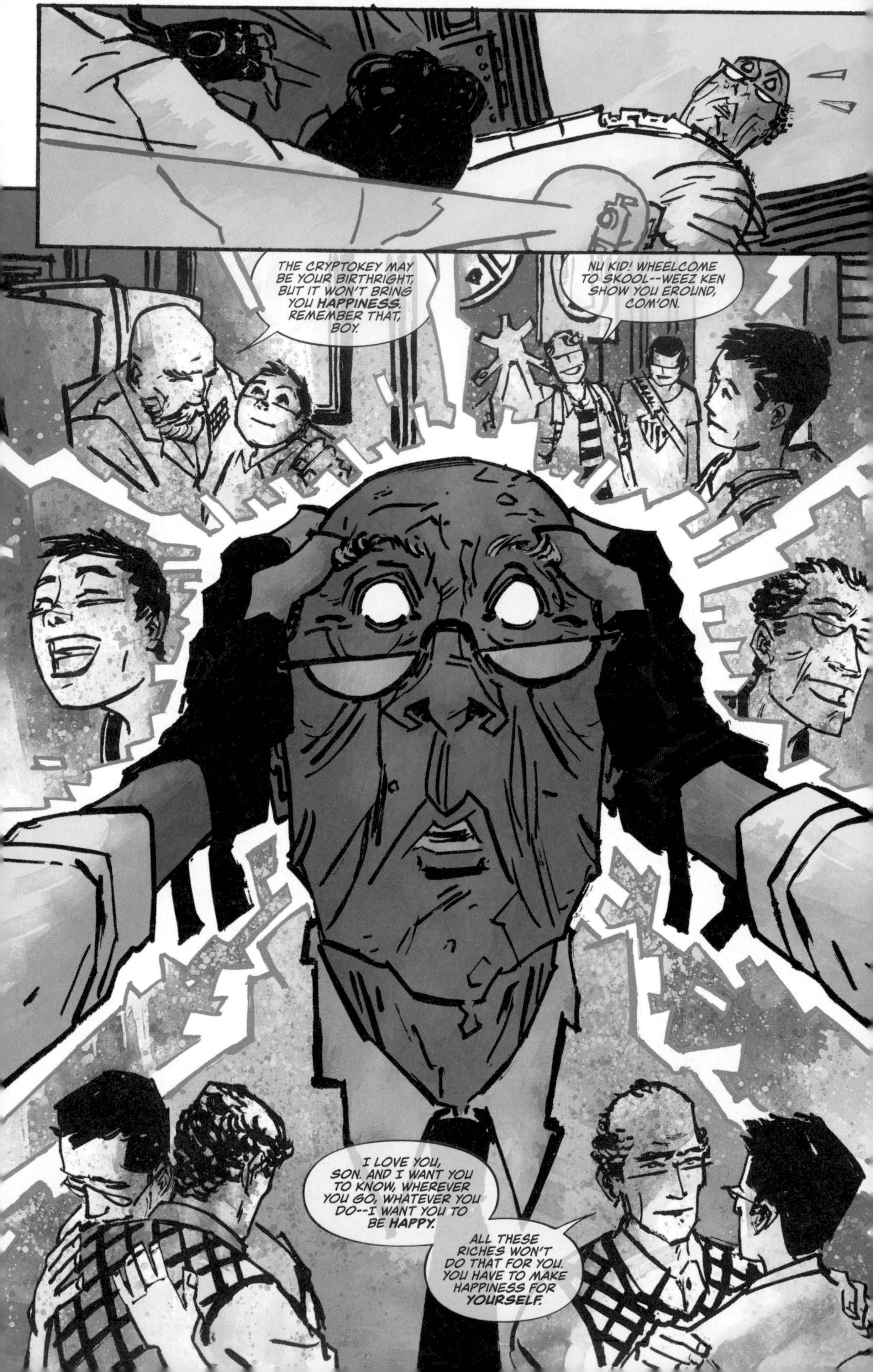
THE CRYPTOKEY MAY BE YOUR BIRTHRIGHT, BUT IT WON'T BRING YOU HAPPINESS. REMEMBER THAT, BOY.
NU KID! WHEELCOME TO SKOOL--WEEZ KEN SHOW YOU EROUND, COM'ON.
I LOVE YOU, SON. AND I WANT YOU TO KNOW, WHEREVER YOU GO, WHATEVER YOU DO--I WANT YOU TO BE HAPPY.
ALL THESE RICHES WON'T DO THAT FOR YOU. YOU HAVE TO MAKE HAPPINESS FOR YOURSELF.

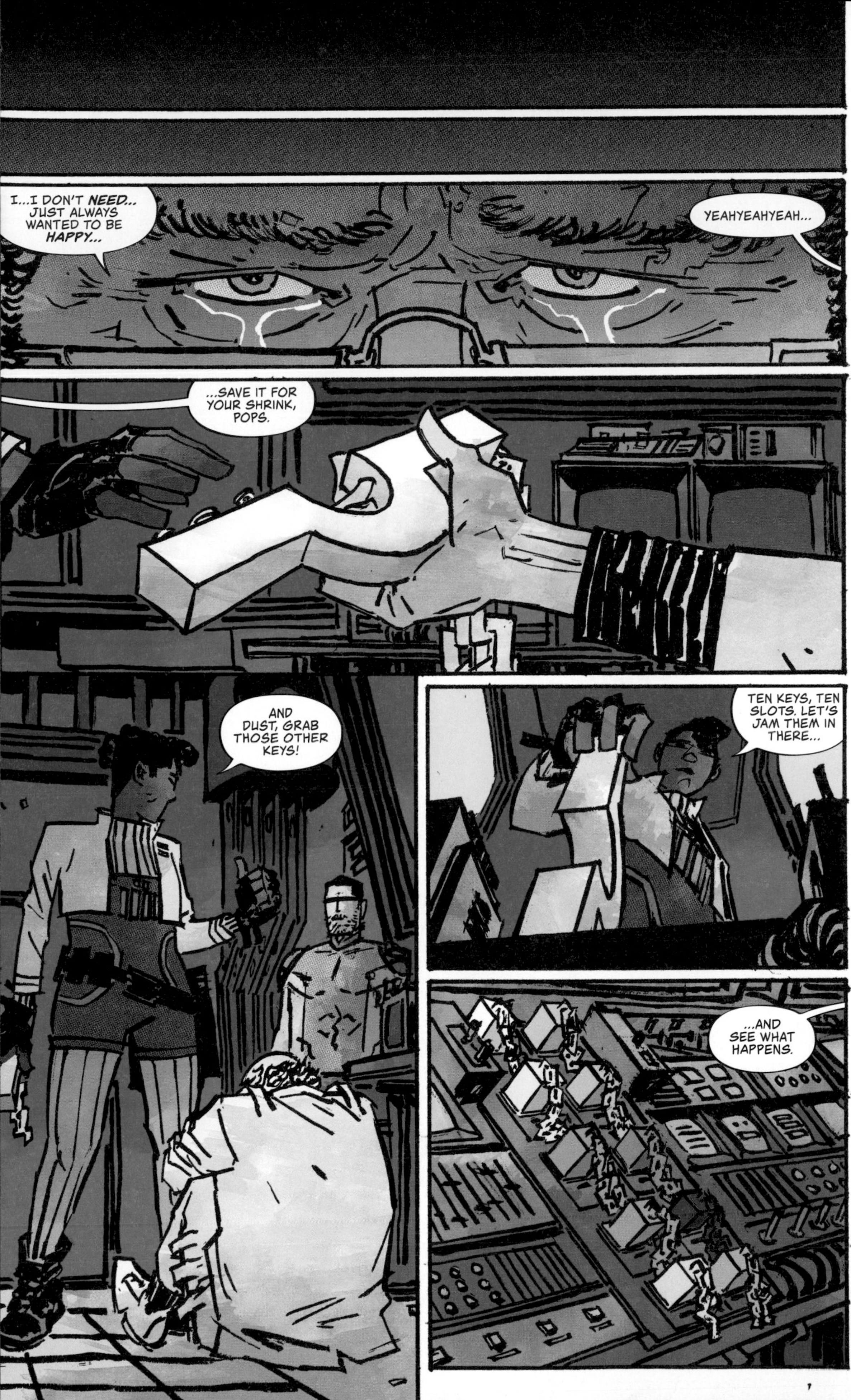
I...I DON'T NEED... JUST ALWAYS WANTED TO BE HAPPY...
YEAHYEAHYEAH...
...SAVE IT FOR YOUR SHRINK, POPS.
AND DUST, GRAB THOSE OTHER KEYS!
TEN KEYS, TEN SLOTS. LET'S JAM THEM IN THERE...
...AND SEE WHAT HAPPENS.

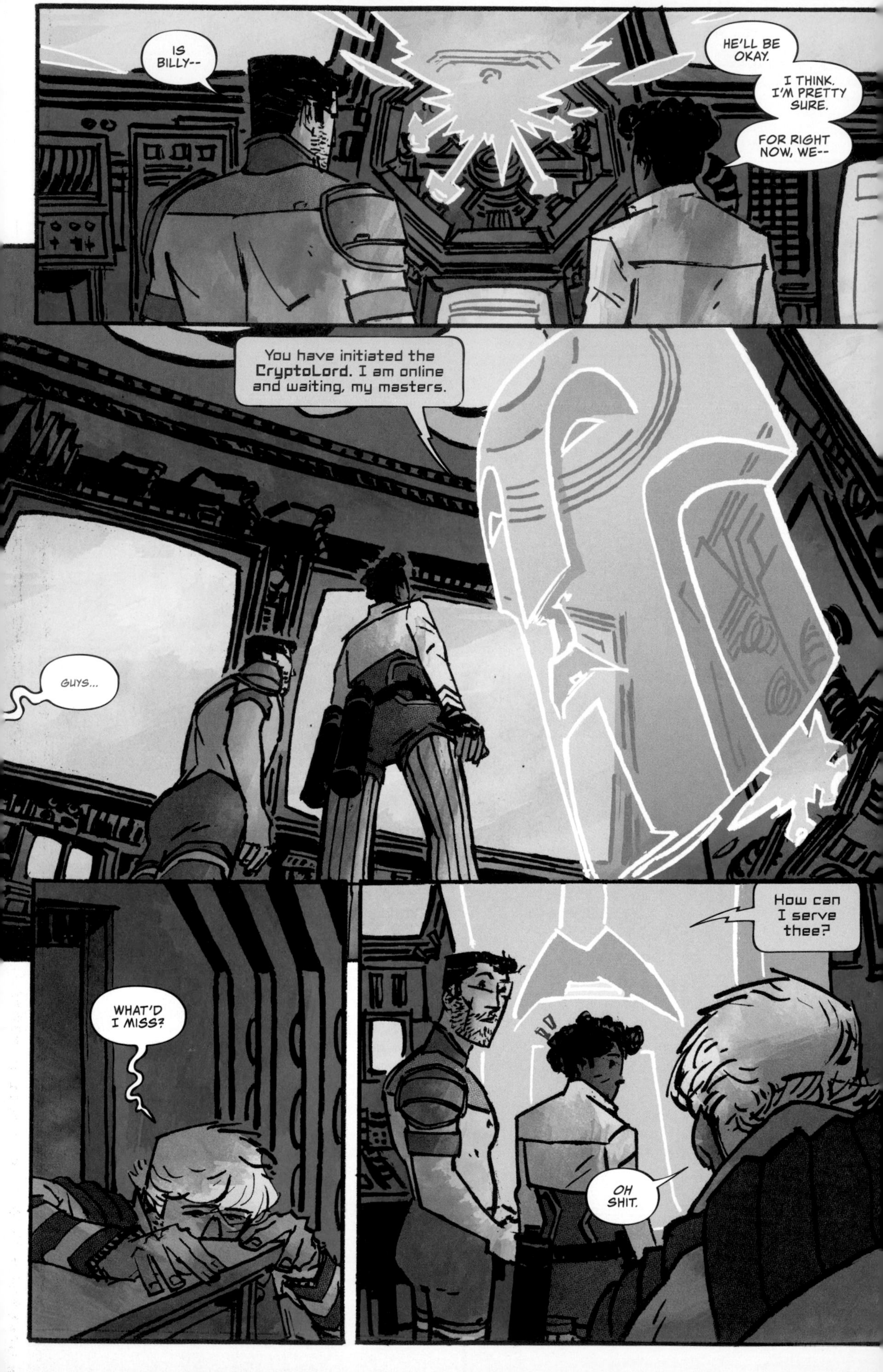
IS BILLY--
HE'LL BE OKAY.
I THINK. I'M PRETTY SURE.
FOR RIGHT NOW, WE--
You have initiated the CryptoLord. I am online and waiting, my masters.
GUYS...
WHAT'D I MISS?
How can I serve thee?
OH SHIT.

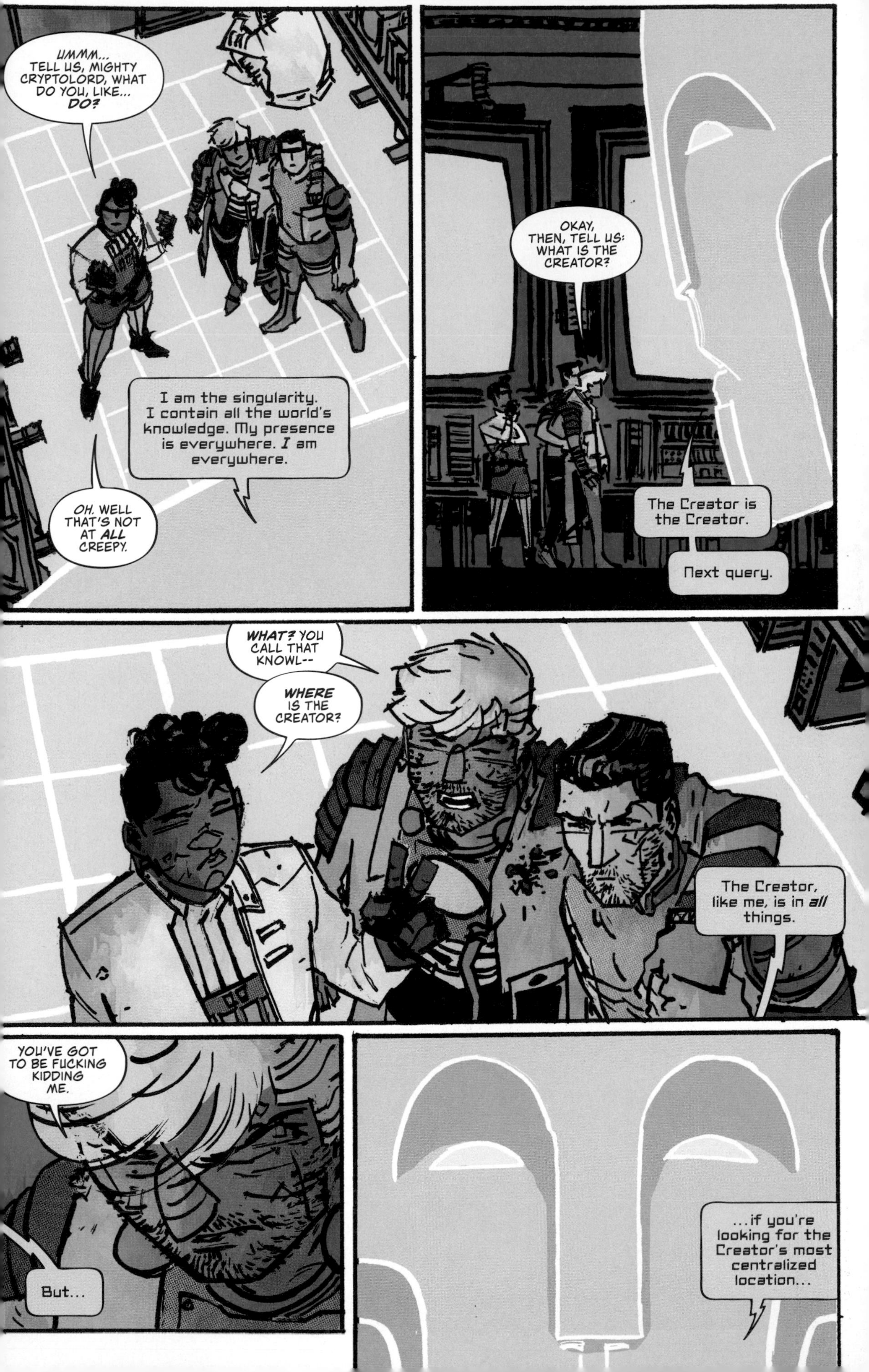
UMMM... TELL US, MIGHTY CRYPTOLORD, WHAT DO YOU, LIKE... DO?
I am the singularity. I contain all the world's knowledge. My presence is everywhere. I am everywhere.
OH. WELL THAT'S NOT AT ALL CREEPY.
OKAY, THEN, TELL US: WHAT IS THE CREATOR?
The Creator is the Creator.
Next query.
WHAT? YOU CALL THAT KNOWL--
WHERE IS THE CREATOR?
The Creator, like me, is in all things.
YOU'VE GOT TO BE FUCKING KIDDING ME.
But...
...if you're looking for the Creator's most centralized location...

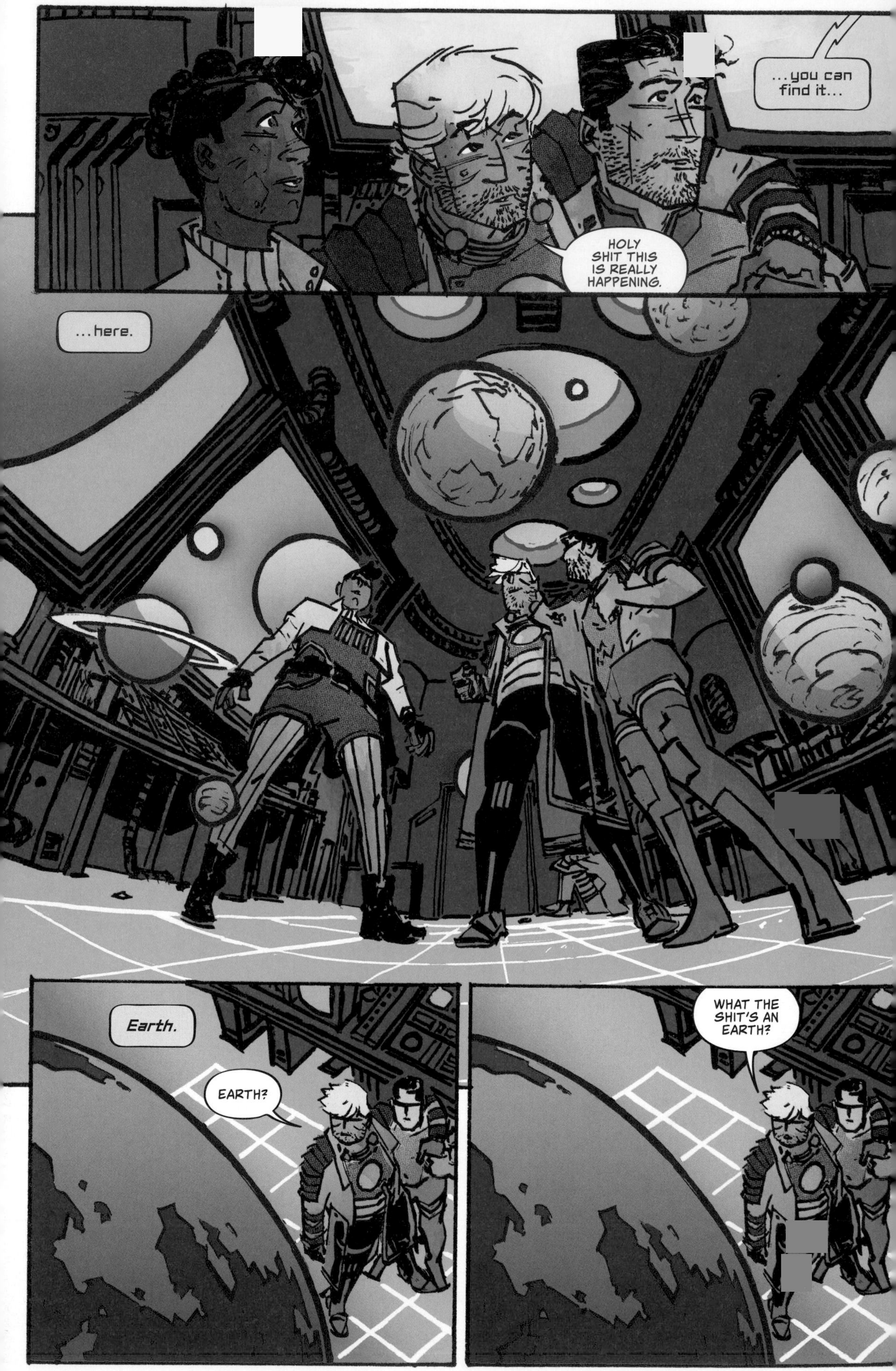
...you can find it...
HOLY SHIT THIS IS REALLY HAPPENING.
...here.
Earth.
EARTH?
WHAT THE SHIT'S AN EARTH?

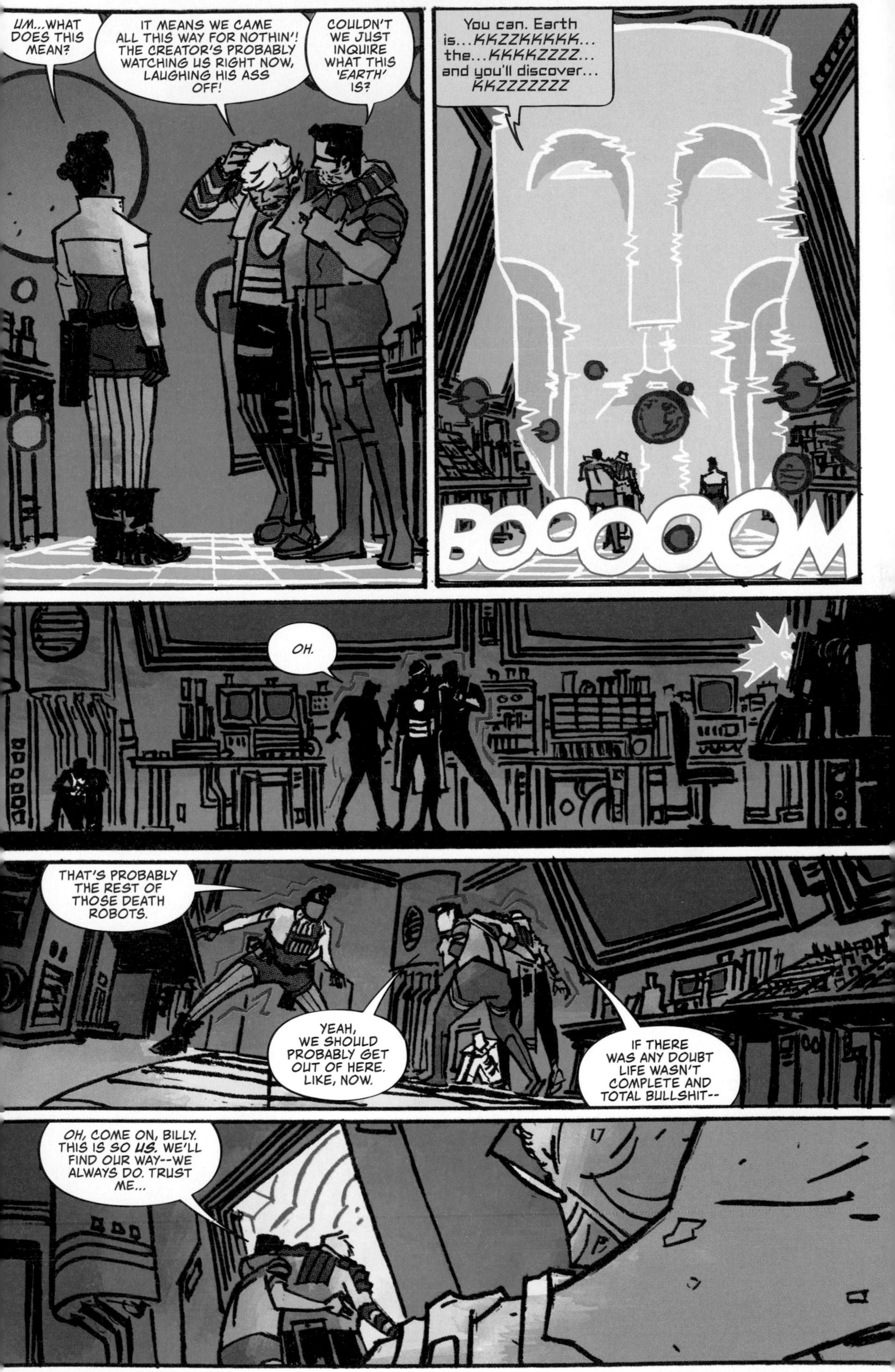
UM...WHAT DOES THIS MEAN?
IT MEANS WE CAME ALL THIS WAY FOR NOTHIN'! THE CREATOR'S PROBABLY WATCHING US RIGHT NOW, LAUGHING HIS ASS OFF!
COULDN'T WE JUST INQUIRE WHAT THIS 'EARTH' IS?
You can. Earth is...KKZZKKKKK... the...KKKKZZZZ... and you'll discover... KKZZZZZZZ
BOOOOOOM
OH.
THAT'S PROBABLY THE REST OF THOSE DEATH ROBOTS.
YEAH, WE SHOULD PROBABLY GET OUT OF HERE. LIKE, NOW.
IF THERE WAS ANY DOUBT LIFE WASN'T COMPLETE AND TOTAL BULLSHIT--
OH, COME ON, BILLY. THIS IS SO US. WE'LL FIND OUR WAY--WE ALWAYS DO. TRUST ME...

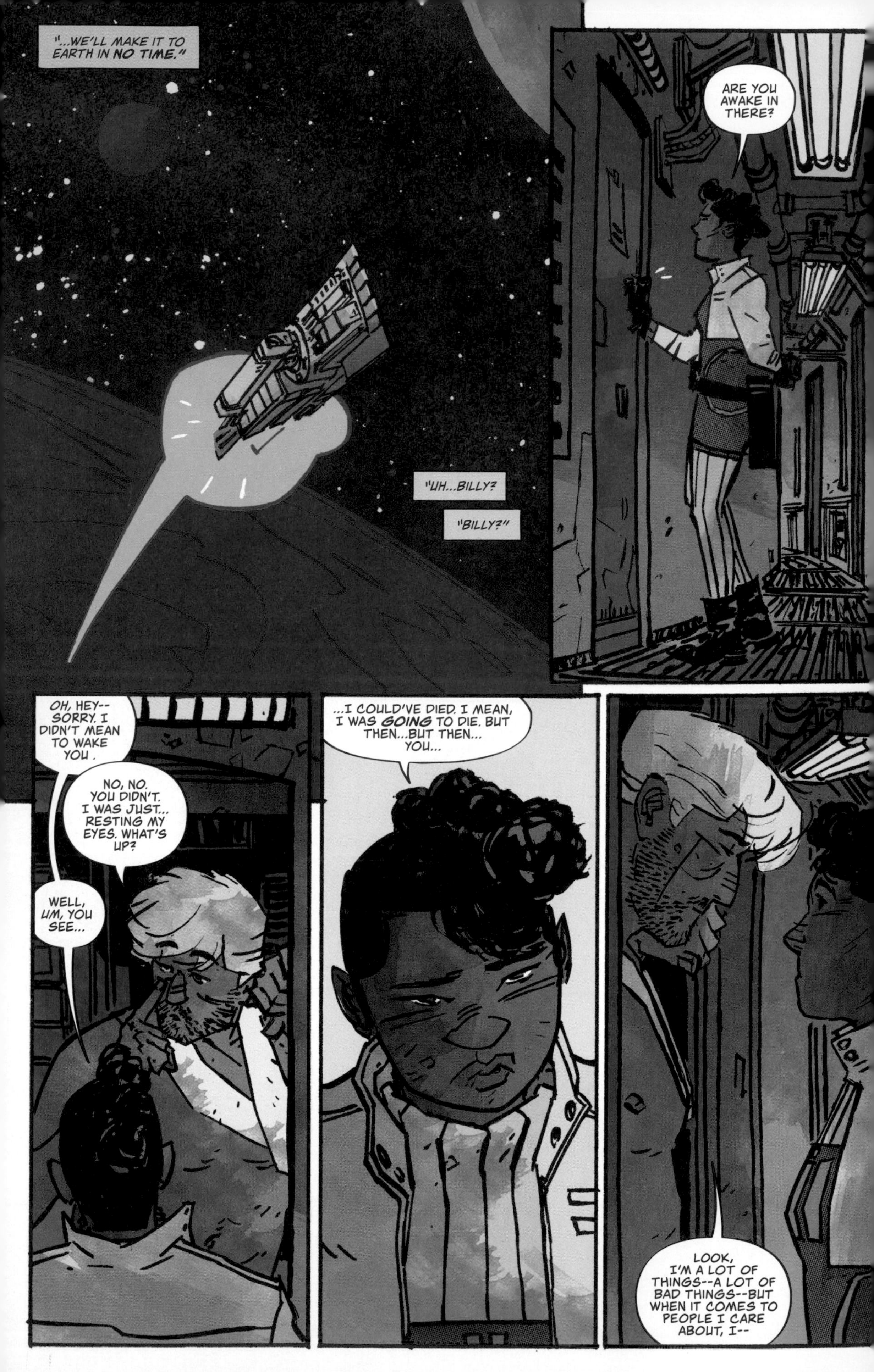
"...WE'LL MAKE IT TO EARTH IN NO TIME."
"UH...BILLY?
"BILLY?"
ARE YOU AWAKE IN THERE?
OH, HEY-- SORRY. I DIDN'T MEAN TO WAKE YOU .
NO, NO. YOU DIDN'T. I WAS JUST... RESTING MY EYES. WHAT'S UP?
WELL, UM, YOU SEE...
...I COULD'VE DIED. I MEAN, I WAS GOING TO DIE. BUT THEN...BUT THEN... YOU...
LOOK, I'M A LOT OF THINGS--A LOT OF BAD THINGS--BUT WHEN IT COMES TO PEOPLE I CARE ABOUT, I--

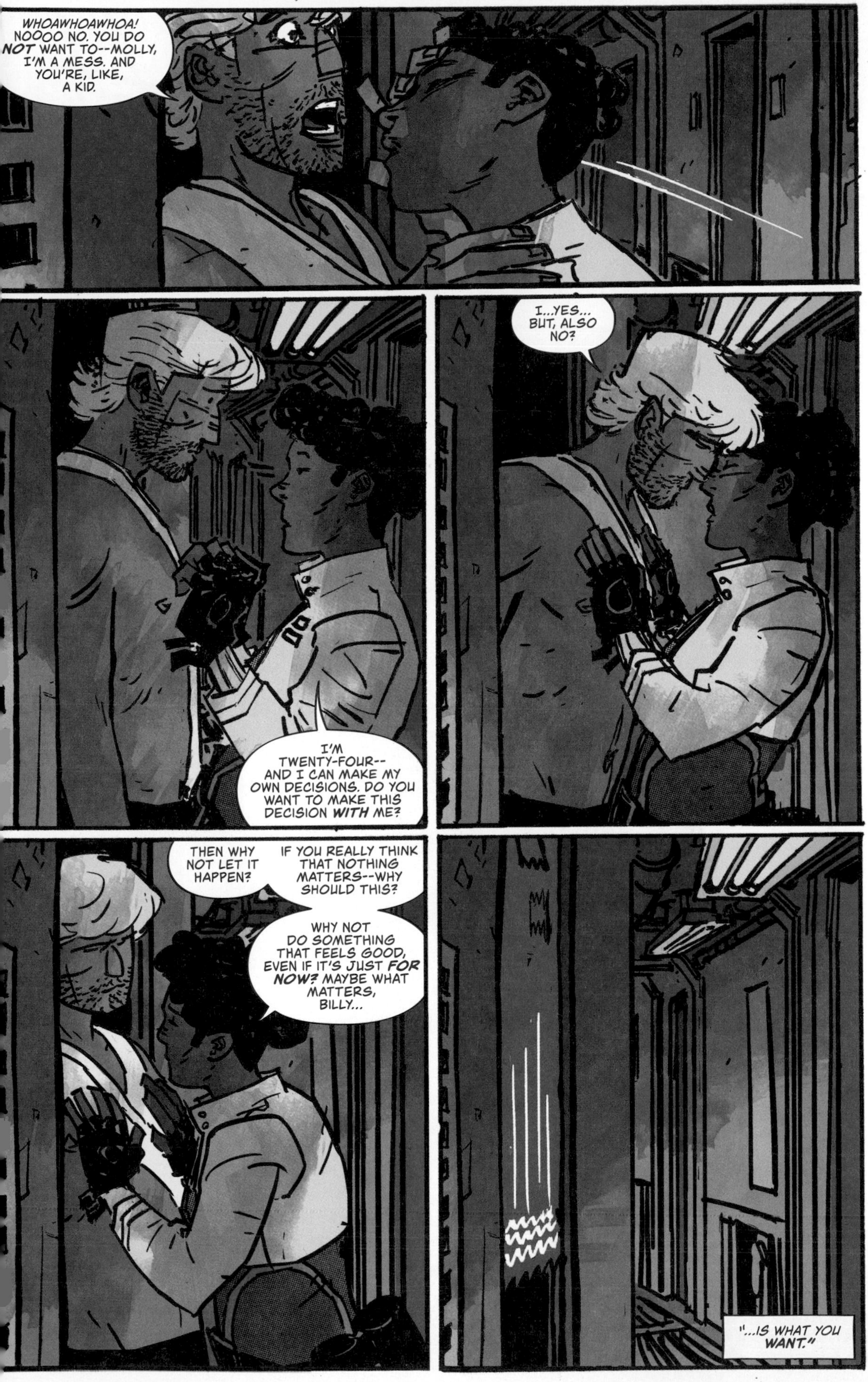
WHOAWHOAWHOA! NOOOO NO. YOU DO NOT WANT TO--MOLLY, I'M A MESS. AND YOU'RE, LIKE, A KID.
I'M TWENTY-FOUR--AND I CAN MAKE MY OWN DECISIONS. DO YOU WANT TO MAKE THIS DECISION WITH ME?
I...YES... BUT, ALSO NO?
THEN WHY NOT LET IT HAPPEN?
IF YOU REALLY THINK THAT NOTHING MATTERS--WHY SHOULD THIS?
WHY NOT DO SOMETHING THAT FEELS GOOD, EVEN IF IT'S JUST FOR NOW? MAYBE WHAT MATTERS, BILLY...
"...IS WHAT YOU WANT."

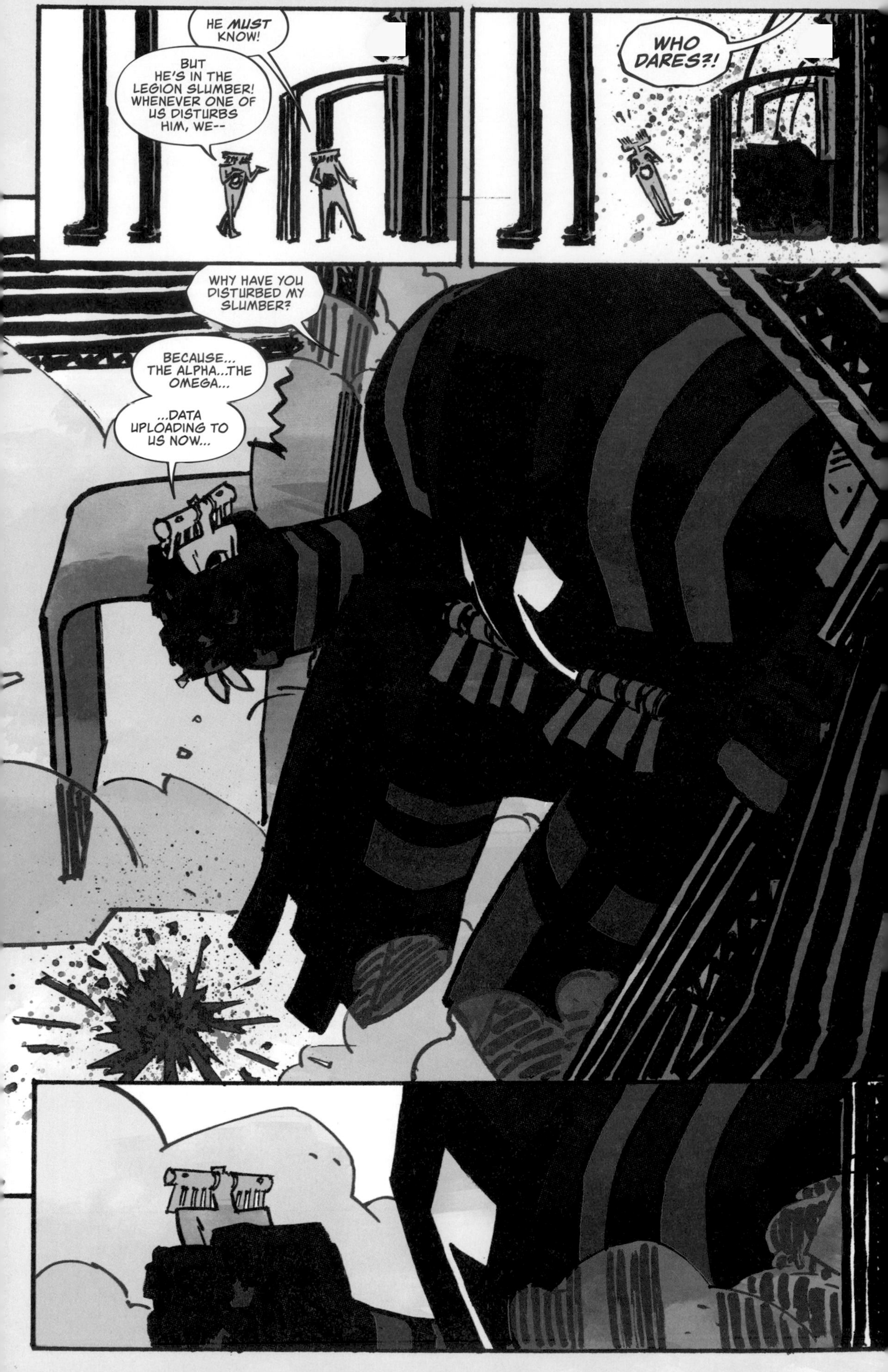
HE MUST KNOW!
BUT HE'S IN THE LEGION SLUMBER! WHENEVER ONE OF US DISTURBS HIM, WE--
WHO DARES?!
WHY HAVE YOU DISTURBED MY SLUMBER?
BECAUSE... THE ALPHA...THE OMEGA...
...DATA UPLOADING TO US NOW...

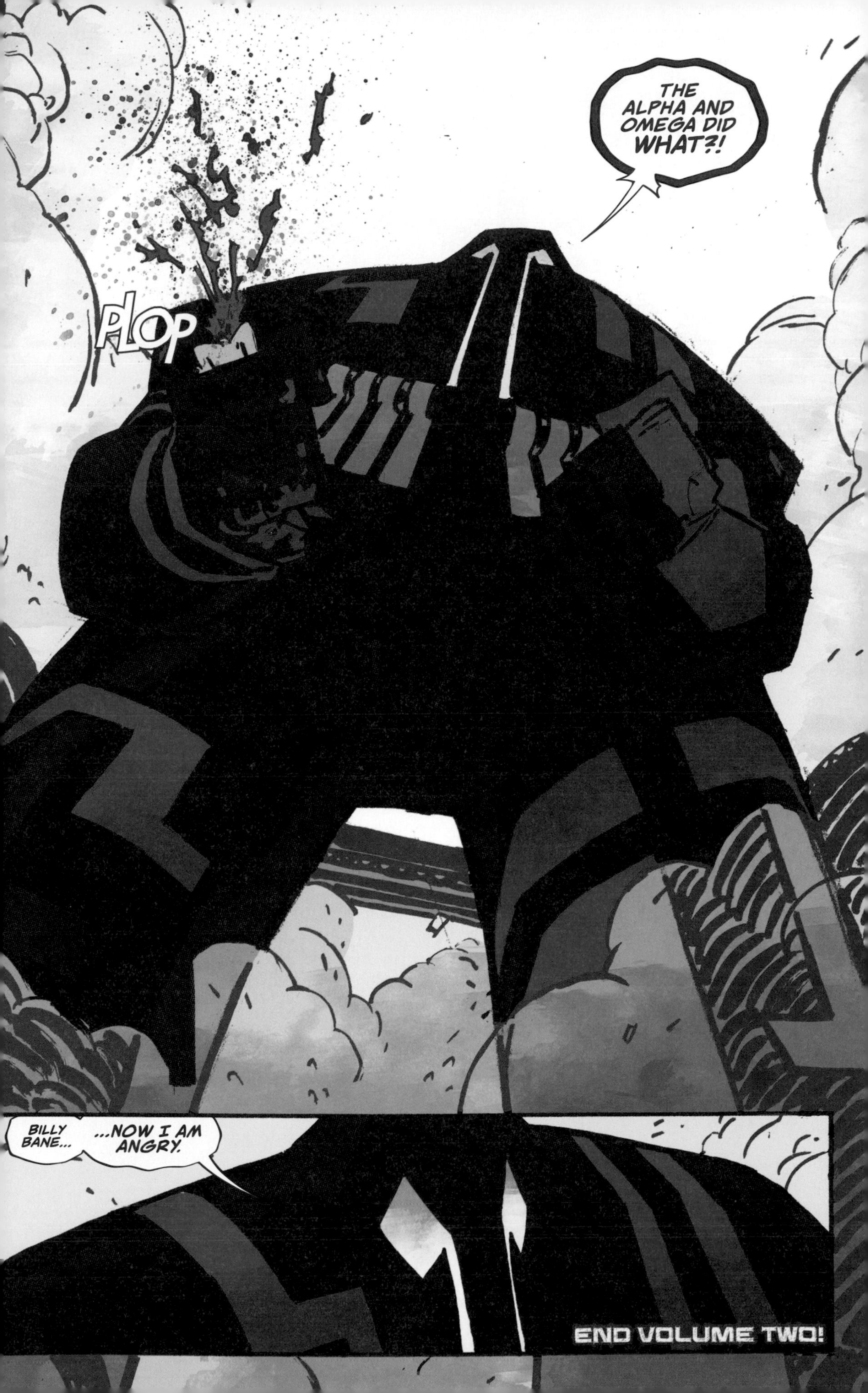
THE ALPHA AND OMEGA DID WHAT?!
PLOP
BILLY BANE...
...NOW I AM ANGRY.
END VOLUME TWO!

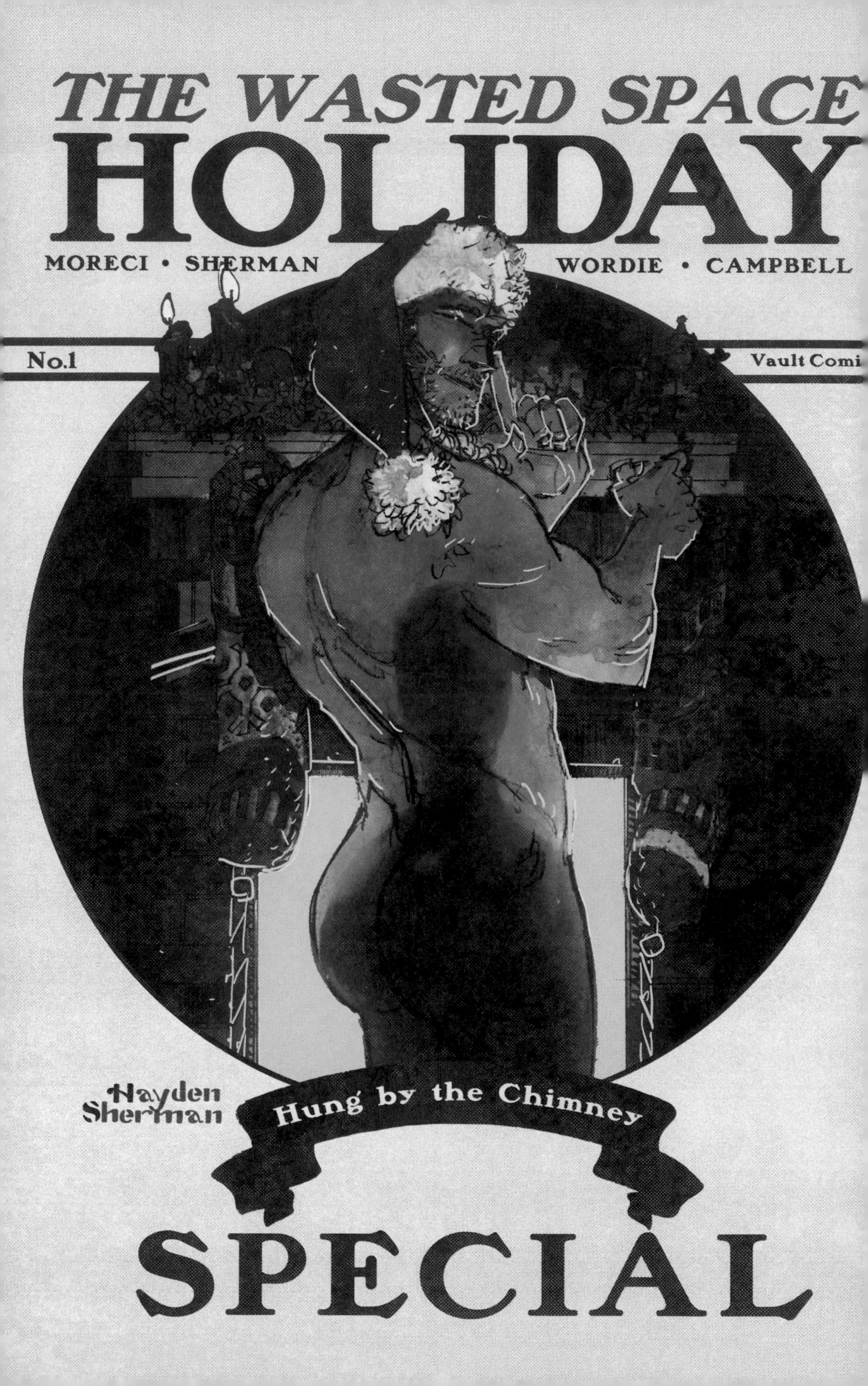
THE WASTED SPACE
HOLIDAY
MORECI • SHERMAN
WORDIE • CAMPBELL
No.1
Vault Comi
Hayden Sherman
Hung by the Chimney
SPECIAL

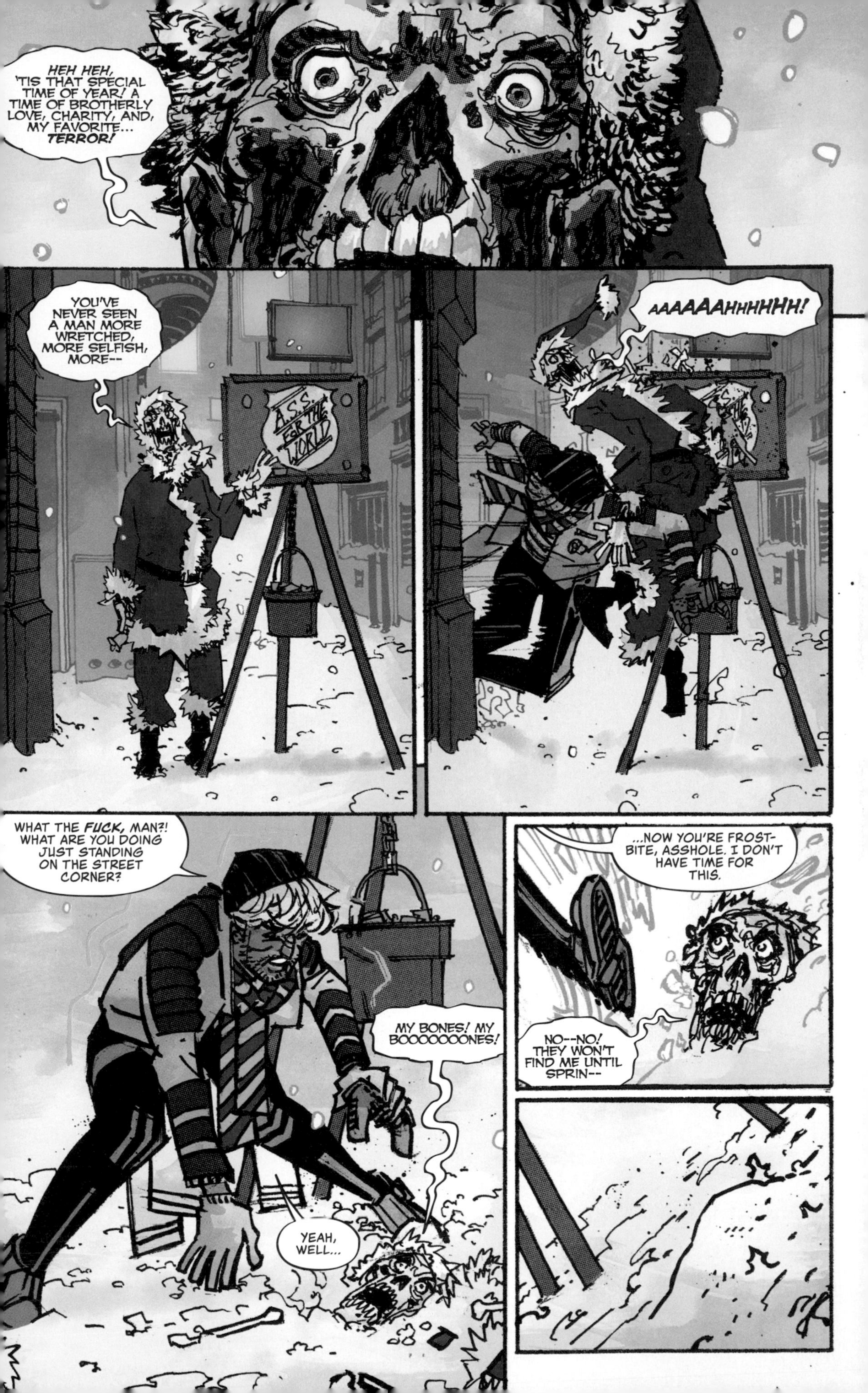
HEH HEH, 'TIS THAT SPECIAL TIME OF YEAR! A TIME OF BROTHERLY LOVE, CHARITY, AND, MY FAVORITE... TERROR!
YOU'VE NEVER SEEN A MAN MORE WRETCHED, MORE SELFISH, MORE--
A.S.S. FOR THE WORLD
AAAAAAHHHHHH!
WHAT THE FUCK, MAN?! WHAT ARE YOU DOING JUST STANDING ON THE STREET CORNER?
MY BONES! MY BOOOOOOOONES!
YEAH, WELL...
...NOW YOU'RE FROST-BITE, ASSHOLE. I DON'T HAVE TIME FOR THIS.
NO--NO! THEY WON'T FIND ME UNTIL SPRIN--

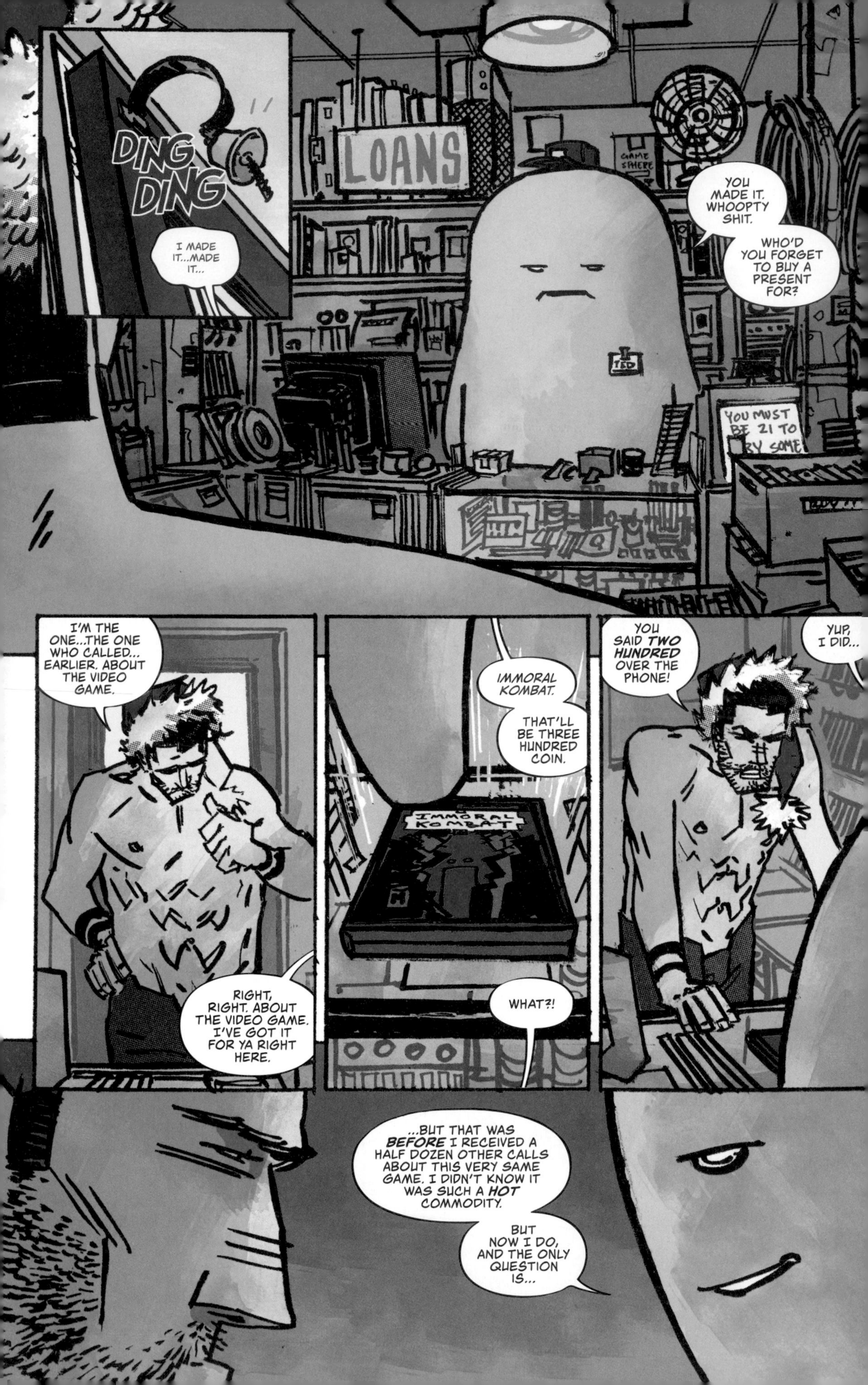
DING DING
I MADE IT...MADE IT...
LOANS
GAME SPHERE
YOU MADE IT. WHOOPTY SHIT.
WHO'D YOU FORGET TO BUY A PRESENT FOR?
TED
I'M THE ONE...THE ONE WHO CALLED... EARLIER. ABOUT THE VIDEO GAME.
RIGHT, RIGHT. ABOUT THE VIDEO GAME. I'VE GOT IT FOR YA RIGHT HERE.
IMMORAL KOMBAT.
THAT'LL BE THREE HUNDRED COIN.
IMMORAL KOMBAT
WHAT?!
YOU SAID **TWO HUNDRED** OVER THE PHONE!
YUP, I DID...
...BUT THAT WAS **BEFORE** I RECEIVED A HALF DOZEN OTHER CALLS ABOUT THIS VERY SAME GAME. I DIDN'T KNOW IT WAS SUCH A **HOT** COMMODITY.
BUT NOW I DO, AND THE ONLY QUESTION IS...

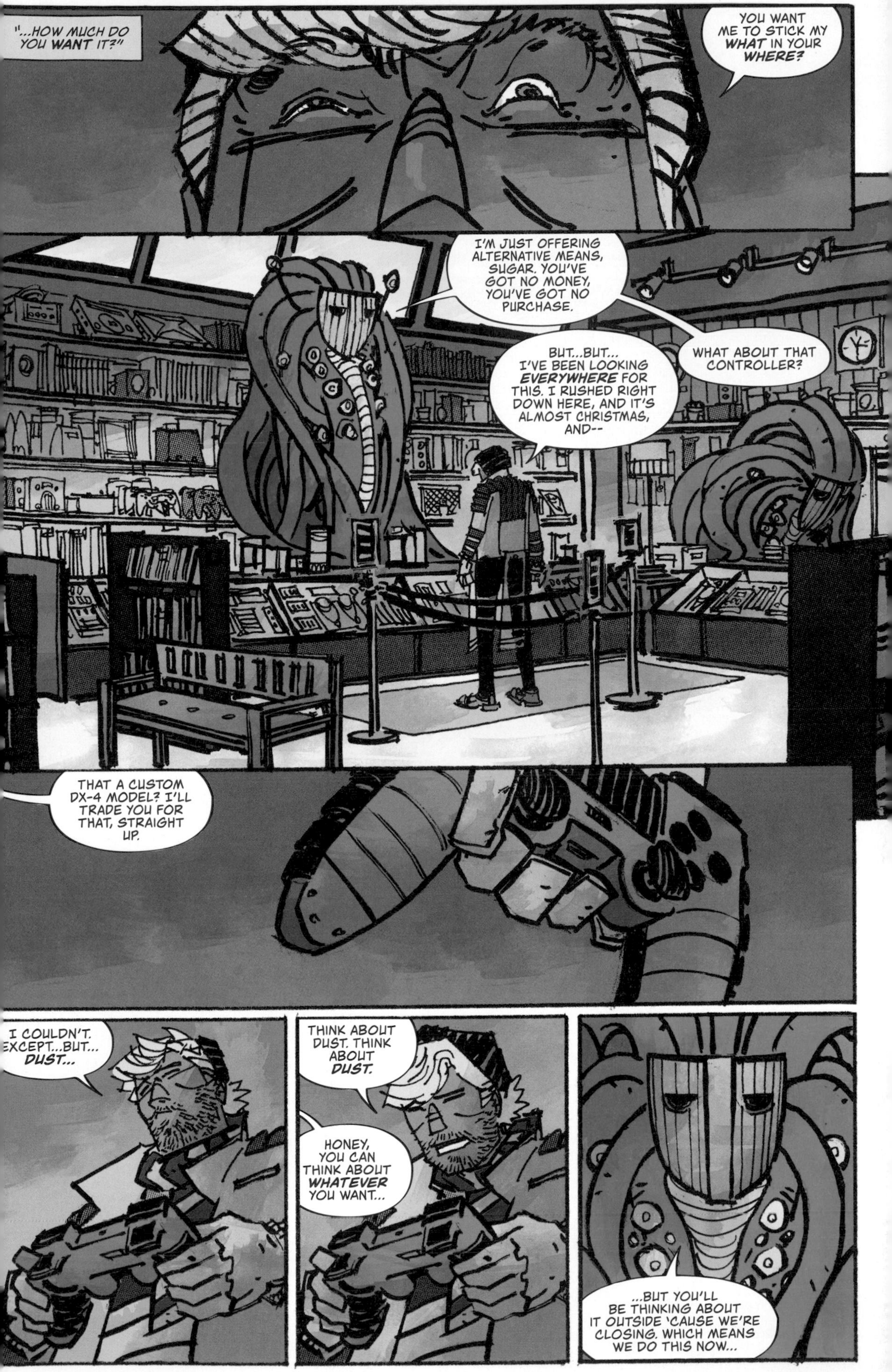
"...HOW MUCH DO YOU *WANT* IT?"
YOU WANT ME TO STICK MY *WHAT* IN YOUR *WHERE?*
I'M JUST OFFERING ALTERNATIVE MEANS, SUGAR. YOU'VE GOT NO MONEY, YOU'VE GOT NO PURCHASE.
BUT...BUT... I'VE BEEN LOOKING *EVERYWHERE* FOR THIS. I RUSHED RIGHT DOWN HERE, AND IT'S ALMOST CHRISTMAS, AND--
WHAT ABOUT THAT CONTROLLER?
THAT A CUSTOM DX-4 MODEL? I'LL TRADE YOU FOR THAT, STRAIGHT UP.
I COULDN'T. EXCEPT...BUT... *DUST...*
THINK ABOUT DUST. THINK ABOUT *DUST.*
HONEY, YOU CAN THINK ABOUT *WHATEVER* YOU WANT...
...BUT YOU'LL BE THINKING ABOUT IT OUTSIDE 'CAUSE WE'RE CLOSING. WHICH MEANS WE DO THIS NOW...

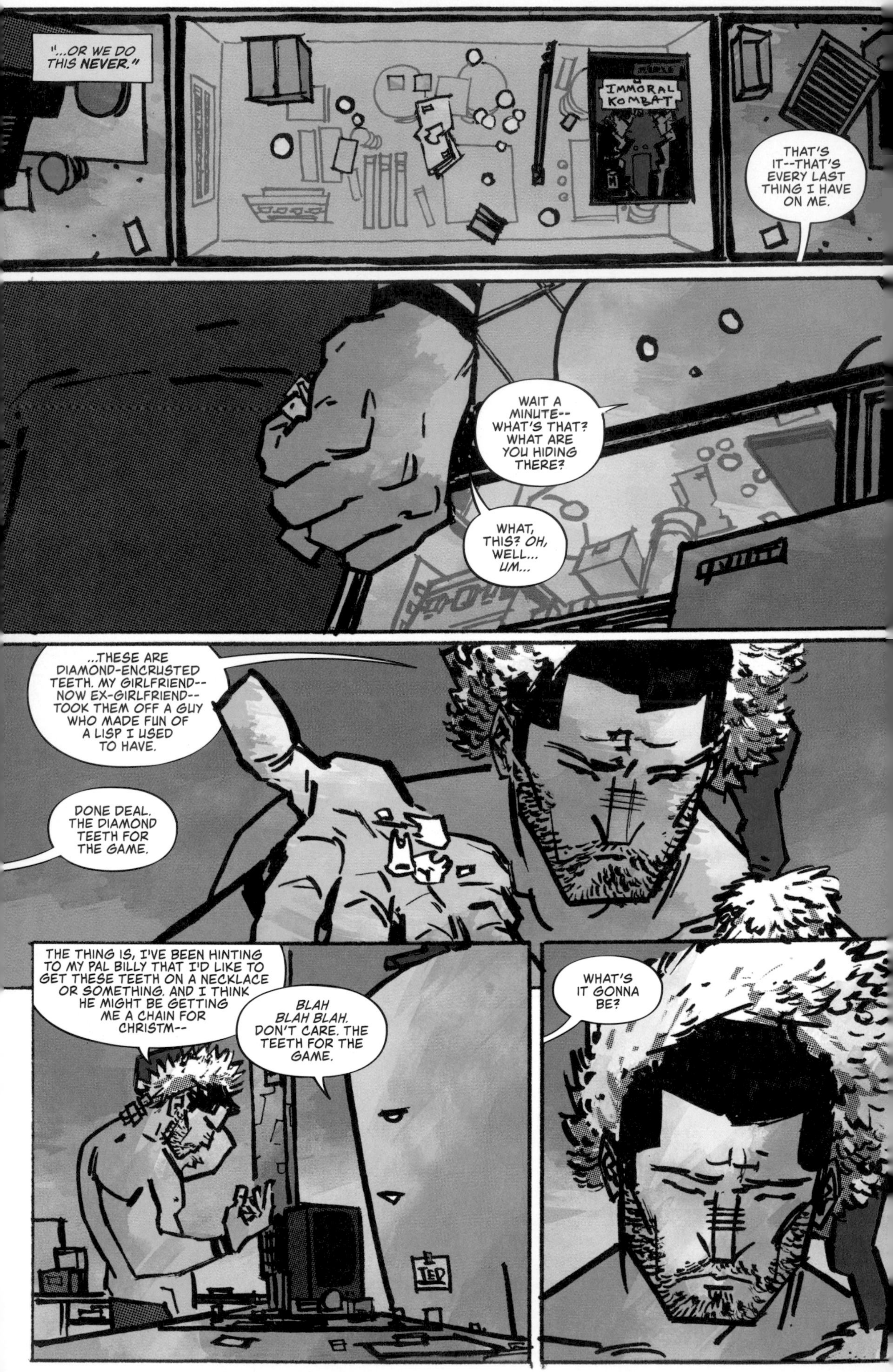
"...OR WE DO THIS NEVER."
IMMORAL KOMBAT
THAT'S IT--THAT'S EVERY LAST THING I HAVE ON ME.
WAIT A MINUTE--WHAT'S THAT? WHAT ARE YOU HIDING THERE?
WHAT, THIS? OH, WELL... UM...
...THESE ARE DIAMOND-ENCRUSTED TEETH. MY GIRLFRIEND--NOW EX-GIRLFRIEND--TOOK THEM OFF A GUY WHO MADE FUN OF A LISP I USED TO HAVE.
DONE DEAL. THE DIAMOND TEETH FOR THE GAME.
THE THING IS, I'VE BEEN HINTING TO MY PAL BILLY THAT I'D LIKE TO GET THESE TEETH ON A NECKLACE OR SOMETHING. AND I THINK HE MIGHT BE GETTING ME A CHAIN FOR CHRISTM--
BLAH BLAH BLAH. DON'T CARE. THE TEETH FOR THE GAME.
WHAT'S IT GONNA BE?

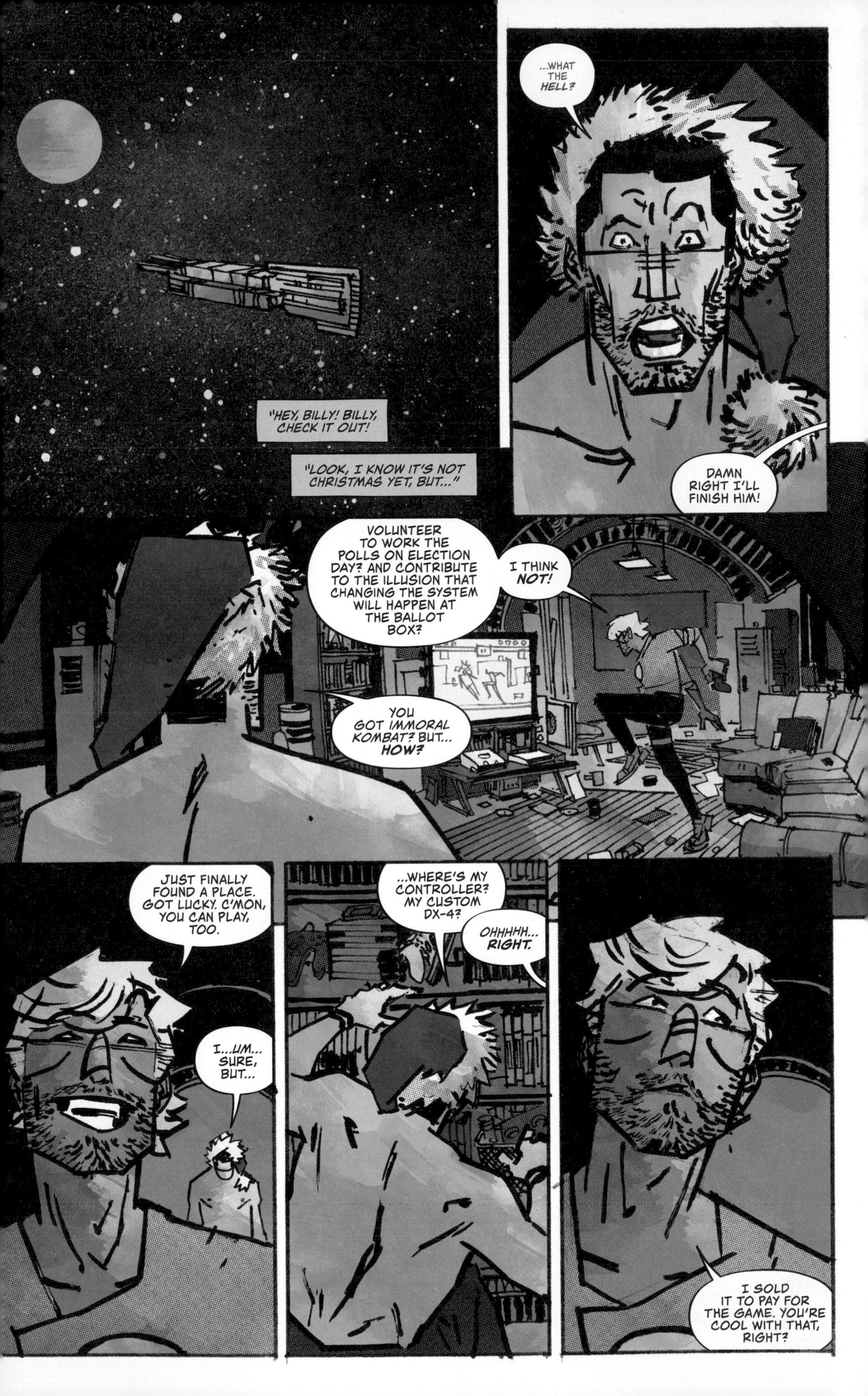

"HEY, BILLY! BILLY, CHECK IT OUT!
"LOOK, I KNOW IT'S NOT CHRISTMAS YET, BUT..."
...WHAT THE HELL?
DAMN RIGHT I'LL FINISH HIM!
VOLUNTEER TO WORK THE POLLS ON ELECTION DAY? AND CONTRIBUTE TO THE ILLUSION THAT CHANGING THE SYSTEM WILL HAPPEN AT THE BALLOT BOX?
I THINK NOT!
YOU GOT IMMORAL KOMBAT? BUT... HOW?
JUST FINALLY FOUND A PLACE. GOT LUCKY. C'MON, YOU CAN PLAY, TOO.
I...UM... SURE, BUT...
...WHERE'S MY CONTROLLER? MY CUSTOM DX-4?
OHHHHH... RIGHT.
I SOLD IT TO PAY FOR THE GAME. YOU'RE COOL WITH THAT, RIGHT?

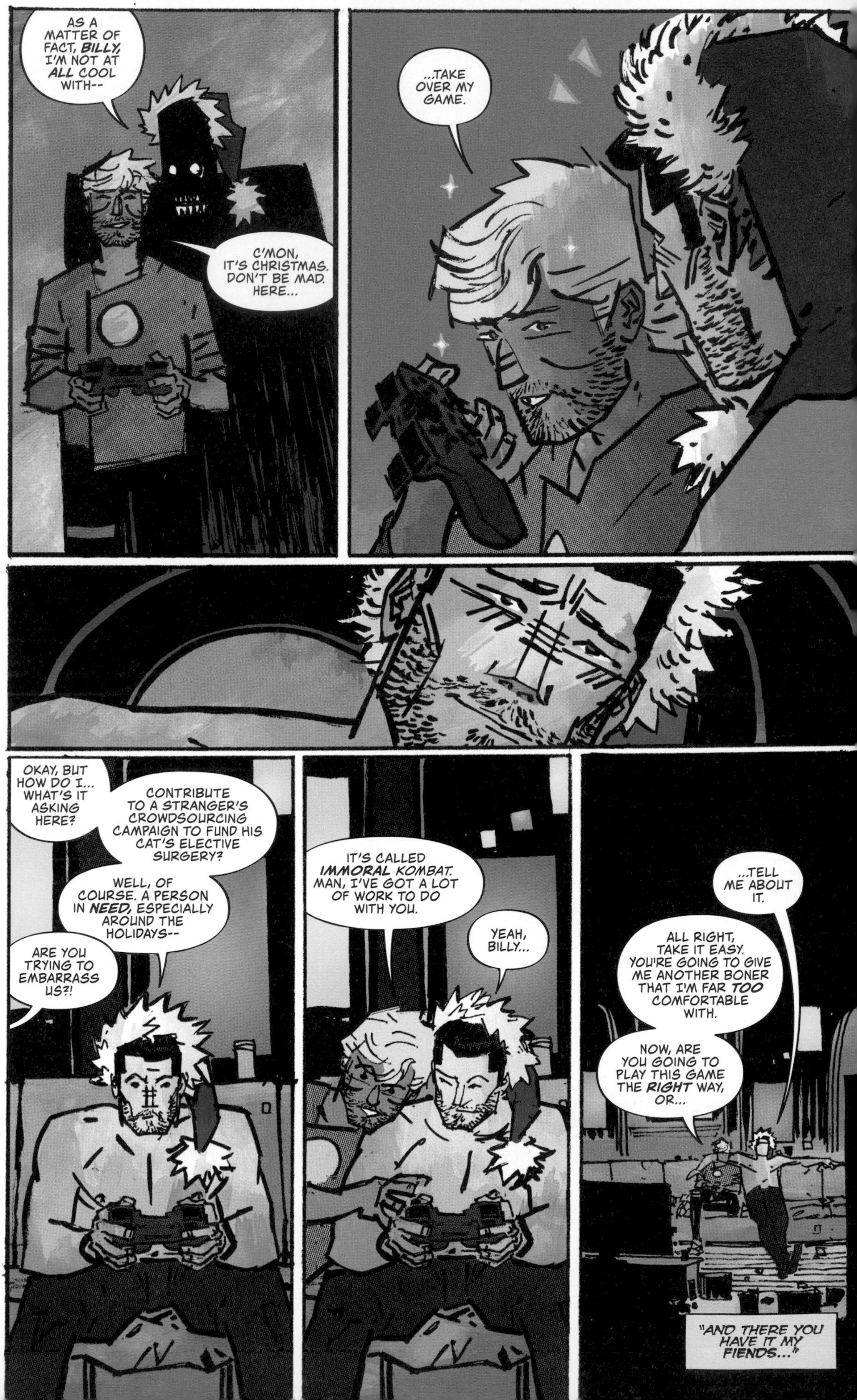
AS A MATTER OF FACT, BILLY, I'M NOT AT ALL COOL WITH--
C'MON, IT'S CHRISTMAS. DON'T BE MAD. HERE...
...TAKE OVER MY GAME.
OKAY, BUT HOW DO I... WHAT'S IT ASKING HERE?
CONTRIBUTE TO A STRANGER'S CROWDSOURCING CAMPAIGN TO FUND HIS CAT'S ELECTIVE SURGERY?
WELL, OF COURSE. A PERSON IN NEED, ESPECIALLY AROUND THE HOLIDAYS--
ARE YOU TRYING TO EMBARRASS US?!
IT'S CALLED IMMORAL KOMBAT. MAN, I'VE GOT A LOT OF WORK TO DO WITH YOU.
YEAH, BILLY...
...TELL ME ABOUT IT.
ALL RIGHT, TAKE IT EASY. YOU'RE GOING TO GIVE ME ANOTHER BONER THAT I'M FAR TOO COMFORTABLE WITH.
NOW, ARE YOU GOING TO PLAY THIS GAME THE RIGHT WAY, OR...
"AND THERE YOU HAVE IT MY FIENDS..."

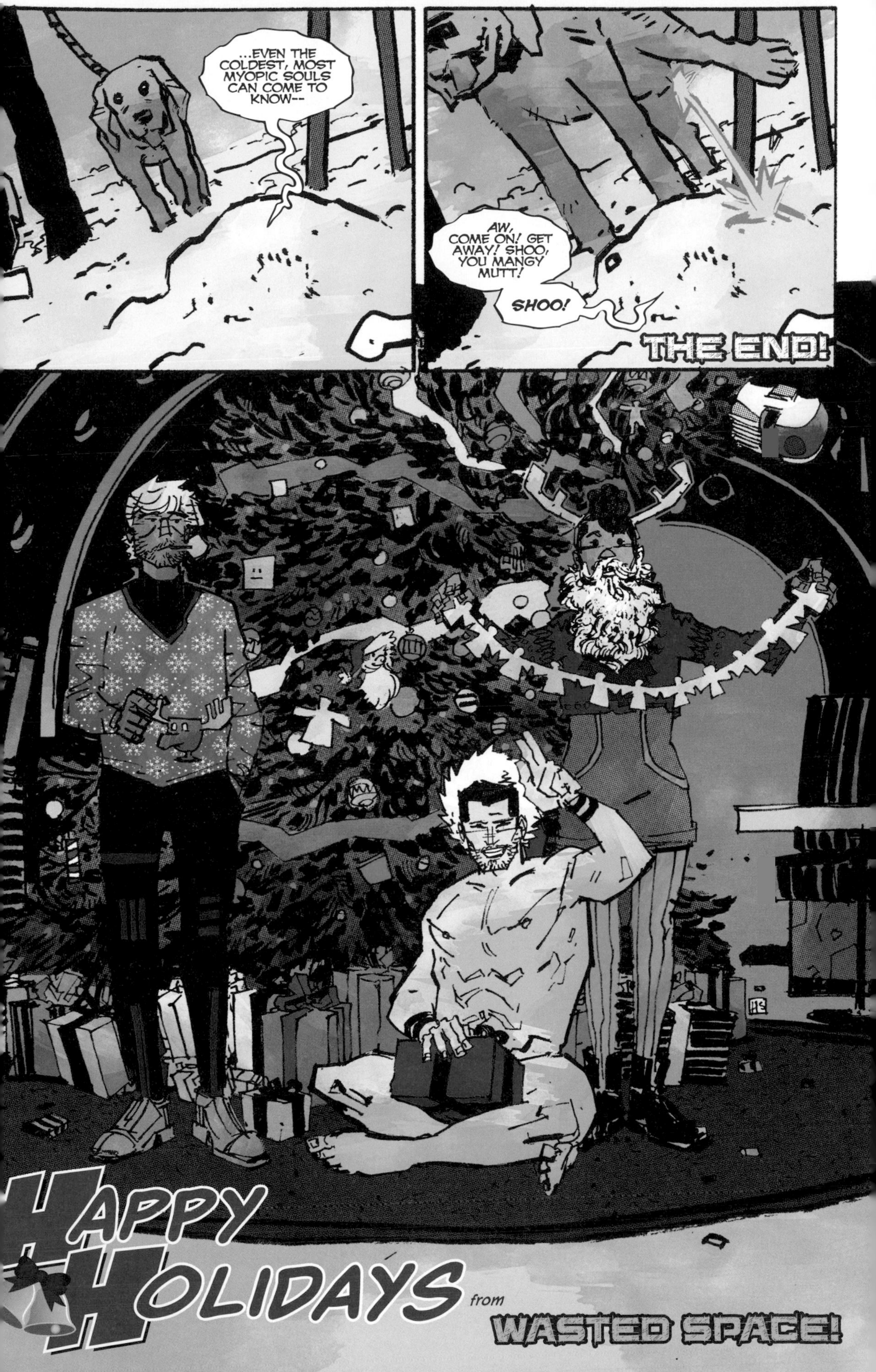
...EVEN THE COLDEST, MOST MYOPIC SOULS CAN COME TO KNOW--
AW, COME ON! GET AWAY! SHOO, YOU MANGY MUTT!
SHOO!
THE END!
HAPPY HOLIDAYS from
WASTED SPACE!

COVER ISSUE 6//HAYDEN SHERMAN

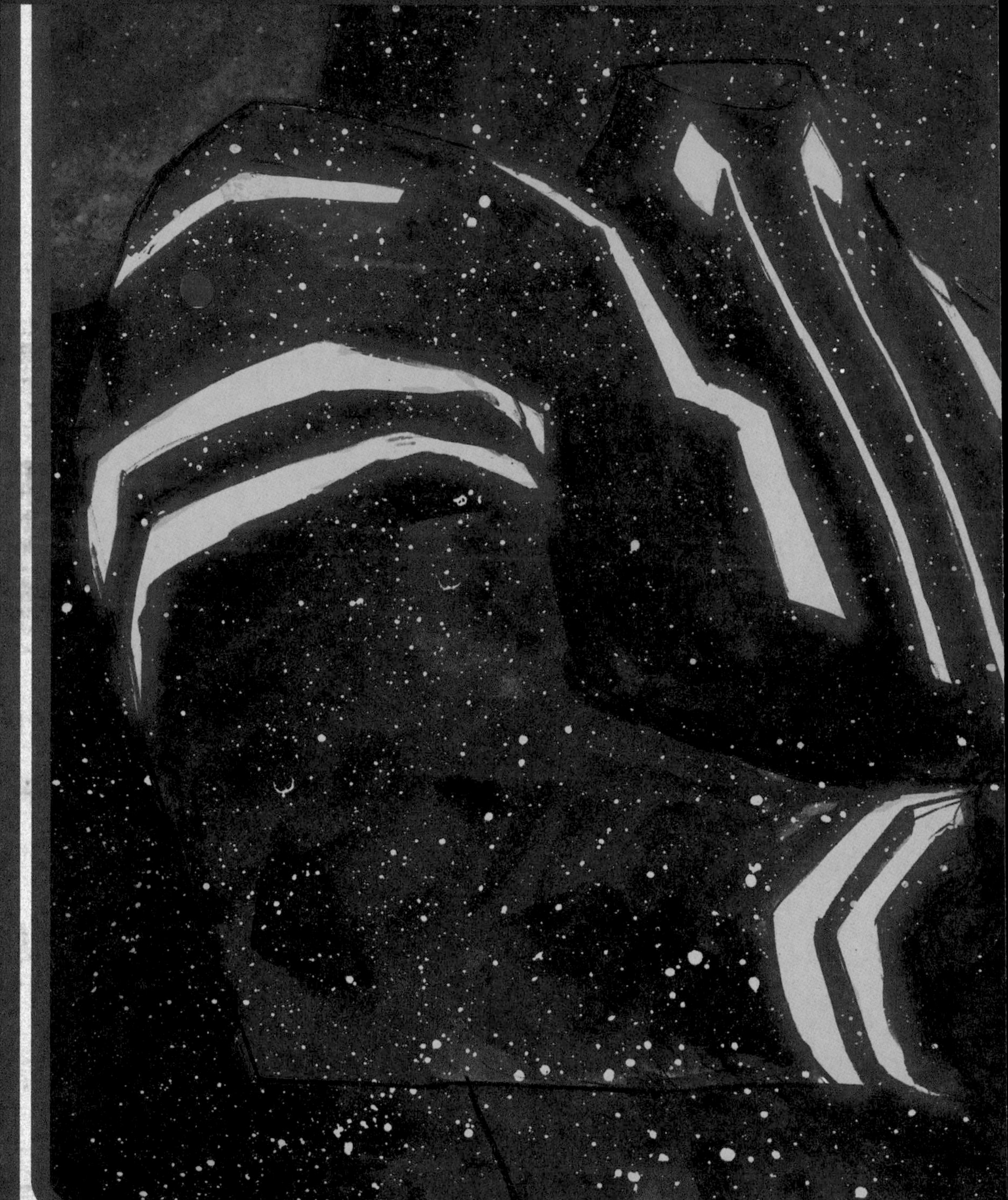

GET WASTED

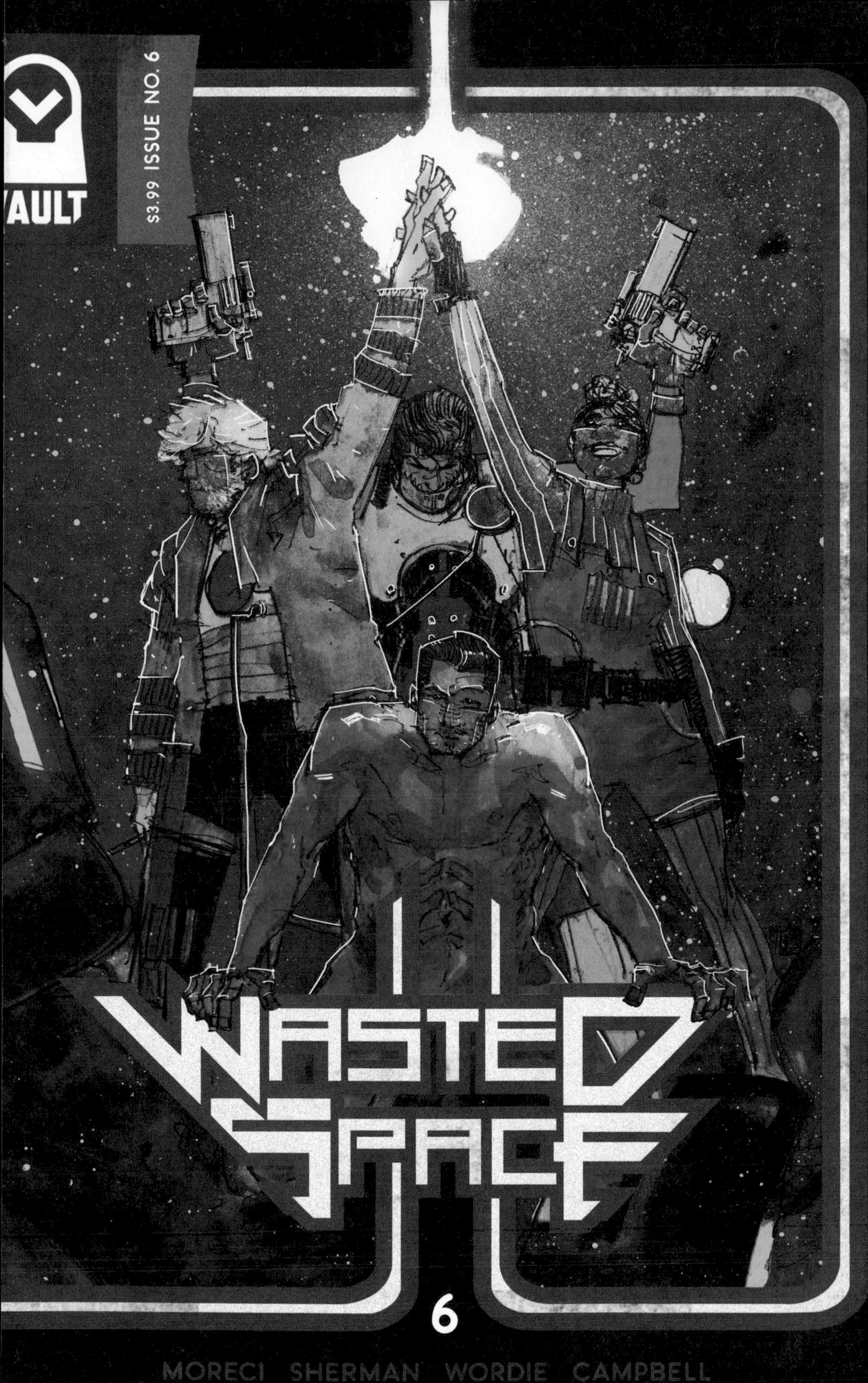
VAULT
$3.99 ISSUE NO. 6
WASTED SPACE
6
MORECI SHERMAN WORDIE CAMPBELL

COVER ISSUE 7//HAYDEN SHERMAN

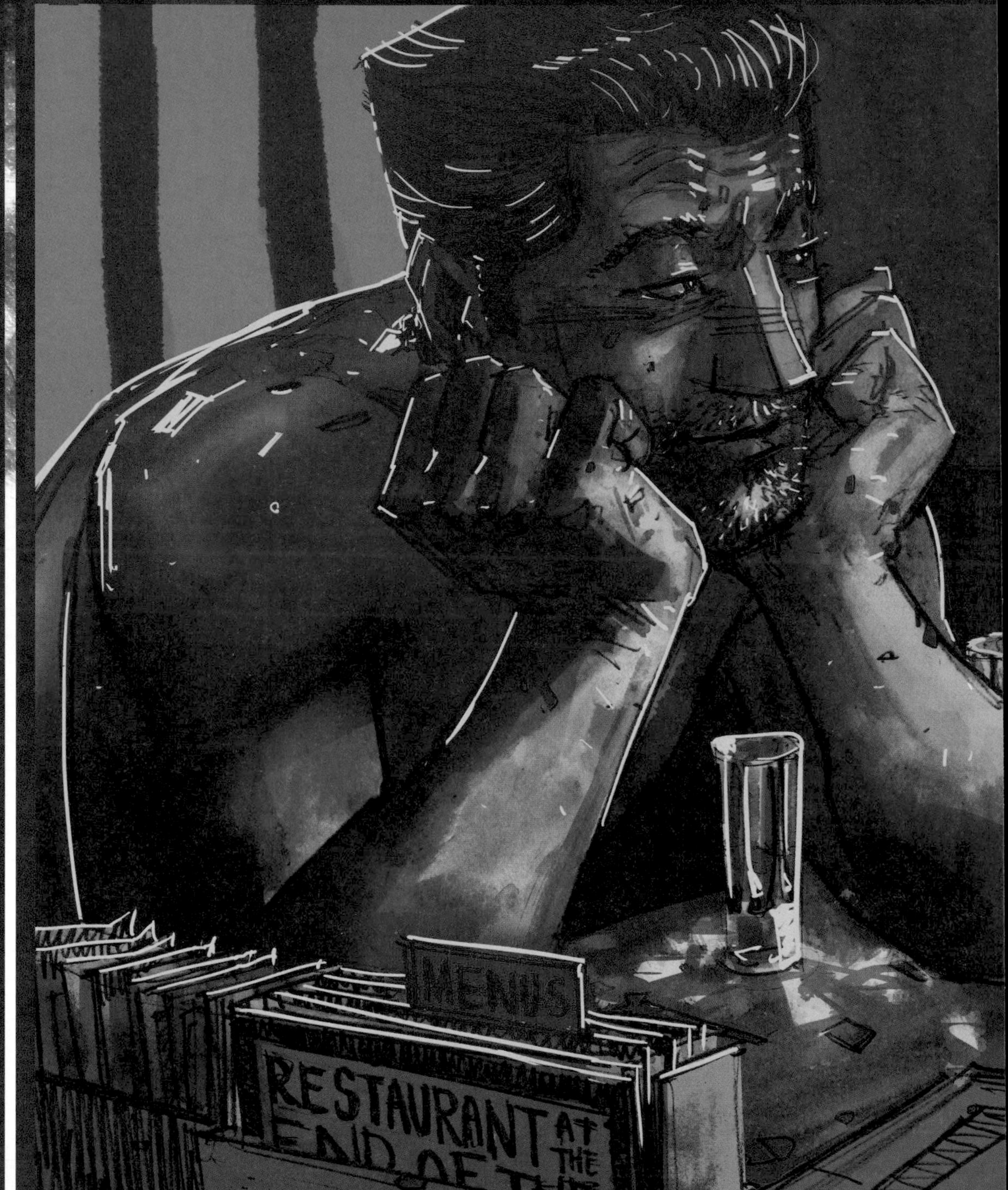
MENUS
RESTAURANT AT THE

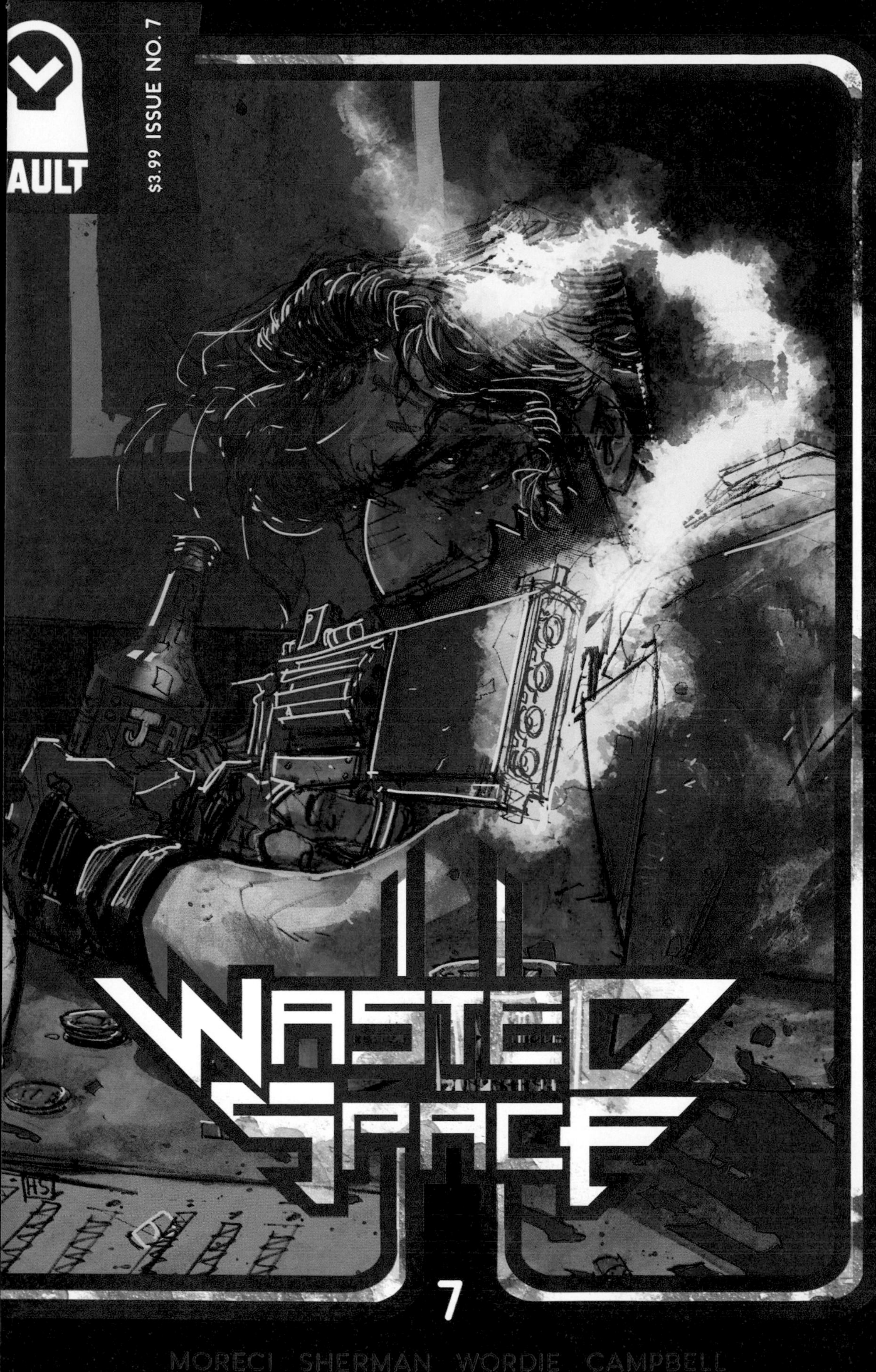
VAULT
$3.99 ISSUE NO. 7
WASTED SPACE
7
MORECI SHERMAN WORDIE CAMPBELL

COVER ISSUE 8//HAYDEN SHERMAN

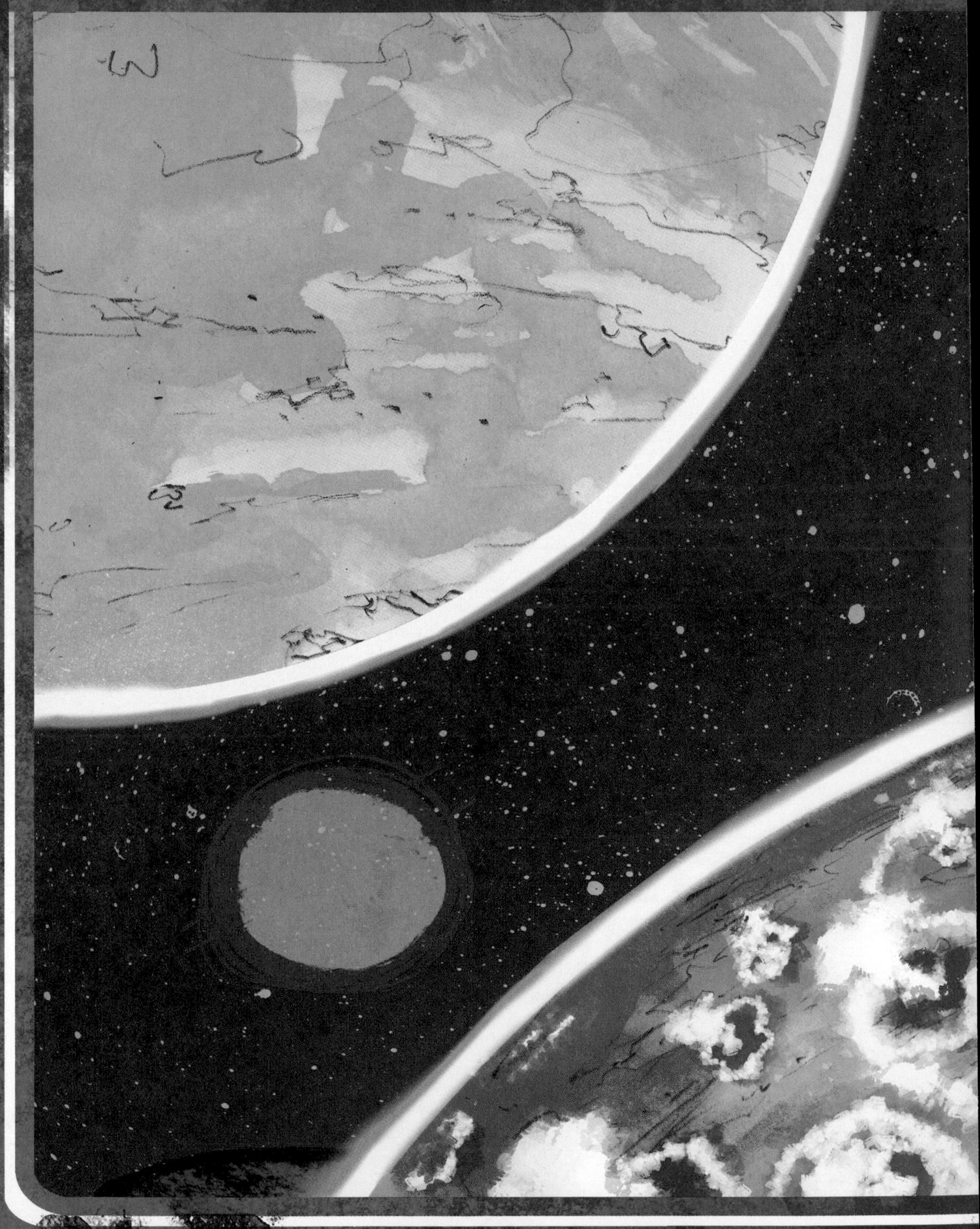

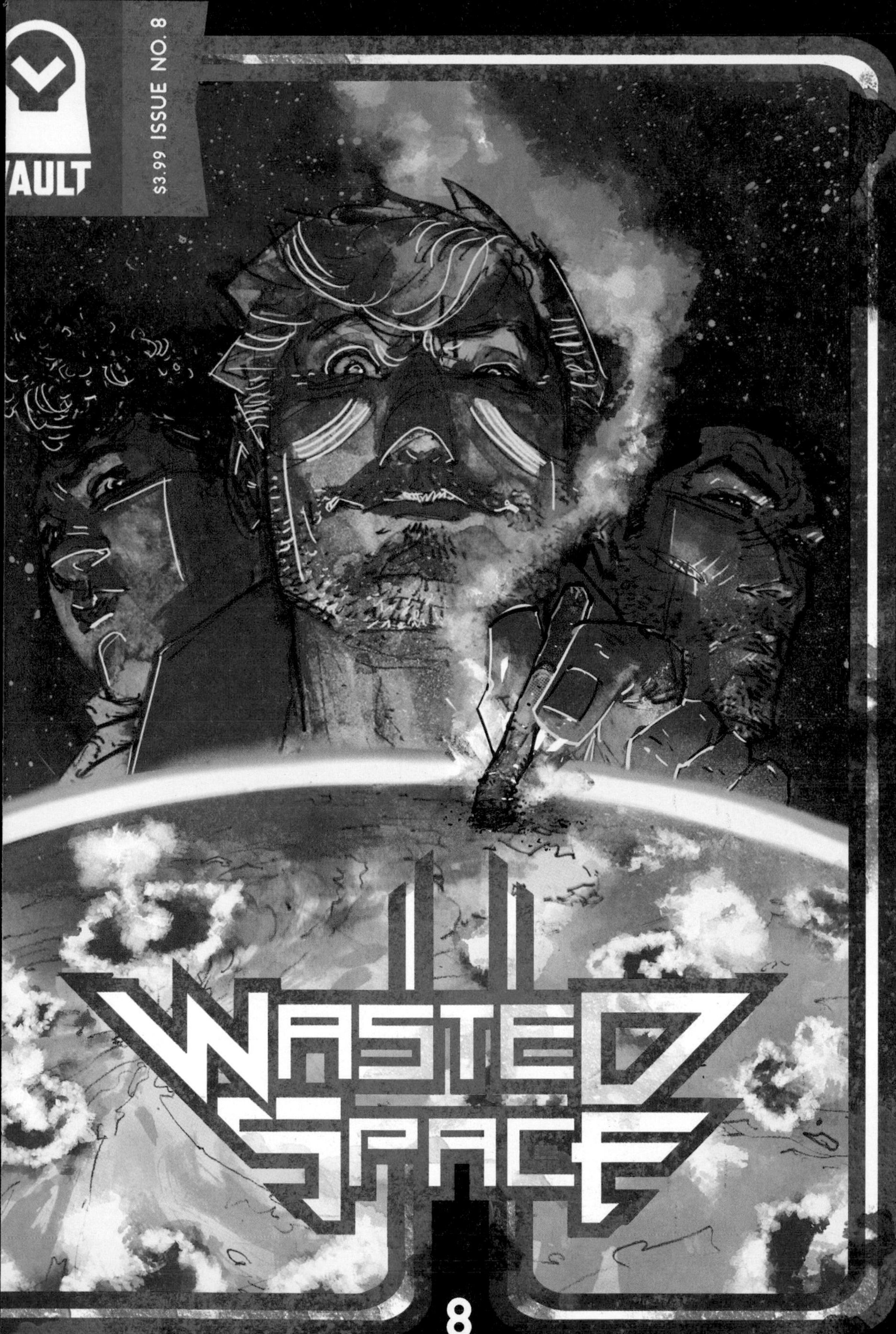
VAULT
$3.99 ISSUE NO. 8
WASTED SPACE
8

COVER ISSUE 9//HAYDEN SHERMAN

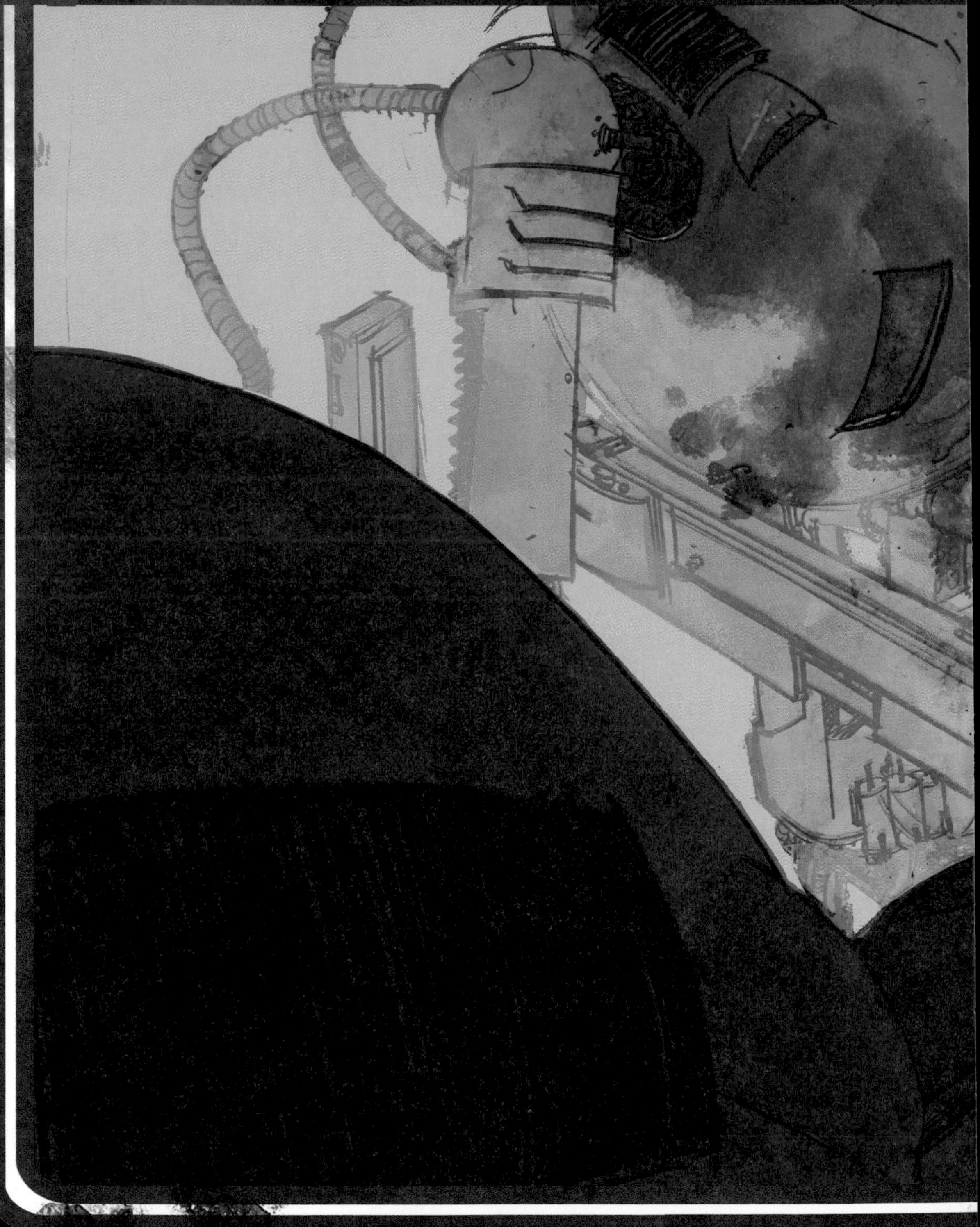

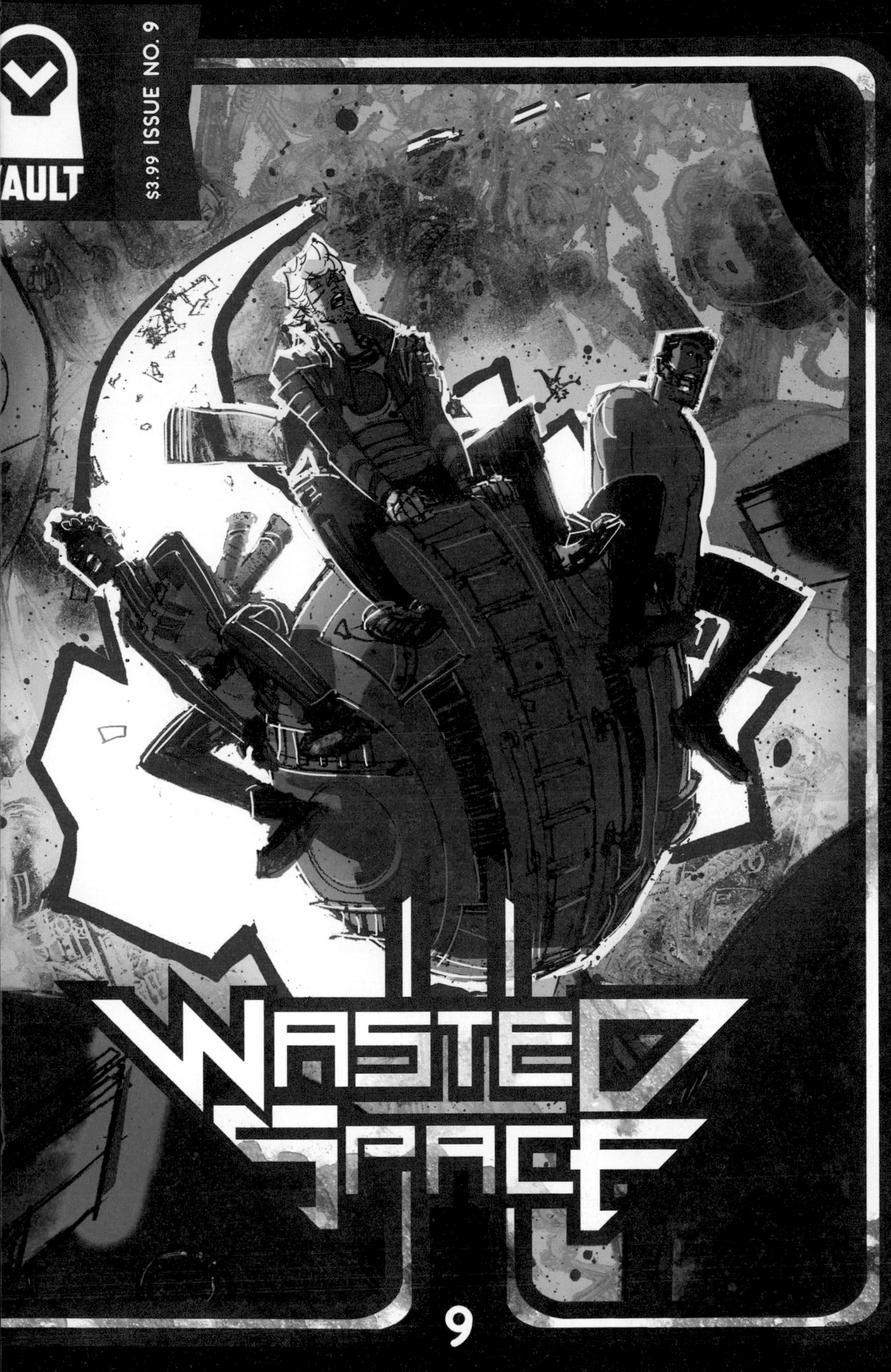
VAULT
$3.99 ISSUE NO. 9
WASTED SPACE
9

MORECI SHERMAN WORDIE CAMPBELL

COVER ISSUE 10//HAYDEN SHERMAN

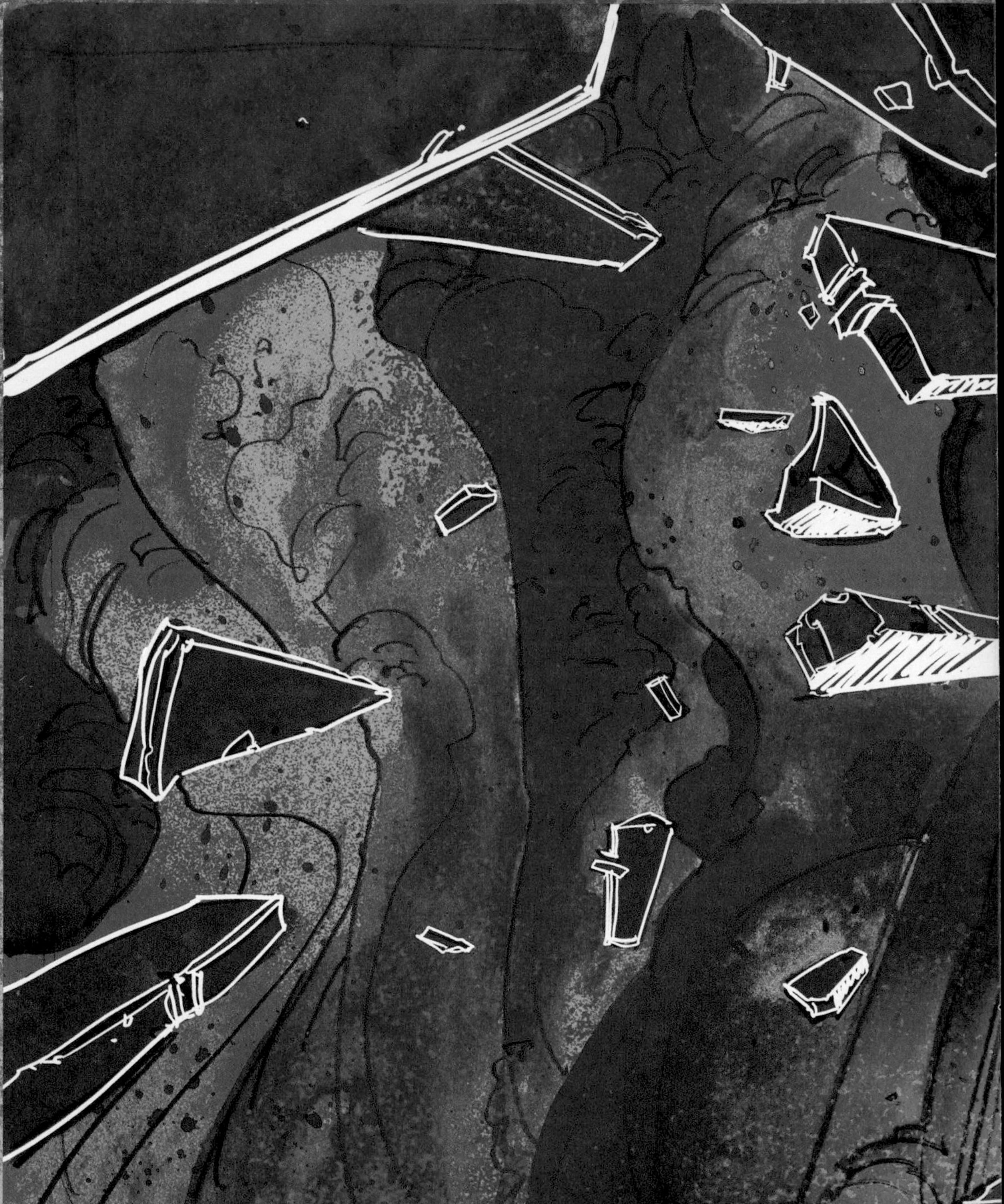

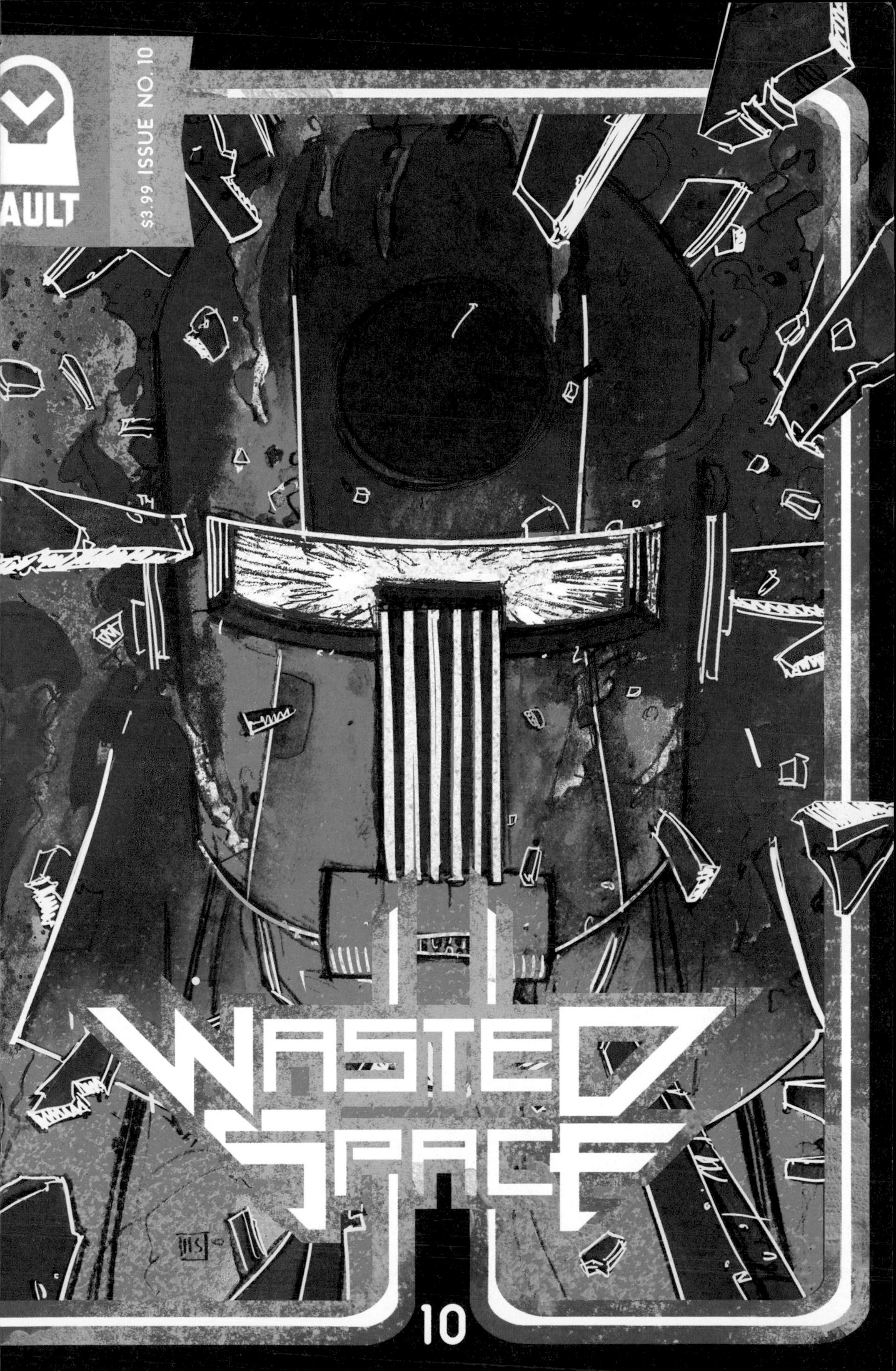
AULT
$3.99 ISSUE NO. 10
WASTED SPACE
10

MORECI SHERMAN WORDIE CAMPBELL

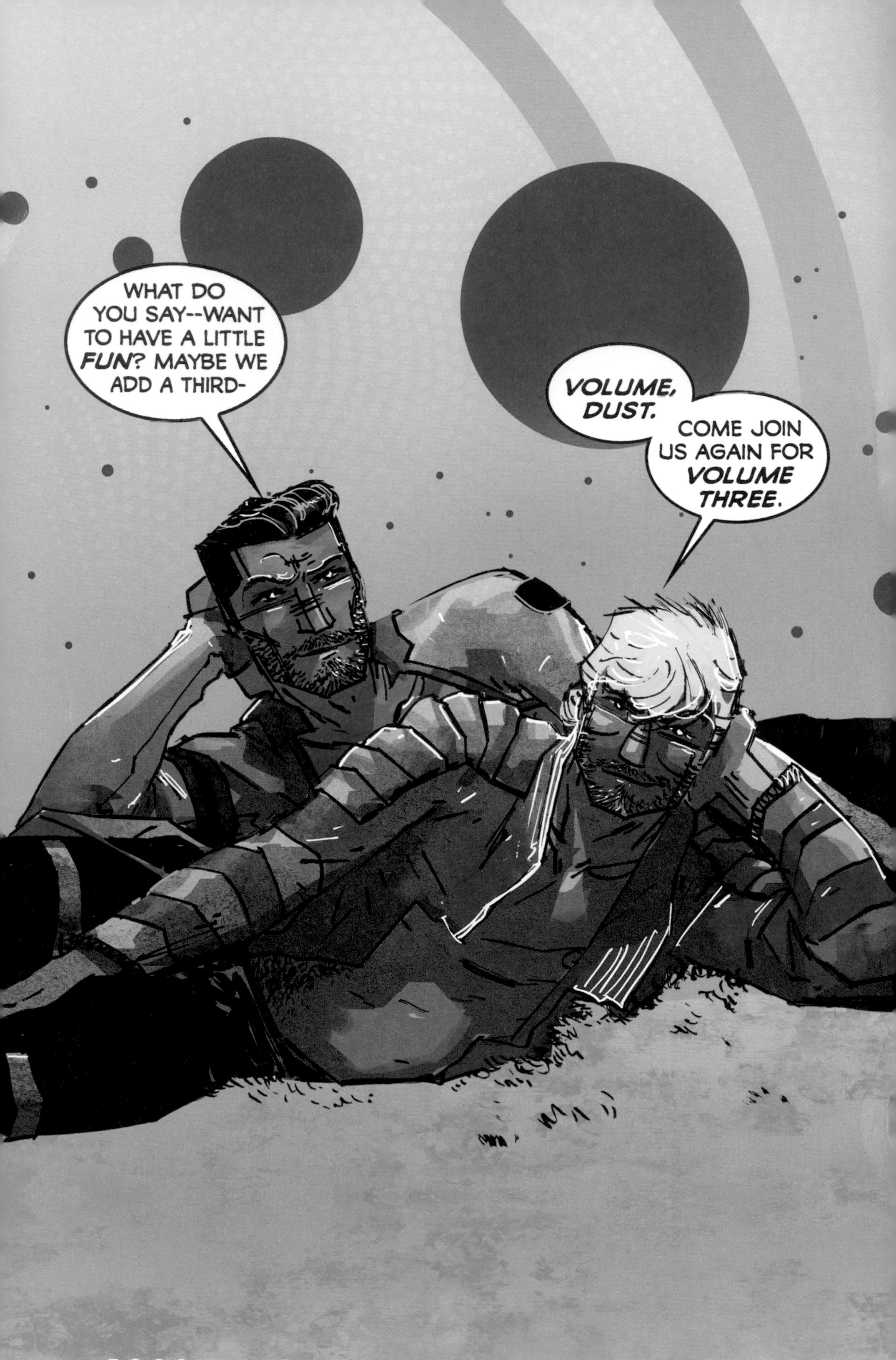
WHAT DO YOU SAY--WANT TO HAVE A LITTLE FUN? MAYBE WE ADD A THIRD-
VOLUME, DUST.
COME JOIN US AGAIN FOR VOLUME THREE.

ECCC 19 BANNER//HAYDEN SHERMAN